"If you really need to lose yourself in lush language for a while, to race between mourning and desire and wander the corridors of a hotel where ordinary people just do not stay, then this is the book for you.
For me it is a very literary treatment of the uncanny, a much more psychologically satisfying handling of grief and shock and unreal realities than most books of terror will brave."

– Danel Olson, Professor of English, Lone Star College and editor of the *Exotic Gothic* anthology series

"As effective as the horror sequences are (and they are – especially the 'King of Cats' chapter, which contains one of the greatest chase sequences in the history of horror literature), at the heart of Deadfall Hotel *is the story of a father doing everything he can to make life the best it can be for his daughter, and his struggles to protect her from the hotel, its guests, and the fear accompanying her burgeoning womanhood. In all of horror literature, I can think of no other novel that explores parental love as effectively or as deeply."*

– *Fearnet.com*

DEADFALL HOTEL

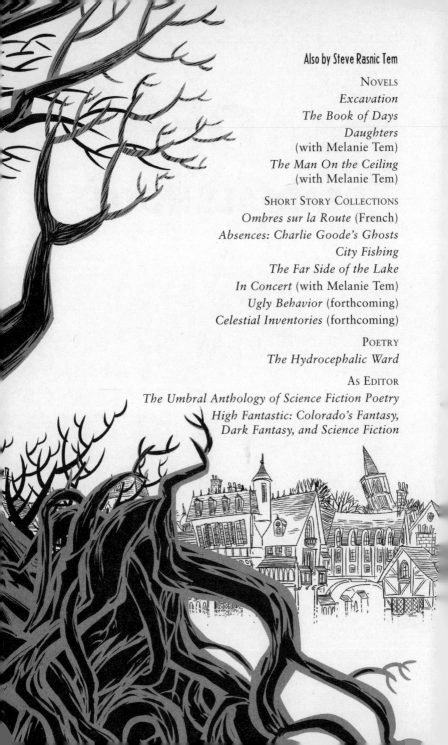

Also by Steve Rasnic Tem

NOVELS
Excavation
The Book of Days
Daughters
(with Melanie Tem)
The Man On the Ceiling
(with Melanie Tem)

SHORT STORY COLLECTIONS
Ombres sur la Route (French)
Absences: Charlie Goode's Ghosts
City Fishing
The Far Side of the Lake
In Concert (with Melanie Tem)
Ugly Behavior (forthcoming)
Celestial Inventories (forthcoming)

POETRY
The Hydrocephalic Ward

AS EDITOR
The Umbral Anthology of Science Fiction Poetry
*High Fantastic: Colorado's Fantasy,
Dark Fantasy, and Science Fiction*

DEADFALL HOTEL

by
STEVE RASNIC TEM

SOLARIS

First published 2012 by Solaris
an imprint of Rebellion Publishing Ltd,
Riverside House, Osney Mead,
Oxford, OX2 0ES, UK

www.solarisbooks.com

US ISBN: 978 1 907992 83 4

Internal illustrations by D'Israeli

10 9 8 7 6 5 4 3 2 1

A CIP catalogue record for this book is available
from the British Library.

Designed & typeset by Rebellion Publishing

Printed in the US

This one's for Charlie Grant

Chapter One
THE FUNHOUSE

Deadfall Hotel. A curtain of gnarled, skeletal oak and pine hides it from the rest of the world. The hotel is not well-lit, there is no sign, and night comes early here. The main highway bypassed its access road nearly half a century ago. From the air (and a few private pilots still venture over, out of curiosity) the hotel appears to follow the jumbled line of a train wreck, cars thrown out at all angles and yet still attached in sequence. Additions have been made haphazardly over the years, torn down, rebuilt, fallen into disuse. Repairs have not always been effective. From the back, facing the lake, boarded-up windows, doors, even entire discarded sections may be seen, coated in slightly different shades of paint, constructed of a miscellanea of materials and in a range of styles. But·the owners ·have always tried to maintain a uniform appearance in the front of the hotel, facing the road; they have established facades, like film-sets, over some sections of the structure.

Although the hotel has more than three hundred rooms, fewer than a third are serviceable at any given time. The staff has always been kept small, and the repairs are too many. Systematic repair schedules have been attempted, but time seems to work its destructions at varying rates throughout the rooms, favoring some and wreaking havoc on others, so that projections as to the decline of any one part are virtually impossible. Walking here, you become disoriented to time, place, even spatial relationships. Unless you have a guide. Unless you are of the right frame of mind, or species.

The current proprietor will not bother you; he will want to respect your solitude and, besides, he will have too much else on his mind. Once again, his predecessor has stayed on as caretaker.

The hotel takes its name from the grove. Those who stay here often complain of the trees in their dreams – long, snake-like, involved limbs they imagine must mirror the tree's root system. Limbs you feel compelled to follow, in and out of shadowed hollows where branches disappear, where nests, newly inhabited or ancient and abandoned, are hidden. In parts of the trees the branches are so interlocked – both within and among individual trees – that the strongest wind will not free them.

Yet when the time comes, and only the grove itself seems to know the secret to this timing (certainly no natural thing; past proprietors have allowed botanists to study the grove, and all have been at a loss to explain its peculiar physics) the branches, the deadfall, fall with rifle-shot sound and abruptness, to join the decades-old clutter layered beneath.

Running such a hotel requires a special calling, or need. There are visitors coming, guests who have nowhere else to go.

– from the diary of Jacob Ascher,
proprietor, Deadfall Hotel, 1969-2000

RICHARD COULD HEAR Serena screaming in the house. He was sure it was her scream, even though there were dozens of other children in there. It was that kind of uneasy scream that could be excitement or terror – impossible to tell, when he couldn't see her or the exact circumstances. He had the impulse to run in and get her out of that house, but of course that would embarrass her. Serena had reached that age when, more often than not, her father embarrassed her. And unfortunately, he thought, lately her father had become legitimately embarrassing.

She had been reluctant to go into the funhouse at first – she didn't like the maze of mirrors at the beginning; all those images of herself gave her the creeps, she said. But the rest of it, she said, was "so *amazing*," that it was worth being a little scared for a time. He'd been so proud of her then, and a little envious. Sometimes his wise child was far wiser than he.

Richard hated funhouses, haunted houses, horror movies, all that. He'd never understood this impulse people had to be frightened out of their wits. This idea that terror constituted entertainment. He'd always considered that inclination vaguely masochistic. He and Abby used to argue about it all the time. She'd been passionate, acutely intelligent, and perhaps no more so than when arguing the value of what he thought, actually, were lower forms of entertainment: circuses, sideshows, funhouses, horror books and movies. Pale, thin, and beautiful, her body betrayed the strength of her feelings. She would pace, swing her arms, snap her fingers to emphasize some point. He'd be convinced she was angry with him, and then she'd break the mood with a quick, thin-lipped smile that widened her mouth so it made her face almost freakishly lovely. Some days she maintained that smile most of the day, until it began to seem pained, even more so given the crystalline intelligence in her eyes, with their sadness of knowing.

She had loved horror books and movies. She would use words like "cathartic," and she'd say how important it was sometimes not to look away.

If she had seen her own face in the mirror at the moment of her death, would she have looked away? He had not looked away, and would regret it the rest of his life.

Now all that horror business just irritated him. Kids in Gothic clothing, people laughing about this and that new movie with the latest, grossest effects, books with drippy lettering on the covers, creepy illustrations of faces losing their flesh. People scared from the safety of their armchairs. Laughing their way through the funhouse. None of it real, none of it to be taken seriously. He felt mocked by it all. Theirs was a comfort and an entertainment denied him.

A little girl's face appeared framed in one of the windows of the funhouse. He couldn't tell if it was Serena or not. It looked like Serena – the face had Serena's eyes, her slight, almost nonexistent nose, pale hair so like her mother's. She screamed at the people milling around outside the house: lounging, waiting for people to come out. Behind her head, red light danced. Her hair suddenly appeared to fan away from her face, rising on agitated air, her head in flames. She screamed as if in agony, and then she screamed again. And then she laughed. Looking directly at Richard, she laughed until she stopped abruptly, as if so exhausted she couldn't make another sound.

Richard felt thought escape him as if pushed out by some high, nervous wind. His chest seizing, his face hot, he ran into the funhouse entrance, a wide opening framed by painted red lips and crooked yellow teeth. Almost immediately he was assailed by the smells of old popcorn grease and trapped body odor. He pushed at a pink wall for balance, pulling his fingers away when he felt its unsteadiness. The first closet-sized room appeared to be walled in plastic panels of varying degrees of redness and translucency, overlapped and layered so that he was witness to a bewildering display of distant and reflected movement, slices of faces multiplied, legs and arms meeting and crossing, children's voices shrieking and malformed as audio waves collided. Somewhere in the depths, music pulsed and a revolving light swept the panels, making them dance as if torched and melting. He looked for an edge that would lead him into the next passageway, and a random gleam appeared to suggest a mirrored surface, so he let himself be drawn there, sick to his stomach and angry with Serena for putting him through this.

His first steps appeared to be successful, however, as he immediately found himself inside the beginning of the maze, faced with mirrors in all directions as if inside the dressing room of a nightmare department store.

He took a deep breath to steady himself and attempted to filter through a labyrinth of near and distant sound. Some of it was recorded music, the crank and whir of hidden machinery, threaded through with children's voices, some younger – as much as he could determine – than Serena's, some possibly male, some giggling out of control, some – if he wasn't reading too much into their choked vocalizations – weeping their grief away. But impossible to tell what might be Serena's sounds, if she were making any sounds at all.

In his attention to sound, he'd let his gaze drop to the floor, which was a fortunate accident as it exposed the geometric patterns of gray tile, well-worn and beginning to separate at the seams, and the places where a mirrored wall made a perpendicular angle with flooring. He had some sense of the beginnings of the maze's layout now. This first cell was more-or-less six-sided, mirrors arranged at approximately sixty degree angles to one another, a triangular grid. One wall of one triangle was missing, which surely meant that was the way into the next cell of mirrors, and so he made himself step that way, even though to his eyes he appeared to be stepping directly into his own reflection. He saw his other face grimace in anticipation, but he discovered himself successfully through once again, confronted by a multitude of himself, all dumb-faced and sweating.

New music slipped wetly from hidden speakers, accompanied by a steady shifting in the lights from red to orange to green. In the walls his body contorted even as he stood statue-still; it seemed these mirrors were some sort of thin metal, and that some device behind the walls was rippling the surface to make the distortion. In front of him, three of his chests appeared to swallow three of his shrunken, alarmed heads.

He turned to get away from the disturbing self-images, and was immediately confronted by a perfectly normal, accurate reflection of himself. In fact, the clarity of his image in the mirror's clean polish was almost hyper-real. The paleness of his face was troubling, more so because of the dark nested eyes, suggesting as they did a dangerous lack of sleep and a frailty of nerve.

Suddenly the lights buzzed to black and his reflection disappeared. Light came up slowly behind the mirror, which was now transparent. The depth exposed behind the panel was impossible, with rows of panels and rectangular borders going back hundreds of yards. A figure made its way from the back swiftly, arms outstretched and mouth open to panic. Thinking he had recognized her, Richard shouted "Serena! Serena, this way!" He was sure there were things in the background chasing her, but although the black shadows boiled, none broke away in pursuit.

As she came closer, pale hair pulled back to expose the high, smooth forehead, brilliant yet fractured eyes fixing him, thin lips stretched into that so-familiar smile, she became Abby, either running to him or running away from something he could not see. The lights flared and bathed her in red, and she was burning.

Richard wasn't sure if he'd closed his eyes, or if the lights had simply gone out. He reached up and massaged his lids, making lightning in the pitch black. He heard a groaning behind him, either something opening, or someone complaining in hurt. He turned to face either.

He saw himself splitting in half, darkness filling the injury. He strolled through the double doors of himself, into rows of men walking away from him, then recognized the clothing. All of these men were himself from behind, somehow captured and projected. Across the reflective ceiling, a dozen or more images of Abby flowed liquidly over, lips parted with a sigh. She withered into a narrow crack, as if all her air had been let out.

Richard could feel her rolling down his face then, captured in a single tear. He closed his eyes in anger, so tired, he thought, that he could easily lose all care for anything. He could feel her take his hand, and he shook it in frustration, but he still held on.

When he opened his eyes and looked down, however, it was Serena looking up at him sadly, holding his trembling hand to her cheek. "Oh, Daddy, I'm sorry!" she said, and led him out of that place.

WHEN THEY CAME out of the funhouse he saw that Serena had the remnants of a chocolate bar smeared around her mouth, making her look like a much younger child, or a senile old lady whose application of lipstick had been clownishly inexact. She appeared slightly stunned. For himself, he felt as if his mind had suddenly cleared itself of noxious debris. He felt like a parent again.

"I think it's time to go, honey," he said, guiding her gently toward the park's exit.

"I'm not ready, Daddy," she said sleepily.

"We have to catch the next bus. Someone's coming to interview me for a job. He's coming right to the house, so he must really be interested in me. That would be great, wouldn't it?"

"I don't want to move again, Daddy."

He patted her shoulder awkwardly, as if he'd never felt her shoulder before, as if he didn't know where to place his hand. Lately, that seemed the best he could do by way of comfort.

They arrived at the house to find an unfamiliar automobile parked in front. The car was an antique, an old Ford, Richard thought, but with his limited knowledge of automobiles it could have been almost anything. Whatever it was, it had been well kept, the black paint glossy as if recently applied. He walked over to the car, admiring the plush interior, admiring all the gleaming bits of it, saw his neighbors across the street looking at it, and he expected them to come over any second to get a closer look themselves. Because that was the way it was with old cars that had been fixed up to look new: people – especially men – were just naturally drawn to them.

But after some time, his neighbors did not come over. They went back inside without even a friendly *hello*. Of course, it might be because he hardly knew them – he and Serena had been in the rental only a few weeks. Neither of them had made any friends. Perhaps they had the natural distrust that people who have lived in a neighborhood a long time have for new renters. It wasn't as if he would buy the place – he didn't think he'd ever own a home again.

But Richard was having odd feelings about this car: everything looked new, but the style of upholstery and trim seemed more suited to a much older vehicle, and Serena had avoided it, going directly into the house.

Something on the driver's side door: was that a scratch? It made him unaccountably sad – why should he care? If Abby could see him now, she'd think he'd finally gone over the edge. It would've made her worry about Serena, of course. But now it was his full-time job to worry about Serena.

He'd caught himself thinking foolishly again. He didn't know why the living felt so compelled to imagine what the dead might think. Richard could imagine the dead looking down from their private apartments in Heaven, gazing with a surfeit of arrogant pity at the poor, uncomprehending families they'd abandoned. *Easier to imagine that, than to imagine nothing.*

Then that place on the door wasn't so much a scratch as a twisting line of rust, working its way through the paint and deep into the metal. That was worse, more disturbing somehow.

He bent close enough to see: reddish gold lettering, no more than a quarter-inch tall. *Deadfall Hotel*, in careful hand-drawn script.

"It's a 1934 Ford, a Fordor they called them. De Luxe Sedan."

Richard stood up too quickly, making himself dizzy. The man's quick, strong hand on his shoulder steadied him. Richard looked up into the old man's face.

"Are you ready for your interview?"

Richard nodded dumbly.

MR. ASCHER WATCHED Serena through the living room window. She was playing by herself, but she was happy. Or at least, she was singing. Richard thought that maybe happy didn't matter as long as you had it in you to sing.

He supposed the man's appearance was ordinary enough, but he found the overall effect to be pretty intimidating. Tall, almost a head taller than Richard. A little on the thin side. There was something odd about his profile. Richard eventually realized that the forehead and chin were pushed forward slightly, the nose pushed back, making the features somewhat moonish. Waxing crescent. He wore a dark, old-fashioned suit that looked too tight for him. A thin material, almost gauzy, close-fitting as if molded on. "Did your wife die by fire, by any chance?" Ascher asked.

Amazement got Richard to his feet, but then he saw what the fellow was looking at out in the yard. He pushed himself roughly to the window. Past Serena and on the other side of a low iron fence their neighbor had set fire to a hornet's nest, which he now held high on its broken-off branch. Long, flowing locks of flame enveloped the darkened paper head.

The burning nest began to open and the hornets rushed out in a scream. Serena looked stricken, and Richard considered, not for the first time, the terrible possibility that she had seen her mother die. But when he'd carried her out of the house, she'd been almost comatose from the smoke. He'd been sure she hadn't seen anything.

Richard stuck his head out the window. "Serena, go play in the back yard, okay, honey?"

Serena gazed at him curiously, but did as he asked. Irritably, Richard moved away from the window, gesturing abruptly toward the nicer of the shabby living room chairs while he sank into the worst one, hiding the torn seat and back with his body. "Our house burned to the ground. My wife was inside. I couldn't get her out. I don't think Serena saw much of what happened, but I can't be positive." It was the bluntest, least emotional description he'd ever given of the event, but at least it was brief.

"I understand," Ascher said, which angered Richard immensely, because it was a lie. "We human beings," he continued, "are known for our inability to completely bury our dead." Which angered Richard even more.

It may have been his anger that encouraged Richard to behave a little less obsequiously than he would have at a normal job interview. "So, you think you might have a job for me?"

Mr. Ascher looked at him with lips pursed, as if considering how to respond to Richard's rudeness. "Possibly," he finally said. "If it's a job you want."

"I can't honestly say I know what I want, right now. At least among the things I can *have*. But I *need* a job. I need to be doing something useful. And as you saw, I have a daughter. But your ad wasn't very specific."

"Lovely young girl," he replied. "A child who is special, I think."

"I think so."

"Permit me to introduce myself. I have been the proprietor of the Deadfall Hotel for over thirty years. Until I placed that small, uninformative ad. The ad which you did respond to, despite its unfortunate lack of detail."

"As I said. I do need a job." Richard knew he was acting like a sullen child, but he couldn't help himself.

"In any case, my former position is now vacant. Currently I am the hotel's, how do you say, caretaker, or perhaps, handy man. I like the sound of that better, I think. Handy man – it sounds so competent."

"So you were demoted, Mr. Ascher," Richard said.

"I prefer Jacob." He smiled.

"Jacob."

"Thank you. And I was not demoted. I merely changed jobs. It is part of the tradition."

"So it's a job with a tradition. I think I may be impressed."

"No need. Do you want the job, Richard?"

"Just like that? You'd hire me just like that? What's wrong with this job, Mister... Jacob?"

Jacob closed his eyes. After an uncomfortable silence he said, "It's not an easy job. It can be a complicated job. At times, it can be a consuming job."

"I have no hotel experience, you know."

"I am aware of that lack in your resume, I assure you. But, how do they say it? No experience necessary. The fact that you even answered my little ad indicates, well, a certain aptitude, strangely enough."

"I did work behind a counter at a convenience store when I was in college." Now he felt ridiculous, an inexperienced youngster desperate for his first job.

"Splendid. The Deadfall has a very nice counter, although I prefer the phrase 'front desk.'"

"My daughter needs special attention these days. I'll need to spend a lot of time with her."

"Certainly. Because of her mother. Old houses contain many secrets in their walls. Sometimes those secrets include faulty wiring. It wasn't your fault, Richard."

Richard stared at Jacob, unable to speak. He made himself change the subject. "What about Serena's schooling? Is there a good local school?"

"Too far to be of any use, I'm afraid. There will be a private tutor – we have had her under contract for many years. Your daughter will have a first-class education, I assure you. Very few, in fact, could afford the quality of instruction we'll be able to provide her at no cost to you."

"She'll miss her schoolmates."

"That is unfortunate, of course. But perhaps this will be a useful time for her, a time of... development? Such close adult attention after a recent loss of this magnitude, it might be of great benefit, do you suppose?"

"I really have no idea. I haven't a clue what might be best for her right now. I just want to do the right thing by her."

"I first came to the Deadfall a number of years after the loss of my own family. In one terrible day, my wife, children, parents and grandparents: all of them, gone. I wandered the world for over two decades before landing in that place. Like you, I answered a small, rather obtuse advertisement. It has done me some good, I think."

"I have no experience," Richard said weakly, and teary-eyed.

"I will be there. It is like swimming, I think. It is like love. It is like grief. An experience of total immersion. You are afraid you may drown, but instead you learn to float, you learn to navigate. When I first came to the Deadfall it was as if I'd been dropped into a foreign country with only my wits to help me. I had to learn the customs, the language, and avoid the taboos. But I will be there to tell you the things you need to know. I can help you, Richard."

*   *   *

HE HAD NEVER really enjoyed driving, and after Abby died, his reluctance to get into an automobile became a prominent factor in their lives; some might have said it became pathological. So for him, the long drive to the Deadfall Hotel required a resolute rearrangement of his daily approach to the world. But he had little choice. No buses or trains went there, and one of the few things Jacob was firm about was that he was not permitted to take a cab or any other form of privately hired transport. Richard had thought to ask why, but he had understood so little in Jacob's vague briefing that such a direct question would have seemed somehow nonsensical. The interview had gone on for hours after his acceptance of the position, but with very few questions asked or answered. Richard had spent most of that time trying to stay awake through Jacob's seemingly pointless ramblings.

"Will there be a staff?" he had asked.

"Besides me, on an as-needed basis," was the reply, "of course, there is Enid the cook, and her son, but I doubt you will see much of them. They like to keep to themselves. Occasionally you will see a housekeeper, a maid or two, but I would suggest that you not attempt conversation. Generally speaking, they dislike conversation. You might advise your daughter accordingly. I wouldn't want her to feel slighted in any way."

"But from what you've said, the hotel is rather large."

"It *can* be, certainly."

Now *that* was a funny way to put it. Richard wondered if Jacob might be foreign-born, or perhaps some variety of self-invented eccentric. It annoyed him, but he was pretty sure he could learn to tolerate it. "So how do you keep a place like that clean and running, with such a minimal staff?"

"I assure you," Jacob replied, "this will not be a problem for you. You may remember, I said our clientele often have special proclivities, special needs."

"As in handicapped?"

"Upon occasion, but that is not precisely the term I would use. In any case, they've usually made their own arrangements regarding food and hygiene matters. I really cannot share much information on these issues – I actually have little such information in my possession. The Deadfall is not merely a physical establishment – it is the embodiment of generations of agreements, understandings, pacts, covenants, promises, traditions enforced or simply encouraged, specific and nonspecific contractual negotiations, religious partnerships, spiritual compromises – the bulk of which occurred long before my own birth. There are important pledges and rituals of privacy which must be adhered to. I have, perhaps, revealed too much already, I'm afraid." For the first time Jacob had seemed somewhat agitated.

"There's no danger, is there?" Richard asked. "I mean, I can't possibly put Serena in any sort of danger."

Jacob looked at him directly then. "No more so than in any larger community. In any city, certainly. I'm afraid we must all look out for the children. That has always been so, I think. But I must get back. I will prepare for your arrival in two weeks. Please" – he moved forward and grasped Richard's hand – "please trust me. In the long term, this will be a good thing for you, and your daughter. I know this from experience, and I pledge my assistance, in any way I can."

And strangely enough, Richard did trust this man whom he knew nothing about. Trusted him enough to pay a local garage to repair Richard's aging station wagon, kept in storage since Abby's funeral. He told the owner-mechanic at the seedy-looking establishment to "ready it for a long, and possibly rough, trip," and a week and two thousand dollars later the mechanic had delivered the vehicle to Richard's front door, exposing an awkward smile when he handed him the keys, which now sported a bright blue rabbit's foot attached to the ring.

At the mechanic's insistence, two additional mirrors were now mounted on the driver's and passenger's side doors. "What with the trailer, and those winding mountain roads, you'll want the extra visibility," he'd said. Richard didn't know if the mountain roads would be 'winding,' but there was no additional charge for the mirrors, so he was inclined to accept the mechanic's good intentions.

The mirrors themselves weren't terribly attractive: tall and extending far out on each side of the vehicle, they resembled the side-mirrors used on trucks. Serena said the station wagon now looked as if it had "big, ugly ears." The new passenger side mirror bore the label: 'Caution: objects in mirror are closer than they appear,' just like the old passenger side mirror, which was still clearly visible, and offered a slightly different perspective, warping the world behind them. In fact, with his rearview mirror, Richard now had five mirrors to contend with. It was overkill. He thought of flying insects and their five eyes. He thought of staring into those eyes for the entire trip.

When Richard and Serena pulled out of the driveway for the last time, dragging the small, used trailer containing the few belongings they cared to keep, the car felt powerful, sounding almost nautical when it surged onto the highway.

Even before Abby's death, Richard would never attempt drives of more than eight hours, but he was determined to make the Deadfall trip in a single effort. If he needed a nap they would pull over in some secluded place, but they would not leave this car except for bathroom breaks or food. He knew that to stop at some wood-sided roadside lodge would be to lose conviction, that doubt would flood in to fill the hesitation, and the next day they'd be on their way back to what passed for their home aboard some shiny bright bus, the car abandoned by the roadside. In a persistent daydream, he imagined a final scene in which the engine of that abandoned car purred at a fast idle as the bus pulled out. And the further away the bus traveled, the louder the engine's roar became, until even miles away he and Serena would still hear it from inside the bus.

So they wouldn't be stopping – they would travel on and on through hills and up into the mountains beyond, and toward the end of that effort the long drive would seem near-hallucinatory, the rising landscape a continuous upward bend on his perceptions, disrupting his thoughts, disorganizing his senses.

Serena was content to sleep most of the trip, which was just fine with him, as long as he could hear the sounds of her breathing from the back seat. Sometimes when he didn't hear those soft, important sounds, or thought he didn't hear them, he'd pull over to the side of the road, turn quickly in his seat, eyes scanning for the steady rise and fall of her beneath the blanket. Once he saw that subtle pulse of the cloth he could pull back onto the dark pavement again.

A few hours outside the city the engine altered its musical pitch, the old station wagon and its attached trailer began to labor ever-so-slightly, although as yet he could detect no other signs of an incline. But the somewhat troubling whine increased in volume, until finally he was aware of the hood of the car gradually tilting upwards. He could feel a pressure in his stomach, a gradual lowering of internal organs. Beyond the dark edge of the dashboard, the mountains massed. He'd had no idea that the mountains would be so close. He could think of only a few streets in the city with a detectable rise to them – he couldn't understand how mountains could erupt so suddenly with so little effect on the tilt of the city close by.

"Daddy?" came Serena's sleepy voice out of the back seat. "We're in the mountains already? Why didn't you wake me up?"

"They're not as close as they look, honey." But he wasn't really positive about that. As long as he'd lived in the city – almost twelve years – he'd traveled into the mountains only once before, and that when Abby forced the issue. No – twice, he corrected himself. And Abby had forced it that time as well, to scatter her ashes.

"When I was little, I used to think all my good dreams

floated up into the mountains," Serena said softly. "But that the bad dreams, the nightmares, they floated down from the mountains, and through the city streets until they found the bedroom they were looking for. Isn't that funny, Daddy?"

"Very," he replied, staring up at the dark, approaching slopes. Minutes later he could hear the regular breathing of her sleep.

So far he'd been pleased, and surprised, by the performance of the old station wagon, even with a trailer attached. Now and again, in fact, he felt compelled to peek into all those mirrors to confirm that the trailer was still there. All the things left from a lifetime, and yet now they seemed to weigh next to nothing, to stack up to nothing. But maybe they hadn't needed to bring even this much. What did you need, really, to make your way through a life? He and Serena had each other – that's what was important.

When Serena was little, the three of them would take these long Sunday drives. It had seemed so delightfully old-fashioned, not the way Richard and Abby had thought of themselves at all. They'd just put a basket of snacks and sandwiches into the car and drive. Sometimes Abby would insist that Richard choose and pack everything himself, so that when they were out on the road she and Serena could paw through the goodies and be surprised, alternately praising him for his unexpectedly good taste, and heaping good-natured scorn on what they considered his odder choices. "Pimento cheese, Richard? Who in this family, pray-tell, has ever eaten pimento cheese?" Then she'd cackle like a mad woman, and from the back seat Serena would try to imitate her with often hilarious results.

On those wonderful days they would head back during sunset, Serena asleep on the backseat, Abby with her head against the window, gazing at the sky, at the houses passing into a stream of line and color, the line of her mouth extending her smile into shadow, and Richard would keep glancing at her, glancing at her, unable to keep his eyes away, even for safety, because never had she been more beautiful, and never had he loved her more.

He glanced now at the large convex passenger mirror, 'Caution: objects in mirror are closer than they appear,' and saw the reflection of a reflection, his beloved wife's face pressing against the inside of the window, staring at him and smiling that so-knowledgeable smile. He jerked his head toward the seat – of course there was nothing there. Nothing there. Abby was just part of all that nothing he had left in the life behind.

He leaned over and switched the radio on, careful to keep the volume low so it wouldn't disturb Serena. Distant radio stations came and went, traveling at high speed into some other time, breaking apart in their haste. *Richard*, she sighed from the dashboard speaker, fogging ever so slightly the windshield above. A flutter and a shudder of bird wings swept through the radio air. *Are you sure this trip is necessary?* The radio whined, then began coughing static.

He looked around at the empty seat. He twisted his head and shoulders, looking for something else on the backseat with his sleeping daughter. He peered into every corner of the five mirrors, trying to ferret out her pale, languid face, her terribly relaxed smile. But she was nothing, and she was behind. *Are you sure?* She still insisted. *Are you sure?*

"Objects in mirror are closer than they appear," he replied, and said it again. And again. "Objects in mirror are closer than they appear," until Abby shut up, and let him drive.

According to Jacob's crude, hand-drawn map, the Deadfall was located somewhere on the edge of a huge lake. But the map did not include any indications of relative altitudes. Richard was bothered by a vaguely anxious, cartoony fantasy of a cliff two miles high, the Deadfall Hotel poised on the edge as if ready to tumble into the dark waters below. He glanced at the map again, half expecting to see 'Here Be Dragons' scrawled into the blank area beyond the rectangle labeled 'Deadfall.'

"We like our privacy," Jacob had said at one point during the interview. Indeed.

In the rear view mirror, Richard could see Serena reverting a few years, clutching her dolls to her chest. Her thumb strayed vaguely toward her mouth and he smiled and she seemed almost horrified to see him looking back at her.

In the side mirrors, the world behind them turned over onto itself, spreading ripples of distortion all the way out to the horizon. Trees crept up to the sides of the car before tumbling away. The station wagon bent itself to better fit the curves.

The road went to gravel, to dirt, to concrete, to asphalt, seemingly at random, with no apparent relation to the amount of traffic or the degree of civilization. At the top of one hill, the narrow gravel and dirt path became smooth black paving for approximately one hundred yards before reverting to gravel and dirt again. There had been no houses in sight. There had been no other vehicles since three turn-offs before. None of the fields had been plowed, but under one tree lay the rusted husk of an ancient tractor.

They passed through several small communities, the largest being Mad Devon, a grouping of perhaps three dozen structures, including a church and a school. Richard noticed people coming out onto their porches to watch, and on the school playground the handful of children halted their games to stare. A short distance outside Mad Devon, they came to a still narrower paved highway leading off at an angle into a patch of ragged woods.

A huge rock outcropping rose – 'King's Head,' according to the map. That's exactly what it resembled: a large-nosed, high-cheek-boned head some thirty feet high, topped by a ragged crown of stone finials and spires. It was obviously natural, but its location here seemed unlikely. Richard hesitated only briefly, then took the road into the woods.

After about a mile, the ancient paved road fell apart into

gravel. "Do people really come here for vacations, Daddy?" Richard could barely hear her.

"Sure they do, sweetheart. Otherwise they wouldn't need a hotel manager, now would they?"

As they drove further, he tried to see through the few narrow gaps exposing daylight, and was tantalized by glimpses of distant walls and windows, roof edges and stone corners. *It must be huge!* he thought. Too huge to be a single structure, in fact. Maybe there was a town by the hotel.

Then suddenly they were passing through the ornate iron gates, traveling the winding driveway that snaked its way between the darkly malformed trees and up the wide slope of lawn spread before the Deadfall Hotel, and Jacob's voice was in his head, describing the Deadfall as he had that day he'd interviewed Richard.

There was the pile of deadfall, much like the woods but older, deader, even more complicated in their involvement with each other, swallowing up the grove of trees struggling to keep its still living extremities up in daylight. The extent of the dark pile appalled him – it was many times the area of the huge hotel itself, like an enormous sore across the hillside. Richard had a sudden, overwhelming urge to destroy the thing, to burn it and bulldoze the remnants, then to change the hotel's name to something more inviting. He remembered words like 'guardian' and 'conservator' from Jacob's rambling talk, and vaguely understood that those words applied to the grounds as a whole, including this abomination of landscaping.

That chaotic pile of deadfall was made all the more alarming by the civilized feel of the rest of the grounds: hundreds of square yards of well-manicured grass, the occasional ornamental tree, ornate iron lawn chairs and benches, several elaborate flower beds in paisley patterns. The only exception to this appearance of gentility was the great gray hulk of a gazebo, in slow-motion collapse into a cluster of trees and bushes.

The hotel itself was beyond impressive, as Richard had expected, although somewhat confusing in its architecture and spatial balance. Every few feet was an angle that appeared wrong, a window out of place, a chimney at an unlikely slant, exterior wall planes which met with vaguely disturbing results. The freeform rhythm of its lines was discomfiting. He could imagine it in a high wind, its odd geometry forcing a strange music through its spaces.

He stopped the car twenty feet or so away from the entrance. He just wanted a few more seconds to take it all in, before the angle became too sharp for a comprehensive view. He would need to drive a little closer for them to unload. But was that what he wanted to do? Or should he just circle back down the driveway and leave? At the moment, that seemed by far the more prudent course.

His hands gripped and ungripped the steering wheel. Then his right hand strayed toward the gear knob.

A sharp tap on the glass. "Welcome." Richard twisted around, stared up into Jacob's narrow face at his driver's side window. "Didn't mean to startle you," the old man said.

For no apparent reason, Richard thought, *he's lying.*

Jacob chatted easily with Serena, helping her unload her 'special things' from the back seat – an old Teddy Bear, dolls, a copy of *Black Beauty*, a box of jewelry that had belonged to her mother. Richard fumbled with a few small boxes and cloth bags on the front passenger side floorboard containing some of Abby's journals, one of her dresses, a few books and knick-knacks most clearly expressive of her personality. Things he could not let go of, and now found he could not leave unguarded in the car.

Jacob and Serena passed him, their arms full of Serena's things. Jacob eyed him appraisingly. They went in ahead of him, Jacob pushing the enormous front door open easily. A hushing sound escaped, a massive exhalation. Richard had a moment to consider whether there were sophisticated hydraulics at play here, when the door squeezed shut in front of him.

He paused with his arms full, waiting for Jacob to realize he didn't have a free hand, and open the door for him. But time passed, the boxes – as small as they were – grew heavy in his arms, and Richard grew annoyed. He leaned back to peer at the carved heads poised over the entrance. He looked back at the door, whose paneling appeared as solid, unmovable, and weathered as stone. A growing sickness climbed the walls of his stomach. *He's taken her*, he thought, when the door eased quietly open.

"Sorry. That door is supposed to stay open a bit. It must require adjustment." Jacob's grayish face floated in the darkness just inside the door. Richard willed his eyes to adjust quickly, but they were stubborn. Not wanting Jacob to see his difficulty, he stepped, unseeing, into the hotel.

A sense of poorly lit ornateness was all that came through as he blinked several times, his eyes tearing. His breath caught in his throat as he feared he might actually weep.

"Here, let me," Jacob's voice said, just before Abby's things were taken from his arms.

"No, wait!" He could see clearly now, Jacob's back receding toward his left.

"I'll just put them on the front desk," Jacob threw back over his shoulder. "Get yourself acclimated before trying to move anything else."

Serena, a serious look on her face, was examining a huge painting on the wall: a hunting scene, a dozen or so dogs attempting to bring down a great, slavering bear. The mounted, cloaked hunters had pale faces expressing shock and awe. She held her old teddy bear dangling by one arm.

He looked around: the entrance was domed, several stories high, studded with interior windows, which he assumed opened onto the upper floors. A huge number of similarly old and dark paintings covered most of the wall area of this space – many hung too high to see in any detail, except perhaps from one of those high, interior windows. The air was hot and dusty. Around the entrance were a number of shadowed recesses, the roots of hallways, and rows of full-length mirrors: carefully placed, it seemed, some of them angled away from the wall so that anyone walking there would be distorted, and their distortions multiplied.

Then he saw there was a wider recess where Jacob now stood, carefully placing Abby's things on a polished redwood counter.

Richard watched him touch her things and held his breath. It wasn't as if he was touching her, there was no her anymore. She wasn't here; he hadn't brought her here. She wasn't in those things; she wasn't anywhere. What people did with the things of the dead was what people did.

He closed his eyes, making himself stop. He opened them again, tried to concentrate on the beautiful counter, the figures carved into the front, the delicate columns on either end up which more figures climbed, to be woven into the design of the bridging valance.

Behind the counter he caught the gleam of mirror, a wall of small partitioned boxes, and more doors in the shadows.

But the most prominent, impossible-to-ignore feature of this grand entrance was the great staircase directly opposite the front door. It spilled down from the second or third floor – difficult to tell which, with the four or five tributary stairs joining it at various points on its height, massing like waves until it flooded most of the area before the door. It pushed the occasional tables and sitting chairs off into the corners by the windows, stealing the bulk of the lobby floor, threatening to ram out the front wall of the hotel. Ridiculously impractical, of course – not content to merely break up the traffic flow through the hotel's first floor, it stopped it all together – it was still, undeniably, eccentrically, magnificent. Richard imagined it as the corpse of some gigantic mythological creature, slain by forces unknown, left to rot here at the center of the hotel.

"Nice stairs, huh, Daddy?" Serena said softly behind him.

"Oh, yes, sweetheart," he practically whispered. "Very nice."

"Enid has made you a meal," Jacob said. Richard looked around, unable to place his voice. Finally he found him: on the wall past the desk, in a corner almost hidden by the great stairs. He stood in the opening to a narrow hallway, beside a very short woman in a dark dress, her face an oval of olive skin, creased severely once for a mouth, and again for a channel to contain the tiny, moving eyes. Her nose was slight, with no detectable underlying structure.

"Thanks. Hi." He raised his hand shyly, but she didn't respond. He moved his hand behind his head as if to stretch.

"It was a long drive. Enid's son can move the rest of your belongings into your new quarters. This hallway will take you there, and to the staff entrance for the kitchen and dining rooms." A broad, squarish man slightly taller than Enid, but with almost identical features, stepped from behind the pair and walked swiftly toward the door. He appeared not to spare a glance for either Serena or Richard, but Serena couldn't keep her eyes off him.

"Where's the rest of the staff?"

Jacob said nothing for a moment, appearing to consider his words. "Actually, this is all the staff with which you will need to concern yourself."

"But a hotel this size, there must be maintenance staff, recreational people and, my god, housekeeping? This place must require an army of housekeepers!"

Jacob's smile was crooked, as if distorted by scar tissue just under the surface. Richard had already determined that this would be the man's most annoying trait. "I personally will serve as your maintenance crew," Jacob replied. "We have found in many cases that the previous managers are often the best-trained to undertake such a role, if they are willing. And frankly, there are always discretionary issues involved when you hire, for lack of a better term, 'outsiders.' Most of our residents provide their own entertainment, as it were. For the occasions when a bit more is required, you will serve a dual role. I assure you that duty will not be an onerous one.

"As I believe I told you during your interview, we *do* employ a cleaning crew. But they prefer working late at night, after the majority of our residents have gone to bed. They are quite shy – I doubt if you will encounter any of them during your tenure here. The advantage to that, of course, is that it gives you one less responsibility. Your challenges will be significant enough without troubling yourself over distracted maids and dirty linens."

Well, Abby, he thought, *I can't even imagine what you'd have to say about all this.*

The night of the Carters' arrival I worked late behind the front desk, arranging the materials I would use to train Richard in his new duties. I had prepared a number of exercises intended to take him through checking guests in, looking up any available data related to their history with our hotel, making notations as to dietary and exercise requirements, and what to do in the case of any glitches that might occur. I studied my diary entries for the early days of my own tenure here, to refresh my memory regarding my initial difficulties with this work. Perhaps I was over-prepared, but despite my long tenure, this was my first opportunity to train new staff. I swore to myself I would not repeat my predecessor's pedagogical mistakes.

I heard an exaggerated throat clearing and was surprised to see Enid standing there. "Enid. Rather late for you, I should think."

"Yes sir, it is. I just wanted to point out that you never told me our new manager would be bringing a child into the Deadfall."

I admit to feeling a certain defensiveness, but I remained professional. "Well, no. I suppose it slipped my mind," I replied.

"Yes sir, I would just like to also point out that it has been a number of decades since a child was in residence here."

"True. And isn't she charming? She veritably brightens the room, don't you agree?"

"Yes sir, I agree. She is very charming. But do you think we're prepared sufficiently to keep her safe?"

"You know my position on safety issues in general, Enid. It applies to children as well. Safety is quite important, but I also believe a child is safer here than on the average, say, New York City street."

"I am aware of your position, sir. I just wanted to make sure you were comfortable with it, when applied in this specific, and not at all theoretical, case. And that was all I had to say." She left without waiting for my reply. She had annoyed me, but she had made me think.

– from the diary of Jacob Ascher,
proprietor, Deadfall Hotel, 1969-2000

Chapter Two
BLOODWOLF

There have been between thirty and thirty-six managers of the Deadfall Hotel during its existence. The exact number is unknown. Their tenure has ranged from one hour to thirty-one years. I have the honor of having the longest employment at this establishment. The name of the unfortunate individual who had its shortest employ has been lost, or perhaps suppressed, but I refuse to pass judgment on how information is handled regarding such matters. The records I have examined simply refer to a 'spontaneous combustion event' shortly after the woman's arrival.

What that poor woman's demise (if 'demise' it was) illustrates is that there is a certain amount of danger involved when one resides in, and indeed is employed by, such an institution. Several past managers terminated their employment as a consequence of physical disappearance. A few others grew ill with undiagnosable maladies that made their sunset years rather uncomfortable. Whether these incidents were the result of disease contracted from a resident, a disorder native to the materials used to construct the hotel itself, or a condition of a personal nature completely unrelated to their employment, we will never know. But the potential for peril would be foolish to deny.

And yet wherever men or women choose to walk or reside, they will be accompanied by danger. And this danger affects not only themselves, but spouses and children as well. It is a simple fact of life. Before my time, several of the managers had families who shared the life of these grounds with them. And in a few cases, tragedies did occur. But wherever we are, whatever we do, there will be children in danger. We can only try our best to protect them. This hotel, ultimately and on average, is no more dangerous than most of the haunts of men and women. I sincerely believe this. It is also evident, unfortunately, that it is the nature of life that no one, at least no one deserving the classification of human being, survives the endeavor.

None of the therapies used by humans upon humans is without pain. I hesitate to call this position therapy, but I do know that for many of the managers, therapy has been the end result. That has certainly been true in my case. Those individuals chosen for this position – and although the basic interviews are conducted by former managers, the candidates come to us by methods often opaque and without comprehension – tend to be men and women who have experienced terrible trauma in their lives. They come haunted by loss, perhaps some terrible deed perpetrated either by them or upon them, and they carry these traumas around with them like fantastic creatures perched on their shoulders who alter the very way they see the outer world. At the end of their tenure many, but certainly not all, have been better off, in some way.

Recruitment can be difficult. Oftentimes you must balance your belief in complete honesty with the higher needs of the institution that employs you, the clientele who depend on you, *and the ultimate needs of the person with whom you have not been completely candid.*

I was not completely honest with Richard Carter concerning the nature of, and potential dangers regarding, his employment at the Deadfall Hotel. I have some regrets about this, but I cannot honestly say I did the wrong thing.

We cannot escape our fears. Ultimately we must deal with them. We are but momentary blips of consciousness on the sea of time – we have but a limited span to do those things we are willing to do, to say those things we are willing to say. Our greatest challenge may be to face the sadness that knowledge entails. I'm afraid it is a test most of us will fail.

– from the diary of Jacob Ascher,
proprietor, Deadfall Hotel, 1969-2000

SPRING WAS A time of pests: small animals nesting in the rooms, insects prowling over the walls and chewing into hand-carved woodwork and flocked wallpaper. Except for their occasional forays into the realm of human anxiety (a peripheral glimpse of a few silverfish might effectively highlight the mood of one of the hotel's more paranoid guests), most of these tenants remained hidden until their deaths, when their bodies might be discovered behind furniture or in hollow sarcophagi eaten out of the decaying structure as part of the creatures' final, instinctive meals. It was a time of grass that grew too quickly to mow, and in nooks and crannies too out of the way to trim. And it was a time of blood. Richard's daughter was becoming a woman.

Richard had largely gotten over the initial panic. A call to a local doctor whose name Jacob had supplied, a call to a distant cousin, female, whom he hadn't seen in years, and Richard was reassured that although this was earlier than the average, it wasn't that unusual. And certainly it appeared to be the only sign of womanhood in his child, much to his relief. He thought the early and sudden maturities of so many children saddening, and occult in their implications. It pleased him that there still remained so much of the little girl in Serena's dress and fantasies. Even now he could hear her in the great side yard, debating loudly with the squirrels concerning some new infraction, perhaps their appetite for doll blankets or their continued abuse of the trees.

Serena had her own theories about the fantastic jumble of deadfall accumulating densely around the grove – she said it was the squirrels, gnawing and hacking and fighting in the trees. She claimed to have seen a squirrel with front teeth some three inches long, and marked by body-length running sores. "A real fighter of a squirrel, Daddy," she had said. His little girl still, at least for the time being.

This was not something he'd ever anticipated going through without his wife. Abby used to complain that Richard did his best to keep Serena a child, that he'd keep her from maturing forever if he could. The tickling and the crazy stories, the mad play – his way of parenting had always made her uncomfortable – she said it was too 'out of control' for her. He realized, now, there had been some truth in what she'd said, but he had no idea how he was supposed to draw the line, how to encourage her to make the most of her childhood, and then to encourage her growth and maturity when the time came. How was he supposed to know when it was the right time?

He didn't think that Abby had ever fully appreciated that once Serena's childhood was gone, it was gone forever.

"The past *is* our world, Richard." She'd been half-asleep when she'd said that, at the end of a long evening of arguments over Serena, what was best for Serena, what they should and should not say to Serena. It had been an odd, tired thing to say, and he would wonder, particularly after her death, if perhaps she'd had more she could have said, more words that would have made him understand, as she had seemed to understand.

"When we breathe, we breathe memory," Jacob said.

Richard started. He'd been daydreaming again. He nodded assent, although he had no idea what the context of this statement had been. But he didn't want Jacob to know he wasn't paying attention to everything he said.

They were stationed at one of the rounded corners made by the lakeside wall of the hotel as it traveled over the harder rock of the cliff. Here the foundation was so old it was sometimes difficult to tell where it left off and the bedrock began. Some of the masonry was obviously in trouble, heavily pocked and missing stones. Jacob was waist-deep in a cavity, blue coveralls turning white with rock dust.

"See anything?" Richard couldn't; the old man made an efficient plug.

"Oh, quite a few things, actually."

The man's obvious tease irritated. Richard had stopped pushing for the details of Jacob's knowledge some weeks ago. The man distributed information only as it suited him, only when he decided it was actually required.

"Got it!"

Suddenly the blue coveralls were backing out, Jacob's shoulders scrubbing frantically against the crumbling stone. He moved fast enough to startle Richard again, who was accustomed to only patient and leisurely movements from the man. He scrambled out of his way.

Jacob came out of the hole with scraped moss and roots sliming his shoulders, powder and cobwebs and dark brown bugs in his silver-gray hair. Something long and many-legged danced around a blue shoulder, then dropped into tall grass and disappeared. Jacob's shoulders did their own dance beneath the coveralls. Then he turned around.

He held out something all black fur and squeal, with ridged, membranous ears and a snout like a rotted apricot. No tail. Richard stepped back farther. The creature's small mouth had suddenly filled with teeth about three inches long.

"Jesus! What is it?"

Jacob had already stuffed the little furred terror into a steel mesh bag, whose sides now warped furiously with the creature's struggles. Richard no longer wondered at the purpose for such an unusual container.

"I find one of these beasties every now and then. A long time ago, years before I came here, one of the guests left several of them behind. They've been living and breeding somewhere inside the hotel since then. I will tell you more about their history and proclivities at some future date when I have more time."

Richard filed that bit of information away, knowing Jacob never would have the time. A few weeks earlier, he'd observed Jacob removing yard after yard of a slick, grayish, rope-like fungus from around the foundation stones on the north side. The fungus had been remarkably tenacious – at one point a large chunk of stone had come away with the growth – and Jacob had worn heavy gloves. But the old man had neglected as yet to fill Richard in on its nature or origins, or whether any cautionary measures were in order for the future. It had become quite apparent that they had very different ideas about training. He was being trained, wasn't he? But for what?

"I imagine Serena will be interested in boys pretty soon."

Richard laughed. "Oh, I doubt *that*."

"She'll be eleven years old in a few days. And girls, of course, mature faster than boys."

"She'll only be eleven, Jacob. She's a little girl still."

"A girl in ways. A woman in ways. 'That is how the young ladies grow,' is the way my mother used to put it. My mother arrived at her fourteenth birthday mere weeks before my birth. You have talked to her in some detail about her period, I imagine."

Richard nodded hesitantly, then said, "I thought I would wait a few weeks."

Jacob looked at Richard over the pipe he'd brought out for lighting. "Or shall I ask Enid to talk to the girl? I am sure I can persuade her."

Richard found it hard to imagine that sour looking woman talking to Serena about such a personal thing. But she was the only woman on the premises, as far as he could determine. "I don't know; that might be best."

"A single father – it can be a difficult thing." Jacob gestured vaguely.

Richard nodded.

"I'll speak to her," Jacob said. "She does well with children, despite the impression she gives."

"Thank you, I appreciate that."

"And I'll ask her about a party. An eleven-year-old should have a birthday party." He walked away, the steel mesh sack bouncing under its own power along his shoulder.

Richard examined the hole in the foundation where Jacob had removed the furry pest. The darkness within the animal's tunneling varied in gradation, in texture, in smell. When that darkness began to move, Richard backed away. He wondered how long it would take him to become a competent caretaker of such a place.

Serena was still chattering amiably with the squirrels, who appeared strangely drawn to her the past few weeks. There seemed to be a faint, coppery scent in the air. From a distance, his blonde daughter looked older than she was. *More like Abby every day.* He hadn't really noticed until they'd come here. Maybe it hadn't even happened until they'd come here. But it was disorienting. At night he would dream of Abby – the exact curve of her face, the way her hair hung over her ear, how her hand fitted on top of his. He would wake up crying, and wonder if there would come a time when the crying would stop, and he could not decide if that would be a good thing or not. And then in the morning he would see his daughter, and see that same curve of face in her, that same drape of hair, and Serena's hand on top of his would feel so like Abby's he did not know how he could bear it. The shadows by the hotel wall became too cool for him; he walked away from their grip and out into the sun.

Dinner was lasagna that night. Serena had made it all by herself. Enid had been coaching her intermittently for several weeks – more often than not, Serena didn't appear to enjoy those sessions much, but she was never late. Tonight they were alone, dining by candlelight. He wished Abby could have seen her – how grown-up she looked. Then he felt a chill, perhaps because of where they were, and the importance of the evening, and found himself thinking that perhaps Abby *did* see her, that she had been watching them the whole time. The few guests in the hotel kept largely to themselves and took meals in their rooms. Jacob was off attending to his own mysterious affairs.

"I'm kind of glad Jacob isn't here tonight," Serena said. "Is that a bad thing to say?" She cut her lasagna expertly, holding the next portion daintily speared on her fork.

"Of course not. I thought maybe you'd be disappointed," Richard said. "He should have been here for your first try at lasagna." He stuffed his mouth with a huge portion, strands of it hanging off his chin, dripping onto his shirt. "Mmm, and isn't it delicious!"

Serena laughed. "Where's your manners, Daddy?" She took a careful bite. "Sometimes it's nice to have dinner with just the two of us. Makes it kind of special. Besides, Jacob's weird sometimes."

"Well, I can't argue with that. But we couldn't do much without him around."

"Daddy?"

"Mmm." Richard's mouth was full again.

"I know what'd be good for my birthday."

"A new car, I suppose."

"Not this year. I thought maybe a razor. For my legs."

Richard looked at her. He was aware that his face must be showing surprise, but he'd actually been expecting this. "Are you sure?"

"Daddy! I've got hair."

"I know, but it's not that much."

"It's embarrassing."

Richard knew she'd been wearing knee-high socks, and tights, even on very warm days. He'd asked her if she wasn't burning up. Now that he thought about it, she hadn't shown her bare legs in months. "I understand, sweetie. I'll see what I can do."

Serena smiled broadly, then returned, with serious concentration, to her meal. She straightened in her chair and raised her chin. In the candlelight, she appeared suddenly to have aged a decade. Richard took a deep breath and tried to finish his meal.

That night Serena was too excited to sleep, feeling all grown up because of the cooking, and the razor, and he did let her stay up a couple of hours past her bedtime. She'd wanted to listen to a comedy show on the radio with him. They'd discovered upon arrival, much to her distress, that there were no televisions here ("Can you imagine our residents watching television?" was the way Jacob had explained it to him), but he had managed to get her interested in the variety of programming available on the radio. For himself, Richard had little tolerance for anything meant to be 'funny' so soon after Abby's death, but he felt he couldn't refuse Serena's request for his company. And it was easier with radio, if he heard anything he could not deal with, to make himself not hear. Serena had tried to be very grownup about the show, laughing loudly just slightly after the jokes were delivered, or when she saw that he was somewhat amused, and furrowing her brow in concentrated study of the parts of the broadcast outside her immediate experience, which was roughly half of it.

He'd been touched by all this, of course, but it also frightened him. He felt in over his head. He was relieved when she finally asked him to read a fairytale for bedtime and tuck her in.

Abby would have known what to do, what to say. She wouldn't have needed Jacob to prod her into doing the right thing.

Richard liked the nights best. This had been a huge surprise – when he had first arrived, the thought of spending the hours of darkness within those chaotic walls had brought an uneasy sensation he hadn't felt since childhood. The first few mornings, he'd awakened with the covers pulled up over his head.

But after a time, the night had become a comfort to him. After dark, the vast sprawl of the hotel began to disappear slowly into the shadows, the lights dimming by means of an apparently complex system of timers, the various wings and rooms falling asleep one by one until only the suite of rooms he and Serena occupied, and the front lobby, were awake and part of the real world. Then he seldom ventured into the other parts of the hotel, save for a few well-lit corridors where the current guests resided (unless they specified that their section of the complex be kept dark). To walk in those dark, sleeping halls would have felt too much like sleepwalking, or like stepping into someone else's dream. With the darkness limiting his world, he could imagine that he still lived in a small house somewhere, with nothing to bother him outside his few, comfortable rooms.

Abby had always said she liked a "small life in a small house." She would never have been happy living in the hotel.

So why did he feel her now? In their island of light, floating amidst the darkness, it was difficult to ignore the thought. Intense grief made you both a believer and a skeptic. You believed you would see her again, when you least expected it, coming around some corner, or the one face you recognized in an anonymous crowd. You would not permit yourself to believe that death was the end. You were skeptical that she could have died in the first place, for how could such a terrible thing have happened to you?

One night, Richard had come up behind Jacob as he was closing the door to an out-of-the-way room. Jacob spoke into the darkness of the room before completely closing the door, just the one short sentence, and Richard could swear it had been, "There now, Abby, you rest now."

He considered the possibility of Serena having some sort of encounter with her dead mother. She would have told him if something like that had occurred. He trusted it wouldn't happen, couldn't happen. He wouldn't know what to say.

One night Richard was sitting in a huge overstuffed chair off to the side of the lobby, the floor lamp by the chair illuminating his lap, the book, and a little of the floor beyond his feet. He'd been thinking about his married life, and the last time he'd made love to Abby. That thin smile of hers, as omnipresent as it was, had a different cast to it during their lovemaking. The fact that it had always suggested pain to him seemed to have added significance when linked to her passion. He did not know if he'd ever feel such sexual desire again, but he cherished the memory.

When he dreamed of sex, it was as if he were haunted by the ghost of his own lust. He'd wake up in the morning drenched, twisted up in his bedclothes, with no clear memory of the dream, and that forgetting seemed to increase its power over him.

A small antique lamp affixed to the wall near the top of the grand staircase illuminated the landing. Most of the steps remained in darkness. He'd have to do something about that. Someone would try to come down those stairs in the middle of the night and break their neck.

And as he thought that, someone paused on the landing.

"Serena, it's way past bedtime."

There was no answer. The figure wavered, then bent forward as if to whisper something from that long distance.

"Serena?"

Then the figure was falling.

"Serena!"

Richard jumped out of his chair and bounded up the stairs. When he reached the landing, no one was there.

That night his dreams were so sharp-edged, his nerves so raw, that each transition of scene was like a raw scrape across the surface of the brain. Something with teeth had broken into the suite of rooms he shared with his daughter, something with a high-pitched squeal, sharp smell, rough edges. But he could not see it. He held his daughter close to him, her flannel pajamas sweet-smelling against his face, and saw nothing as the creature's wail rose and her soft pajamas filled with red. He could do nothing, even as the pajamas he embraced so fiercely began to empty, until finally all he was holding were rags.

Serena came into his room later that night, sobbing from a terrible dream. He should have asked her for details. Abby would have. He should have encouraged her to talk about it, talked it through with her. But he was afraid to hear what she might say. He hushed her, told her it was just a bad dream, and held her close as she cried herself to sleep.

THE NEXT AFTERNOON, a new guest arrived at the Deadfall. It was unusually hot that day, especially for spring. The hydraulics in the front door had malfunctioned, requiring focused effort by both Richard and Jacob together to open it. Jacob had been struggling over the repair all morning, uncharacteristically garbed in T-shirt and yellow-and-green Bermuda shorts. Serena overcame her embarrassment over her hairy legs and came out of her room shortly after noon in a bathing suit. Seeing Jacob in shorts, she fell apart into giggles, hiding behind the front desk until she could control herself.

So the fact that this new guest arrived in a fur coat gave Richard pause.

An ancient white Cadillac pulled up, polished and gleaming as if it had just come off the showroom floor. A large set of silver antlers ornamented the hood. The driver – a tall, skinny woman with white-blonde hair in a tight-fitting black pants suit – strode around the car and stood by the right rear door. She surveyed the surroundings with a studied casualness, but anxiety betrayed itself in the set of her mouth, the quick dart of her eyes. After a few seconds she bent awkwardly and opened the door.

An elderly man slipped out of the car, his head dropping low over the pavement. Richard thought he might be infirm, but, although he appeared bowed, there was something of a muscular crouch in his posture. And once he was fully out of the car, the man suddenly went electrically erect.

He was enveloped in a voluminous, thick fur coat. Richard didn't recognize the species of the pelt. It was a reddish brown, but with highlights of silver, yellow, and black.

The woman opened the hotel door with one hand. Jacob hadn't been paying attention, and jumped away from the rapidly swinging door as it hit the great bumpers protecting the wall. Richard stared. The hydraulics weren't fixed yet. She'd shown no strain at all.

Richard opened up the registry as they approached the desk. He made himself smile. That was the hardest part of the job – faking friendly. The elderly man stopped and stared at him, his eyes wide and pinkish beneath bushy eyebrows. Deep creases runneled his face, leaving long, rough pouches of flesh between the lines. Every few seconds a portion of skin would twitch, and there would be a generalized shiver across the face, as of something barely controlled. And then the man's face would pale, as if chilled. His hair was a rusty brown, streaked with gray, and very thick.

"I'm not accustomed to signing." His voice was old, yet unusually strong, like a Shakespearean actor's.

Richard closed the book. "We don't require it. Jacob says..."

"I will pay you when I decide to terminate my stay. I require a key," the man said.

"Of course." Richard retrieved a key from the 'good' row, the one Jacob had identified as being for 'impressive' guests. He was pretty sure this guest fit the category.

The woman helped the man remove his fur coat. He wore a three-piece black suit underneath. Wool. Some two feet of thick, luxurious hair billowed out over his shoulders when she pulled the coat away. As it unfurled, layers of hair were revealed, redder and redder, to a dazzling, crimson-copper sheen.

The man stretched his arms, his shoulders straining under the tight seams of his suit. His head fell back slightly; he sniffed the Deadfall air with a narrow-bridged nose that broadened as his nostrils expanded.

Once the woman took the key, the pair moved quickly toward the stairs. The old man's stride did not falter as they headed up.

"I see Arthur is back with us again." Jacob came around the corner and leaned on the desk. It startled Richard – he realized then that Jacob had disappeared during the check-in, perhaps wanting to see if Richard could handle it on his own.

"He didn't want to sign his name. I take it he's been here before?"

"Oh yes, Arthur's a regular guest. Arthur Lovelace. He's been coming here more years than you would believe." He paused. "He has a new driver. You will find that he never has the same driver two years in a row. They are always women. Tall ones." Another pause. Then, abruptly, "Did he say how long he was staying?"

"No, just that he'd pay me when he decides to leave."

Jacob gave a little snort. Then his voice became soft, almost sad. "Keep Serena away from him, Richard."

Richard touched the old caretaker's sleeve. "Why? What's wrong here, Jacob?"

Jacob studied his hands. "Just do as I ask. Nothing to be concerned about, really. You just have to be careful sometimes, running this hotel. I have told you that before. Please, just keep Serena away from him."

"If she's going to be in danger then he'll have to leave!"

Jacob looked at him sharply. "You know that is not an option. We do not turn guests away from the Deadfall. There are very few exceptions. Besides, I did not say she was in danger. She *is* safe; we are all safe, as long as we remain cautious. And most of our guests understand the protocols involved in staying here. With a few, such as Arthur Lovelace, I like to be a bit more careful. More circumspect. More because he is getting old than because of what he is. Sometimes, as they grow older, they become less predictable. We all have elderly relatives who are less – thoughtful, let us say – than they once were, do we not? Less predictable in their behavior? Trust me, Richard. Just keep Serena away from him. She is... on her way to womanhood."

"What does that have to do with it?" He thought of sexual predators, and all the cautions he had instilled in her over the years regarding strangers.

Jacob shook his head. "I will watch him, Richard. Nothing untoward will occur. I am quite fond of the child. And I am a careful man."

Richard wanted more – he was always wanting more from Jacob – but Jacob ended the conversation by walking away.

He could hear Serena playing right outside the front door. He'd have to watch her. He'd keep her inside all day, have her sit right next to him, if it came to it. He stared at the Cadillac through the window. The glare of sun obscured its lines, so that all he could really see was the grill, sharp-edged and shining.

"Jacob! Jacob, come back here!" He couldn't stop himself. "This can't be *right!* How can you be so *calm* about this? Hell, how can *I* be so calm? Do you hear me? This isn't making any sense!"

Jacob stepped out of the shadows. "I am listening, Richard."

"This is all pretty bizarre, don't you think? How am I supposed to take all this in stride? How can we live like this? Things could go terribly wrong at any moment. You take a wrong turn in the hall and your life changes forever! How can I accept that?"

Jacob made a vague, sad gesture. "I had a friend at one time, with cancer. End stage, a terrible thing. He could not understand his own body anymore. He became convinced it *was not* his own body anymore, that someone had stolen his body, taken his brain, transplanted it. He did not understand how he could live that way."

"How did you help him with that?"

"I didn't. I was useless. I told him what I would tell you. 'That is what we have,' I said. 'That is what we have.'"

"So get used to it, right? Stop complaining and get used to it."

"No, Richard, learn to treasure it."

RICHARD AND SERENA sat out in the front lobby that night, talking, reading to each other. Serena would ask him to read her an article in one of the news magazines he'd been perusing, and in return she'd read him a passage from C.S. Lewis or E.B. White. He knew it made her feel grown up, and he usually enjoyed it immensely, although sometimes it went on too long for his tastes – some nights, Serena's tolerance for these readings seemed boundless.

Richard glanced at the staircase, where a shadow slipped down the carpeted steps.

"Serena, it's bedtime."

"Daddy."

The shadow rose and shook its head.

"Serena, it's time to go to bed."

"Daddy! It's only eight o'clock!"

"Serena."

She stood up and flounced away to their quarters behind the desk. Arthur Lovelace eased off the last two stairs, stepped silently across the floor, and entered the enclosed circle of furniture. "A lovely child," he said with a slight rasp.

Richard stiffened. The old man stepped up into one of the soft upholstered chairs, then sank slowly into the seat, curling his legs beneath him. Light from the wall sconces filtered through his hair, casting reddish shadows across the skin pouches hiding his cheekbones. His eyes were dark pits. "Thank you," Richard murmured.

"The young ones break your heart, do they not? I suppose it is because you know they cannot remain young. All too soon they – mature, would be the word, I suppose. They change, into young men, young women. Their bodies become unfamiliar things to you, and to themselves. The boy transitions into manhood. And even more mysteriously, a tide of blood erases a young girl's face, and a woman's features are suddenly detectable beneath the coagulation."

Richard was reluctant to make any sudden movements in the man's – he searched for the right word, settling on 'deadly' – presence. Richard sensed a burning in the man's shadowed face as he spoke, a layer of pain just beneath the surface. Pinkish gums and a redder lining of the mouth, and an even redder tongue, as Lovelace stretched his lips too wide in the articulation of each word, so that Richard was seeing far too much for comfort of the man's oral workings.

"A lovely child, a lovely child," the red mouth said.

"Yes, yes she is. Thank you very much." Richard was giddy with anxiety.

"Do you suppose I might have something to drink, this evening?" Lovelace said, almost coquettishly. "Perhaps some sherry? My tongue becomes rather dry in spring. The climate, I suppose."

"Of course. I'll bring you some sherry."

"No water for me, thank you. It seems to irritate my throat."

"Of course, of course."

"Makes me a bit irritable, as well." Lovelace chuckled dryly. Richard decided he'd get the sherry right away, to wet that dry chuckle. Starting for the bar by the dining room, he staggered slightly as if exhausted or drunk.

"Such a good child," Lovelace called after him.

Richard could see the old man's eyes now, suddenly pushed out of the shadows. As if on wheels, he thought crazily. The eyes looked almost too human, exaggerated, like a manikin's eyes.

"Such a good child," the mouth said again.

Richard almost ran to get the man's sherry, feeling crazed and sick with himself. Abby would have known what to do. She'd always known how to take care of things.

RICHARD WAS SURPRISED to encounter Jacob trotting rapidly down the second floor hallway with a wheelbarrow full of books. Jacob, red-faced, stopped as soon as he saw him. Several dusty hardbound volumes tumbled out of the front of the wheelbarrow onto the scarlet carpet.

Richard began picking them up: *A History of Czarist Russia, The Autobiography of Benjamin Franklin, Beginning English Composition.* "These are from the library?"

"I thought I would set up Serena's classroom today. We always have more than enough empty rooms, and she needs her own space for lessons and study. I've already moved two desks in, and a blackboard. I would not want her to fall behind in her studies." Jacob still did not look directly at him.

"*Two* desks?"

"One is for the tutor."

"Oh, of course. Miss Dandridge. I'm anxious to meet her. Is she starting next week? I'd probably better prepare Serena – I'm afraid she's beginning to think that since we're in a hotel, she must be on vacation."

"Yes, well, I'm afraid Miss Dandridge is unable to help us out this year."

Richard frowned. "This is an important school year for Serena. I trust you've found a competent replacement?"

Jacob straightened, looking at him directly now. "I will be Serena's tutor. At least for the year."

It was Richard's turn to drop his eyes and stare at the books in the wheelbarrow: old volumes of math and social studies, a newer geography, *Huckleberry Finn, On the Road*. "Well, you're obviously a very intelligent man." He looked up shyly. "I mean, obviously. But have you ever *taught* anyone before?"

"Three years in Belgium, in fact. A year in Switzerland. I may be a bit rusty, Richard, but I *will* do a good job. I would not risk your daughter's education, if I were not confident in this."

"Of course. I'm sure. I was just caught off guard."

"As was I," Jacob replied, picking up the long handles of the wheelbarrow again. "Now if you'll excuse me, I'd best get these books onto the shelves."

The next morning, Richard donned his Deadfall Recreation Director's headwear and went out to the tennis courts. Jacob had presented the cap to him with an uncharacteristically broad smile: a baseball-style cap, crimson with black script lettering, the brim too large and too soft to be stylish. The sweatband was cracked and stained, according to Jacob, "with the sweat from every proprietor of the hotel since the early forties." Richard didn't want to appear ungracious, but when he slipped it on he could feel his neck muscles contract involuntarily. But it proved to be remarkably comfortable – he expected to wear it a great deal over the coming months.

The accompanying T-shirt – bearing the same lettering style and similar, although not precisely identical, color scheme – had been Jacob's innovation when he'd been in charge. Thankfully, he hadn't insisted that Richard wear his hand-me-down, but had a little shop in one of the local hamlets make up a new one.

Two old women, draped like unused furniture in dark cloth, swatted at a shuttlecock out on a close-clipped grass court. Black silk scarves hooded their heads so that Richard couldn't see their faces. He stood by the edge of the court and watched them for a while, his arms folded across his chest. He felt silly in his gaudy T-shirt and sports cap in the presence of these dark-clothed, grim players. They didn't so much play, actually, as participate in a predefined ritual. He'd seen them out here before – apparently they were the closest thing the Deadfall had to permanent residents. Jacob said they had moved in sometime before his tenure. They were amazingly accurate in their volley, never missing over the short distance that separated them. They stood stock-still, monk-like, the tilt of their heads following the flight of the shuttlecock.

Then one of the women let the shuttlecock fall to the court, and they left together, the long-stemmed rackets held delicately upright, as they had every other time Richard had watched them. The fallen shuttlecock was forgotten – they used a new one each day. Richard wondered where they got them; they'd never asked him for one. In fact, like most of the guests, they made him feel fairly useless.

He turned his back on the court, watching their smooth, unlabored progress up the slope toward the hotel. He heard a quick flap of wings, and discovered that the shuttlecock was gone.

Few who came here were at all interested in recreation, at least of the sort the hotel sponsored in any official capacity. There was the occasional jogger, sometimes a swimmer, and once an old, hunchbacked man who shot baskets most of every afternoon. But none who really needed any sort of director.

Jacob once told him that they used to have large tennis tournaments here, but that the 'uncomfortable' charge in the atmosphere as hotel guests watched locals and locals stared in return made things so uncomfortable that the local people stopped coming, and the tournament died.

The branches hanging just over the courts stirred, birds flew, something dropped at the far end of the manicured grass and burst through the underbrush, and was soon moving aggressively through the trees beyond.

Richard jogged to the side of the courts and circled around the trees. In the distant green pasture bordering the hotel grounds on the north a figure was running, break-neck, charging. A long banner of red-brown hair flew behind the runner's shoulders.

SOMETHING CAME INTO his dreams: faster than thought, swift and full of rage. Once again, he'd been dreaming of Abby, but the thing swallowed her whole, his memories of her divided again and again until only a fine, red mist remained. Something slipped through the dark corridors of the Deadfall Hotel, which had become the secret passages through Richard's dreams, and, although it could not be seen, it could be felt. It made the dark air electric. It left the belly ill. It made the nerves and muscles dance. Richard tried to shout in his dream, tried to cry warning, but the thing had already stolen his breath away. He had become empty and hopelessly inadequate. A fool.

The thing's swift dance through his dream became playful. A light chuckle left behind in its passing.

SERENA'S PARTY WAS to be held in the gazebo – just the right size for a small, intimate affair. Jacob had been busy washing down the structure and making small repairs since early that morning. Right after lunch, Richard found him up on the gazebo roof.

"You're going to have a heart attack, working so hard!" Richard called. Jacob snorted. Richard knew full well that the old man was much healthier than he was. It touched him that Jacob would expend such effort on Serena's behalf.

"I can't remember the last time this Gazebo was used," Jacob said. "A marriage in the early eighties, I believe."

"What kind of shape is it in?"

"It *was* in terrible shape! I had to replace half of the floor supports – that floor wouldn't have held for a five-year-old, and certainly not Serena and her guests."

Richard nodded, walking around the bright white and red perimeter. Everything was freshly-painted. Jacob had worked a miracle – the gazebo didn't appear ill-used in the least. There remained but a trace of the off-centeredness, the lean, and a faint scent of decay beneath the renewed colors.

The gazebo had been one of the first things Richard noticed when he moved into the Deadfall, after the suicide cascade of tree limbs. Its awkward proportions drew the eye, the pointed gray roof too high for the diameter of its base, and the side-rails too high up on its eight support members. The boards had been warped, cracking with age and damp.

Richard walked around and around the gazebo self-consciously as Jacob worked. He knew he was really looking for flaws, some excuse for Serena not to have her party here, even though that was what she wanted so badly. And Jacob would recognize exactly what he was doing.

"Have you read the paper lately?" Jacob leaned over the railing so far that Richard was startled.

"Which paper?" The question surprised him. Jacob would know that Richard hadn't bought a paper since moving into the Deadfall.

"*The Mad Devon Daily*. Murders. Two in two days. The local authorities are baffled, but of course *that* is hardly news." He handed down a heavily-creased clipping. They were brutal, bloody killings. Although the paper didn't really spell it out, he could surmise that some dismemberment had been involved. "Youngsters, really," Jacob said, "Teenagers. Not wanting to jump to any conclusions, of course, but I would be remiss if I did not consider the possibility that Arthur, due to the mental deterioration common to his kind in their later years, has broken the rules."

Richard stared at him. "He wouldn't."

"Some have. You know that. I have cautioned you."

"We can't let this –"

"Of course not. But I emphasize that we do not *know* this breach has occurred, simply that it is a possibility. We have to be informed, we have to be cautious, but we must be fair about this. It is our obligation. I just wanted you to be aware, so that you will remain on the alert. If Arthur has suffered some kind of breakdown, then I assure you we will act; there are policies in place for just such an occurrence, which all parties have agreed to. But just be cautious. Keep on the alert. Keep Serena close to you. Arthur may be old, but an undiminished *wildness* resides there, as has always been the case. He's not to be played with."

Jacob retrieved his clipping, stuck it into his back pocket, and with his usual abruptness returned to work.

Something rustled the dried vegetation beneath the gazebo. Richard leaned and peered past the latticework surrounding the gazebo's base. Cold stared out at him. Cold blinked its eyes, then went away before Richard could decide exactly what had been there.

He straightened and looked around. He could see Serena out in the field, sitting up on an outcropping of black rock. Richard looked around for the running figure with the long red hair, the loping old man, but didn't see him. He began striding briskly in Serena's direction.

He was almost at her side when he saw the blood spot on her bright yellow shorts. Her face was washed out, pained looking. He felt a sudden panic, reached for her shoulder, started to say something, then realized where the blood came from. He was embarrassed. He drew his hand back, and then was ashamed of himself.

"It hurts, Daddy."

Richard eased up on the rock beside her. "I know, sweetie. It's" – he gestured awkwardly – "it's what happens to you when you become a woman." The words sounded awkward to his own ears, stupid, but he had no others to offer her.

"And that old man scared me."

He stared at her. "What old man?" he asked as softly as he could.

"That old man. He ran right by me, and I didn't even hear him coming. Like he was nothing but wind."

Richard followed her gesture. Lovelace was running by the trees. At that distance his stride looked impossibly broad, his legs inhumanly long. "Did he touch you?"

"What?"

"Did he *touch* you?!"

Serena looked up at him, startled. "No, daddy." Her voice quavered.

Richard hugged her to him, feeling clumsy and ridiculous. He tried to ignore the faint scent of her blood.

In the distance he could see Arthur Lovelace standing against the backdrop of dark trees, watching them, his blood-colored hair billowing in the wind.

"THIS IS MY eighteenth – no, twentieth year here. I imagine it must feel odd at times, Mister – oh, may I call you Richard?" Richard nodded his assent. "Very good. I was simply saying, Richard – I do prefer referring to the Deadfall's various proprietors by their first names – it must feel odd to have guests who know far more about the Deadfall than you may ever be privy to."

Lovelace had taken the chair next to him so quietly that Richard was startled to see his sudden appearance. Certainly in his formal smoke-gray suit, his long hair blown out like a copper-colored cloud, he appeared nothing less than a hallucination.

Enid had just handed Richard a cup of tea. Escape would have been awkward. He looked up – she was still there, waiting for... what? His dismissal? It wasn't like her – usually she was gone by the time he'd realized she was there. But she wasn't looking at him – she was gazing at Lovelace, her eyebrows raised, mouth slightly pouted. He could detect no fearfulness in her. On the contrary, she appeared curious, slightly disapproving of what she saw, and maybe – if he wasn't reading into it – somewhat disgusted.

"Thank you, Enid."

She nodded, then much to his surprise, smiled, replying, "Of course, sir," curtsied and left. Richard almost spilled his tea at her obeisance. Clearly an act for Lovelace's benefit.

"For me as well, if you don't *mind*." Lovelace growled the words.

Enid paused in the distance, and without turning replied, "Of course."

Richard glanced over at Lovelace, who looked displeased. "It *does* feel strange at times. But Jacob has shown me a great deal, Mr. Lovelace. More than you would know."

Lovelace looked at him quizzically, then let a mild chuckle slip. Richard felt foolish, a bragging boy caught in his bravado.

Enid brought Lovelace a cup of tea. She stretched out her arms to deliver it into his palms. Steam billowed from the liquid but he did not wince. The skin of his palms looked worn, rock-like. "I trust this is strong, undiluted by condiments?" Lovelace asked. Enid nodded curtly and escaped.

As Lovelace drank the tea, in surprisingly delicate sips, Richard noted subtle changes in the man. The cheeks flushed even more, as if the mere sensation of liquid in his mouth was exciting him. The nostrils flared to an almost grotesque width. Lovelace's head eased back and his mouth fell open, as if he had fallen asleep, although Richard knew he was wide awake – the body appeared tense, expectant.

Across the lobby, Serena was poised by the front desk, her elbow draped casually on the counter, watching. Lovelace's eyes were pointed decidedly in her direction, his nostrils expanded ever wider, smelling her.

Richard leaned forward slightly and tried to see Lovelace's teeth. They weren't unduly long, but the surfaces seemed to have more sharp edges than normal teeth – he could imagine them scratching the inside of their own mouth. They appeared meticulously cared for.

And then Lovelace was speaking to him again. "The first time I stayed here, it was a Mr. Grant who was the manager. William. A quiet, dark man, that one, said almost nothing. As 'other' as his guests. That one didn't die, I believe. He was simply lost on a midnight's journey to the lavatory. Perhaps he booked himself into a room." Lovelace's chuckle made no sound this time.

Richard remained silent for a long time. His tea was cold when he began drinking it again. Then, "Why do you come here, Mr. Lovelace?"

Lovelace turned his head and stared at Richard – a rotation seemingly independent of the rest of his body. "A manager has never asked me that before. I'm not even sure if it would be considered bad manners." He tilted his head slightly. The mouth grew redder. "I can be myself here, young man. I do not normally have such luxury. Surely you can understand that much?"

"I can. But are you trying to tell me you never show yourself away from this hotel? I'd find that hard to believe."

"I'm an old man. There is little I can do."

"Come now. I've seen you run."

He grinned. His lips seemed too loose, too mobile. "I *do* enjoy my running. But I'm an old man. Where else could I run so freely and fail to attract attention? Away from here I am the old man again – I keep my hair tight under a wig. My cheeks fall inward. I am wound tight. I can hardly move, I am so... inside myself. Away from here I am a *safe* old man."

RICHARD'S ATTEMPTS TO go to sleep that night were thwarted again and again by glimpses of Abby's face, Abby's body, her hair flowing long as curtains, ending bloodily, ending in ash and a charred skull. He sat up in bed, staring across the room, mesmerized by the strands of hair twisted through the dark, unraveling, vanishing beneath the door. He made himself climb out of bed. When he opened the door, he saw traces of the hair slipping around the corner that led to the back staircase and the upper floors. He struggled to keep up. The hair had vanished by the time he reached the second floor. But he knew where to go.

He stood outside that room on the far corner of a dog-leg wing, that door which he had seen Jacob closing, whispering so softly to (*"Abby, you rest now"*). When he rested his hand on the knob, its coldness sent a thrill through his arm, but still he curved his fingers gently around it, and pushed.

Things stirred as he walked inside. The ancient bedclothes, unused, rose and fell. The window glass fogged with the sudden temperature change, with breath. There was a gentle sigh, as of something holding onto its emotion, trying not to betray too much.

He sat down on the bed. He could smell Abby all around him, the saltiness of her sweat mixed with her perfume, and the same shampoo she'd used all the years of their marriage. He leaned forward, put his face in his hands. "I don't know what I'm going to do." He said it in a whisper, not feeling the need, or afraid, to speak any louder than this. "I think maybe we should leave. He says it is safe, as safe as –" He chuckled grimly to himself. "As safe as houses."

A sound like the release of tears, a sadness not quite unbearable. In this room he could not tell if the emotion came from inside.

"I've moved her around, I know that isn't good. I just don't know, could this be any more dangerous than anyplace we've been, or less?"

A rustle in the walls. Paper separating from plaster. Rats or insects?

"And I think you're here, I'm almost sure, but I can't imagine how."

A change in the light, shadows drifting.

"Would you be going with us? How can I even think of leaving you behind, again?"

Soft sighs under the dry whisper of sheets.

THE DEADFALL WAS periodically infested by what Jacob referred to as "inch worms." These were not the small caterpillars or moth larva that Richard had always associated with the term, but long, ropy creatures an inch thick which liked to wrap around things, especially heat and light sources. One of his regular chores became removing these creatures from the hallway light fixtures. As far as he knew, they were harmless, but they greatly lowered the life expectancy of the bulbs.

Jacob had provided him with a special tool for the task: a long pole with three hooks on the end, the points blunted so as not to hurt the worm. But the tool had gone missing again, a regular occurrence. He might have mislaid it once or twice – left it behind a door or in a corner – but clearly someone had another use for the device.

He was searching for the tool outside Serena's classroom when he heard Jacob's voice. "Stalin could be particularly cruel to some of the old Bolsheviks, anyone who had known him in the old days. He would have them arrested, with their wives, send them off to Siberia. When relatives protested, he would claim it was someone else's doing, that his hands were tied, that even he was not above the law.

The victims would not be told the specifics of their crimes, they would have no idea how they had offended him. Some were convinced he couldn't possibly know, and if they were only able to inform him of their plight, he would save them. Sometimes he would bring them back to Moscow suddenly, promote them, sit them down for a special meal, and then that same day take offense at the smallest thing, something he'd just manufactured, and send them right back to Siberia. That was his idea of a joke."

"Ooh, that's *horrible*," Serena said.

"Quite," Jacob replied. "We'll be discussing the purges and Stalin's particular brand of cruelty in more detail next week. For tomorrow I'd like you to read in the Hitler book, the chapter entitled 'Rearmament.'"

After Jacob left Serena to her studies, Richard caught up with him out in the hall. "Stalin? Isn't that a bit much for a kid her age?"

Jacob nodded. "She is a precocious child. I believe her time here has made her more curious about the outside world."

"So Hitler tomorrow? Do you have a name for this course?"

"As a matter of fact I do. *A History of Cruelty in the Twentieth Century.*"

"I want to trust your judgment, but I'm not so sure about this. I have to insist – you're not to show her *any* concentration camp pictures, okay? I won't have that."

"Why, Richard, of course not. A child her age."

"Hey, I don't know. She might be ready, but I'm certainly not."

"She is ready, I think, to know that such horrors exist. Children, I believe, need a basic arsenal of emotional tools, in the event that they do encounter death, tragedy, in the event that true *horror* does walk into their lives. They do not develop these tools, however, as a result of being overwhelmed."

"So no sugarcoating history, is that your meaning? No fairytales?"

"Only original, unsanitized fairytales. We discussed those a couple of days ago as part of a Folklore unit. The original Red Riding Hood, that sort of thing. Perhaps I should have kept you better informed."

"No, no, I'm sure you're doing fine. I'm a nervous dad, that's all. I take it you don't care for the rewrites? The Disney versions?"

He shook his head. "Actually, I enjoy many of those films. Animation has always… pleased me. I simply believe that the original storytellers who shared those rather gruesome tales around a campfire understood some things about psychology and emotional survival which we have unfortunately forgotten."

Richard nodded. "By the way, have you seen the worm stick?"

"First floor closet, left side, beneath the stair case."

"Thanks." He started to leave. "What did she think of the original Red Riding Hood?"

Jacob considered, then, "She said she keeps thinking about the wolf in the story. She says she thinks about him every day."

"LET'S HAVE YOUR party in town."

"But I want the party here, Daddy. In the gazebo. I've always wanted it here. And you promised I could."

"I could hire out an entire restaurant. An entire restaurant just for *you*." He sounded foolish even to himself. He had no idea how he could even get that much money; Serena must know he didn't have it.

"I don't understand why we just can't have it *here*."

"Maybe Jacob won't have the gazebo finished in time. You did want the gazebo."

"He's almost finished. You *know* he's almost finished."

"He's pretty busy. I haven't seen him at all the last two days."

He felt something cool against his hand. He stiffened, and

looked down at the small hand that had reached inside his own. "It's okay, Daddy," she said. "I'm older now. I like it here."

ON MOST DAYS, visitors to the Deadfall might think they had come into a virtually empty hotel. Richard might have thought so as well, if he hadn't had access to the hotel register, which indicated a thirty-five to fifty per cent occupancy rate, on average. Many of those, as he now understood, were long-term residents. There were others whose names simply appeared in the registry one morning, without Richard having made any sort of contact. Some of the guests were slightly more visible, and he might pass those in a hall, or encounter them on the tennis court or in one of the kitchens, or more often see them walking the grounds some distance away, singly or in pairs.

A couple of weeks before Serena's birthday, Richard was coming around the side of the staircase when he saw the remarkably tall man with the pale complexion sitting in one of the chairs in the lobby. From his stiff-posture and quiet manner, Richard assumed the man was patiently waiting for someone. He had never seen the man around the hotel before, but that certainly didn't mean anything.

"May I help you with something?" Richard approached with his best managerial smile.

He felt his smile warping when he saw that the figure was in fact a mannequin, whose painted face did not even attempt to be life-like, resembling more a figurative abstract out of Picasso or Miro. He looked around for whoever had placed the figure, then heard the whisper of movement, and looked down at the figure's chest.

Two yellow arms and hands had been thrust from between the buttons down the red-checkered shirt. They held a local newspaper, spread for reading. Richard stepped closer, leaned over for a better look. He could see a pale gray eye through another gap between buttons. It rotated up, blinked.

"Oh," Richard said, feeling his face flush. "I'm sorry to intrude."

The gray eye appeared to roll in its socket. The hands threw the paper aside, then disappeared. The figure stood up, the painted head rocking side to side as it walked out of the lobby.

"You rarely see him," Jacob said, from behind the desk. "I wouldn't worry about offending him – he's always offended. It's part of his nature."

Five women walked down the stairs, speaking in a language Richard had never heard before. They all had high foreheads, and rough patches of skin above their halter tops.

"Ladies," Jacob called.

The women turned their heads and chattered something back in unison. At the front door they struggled with each other briefly before the tallest woman won and went through the door first. The rest then followed silently, their heads bowed.

"It's Serena's birthday," Jacob said. "A number of the residents seem able to perceive when a birth date is near, and you see them much more frequently in the weeks beforehand. After the birthday has passed you don't see them again until the next one. I have no idea of the mechanism involved, but I have to say the talent would come in handy sometimes."

SOMETHING HAD BEEN bothering Richard all night, worrying its way through the shadowed regions of his dreams, gnawing at the edges of the visual frame, eating through bittersweet memories of Abby. He woke, sat straight up in bed, and found he could *hear* the gnawing. "Jesus Christ," he whispered, and wished he hadn't spoken. The gnawing suddenly stopped, as if the hungry thing were waiting, listening.

Something hard and dark dropped onto his bed. He went rigid, holding in a frightened breath so that it throbbed painfully against his ribcage. The animal started moving up the covers. He could feel its claws through the sheets.

He'd been holding his head stiffly to one side. He stared at the wall, trying to force his eyes to acclimate to the light. Now, as slowly as possible, he moved, turning his head and looking at the creature perched on the thin sheets that separated the darkness of the thing from the tender flesh of his belly. It opened its mouth and revealed rows of teeth; it was one of those things Jacob had removed from inside the foundation stones. It doubled up its neck and hissed at him, its teeth extending even farther into the dim light from the window.

Then a baseball bat came out of the darkness and swatted the beast off the covers. Jacob materialized out of the dark and stood by the bed. "I do apologize. There's no excuse really, although I'm sure you'd rather not share your bed with such an ungrateful guest. I've been chasing this nasty bit of fur and claw the breadth and length of the hotel. I believe this is the last one. So sorry."

Then the creature was scrabbling at the door, its teeth prying at the frame. Then the door was open, the mad ball of animal rocketing into the hall.

"What ho!" Jacob shouted, jumping onto Richard's bed. "Again, I beg your pardon," he said, then bounded after the animal.

Somewhat incoherently, Richard thought of Serena, asleep in her room with this beastie roaming the halls, and how Jacob seemed to be making a game of the whole thing, and it made him furious, more so because he didn't exactly know what to do about it all. And it seemed strange to be worrying over this small creature, however ferocious it might be, when there were other things, his guests, who might be far worse. And he felt a rage toward himself, for bringing his young daughter into this terrible place, where there were things with teeth and things with claws, and worse.

He jerked himself out of bed and ran after Jacob and the small aggressive intruder.

He could hear, somewhere in the darkness ahead of him, the rhythmic pound of Jacob's shoes on the carpeted hallway. And beyond that, the fading but still nerve-tickling scrape of claw and tooth against walls and baseboards.

Richard followed the sound to the staircase, over the landing, and to the rear hallways of the second floor. Here, the electricity was rationed. Two of the rooms in this section were more or less permanently occupied, but Richard hadn't yet met those occupants. Jacob had told him he might never meet them, that he himself had caught only a brief glimpse of a single member of the pair, and that years ago. "I hear them, now and then, one of them crying occasionally, the other tapping the bed with something metal," was all he could say. There were only nightlights protruding here and there, like glowing tumors from the baseboards to light the way. "Those two are quite intolerant of the light," Jacob had said.

Richard's bare feet appeared to float from shadow to pooled light to shadow again – each reappearance was almost a surprise. They might have been someone else's feet, and he just an anxious head drifting through the dark.

You just don't think, Richard, she whispered inside his head.

He concentrated on the audible trail of pounds and scrapes.

What did you think you were trying to do, Richard, bringing her here? Look at the danger you've put her in.

He tried not to speak it, but softly he was saying, "No, dear. Not now." He tried not to plead, but even more softly he found himself saying, "please."

The air around him shimmered. *You've no sense anymore,* she said, and the voice was sad now. *You'll get the both of you killed.*

"I'm her parent," he said, straining to hear what might be ahead of him. "The only one she has now."

The air was suddenly ice that adhered to his skin. His boxers became slightly abrasive. A cold wind caressed his numb face.

He was in the red corridor on the third floor now, the walls a dark burgundy, the long crimson rug glowing. He didn't understand how he could have gotten here – he hadn't climbed any more stairs. But he had to listen for the trail. Serena depended on him, perhaps more than he could manage. But he was all she had.

The burgundy walls lightened and ran. The ice evaporated from his skin.

Bathed in sweat, he ran around a bend in the corridor he did not recognize. He could hear a dry scrambling in the walls.

Dust spread like lace over his cheeks and forehead. Debris carpeted the hall. He stumbled. Something warm and wet smeared across the bottoms of his feet, collecting grit as he ran. He realized he'd never been in this part of the hotel before.

He passed under a low arch into a night cool and wet with earth. The flavor of it filled his lungs, then became candy-sweet, burning up his sinuses.

He paced through rooms and corridors burned into a pale, geometric skeleton, and clamped his lips against the flying ash. He passed indistinct sleepwalkers, clothed and bare.

It was only when he found himself in a great emptiness, when he had lost the very walls of the Deadfall, and the sound of the trail, that he stopped to consider. Where was Serena?

He had left her back there alone in their suite of rooms while he chased shadows through the multitudinous intersections of the Deadfall's skewed geometry. He had run off half-crazed in his underwear, he had ignored his dead wife's prodding and thereby proved her doubts correct. Where was Lovelace?

Richard had begun to turn, crouching, seeking the clearest way back.

"Got you, you devil!" It was Jacob's shout, close by. Richard moved to the left and strained forward. An inestimable distance away, he could see a vague rectangular outline in the darkness. He walked toward it. The floor felt seamless and without texture under his feet. He encountered no furniture, no obstacles of any kind.

Richard ran his fingers along the vertical edges of the outline. His hand found an irregularly-shaped lump of metal – he clutched it in both hands and yanked. The door scraped and whined. He yanked it again.

The door jerked opened with the sound of breaking rust. Jacob sat on the floor with his back against the blue-papered wall, stoking his pipe. At his feet lay a grass sack decorated with spreading bright red spots. Some of the red had dripped out and stained the indigo rug. The baseball bat lay a short distance away, several inches missing from the business end.

Jacob slipped the pipe from his mouth and sighed. "I do hope this last one didn't have offspring." They were back on the second floor, the wing above his quarters. Jacob stared at the ancient door behind Richard and nodded. "Myself, I haven't used that way in years." He looked down at Richard's bleeding feet. "Where's your daughter, Richard? Where's Serena?"

"I – I was following *you*." His own voice sounded ragged to him, with an edge of hysteria.

He'd barely gotten it out before Jacob was on his feet. "This way!" The sudden quickness frightened him.

This section of the hotel was familiar, but after only a couple of turns he felt confused. He wondered if he would ever feel at ease again, even in the most used sections of the Deadfall. In minutes, they were standing in front of one of the closets. Jacob dragged him inside. The closet appeared to be empty. Jacob felt the wallpaper on one side. "I do not like doing this, mind you. But it is necessary." A horizontal split of gray light opened in the dark wall. Jacob put one eye to it. "Come here," he whispered.

Richard awkwardly pushed his head alongside Jacob's. On the other side was one of the better rooms. A dark form had spread itself over the bed. The head of the dark form fell slowly to the side. Richard felt his breath swell in his throat. "Lovelace."

In sleep, he looked like an old man. His long red hair had been pulled back from his face and lay trapped under his head and shoulders. What little of it Richard could see appeared pale, a silver color. The many lines of the face were thin and long, and fell together into a sharp bundle when he snored. It was an old man's snore – congested and throaty – and it made the man's narrow chest tremble.

"Not so threatening now, is he? Not the broad-chested, flame-haired terror?" Jacob whispered.

"He hardly looks like the same person."

Jacob snorted softly. "Our residents seldom do. They are so like children, asleep. Until they dream. They may hunt safely in their dreams. They may howl at the darkness in their dreams without betraying themselves. And most of them carry those dreams down into their days, I think, where they may seem no different from you or me. And, indeed, perhaps in their days they are *not* that different from you or me."

Richard didn't really buy that, but he didn't have the words to argue with Jacob. And something was happening to Lovelace now, which made it impossible to see any such resemblance.

Arthur Lovelace was apparently dreaming. His head moved slowly from side to side, as if in denial. His hands clutched and unclutched. His brow gleamed. A low moan stirred in his throat. His bare feet made small kicking motions, as if running in some other world. And his hair had begun to redden again, transitioning back to its familiar daylight color of flame, like blood oozing out of the scalp, out of the brain.

"The old tales have it wrong," Jacob said.

Richard pressed his eyes against the slit. Lovelace's motions of denial had grown more vigorous; the fine red hair filled the air above his head like a mist of exploded blood. The lines of his face blurred and doubled.

"Richard, behind the bed."

Richard looked beyond Lovelace's thrashing form to the far wall. A vague oval stared at him: a pale face, with patches of skin missing from cheeks and forehead. A wide red mouth. Dark, obscured eyes. And the tatters of uniform. "The chauffeur."

Richard felt a flash of anger. "Isn't that enough, Jacob?"

"No, my friend, not necessarily. As distasteful as it certainly is, there is always the possibility the driver knew exactly what she was getting into, that some sort of bargain had been made. I've known Arthur to make such arrangements before."

Lovelace's mouth had fallen back, and now it filled with an odd combination of sounds, guttural background accented by occasional high-pitched notes. His skin broke out into a heavy, syrupy sweat that made his flesh appear to melt. His long, crooked fingers pulled at collar, at sleeves. His ears fell back. His face fell back. And something like a ghost of skin, like flesh turned to vapor, began to separate out of him, began to spread like wings from shoulders and head and hips, wrapping him in mist, all his secret fluids suddenly taken flight, fleeing the body.

Richard felt his own back straighten, his shoulders curl forward, as if he had suddenly lost control of his body. His tongue was dry; anxiety wracked him. Distantly, he could feel Jacob's fingers wrapping around his arm, steadying him.

The white vapor floating over Lovelace began to congeal. The lines of the form grew more distinct. Jagged edges rose out of the mist. The lines appeared luminous, electrified.

The white form twisted its head. Eyes burned like dark coals in hollows of ice. The pale wolf raked its claws derisively across the old man's puny, laboring chest. Shallow rivulets of blood welled. Then the wolf was leaping in slow motion out of Lovelace's body, pulling a film of blood out of the flesh, splattering walls and sheets, the lines of the room distorting with its passage.

Richard couldn't make himself turn away, but Jacob was already pulling him from the closet and across to another door. "We have to beat it to Serena's room!"

He dragged Richard down a narrow spiral staircase, through a room empty of furniture except for hundreds of glass bottles filled with a murky green liquid, and, suddenly, into Serena's room. She was sound asleep, two rag dolls tucked against her chin. She always tried to hide them when he was in the room – he wasn't supposed to know she still slept with them.

A fierce scratching came from the door. Jacob moved quickly and grabbed the knob. "Jacob?" Richard moved in front of Serena's bed. Jacob began to open the door. "Jacob! Are you crazy?"

But he had already flung it open. The wolf crouched there, back rising like a white, foamy wave. Jacob clapped his hands together sharply in front of its face.

The clouded face of the wolf appeared to separate slightly. The wolf howled – not from its mouth but from somewhere inside its head – a cry something between a baby's scream and an electronic whine. The wolf twisted up into the air like the tail of a tornado and then was gone.

Serena cried softly in her sleep. Richard stroked her hair. "It's gone, then?"

"He is a creature of dreams, do you understand? Such things are essentially cowards when surprised by those of us in the waking world. But that does not mean they are harmless. Once you fall asleep you are vulnerable to them. And of course you cannot stay awake all the time."

Richard gathered his daughter closer to him. "So what do we *do*?"

Jacob looked at him as if the answer should be obvious. "Tomorrow is Serena's birthday. We will have a party."

THE PARTY WAS to be held at twilight. Serena said the sky behind the gazebo was prettiest then, the light just the way she wanted it. She had her mother's eye for the small details.

That timing, of course, made Richard anxious. The Deadfall was at its most ethereal then, its most ambiguous. At that time of day, it might look most like a normal hotel, but only because the gray shadows obscured it. But it also made it easier to lose your way. Walls suddenly became new passages. Passages suddenly became solid walls.

In the shadows under the trees, long hair waved, flapped. Abby's face flashed suddenly from beneath the hair, her eyes fixed on him. What did she want him to do? Did she miss him? Sometimes it seemed all he could think of was her, how it had been like to make love to her, and he wondered how it could be possible to make love to another woman ever again.

Sometimes, in bed, she'd been a huge, beautiful monster to him. Her body had seemed to fill the bed, to stretch as far as he could touch, and he had been a little boy struggling to explore it, to discover all the forbidden places, the secret regions that had filled him with both dread and longing. He had felt enslaved by her, consumed by her, his monster, draining him of thought, tucking it away inside her vastness.

ALL THAT DAY Richard had tried to find out more of what Jacob knew, if indeed he knew anything concrete at all, about what to do about Lovelace.

"We must watch him, Richard. I am still weighing our options. This is a delicate matter, given our mission here. Act, if it seems absolutely necessary, but only at the appropriate time."

"Then you have some sort of plan?"

"I assure you I am always making plans. You will learn that habit as well, running the Deadfall."

Richard thought then that running the Deadfall was the last thing he wanted to do. They would pack a few belongings, then they would get in the car and leave. Jacob could keep the rest of their things. Serena would be safe.

But what to do with Abby? They'd be leaving her behind as well. How could they do that? Jacob had been here for many years – he seemed to know what he was doing. Couldn't Richard just trust him? Because he certainly couldn't trust himself.

Richard watched for any trace of the wolf, but Lovelace had proved difficult to find, most of that day. Richard had used his passkey to enter Lovelace's room, and been relieved to find the chauffeur's body gone, but there had been no signs of Lovelace, except for small threads of bloodstain on the quilt. Then, at lunch, Lovelace suddenly appeared in the dining room as if nothing unusual were going on. The old man ate a hearty meal.

"You realize, he may remember little, if anything, of last night," Jacob said, as they watched Lovelace devour his food. Richard wasn't comforted by Jacob's information – it made Lovelace seem even more out of control. And he himself felt increasingly impotent.

He sometimes wondered if Jacob had seen a certain passivity, a certain pliancy in his character that had led to his choice as successor. Certainly he treated him like a child much of the time, withholding information as if it were gold and he a miser, as if he couldn't trust Richard with the responsibility of knowing. Someone with backbone might have left a long time ago. Someone with backbone probably wouldn't have taken the job in the first place. Not with all the restrictions.

"There are certain rooms, certain locks, where you'll find your passkey useless," Jacob had said. "In due time you'll receive the keys to some of those locks, but perhaps never for others."

He had come into the hotel assuming that he was to be part of management, with privileged access. But they hadn't signed anything, and no money actually changed hands. It was a ridiculous way to do business, but then Richard had never been much of a businessman.

And how could he live with the madness of the night before? He desperately, desperately needed to trust Jacob. He could not do this himself; he couldn't even run his own life. He needed someone to tell him what he should do.

For all his anxiety, Serena's party was actually a pleasant affair. Serena and Enid had baked several platters full of cookies, far more than the small party of staff and a few locals (all of them related to Enid, apparently) could possibly eat. Serena kept pushing the cookies on Richard, and he ate far too many, enough to make him even more jittery than before. She wore a rather grownup dress Enid had made for her. She looked gorgeous. And sometimes when she looked at him, his heart seized, because they were Abby's eyes. Richard had felt somewhat self-conscious about the meager gifts he had selected – a small flute and a stuffed giraffe – but she was enthusiastic about both. Her delight seemed genuine – she was a joy to give things to. He was very proud of her.

Jacob's gift was an intricately-carved wooden necklace, primitive looking, with highly-stylized fruits and animals. He also provided the musical entertainment: an ancient accordion he hauled out of a trunk that had been hidden in one of the storage closets under the stairs. It possessed a strange, tinny sound. When Jacob squeezed it, great dark clouds of dust blew out. Serena laughed until she cried, and after a moment of false consternation, Jacob laughed with her.

The clouds were dark that evening. The final rays of sunlight left a liquid crimson rim around them that gradually blackened, blending with the night.

An hour after dark, they all gathered the things from the

party and went inside. Serena seemed mildly disappointed, but when Enid suggested tea in the formal parlor her mood quickly picked up again.

"I'm going to go change for the parlor, Father."

Richard looked at her, amused. "*Father*, eh?"

Serena laughed. "I'll just be a minute. Enid made me *two* dresses! Can you believe it?" She could barely contain herself.

"Well, Lord knows a woman needs to look her best on important occasions like this. But don't be too long."

"I won't. Promise." She went around the front desk at a dead run.

Richard settled into a chair in the lobby to wait. The dim light over the lobby reddened. Richard was already out of his chair when he heard Serena's scream.

When he got to her room, Serena was standing behind her bed. Jacob was standing beside her, whispering to her, apparently trying to calm her by stroking the side of her head.

Richard was furious, as much with himself as with Jacob. "I thought you were going to be watching her?"

"I was," Jacob said softly. "I was right here." He nodded toward her closet.

Richard could feel the thing before he actually saw it. Standing inside the closet door, its back drifting upward like an arch of smoke, was the wolf. Its jaws drifted apart. The mist inside them was burning. Richard raised his hands stiffly and clapped them together with as much force as he could muster.

The wolf's eyes burned a brighter red. Its head twisted on its neck like a snake, whining and snarling. The edges of its form grew firmer as it began to slice the rug apart with its claws.

"That won't work, Richard. How can I explain this? It is deep in *thrall*. Arthur must have deteriorated rapidly for this to occur."

The wolf crept forward, leaving a trail of mist that settled into the floor like a stain.

"Pull back with us, Richard. Behind the bed."

Richard did as he was told.

The wolf raked its ghost teeth against the steel bedpost. Sparks flew. Richard began to worry about a fire, when Jacob pulled all three of them down to the floor and forced them to roll. The power in the move astonished Richard. Suddenly they were under Serena's bed, staring up at the springs.

"Jacob?" He could hear Serena whimpering, but he couldn't see her. A white muzzle suddenly gaped open a few inches from his face at the side of the bed. "Jacob!"

White fire roasted his face. He began to scream.

And then he was falling through darkness. He could feel Serena next to him. He grabbed her and waited for the fall to end. It seemed to go on for a very long time.

At the bottom there was light. And a hallway. Before he could think about the implications, Jacob had them running again, down a snakework of tangled passages and stairs.

And into the room of Arthur Lovelace.

"Daddy! That poor man."

Lovelace was spread-eagle on the bed, head back, mouth peeled open. His skin appeared shrunken, pulled tight enough to break the underlying bone.

"Grab his feet!"

Richard hesitated. He imagined touching the man's paper-thin flesh, the skin breaking open, and... things... coming out.

"Richard! Do it now!"

Together they pulled the old man off the bed. He was stiff, and he spasmed as they moved him, almost bringing them down. Serena helped where she could. Jacob led the way down the corridor. Again, Richard was amazed by Jacob's strength: he practically dragged the rest of them with him.

They followed two bends of the corridor, and at the third bend Jacob stopped and backed through a solid wall. Richard and Serena slowed, confused, but Jacob pulled them through as well.

They were suddenly within a passageway lined with ornate doors, with elaborate carvings over each doorway. It was too dark to make out many of the details, but Richard had the sensation of being stared upon by hundreds of tiny faces. Jacob opened one of the doors and they entered.

The room was empty except for a rough plank laid across two ancient sawhorses. Jacob guided them as they laid Lovelace's body on its length. Richard and Serena stood holding each other, exhausted, unable to move. Jacob pushed them back toward the door, and they stumbled awkwardly in that direction.

The wolf drifted through the doorway. Its face howled and vibrated, the misty contours of its head breaking apart, then drifting back together again. Jacob tried to push Richard and Serena back, but they couldn't keep their eyes off the thing.

The wolf's teeth grew like fast-forming icicles. Its head spun madly around. It reached back with teeth grown too long for its mouth and began ripping pieces out of its own torso. Luminescent blood filmed the room. The wolf's head stared at them; it stopped, statue-like, and stared at them.

Then the wolf began its leap.

Suddenly Arthur Lovelace's emaciated arm reached out and grabbed the thing, pulling it to him. The wolf thrashed and bit. Blood flooded Lovelace's face. "Go."

Jacob was the last one out. He slammed the ornate door and locked it. In the shadows, the elaborate carvings writhed. Sculptured eyes blinked. He pushed Richard and Serena through several more doors before they could no longer hear the wolf's frenzy, the snap and splash of Lovelace's embrace.

"THAT MAN," SERENA said later. "Mr. Lovelace. He still isn't dead, is he?"

Richard stared at Jacob.

"No, he isn't, my dear," Jacob replied. "But as terrible as that might seem, he is where he wanted to be. In that room, where he cannot leave. I suspect he had that half in mind when he came, this season."

Richard held his daughter in his arms. He looked down at her: she seemed noticeably older.

"She has changed, but you did not lose her," Jacob said softly.

But Richard wasn't listening to him. There were other sounds to hear. There was the soft inner breath that drifted through the Deadfall, higher pitched through the halls, dropping lower in the stairs and secret passages. There was the light tapping of guests who never left their rooms, their frenetic thoughts in tune with that breath. There was the distant crying of a white wolf with dying eyes. And there was the nearly inaudible laughter of his wife, his beautiful wife Abby, growing madder with every passing day of her death.

I never imagined that training a replacement would prove to be so difficult. I find I have increased respect for what my own predecessor must have gone through. It is a delicate balance, managing a new member of our family – we want him to be able to act independently, and yet we also want him to do what we want. Prospective managers are selected from a pool of the traumatized, the wounded and damaged. And yet we expect them to be brave. We expect them to protect themselves and their families and yet be brave, to do what needs to be done.

Sometimes when I look at Richard Carter I see a frozen man, stilled by grief and impossible dilemma. How can he protect his daughter? How can he leave his wife behind a second time? *My heart goes out to him. I will do what I can to protect him and his daughter.*

Perhaps we expect too much.

– from the diary of Jacob Ascher,
proprietor, Deadfall Hotel, 1969-2000

Chapter Three

THE KING OF THE CATS

"And death shall have no dominion," at least that was his hope, that Dylan Thomas who drank and sang and insulted and roared and made immortal poetry. We write, we sing, we have our children and have our way, all in an attempt to defeat that fatal king. Perhaps the famous succeed – I can't really say. But certainly it isn't their true selves the people remember, but rather the great and interesting lies they told about themselves. And whose children remember them as they really were? Your children remember you too harshly, too well, or seemingly not at all.

The dead should be grateful that we live our lives so poorly, that we have so much trouble actually being where we are and when we are. It is the dead who fill in the blanks, who occupy the empty spaces in our minds and hearts. If you see someone living their life as if their life were living them, if the most remarkable aspect of their day is their lack of participation in it, then I wager if you look closely enough you will find one or more of the dead buried waist-deep in that life, gazing about in wonder as the poor soul wanders from event to event.

It is the dead who benefit from our lack of care. And they fully understand on what side of the bread their butter lies. I must admit that I was so taken by Richard Carter's daughter Serena that I was compelled to discuss their situation with Abigail Carter, the dead wife and mother who tagged along for the ride. I attempted to explain to her that a dead mother was no help for such a child, and that whatever she might be feeling about her recent demise (and, yes, the dead have feelings – in fact emotion is the sum total of most of them), she was doing her daughter no favors by lingering about.

Mine was a futile endeavor, of course, as the dead are remarkably self-centered and narrow-minded.

My own dead wife and children have never appeared here. I cannot honestly say whether I am relieved or disappointed. I wonder if I may have so expunged them from my growing list of heartbreaks that they feel no need to make an appearance. Does that make me a terrible husband and father? I have no answer for that.

We carry our fears with us wherever we go. We pack them neatly, holding them close because if we lost them, where would we be? Lost in some foreign land without proper clothing, I suppose. Our current and past guests have brought their fears to the Deadfall, and so many of them have left theirs behind. I sometimes wonder if these missing items are mourned, or if the visitors are aware of an unburdening, a lightening of attitude due to a mysterious cause they cannot quite put their finger on. This hotel has become a warehouse of such items, and we take our duties as conservators quite seriously. From time to time some group which does not understand attempts to rent the Deadfall for parties, particularly around the season of Halloween, as if this establishment might function as some sort of funhouse. Such applications are, without exception, denied.

The strongest presence is so often an absence. Life here underscores this point almost daily. Yesterday I was up on the third floor when I became aware of the odor coming from #302. I had almost forgotten – it has been almost a decade since I thought of the tenant residing there. I stood outside the door and breathed in the stray wisps of perfume, that particular tobacco-and-fried-food aroma. No actual physical being resides in that room, but it has long been occupied by a lingering aftersmell of the man who lived there in the 'forties and 'fifties. The room is sealed so that a sufficient quantity of the smell may be preserved. We do not rent the room, nor do we enter to clean.

After the summer break I intend to intensify Serena's home-schooling. I had originally been reluctant to take on the job, hoping eventually to replace myself with a tutor lured away from some institute of higher learning. But I have been surprised to discover an unexpected enthusiasm in myself for the project. Since the beginning of the summer I have read a number of volumes of educational theory, and made hundreds of pages of notes concerning strategies and exercises I intend to try out in the fall. I believe there is much I can teach her in a relatively short span of time. In the meantime I have filled her summer with books taken from our magnificent Deadfall library. I feel confident that Richard Carter will be satisfied with the richness this educational mixture has to offer.

There is a seasonal aspect to learning, I believe, and we do our best when we respect this. Now is her season to explore, to let her fancies guide her to whatever knowledge she might find.

This spring, the Deadfall revived from its long winter sleep. By the end of summer we will see exactly what has been awakened.

– from the diary of Jacob Ascher,
proprietor, Deadfall Hotel, 1969-2000

LIFE IN THE hotel was a bumpy ride. Each arrival brought some new story. Each checkout left yet another narrative incomplete, demanding that Richard's imagination supply some sort of conclusion or at least a few seconds of summation. His and Serena's time here felt splintered, jiggered by rising and falling excitements and stray, inconclusive climaxes. Only their consistent presence, and that of the hotel, with its minimal staff, provided some sort of stability. But that was human life, wasn't it? The sadness and the thrill of it. If people did their jobs properly, they would never outlive their own homes, the places they met and studied in, made love in, sculpted their destinies in. It was all a collection of incomplete, yet meaningful tales.

Abby, of course, would have loved it here. It was an attitude and an interpretation so much in sympathy with her own. She would have loved the excitement and the anticipation, even the strangeness of it all. Richard thought she belonged in this setting much more than he.

Not that she wasn't here, of course. There was this *remnant*, this reminder, a pale simulacrum of what his wife had been, walking these halls, peering into things, taking the air.

Perhaps he had no business thinking that way. Even the living changed, went their separate ways, disappointed. And what bigger change than that turning from life into death? It wasn't her fault. But still, he found that he harbored resentment.

He saw her often in the halls, particularly around bedtime, looking under and around things, testing chairs, sometimes lying down on a step or underneath a table as if to test the comfort of a rug, measuring windows and doors with her pale, nearly-transparent hands. Always smiling. Always using those intelligent eyes which seemed to burn with their own, independent light. There was a sadness in it, but there had always been a beautiful sadness in Abby. Death seemed not to have changed her that much, in this regard.

What he felt when he saw her, besides his own sadness, was a certain irretrievable disconnection. It must be the way divorced couples view each other, he thought, if the divorce has been relatively amicable. She was no longer part of his life, really. He might wave to her in the hall; she might smile his way. But she was no longer part of his life. She had moved on. He needed to move on as well.

If only there hadn't been Serena to consider. As far as he could tell, Abby made little contact with their daughter. Maybe Abby thought that best; maybe it was for Serena's benefit. Did Abby think, now? Richard understood none of it.

THE HOTEL AND surrounding wood had baked for two months. Each day the heat built without leveling, before night or the rare downpour discouraged it until the following morning, when the climb started all over again. Guests and the occasional delivery driver sat with their heads lowered. Small animals made noises like babies calling for their lost mothers, and Richard stayed awake nights, trying to make sure in his own mind that they were not, indeed, babies. Insects danced madly in silence. Richard spent his days worrying over Serena, who filled her mornings with imaginary playmates – but wasn't she too old for that sort of thing? – and in any case who might say that an invisible Deadfall playmate was truly, unquestionably imaginary?

"Here, we'll provide these gentlemen with some lemonade and send them on their way," Jacob said, gesturing to the row of uniformed men sitting on chairs on the Deadfall porch. Bus drivers: staring out at the wide lawn, their faces dripping sweat. Jacob had told him how large numbers of these bus drivers had shown up at the Deadfall over the years, in uniform, with their empty buses, having just walked off – or driven off – their jobs. "This year, well, I believe this year will be a good year for bus drivers," Jacob had said, a few weeks earlier. And he had been right. They'd been showing up all week.

There'd been fewer official check-ins than usual, however. Jacob didn't appear surprised. A few guests had shipped themselves to the hotel in crates and barrels, and Jacob had wheeled the containers up to their reserved rooms without fuss. A family had checked in: short people in tight brown coats, the parents no bigger than the small children. And then there was the naked man covered in bite marks and sutures, who'd wandered in from the woods without baggage, and Jacob had taken him up to a room immediately. Richard was glad Serena hadn't been down in the lobby for that one.

During the afternoons, Serena spoke obsessively of babies and of more than babies – of embryos and fetuses and how there might be hundreds of thousands of them hidden in the world around us, so tiny we can't see them, floating into our open mouths and gathering into our soup spoons and crushing under our bodies when we rolled sleepless in bed, and how angry they all must be at not having a chance to be born. Of course, it made him uneasy. She was *his* baby, after all. She asked her father if maybe the Deadfall and its grounds contained more of these invisible lives than most places, and he had no idea how to answer her.

Then, after dark, there was the Serena of mercurial mood. She'd suddenly be angry at him with no reason, talking so loudly, so rapidly she was spitting. Over nothing. Over things

Richard couldn't even recall having said. Over things Serena said he *would* have said, if she'd only given him half a chance.

And still the heat intensified. What had begun as a warm welcome to the sunniest part of the year had exaggerated itself without relief, until the sun was an eye in flames and breathing became a miserable chore. Then came an afternoon when the season collapsed suddenly, parched and exhausted, falling hard into what Richard's grandmother had always inexplicably called the dog days of summer.

"The expression comes from Sirius, the dog star," Jacob offered. Providing explanations was second nature to him. Whether his explanations actually explained anything was another matter entirely. "The brightest star in the night sky. The Romans thought Sirius rose with the sun this time of year and added its heat to the sun's heat. Thereby making the dog days the hottest time of the year."

From the sound of it, you might think this was supposed to be the best time for dogs. But mid-July through August had always been unbearably, impossibly hot where he'd grown up, and he remembered rarely seeing dogs during this time, and wondering if maybe they'd retreated below ground, into vast underground dog runs and chambers where they had their own government, queens, dukes, and kings.

Every now and then, through the years, his interest would bubble over when he spied a dog digging in an out-of-the-way patch of ground, so that he could hardly contain himself. He would wait for hours sometimes, hoping the dog might suddenly disappear into the earth.

He'd also wondered if there might be special times of the year for other animals, which had heretofore gone unrecognized by the human world. Cat days and mouse days. And maybe they had places of their own, lives human beings knew nothing about, seasons and cycles and natural rhythms that affected humans, even though humans took no notice of their effects. Maybe there were realms of birds, empires of ants, counties of rabbits, kingdoms of cats. Bat weeks and months for deer. Who could know? Sometimes it seemed only human beings, with their all-too-unfocused lives, their chronic social awkwardness, had no calendrical dominion they might call their own.

These were the thoughts of a man suffering from too much heat, he supposed. No new guests had arrived, the past few days, and those who were already buried within the walls of the Deadfall appeared to have become more deeply buried still. He imagined them sitting naked in their rooms, their usually hidden deformities at home in the shadows, occasionally getting up to gulp cool air down by the grates in the floor.

The Deadfall's cooling system appeared to work well enough. Despite the heat outside, it was possible to sleep the night through, if that's what you wanted to do. Jacob had told him that sections of the upper level lacked air conditioning, but that these rooms were by special request only, this time of year. He couldn't imagine it. Even the relatively cool Deadfall interior held pockets of cooked, pressurized air. Sometimes he would be sitting, thinking idly, and it was as if the ideas adhered to the stale air around him – for hours he might watch their afterimages float languidly about his head.

A few weeks earlier Jacob had informed him that the time was fast approaching for the Deadfall's more or less comprehensive biannual cleaning.

"Now, please remain calm. There is no need for panic," Jacob had told him. "We'll be hiring what local crew we can obtain, and I have a list of past laborers who will travel this far out just for the money we will be paying them. All you have to do is provide a little supervision, and keep them out of those rooms, and floors, where they do not belong, or for some reason we do not wish to be cleaned." Richard understood there was a fund available for such work, but Jacob had never bothered to reveal its source.

Richard hadn't thought any more about it – maybe because it seemed too much to think about, a cleaning task beyond any he could imagine, particularly during the hottest, most miserable time of the year – and why choose this time of year in any case? – until one morning, when Jacob off-handedly informed him he'd already made all the arrangements, and that the workers would be arriving that afternoon. Well, let the old man do what he wanted. He couldn't be responsible for the consequences. He couldn't even think clearly. If things continued like this, soon he'd be seeing Serena's invisible fetuses and embryos himself.

AT LUNCH TIME, Richard went into the kitchens to ask Enid if she would make him a sandwich. Serena liked making her own (no self-respecting cook would serve up such unattractive combinations), and part of the fun for her was taking the sandwich somewhere she didn't belong and curling up with a book to read and eat, dripping unidentifiable juices on book, clothing, carpeting and furniture. He'd decided not to stop her – you had to choose your battles, and Jacob didn't seem to mind. Besides, the secret army of housekeepers always had things spotless by the next morning, and he had never received any notes of complaint.

He really should learn to make his own sandwiches, he thought, but he wouldn't be able to top Enid's wonderful lunches in a hundred years, so why bother? And she obviously thought fixing him lunch was just part of her job.

He walked in to find Enid packing utensils and gear into two large canvas bags. Her son stood impassively nearby, suitcases hanging from each hand. He blinked acknowledgement in Richard's direction, but said nothing.

"You're not leaving us, are you?" he asked her, unsuccessfully trying to keep alarm out of his voice.

"I always leave during The Big Cleaning," she replied, "go down to spend some time with my sister. Besides, I just can't abide this heat! I'll be back by the first snow. This is the slow season; didn't Jacob tell you?"

Richard thought that the hotel always seemed to be a bit on the slow side, but he said nothing. It wasn't his place. "I would have thought you'd want to stick around, make sure they didn't mess up your kitchens."

"Hmpf. They do what Jacob says. It's all down on that list of his, been done the same way for decades, way before he came. He never asks for my input. He probably can't – asking for my input isn't on the list, I bet."

"What about the housekeepers? Do they help out, or do they go away as well?"

"The housekeepers… do what they do, that's all anybody can say. We don't interact. Now, you have a good couple of months, and take good care of that sweet child of yours."

She nodded at her son, picked up the bags, and they left. Her saying "sweet child" had been an unexpected and endearing gift.

WHEN THE WORKERS pulled up to the hotel in assorted pickups, vans, rusted Volkswagen Bugs, and stripped-down and sloppily-puttied old Cadillacs, Richard was ready for them. He'd prepared a rough map of the hotel, breaking it down into areas and assigning so many workers to each area, accompanied by a specific list of tasks. That had required some occasionally puzzling input from Jacob. The full meaning of such tasks as 'wrap the yellow vase at the end of the hall in #14 copper wire' and 'dip the fringe of the triangular area rug with the red cat pattern into a solution of 3 parts graphite and 1 part lemon juice, but under *no* circumstances do the same to the similar rug with the green cat pattern' was not immediately apparent.

"So what does this one mean? 'Stand with your back to the closet door while rubbing two ounces of butter on the back side of the lower right-hand door frame.'"

Jacob studied the note on the map, hastily scribbled in his own handwriting, and said, "You had best obtain someone unusually limber for this particular task. I saw a couple of tall young men; perhaps one of them will do."

"So what does it mean?"

"I have no idea, Richard."

"Terrific."

"That is simply the way it has always been done. I received those instructions from the manager before me; now I'm giving them to you. There are rituals about these things, precautions to take, restrictions to be respected. It has all been passed down."

"I just wonder how I'm going to remember all this when you aren't here anymore."

"You just will. I did. You'll find you have to."

But the nature of the Deadfall seemed increasingly unreal and arbitrary, something to be memorized, to deal with ritualistically, to be accepted as a matter of faith. Working on that map made it clear how confused Richard's sense of the hotel's structure actually was. He thought he knew where most of the rooms were by now, and their relationship to the various central architectural features – halls, chimneys, and staircases – but once he started diagramming them, the pieces didn't all fit.

It appeared impossible to capture the hotel on paper. Rooms were either larger or smaller than they should have been, and the separate pieces of the hotel seemed incapable of forming a coherent whole. Chimneys did not flow unbroken from floor to floor as they should have. Tracing one such chimney all the way up from the basement, Richard discovered that it took several impossible jogs, changing its position a full ten feet from floor two to floor three (as well as the type of brick from which it had been constructed) and in no way matching the apparently corresponding chimney leaning precariously from one side of the Deadfall's roof. He had similar problems making sense of the construction of staircases, and the arrangement of pipes and ductwork moving between rooms and floors was an impossible tangle.

"We have to clean all the ducts somehow," Jacob muttered in passing. "I shudder to imagine all that might be growing inside them."

Richard got the bright idea of attaching a long cord to a heavy wheel taken from a toy wagon, and tossing that down the ducts to see where it might lead. He could hear it clanging in the metal shafts for a long time, bouncing off walls, taking long drops. Then silence. Then the cord burned its entire length through his hands, the whole of it disappearing into the dark mouth of the duct. Every few hours he would hear it in some distant wall, or rattling the boards under his feet, or making a brief appearance at the bottom of a toilet bowl before disappearing again.

He and Jacob tried to pay the smaller workers to climb into the ducts with a sponge, a bucket, and a net, but they got no takers at any price. Finally they decided to clean the best they could with mop heads attached to long limber poles, and leave it at that.

The used mop heads were dumped into a pile by the driveway. Now and then Richard would prod it with one of the long poles. There was always some arousal of movement, and tiny things scuttled or slithered out of the pile into the tall grass. Once Richard had read a book all about house mites, how they fed on tiny flakes of human skin, how millions of them lived in even the cleanest of houses. He imagined those mites nourished in the perfect environment, and magnified hundreds of times. Deadfall mites.

House mites were not something he could ever have talked to Abby about. Someone looking into their house from the outside might have called her a meticulous housekeeper. But the word he would have used was 'frightened.' She was frightened of dirt, not just because she was afraid that people would judge her on the basis of her housecleaning, or that she would be a bad mother if she didn't maintain a filth-free environment for her child (although she believed both of these things), but because of what she couldn't see, and of what she didn't know.

"There are *things* in dirt," was all she would say about it. He thought of the vigor with which she wiped everything down before the baby Serena was permitted into a room, and the way she studied newspaper stories having to do with disease and freak accidents as if they were biblical texts, and the constant journeys she made to the doctors, and how she tried every new remedy on the market until cautioning newspaper stories kept her away from medicines and chemicals of any kind for a while.

Chemicals, molecules, microbes – all bits of the unseen world were like ghosts to her. They haunted her to distraction.

He'd sometimes wondered if it had something to do with the baby – not Serena, but the one who hadn't made it. The one she'd been told was dying in her womb after six months, and then was dead, and had to be pulled out like a bad tooth. Abby had been a woman who couldn't even say the words *fetus*, or *embryo*. Early in her pregnancy, she'd sat up in bed one night and said, "There's a secret growing inside me." He'd switched on the light, expecting to see a silly smile on her face, but she hadn't been smiling at all.

He didn't think she should see it, but she'd insisted, and she said it looked like a dark doll, like an unfinished sculpture, and she had been right. But then she had said it *couldn't* be human, its fingers weren't right and she was sure there had been claws, and that the doctors had planted this *thing* inside her, and she'd never been pregnant at all. They'd had to sedate her, and he'd gone home alone to drink and cry all night.

Embryos and fetuses. For the past two years, Serena's interest in babies had remained constant. She clipped their pictures from magazines and hung them on her wall. When she tired of talking about babies, then she talked about animal babies instead, which she might always have access to, which she could hold. So unlike her mother, she had no fear of small, hidden things, even the things that smelled, crawled, and bit. But Richard had never told her about the older brother she'd almost had.

JACOB ASSIGNED RICHARD the task of inspecting the cleaned areas of the hotel.

"Don't you think you should do that? I mean, I'd like to make the rounds with you to see what I can learn, but that's my point – I don't know enough about what's right, what's wrong. Christ, I hardly know what's up or down, left or right in the Deadfall yet."

Jacob looked harried, his normally neatly-combed hair sticking up in all directions, his belt askew, cuffs spotted with black dust. "I appreciate that," he said, distractedly, "but I can't really take the time right now, and I do believe it might be beneficial if you were to examine the hotel with new eyes, without the influence of my observations."

"So you're teaching me to swim by just throwing me into the water."

"A bit of an exaggeration, but if you wish. Necessity is the great teacher, and all that."

In Richard's experience, there had always been some buildings that looked huge on the outside but proved cramped and impossible to navigate inside. In turn, smaller-looking structures appeared to go on forever for those taking a first-time tour.

He'd noticed it from the beginning, but today underscored the impression: the Deadfall managed to be too big both outside and in. From the outside, the main building resembled one of those grand old mansions from the South, with large white columns framing the enormous hard-carved front doors. The columns supported an elaborately sculpted porch roof two stories off the ground, and small windows like peepholes had been carved out of the wall above the doors in an arc. On either side of the columns were the great front windows, four to a floor, running practically floor to ceiling to maximize light and impressiveness.

Out of this central bulk the wings spread, in smaller blocks that stepped back from the main building at random angles, following the slope and irregularities of the hillside, so that the farther from the front doors the structure went, groping for stability, the more chaotic (and less elegant) it became, and the natural stresses of gravity pulled walls and framing out of alignment, until you arrived at the last segment, which should have been condemned. In fact, many sections were boarded up and isolated from the rest of the hotel.

Richard thought the Deadfall looked not so much constructed as landed, the body of some great creature fallen to ground and into its final resting place.

He had been assembling a rough interior map of the hotel since his first few days here, surprised that one didn't already exist. ("Every new manager starts one," Jacob explained. "But all eventually quit the enterprise. You will, too, I assure you.") Richard's map was now several sheets taped together, walls drawn with pencil, erased, and redrawn, arrows used to indicate geometries that made no logical sense.

He did the main structure first, which was straightforward

enough, although he did have trouble in the southeast corner of the third floor, where one room featured a closet within a closet within a closet, the final closet leading him out to the middle of the second floor hall, with no sensation of having descended. He entered a number on the sheet for each room or hall, described its location as best he could, added notations regarding closets, private baths, and similar utility spaces, and attempted some critique of the cleanliness ('Floors spotless, ceiling could use some work, mirror over the fireplace filthy, or severely corroded').

Sometimes he caught a glimpse of residents (gray flesh, curled claw, balding, rash-eaten head) as they quickly entered a closet or hid behind a curtain while he made his inspections. This always embarrassed him, even made him feel slightly ashamed of himself. Many residents didn't let him in at all, of course, and these he duly noted and went on his way. Jacob had told him that a number of them chose to travel during the annual cleaning period, and in their rooms Richard often found personal possessions awaiting their owners' return: odd, unshapely garments, twisted bits of toys, elaborate wrappings, ornate brushes and combs, scissors, and other grooming devices of unimaginable purpose. There were also pets in covered cages whose plaintive, ominous cries he decided it best to ignore.

The wings proved more difficult, as he had expected. The halls seldom followed straight lines, and the twists, turns, and doublings back made him abandon his descriptions of location in favor of relative descriptions ('eighteen steps down the hall from the previous door'). Ceiling heights were unpredictable, so that sometimes he had to crouch and other times, while there was too little light to tell him the ceiling's height, he knew it was some distance because he could hear things flying up there.

Furnishings also varied greatly in the wings. In some rooms he had to walk over the tops of beds and sideboards just to reach the other side. Others were completely bare of furniture, even though the room was still occupied ('coughs and throat clearings from the closet suggesting more than one guest').

At the end of three days, Richard had gotten up to 232 on his numbered list, and couldn't really tell how much more he had to do. This confusion of scope was further complicated when he discovered he had somehow skipped a string of rooms – as many as twenty doors – from the first day's inspections. His map was falling apart from pencil corrections and arrowed notations, indecipherable worn and smudged sections, torn bits from anxious handling.

After a week with no clear end in sight, Jacob stopped him in the hall. "Perhaps it's time for a rest. Do the rooms appear to be being cleaned, or at least dealt with?"

Richard nodded wearily.

"Then so be it. Go spend some time with your daughter."

ONE OF THE cleaning crew found the thing. The jittery old fellow brought a bucket of red paint over and set it down where Richard and Jacob were standing. At first its only movement was a slow, wet, explosion of breath, and with everything tucked in so, it resembled a heart pulled out of somebody's chest, still determinedly beating. He looked over at Jacob, thinking, *explain this one, will you please?* Then he noticed the edges of dark fur beneath the red paint and just for a moment tried to remember if there were any creatures with fur on the *inside*, then thinking *werewolf*, of course, he amazingly felt as if he were back on known, comfortable ground, and tried to smile at Jacob as if to say, *See how I've adjusted?* But Jacob continued to stare down at the heart now thrashing around, now spinning like a fur-covered top, now screeching through the goopey layers of blood-red latex enamel.

"Still alive," Jacob said. "I suppose now we must clean

the poor creature." Then glancing at Richard, "It looks as if Serena is about to have a pet. I hope you don't mind."

"Not on your life, Jacob. Get rid of that thing."

"Just bear with me, please," Jacob replied. He reached down into the bucket carefully, and to Richard's continued amazement, clutched the creature on both sides behind the head, squeezing a bit until it stopped struggling, and lifted it out of the can and onto the grass. "I don't believe he will be going anywhere," he said, and as predicted, the thing – a rat, a ferret, a squirrel, what? – sat and shivered and shook off the excess paint in long ropy strands that made it appear to be flying apart. Richard stepped back so his shoes and pants wouldn't be splattered. Jacob didn't appear to mind.

Jacob said they should get as much paint out of its fur as they could and check out the mouth and nasal passages to make sure the creature was going to live – and Richard nodded dumbly. It looked up at Richard with a broad, flat head, bloody tears barring its face. Behind the red streaks were eyes like blackened portholes, a dim glow barely detectable as if from far back in the creature's brain.

"We'll need a mixture of relatively mild solvents to get the bulk of it out. This heavy-duty paint will not come out easily. Scissors will take care of most of the rest. If there are still streaks of paint here and there, well, I suppose Serena will find it that much more appealing."

"Jacob, we're not bringing this monster any where near my daughter."

The creature opened its mouth and coughed out bright red mucous. Then it stretched its body, so that the paint-stiffened fur stood out up and down the length of it, bare patches of grayish hide showing between the spikes. It snapped its head back suddenly, staring at Richard, opened its mouth and hissed, and more red mucous and pink foam and clots of paint came flying out. Richard stepped back out of the way.

"Jesus, what is it?" he said, watching as Jacob began gently rubbing moist rags over its skin. A murmur came from deep within the animal, rising into a remarkable, engine-like rumble, almost appalling coming from something so small and thin. "You wanted to give *that* to my daughter?"

Jacob glanced up quizzically. Then, speaking so softly Richard could barely hear him above the creature's throaty vibrations, "I'm sorry to disappoint you. Richard – it's just a little kitty cat."

JACOB HAD THE notion that they should present the cat to Serena in the cleaned-out paint can he had been found in, nested in black and red tissue paper. Richard didn't think twice about it until he held the can in his hands, its exterior encased in thick, layered webs of bright red paint.

The cat had torn the edges of the tissue paper to tatters, chewed it up until it was wet and twisted. As Richard carried him toward Serena's room he wriggled and heaved, looking like a dark parasite writhing within the center of a great plague boil.

Richard knocked on her door. Like all the other carved doors in the hotel, it bore a large dragon's crest, with a massive doorknob and hinge hardware patterned after a lion's paws, a lion's face with roaring mouth for a keyhole. But this door had been painted glossy white to distinguish it from the others, and there was a small cardboard sign inscribed in bright pink marker: SERENA'S ROOM – ALL YOU CHARACTERS KEEP OUT!!

Richard again knocked lightly. "Come in," she said softly, from a distance.

Richard opened the door and stepped through two layers of soft music: she had both her portable radio and the stereo he'd given her for Christmas on, playing 'mush' music, as she liked to call it. Serena lay sprawled across her four-poster bed as if she'd been shot. Around the room were posters of a variety of animals, and pictures of babies cut out of magazines and thumb tacked to the wallpaper. Jacob said it was okay – family quarters could be decorated in any way they saw fit.

"I've got something for you, honey," he said, and then hesitated, for some reason not quite ready to bring out the cat, in that hideous packaging, from behind his back.

But the cat had already jumped down and padded across the baby blue carpet, and was now nuzzling Serena's bare toes. "Daddy!" she gasped. "Oh, it's precious!" The cat of many colors attacked her toes as she moved them, then rolled onto his back to offer some belly to her, but as she reached to stroke him he twisted around again and batted at her fingers.

What a ham, Richard thought. Serena laughed. "He's as ferocious as a little dragon. That's what I'll call him – Dragon!" Dragon stopped as if he'd recognized his name, then glided up the length of the bed to nuzzle her neck. He allowed her to scoop him up and rub her face into his fur. *This cat knows exactly what to do.* The thought vaguely troubled Richard, but he had never particularly liked cats. Then he was distracted by the weight of the ugly can and tissue monstrosity he held behind him. He didn't want Serena to see it, so he backed out quietly. She was too busy with Dragon even to notice him leaving. He knew she'd ask about the can once she'd heard the story of Dragon's discovery. But Richard didn't like the look of it, and planned to throw it away.

BY THE END of the third week, Dragon had become a well-established member of the Deadfall staff. It was remarkable how quickly the cat became attached, and trained, or at least as trained as a cat could possibly be. It amused him to see Serena walking with her kitty in tow, stopping, glancing back over her shoulder, and waiting for Dragon to come trotting.

He discovered that besides reading everything she could find concerning babies and small animals, her personal studies had recently turned to volumes of folklore concerning dragons. The Deadfall library had a number of these. Now and then he would come into the library to do researches of his own – into former owners, unusual guests of the past, highly speculative histories of the hotel itself – and coming out of the low-ceilinged, claustrophobic entrance passage, which always gave Richard the sensation of being in one of those World War II era submarines, he would find her around the corner in the L, sitting cross-legged in a high winged-back Queen Anne chair, some dusty tome spread across her lap. Dragon was always close by, making only occasional forays to search for mice among the crumbling volumes on the bottom shelves, or to bat at a bug tapping against one of the tall windows over the reading chairs. Serena couldn't see Richard from her position, and more often than he could feel good about, he'd make no attempt to let her know he was there.

Dragon stalked like a tiger. Dragon leapt and rolled like a fox. Dragon curled around her legs like a snake. Dragon widened his mouth and came hissing in Richard's direction like a great walking bat.

"Dragon! Come here! I have a story to read you," Serena called. And Dragon slunk back, all disappointment. "It's a story about the king of the cats!"

Richard couldn't help marveling at how nicely his daughter read, and assumed it had much to do with Jacob's recent tutelage. All her childhood hesitations seemed to have vanished here, the earlier signs of a stutter absorbed into a slightly nasal accent she affected during the stereotypical male parts of the piece. But then he listened more carefully to the story she read, and found it troubled him.

"So he roasted them and toasted them. He baked them 'til they flaked. Thousands of living cats were lost this way, and the man cared not a jot, for he was a man and believed he owned the world.

"But finally, after days, he had to sleep, and as he slept the spirits of all the cats he had killed entered his house like streams of dark water through every window, chimney opening, and door. Even the calicos, even the white cats were black in spirit, and they were so many they filled every room in his house with their bodies of night and hundreds of them sat on his bed, sat on his legs and chest waiting for him to awaken.

"When he did awaken and opened his mouth to scream, the black cats entered his mouth just like another door, and one after the other they marched down his tongue and down his throat until they reached his secret places, all the time making a terrible din.

"The last thing he saw, they say, back in the shadows and surrounded by his smaller kin, was the monstrous cat Cluasa Leabhra, old Big Ears, the king of all the cats."

As Serena read these passages aloud, Dragon glided back and forth across the top of the chair, pausing now and then to perch on his hind legs and stare at her and sway with the sound of her, as if he actually understood what she was reading to him, as if he were mesmerized by the words. But if she paused for a moment to catch her breath, to admire a particular description, or to puzzle out a word, Dragon resumed his incessant movement, his stalking of things invisible.

After a few weeks of Serena's constant grooming, the cat had become something extraordinary. Extraordinarily beautiful or extraordinarily ugly, Richard couldn't quite decide. He supposed it depended on his mood, and/or the weather.

Much to his surprise, the cat revealed itself to be of a long-haired variety. As the days had passed and the paint turned to powder and the hide was scraped clean, long strands of fur appeared to erupt from hidden pockets all over the cat's body, uncoiling a good inch and a half on the hottest days. The hair was fine, the texture silky, in places more like down than feline fur. Unlike any other cat Richard had ever encountered, Dragon seemed to have no interest in grooming himself, content to let someone else do the job. This cat seemed to *expect* Serena to groom him.

Generally speaking, the cat's coloring made him a calico, with the usual bright patches of brown, orange, black and white irregularly distributed from the roots to the outermost edges of the hair, so that a variation in the stroke of Serena's brush resulted in a quite different pattern of colors. This varied the cat's appearance so drastically from one moment to the next, from one posture or ruffling of fur to the next, that this one calico became a pattern book for any calico imaginable.

The cat leapt from the back of the chair as if in slow motion, twisting his body until he resembled a bird, a hawk in attack. He severed the mouse that had risked the open rug, ate the front half quickly, leaving the thick hindquarters at Serena's feet as a kind of offering. She uttered an unconvincing "yuck," and went back to her reading, but silently this time.

Dragon was a master at mimicking birds in his leaps, bears in his bulk and power, sea creatures in his floating grace, wolverines in his snap and bite. Wandering among the twisting trunks of the Deadfall grove, Richard had been startled to see the cat leaping from one tree to the next almost directly over his head. Seen from underneath, Dragon was another thing entirely – dark lines of fur outlining ribs and pelvic bones on stomach fur a shimmering blend of pink and brilliant white fibers – so that when Dragon lounged belly-up in the grass, Richard could think of little but butcher's charts and antique anatomical engravings, x-rays and transparent models.

To see the cat in Serena's lap, the way she stroked him so slowly, Dragon's purr thrumming up into the still, hot air, Serena's eyes and the cat's eyes half-closed, his claws slightly extended onto her pants' leg but promising much more, made Richard feel anxious and foolish, but he could not stop himself from spying on them, sneaking glances wherever possible.

He could not bear to pick up the cat himself, imagining terrible claws hidden within Dragon's paw pads. The few times the cat passed by him close enough for those impossibly long whiskers to brush him, their stiff edge sent him to the mirror to search his flesh for scratches.

Then, one afternoon, Dragon disappeared, and Richard thought for a time his unease had vanished with the beast. Serena was inconsolable.

"He's just a kitty, Daddy!"

Richard felt badly for her, but he'd never felt entirely comfortable with the 'kitty.' Sometimes when he came into her room at night to check on her (which was every night, had been every night since Abby had died), he'd find Serena asleep and the cat curled around the top of her head.

That should have been a touching, a comforting portrait of his daughter, but it was not. There was a peculiar sort of tension evident in the cat's body, a coiling so unlike the image of the plush toy he appeared to be emulating. As if he might explode at any moment, ramming his claws into her scalp. As if he were simply biding his time.

There was the obligatory search party, and Richard made a show of looking in every hiding place imaginable. After a couple of days, Jacob joined in. After two weeks, the search seemed to be at an end.

"There are quite a few places for a cat to hide," Jacob said softly, stroking Serena's hair as if the cat might be hiding some place in her head. "Thousands of places. There are all these rooms and ducts and chimneys and air passages, not to mention the attics and cellars and miscellaneous crawl spaces."

This is supposed to make her feel better? But Richard said nothing.

"Of course there is the deadfall as well," Jacob said, jerking his head in that direction. "Kitty could wander around that massive old tangle a long time without losing interest. Kitty could find plenty to hunt, and eat, enough to satisfy most appetites. Kitty could spend a year or two exploring that deadfall and we would not even know he was there."

"Then that's where I'm going!" Serena stomped away. Richard just stood there. His little girl was slinging her arms with real, teeth-clenching rage. Then she stopped and turned around, "Are you two coming or not?" Then she spat on the ground.

Richard was so surprised he didn't say anything, just stood there while his child walked away from him toward that twisted mass of trees. Then Jacob touched his arm. "You cannot let her go in there, Richard." And that was enough to galvanize him, sending him running after her. He reached out and touched her back. She spun and snarled as if ready to attack.

"Don't touch me!" she screamed.

Richard stared at her. She was reaching that temperamental age, of course. But she'd always been remarkably sweet for all that. He backed away a step, but he felt in charge again, maybe a little angry.

"Calm down. I'm still your dad."

"Did I say –"

"You're not going in there, sweetie. You're going back into the house to wait. I'll search the deadfall myself, and I promise I'll go over every foot of it. I *mean* it. Every foot."

Her face fell. "Daddy, I'm sorry, but–"

"It's okay. Don't apologize – I understand. Just go in the house. Read a book, whatever. I'll come inside when I'm finished."

And, just as quickly, Serena was a little girl again. Sadly, he watched her go inside the hotel, looking smaller, less sure.

He looked around for Jacob, hoping to get some clever suggestions as to how he should proceed into the deadfall, but the old man had disappeared. He was getting used to that.

He walked across the wide lawn that sloped down to the deadfall like an erasure, noting how brown and wispy the grass was, vaguely wondering if it would recover but knowing that things had no trouble growing here. You could burn, blast, strip away – there were always deep roots you could never touch. In fact, the grass had a pleasing, tamed look to it. It was only as he neared the vast tangle of limbs that he found himself pausing to look at the stray, burnt flowers, their heads blackened and crusted, ruptured, the seeds popped.

On this side of the deadfall, the limbs were piled almost two feet high. The layers were shallower around the curve near the cliff's edge, but he didn't want to walk that far. Besides, he didn't much care for the cliff. He stepped up onto a thick branch, and then teetered over to one even thicker. Then he was able to stand, however unsteadily, and get a better look at where he should be going.

The tangle did not make a consistent spread below the skeletal network of trunks and limbs overhead. There were paths and partial paths through the complexity, as well as areas of two or three square feet which appeared to have avoided coverage completely. He really couldn't see all that far into the deadfall. Deeper into the tangle, sunlight was only intermittent. Despite the fact that the branches were almost totally devoid of leaves – just occasional triangular green things at the ends of long, limber stems, that fluttered in the slightest breeze, that fluttered even when there was no breeze – the trees were so closely packed, the network of interlocking twigs and branches and limbs so complex, that they made an almost opaque canopy, the little light that did escape becoming almost suspect in the vague way it illuminated hidden recesses and deformities in the fallen branches.

As Richard stepped off the thicker limbs into the snarl of narrow, brittle wood that cracked and disintegrated beneath his heavy boots, here and there was a shifting, a repositioning which could not be accounted for by his own progress through the deadfall. As quickly as he could, he made for one of those bare paths through the branches. Some of the larger branches were slippery, slowing him down as he thought about pitching face-first into the snags and spines. Sudden movements to his left made him turn too quickly and he lost his balance. Thrusting out for any feasible support, he left half an inch of skin from the back of his hand on a greedy reach of limb. He crawled out of a nest of branches left broken and sharpened by his fall into a relatively clear pathway.

The regular travel of animals had made the path, such as it was. Droppings of various sizes displayed a range of diets. There were scattered snags of brown, red, white, black and – if he was not mistaken – dark blue fur. There were also prints: broad and narrow footpads, three-toed, four-toed, five, claws and more than claws, bits of teeth and bone, buttons and shoelaces and shoes and here and there a human footprint as well. Barefoot. About Serena's size. And, more disturbing, sizes even smaller, making him wonder about feral children. Feral babies. If Serena had any idea there might be babies in here, of whatever kind.

Then, around a thick trunk directly ahead, a flash of calico fur, changing patterns iridescently as it moved, a soft murmur building into a full-throated engine purr.

"Hey! Kitty!" Richard called out in surprise, recklessly dashing forward.

After only a few steps, he snagged a foot. He threw his arms in front of him to break his fall, curling his hands away to shield them from the wooden fingers and teeth.

"Myyaaaaaahhhhh." Something dashed around his head,

digging a claw into his cheek just before he crashed into the branches.

"Jesus!" A flurry of winged insects exploded from the mass of dead brush and filled his face. He flailed at them with the arm that wasn't jammed elbow-deep into the branches, hit something a bit larger but still winged, beating against his hand, and he figured it for either a bat or a bird but he couldn't see because things were crawling in his eyes. "Oh, Christ!" Something bit him near the wrist. Something squealed and raced down his back. Something heavy for its size. "Christ, oh, Christ, oh, Christ!" He thrashed around, forced himself over onto his back, flung his arms to detach the squealing, clinging weights and forced his eyes open, even though for a moment something was caught, struggling beneath the edge of his left eyelid.

The thing moving through the skeletal branches was a sharp-edged shadow under the glare of the afternoon sun. But even denied the fine details of its appearance, Richard could detect something distinctly primitive about the animal. It was short-legged, long-bodied, about the size of a weasel or a small wolf. It moved in and out of the fallen limbs of the deadfall with ease, as if it had been born there. Its large front teeth stabbed down through the neck of some sort of small rodent.

Suddenly the animal raised its head high into the glare of sun, and from its silhouette Richard could see it was some type of cat. But the light illuminating the back of its head gave it the glow of decay, its eyes the sheen of a dead thing's.

It stared at Richard, then leapt once, twice, and Richard knew that a third would bring it right on top of him. He struggled with the branches holding him down, tore his hands open untangling himself. Then the cat struck him high in the forehead and he was down again, torn hands trying to shield his face. He looked between his fingers through a haze of blood, and the creature seemed somehow clearer, more definable.

Hanging upside down from the limb overhead was a gray mass of anger, the fur standing out in silver-tipped spikes, and though the thing was half in shadow, Richard was sure he could detect traces of orange and brown, traces of calico, blended into the gray.

"Myyyaaaaahhhh!"

The jaw wobbled weirdly on its hinge, then opened even farther. Richard saw a tongue caked in garbage before the cat started spitting at him. He moved his head to the side and sticky glop splattered the side of his face. He stared up and saw how its coat was veined first in silver, then in red, saw how its sides heaved, how its muscles had expanded, how its teeth had grown.

"Dragon?"

The cat looked down at him with eyes like stones. Then the animal leapt. Richard cried out and tried desperately to shield his face. But then nothing happened; the cat was gone.

He'd have to tell Serena he could not find her cat. He would make some pretense of looking in other places, but he would make sure this cat was not found again.

THE CHAOS OF the cleaning (and, he thought, perhaps the chaos generated by the cat as well) had kept the hotel's residents almost completely absent the past few weeks. Occasionally Richard might hear a footfall overhead, or hear cabinet doors opening and closing as he passed a kitchen, but otherwise the residents had made no appearances.

And now that the big cleanup was over, caution still appeared to be the order of the day at the Deadfall. One afternoon Richard watched as two figures covered head to foot in matching suits of stained canvas crept around the front lawn with badminton rackets in their hands, swinging at low-lying branches and into the shadows beneath bushes. There was also the incident in which he was stopped walking down the third floor hall by a voice behind a door.

"Sir? Sir! A moment, if you will." The voice was gravelly, garbled, and wet, as if the speaker's mouth were just under the edge of water.

Richard went over to the door, putting his ear against the panel to listen. "Yes? I'm Richard, the manager. Can I help you?"

"Just a piece of information I would like to share with you."

"Yes?" He could hear a soft, pleasant splashing sound from inside the room.

"I – cannot – *abide* – a cat."

And try as he might, he could not get the speaker to say more.

The oppressive heat slowly leaked out of the Deadfall over the next two weeks, supplanted by a cool, which, thanks to the contrast, actually seemed uncomfortable at times. Life was strangely slow now, as if the heat had used up all available energy.

For all Richard's doubts and ignorance as to the efficacy of their cleaning efforts, the hotel *did* feel like a much more sanitary environment these days. He breathed more easily, slept more soundly, and the hotel in general was a less gloomy, less shadowy place. The windows must have been rather grimy for there to be such a difference, and yet he didn't remember anyone actually cleaning the windows. In the midst of all those odd and complicated instructions, no one had even been assigned them.

"I can't believe how fresh everything feels and *smells* around here lately," he said to Jacob one morning as the old man busily sprinkled a green powder around the flower beds out front. "Not so much like a mausoleum."

"Well," Jacob stopped now and then and dug a small hole with his trowel, filling it with a portion of the powder. "Even with a structure like the Deadfall, sometimes you just have to clean some of the dread out of a place, before the situation becomes critical."

Richard watched for a time. "Is that green stuff meant to encourage growth?"

Jacob hunched his back, vigorously attacking one corner of the bed with his trowel. "No," he said, as stems and petals slapped at his hands and shoes. "It is to keep them a bit less active."

Richard meant to ask what exactly he meant by that, but never got around to it.

Serena spent a great deal of time to herself these days, brooding in her room, or curled up in a library chair reading. There was no peace in the way she held herself – she looked edgy, ready to spring. She wouldn't talk to him about it; when he tried, she snapped at him. But he'd been the same way at her age. No one *really* liked growing up, the way the body, the mind, changed. He remembered feeling like some sort of animal. In fact, he remembered *smelling* like some sort of animal. Cornered and in a constant state of confusion. Transformed. As if you didn't know what kind of animal you were going to turn out to be.

The next cat showed up around sunset one evening. Richard had been out on the front lawn trying to track down the source of a sound: an elusive whining somewhere between a baby's cry and the soft keen of an injured animal grieving for itself. Usually he ignored the various mysterious sounds that traveled through the Deadfall. They were too far displaced in time and location – to pursue every one of them would have been maddening. But this particular sound was especially distressing to him. It had gone on most of the day and by mid-afternoon Richard had felt a heavy depression descending through his body. He'd gone out looking for the source of the sound, less to render aid than to stop the outcry.

He was approaching a line of singular bushes – their tiny brownish leaves recently having burst back into a fiery kind of life, having become so red he could almost feel the heat from them – when a portion of one bush flared up into a roughly ball-shaped cloud of fire which fell to the ground and rolled on to the next bush. It was only after it merged with the flame-colored leaves that Richard realized it had been a cat: a red tabby Persian with bright copper eyes discernible among the brilliant red foliage. Watching him, and wanting him to know it was watching him.

For a few brief moments Richard actually thought about calling Serena so that together they might coax the cat out; she would have a replacement for Dragon, which could only cheer her up again. But then he knew he wouldn't mention it to her at all, and hoped that this new cat would make no further dramatic appearances while she was around.

Less than a half hour later, he caught sight of a huge blue cat perched on the edge of the porch roof. A Russian Blue, if he wasn't mistaken. He'd once dated a woman with a Russian Blue, and this one could have been the twin. That one had been an incredibly gentle cat. This cat had a presence which projected anything but.

Its eyes seemed unnaturally light, large and flat as if painted on. But it was the mouth that was impossible: fluid and mobile, like the mouths of talking cartoon cats. It screamed silently at him and leapt. Richard instinctively covered his face; when next he looked around, the cat had disappeared.

But the deepening shadows around the edges of the front lawn were shifting. There was a nervousness in the way Richard was looking at things. Then he realized it wasn't his eyes: the landscape had grown agitated, a fierceness barely contained.

Cats in twos and threes suddenly sprouted from the bushes, slunk out of the shadows spread under the trees, dropped from darkened eaves, jumped into the warmth of windows. Then there was a scream like a baby's scream and all movement stopped, the cats became shadows and stone, and a cat very much like Serena's Dragon crept slowly up the Deadfall drive toward Richard.

The cat halted a couple of feet in front of him, tilted his head and gazed up and held Richard's eyes, then murmured and moved his pink tongue in and out, yawned enormously and moved a paw up to rub his face. That was all that was required to make Richard feel utterly foolish: this was a kitten after all. No demon. No fire-breathing dragon, either, but unmistakably Dragon, Serena's lost cat. Richard stepped forward and crouched. "Here, kitty, kitty," with one hand outstretched. Serena would be so pleased.

But Dragon moved, first side to side like a weaving snake, which made Richard hesitate and draw back, then the cat bounded away, batting at fireflies as he went, leaping to snap at a flapping moth, running and tumbling across the blackening lawn. "Kitty, kitty," Richard called again, thinking how stupid he must sound, how he had never called the cat this way, and walked briskly after, thinking he could deliver Dragon into Serena's arms before she went to bed.

Richard tried following the cat as he shuttled across the lawn, in and out of bushes and clumps of vegetation, up one tree and down another, passing through light and passing through dark. Sometimes Richard could hold the cat in his eyes and sometimes he could not. When he could not, he imagined the animal's progress, dreamed the dance in and out of this world and the worlds beyond and in between. The cat was some sort of messenger, but Richard wondered if it was a message he really wanted to hear.

Then he came upon the cat again, cast in the circle of a security light that had just switched on in the thickening gloom. There were four or five working lights scattered somewhat randomly along the Deadfall roofline; there were many more, which did not work, had been painted over, or had things growing out of the sockets.

Dragon was playing with another cat, wrestling, mock stalking, embracing. But as Richard grew closer he realized this wasn't another cat at all, but a light-gray, emaciated squirrel, struggling to get away but caught and dragged back by Dragon's delicate but amazingly strong paws. The squirrel began to squeal, a noise Richard didn't think he'd ever heard a squirrel make before.

Richard watched Serena's Dragon as he played with the squirrel, but a squirrel was so much bigger than a mouse, so much wilder, surely a kitten could not play with a squirrel as it did with a mouse, but Dragon did, tormenting the squirrel, torturing it. Richard was glad Serena wasn't seeing this – what might she make of *this*, Dragon scratching away at the squirrel's belly just enough to expose the most sensitive layers of skin, but not enough to kill it, just enough to precisely heighten its agony? He didn't want her to see things like this, to even know about things like this, even though it was everywhere. Cruelty that came unplanned, that came out of a creature's nature.

With a final bite to the neck, Dragon ended it, and then almost immediately there came a murmuring and a rustle that stiffened Richard's neck. He turned around as the surrounding dark began to move again, and cat after cat came out to witness Dragon shred and devour the squirrel inside the circle of light.

He had never seen so many different types of cats gathered together in one place. He recognized several Burmese: a brown, like his neighbors used to have, then a lilac, then a red. Then, bounding in front, a Siamese with a glacial white coat which shaded into a light blue as it twisted in apparent ecstasy and displayed its back.

There were more breeds here, he realized, than he could recognize. He could identify a large, plump Angora in the crowd. A couple of others might have been Turkish. There were several long-haired tabbies. A huge, raccoon-like animal slunk up the rear – he'd seen pictures of the breed. A Maine

Coon cat. Several black cats of different varieties – both short- and long-haired – blended in with the others to make a neutral background of night.

Then three aristocratic-looking cats with fur a blend of gray shades strolled in front of him. They looked at him with a precise, synchronous turning of heads, and he could feel an electric charge of anxiety passing across his nerves. They twisted around and displayed their double tails.

Pieces of the dark started breaking off around him. He made a staggered turn and tried to walk swiftly, but not too obviously, away.

His foot kicked into softness with a hard center. He looked down at a rag doll cat chewing at the offending shoe. Feeling the cats behind him beginning to turn, he glanced back at hundreds of bright, focused eyes.

The cats had been focused on the squirrel, leading and playing with the squirrel. Now they were focused on him. He jerked his shoe away from the snarling ragdoll and started trotting toward the front door.

Several brightly-colored bodies shot past him, then slowed down to keep pace. Other cats shouldered them aside and trotted along, grinning up at him. Soon there were a dozen cats keeping pace with him, running ahead, falling back. As if they knew, with amused confidence, they were in a race they were going to win. At the middle of the group were a couple of larger cats – mountain cats, wild cats – cats you might expect to see in a zoo.

Richard reached the front apron of the Deadfall and started up the porch when the dance of light and shadow overhead made him look up. The line of the porch roof was jammed whisker to tail with cats. They peered down at him as one creature, their numbers thickening the shadows massed above the Deadfall.

Cats crowded so closely to the edge of the roof that the

ones in front began tumbling off, twisting and stretching out their backs during their descent until the legs came around, feet ready to cushion their landing. They dropped in front of Richard and shot behind him, gathering together again so that he was surrounded.

Suddenly he felt a sharp tearing at the back of his ankle – he twisted around and found Dragon clamped onto his lower leg, biting down with all his might. Richard kicked and kicked, but could not shake the cat loose. He dragged his leg, cat attached, to a wooden box beside the front steps where they kept a variety of brooms, clippers, shovels. He reached in, grabbed a shovel, and tried beating on the cat without hitting his own leg. The cat howled and dug deeper with teeth and claws, until in agony Richard dropped the long-handled tool.

At that moment the front door of the Deadfall slammed open and a ball of fire shot out, made a high, brilliant arch and landed in the middle of the cats with an explosion of sparks. With a ragged howl that chorused and echoed throughout the feline mass, the cats scattered to shadow.

"Richard! Come on! Move your feet!" Dazed, Richard looked up at the doorway. Jacob stood there, motioning vigorously with both hands. "Come on! Before they understand it was just a burning ball of rags!"

Dragon released him and went after them.

Richard trotted up to the porch and leapt to the first step, then through the door past Jacob, who smelled strongly of gasoline. "All those cats –"

"A field of kitties," Jacob said. "It appears that Serena's Dragon has turned out to be King of the Cats!"

"King of the Cats?"

Jacob's eyes were brilliant in his soot-coated face. "Surely you don't imagine human beings are the only ones to engage in politics? I know you must have heard of alpha males and such."

"But that's hardly politics."

"Politics was born the day the first creature opened its eyes to the realization that it wasn't a physical part of everything else. That made it lonely, and that made it angry. That was the day the real darkness first came, the beast was born, and politics along with it."

"So we have a political problem here?"

"At least. And a pest control problem of somewhat major proportions. I would have suggested that we throw out a few mice to pacify them, but I think one of our guests has eaten them all."

Richard glanced down at his hands, which had been feeling alternately hot and clammy. He hadn't felt the claws go in, but the backs of his hands were criss-crossed with thin lines of blood. He looked back up at Jacob. "Maybe one of the guests might help."

"No, Richard – that runs counter to the contractual understandings we have here. We're staff, they're guests – the lines don't cross. Besides, most of the guests would not help in any case. Remember that they are of a different world – it simply rubs up against ours now and again. Most of them would be quite unable to parse what the fuss was all about."

"So what do we do? Bring out the flame throwers? Stay inside our rooms with the doors locked? I'm about ready to do that."

"We do what people have done throughout the ages when serious political problems arise – we take out the king."

Richard glanced around warily. He could hear a distant, directionless scratching. "So do you have a shotgun?"

Jacob shook his head. "The first time we had him in our sights there would be a dozen other cats throwing themselves into the line of fire, and a few dozen more clawing up our backsides before we knew it. No, we'll have to be cleverer than that. We're going to have to get up close to Dragon with someone he already trusts."

Richard had been distracted, listening for the vague scratching that moved in and out of his hearing in waves. Then suddenly Jacob's words registered. "You're out of your mind."

"She's not just a little girl, Richard. There are limits to what you can protect her from."

"I'm not sending Serena out to face that thing! We'll find another way! If you were a father yourself, you wouldn't even suggest it."

Jacob stared at him, then he opened a hand and shrugged. "Then we look for another way."

"Fine, then. I'm going to wash this blood off and check on her." Then, seeing Jacob purse his lips, "Because I don't want to alarm her. I'm alarmed enough for the both of us, goddammit."

Richard scrubbed and disinfected his hands vigorously. The skin burned and reddened, then paled amazingly, the surface looking like skate tracks in ice. Maybe she wouldn't notice, he thought, knowing full well that these days Serena noticed everything. He threw cold water on his face then ran down the hall.

In the corridor outside Serena's room, two cats stood guard: a tall, thin black, a short stout gray. Wide mouths, slightly goofy expressions. Richard thought immediately of Laurel and Hardy. He forced himself to smile down at them as he started past, putting his hands palm down as if to placate or pat.

The short cat approached him with tail and ears erect: friendly, interested. But as it climbed onto his shoes, its tail suddenly began lashing side to side, the tip twitching, and then the claws came out, and Richard started kicking when the claws entered his pants leg. The cat landed against the cushiony flocked wall and commenced a deep, harsh purring.

Then the tall cat rubbed up against him, its fur electric, and Richard tried to pull away, but could not. It was as if he'd grabbed hold of an electrified fence and his charged muscles would not permit him to let go. But the Hardy cat broke the connection by barreling between them, then lolling playfully on its back to expose its huge belly, looking up with an invitation for Richard to scratch. Richard declined.

The Laurel cat took one swat at Hardy's belly, opening it in a broadening red line. Hardy looked surprised, and then sprayed the air with fur and phlegm. The emaciated Laurel leapt up into a small open window and crouched there, ready for any retaliation from Hardy. Laurel kept turning its head toward the outside, sniffing at the air, then when it seemed to find a particular direction of interest it opened its mouth and gasped in more air.

Meanwhile Hardy spread itself wide in front of Serena's door, its eyes mad with fury and pain, obviously determined to bar entrance even with its ropy guts hanging out. Richard would need something more than his feet and his unprotected hands to get through to Serena. He ran back down the corridor to the closet in his own room, groping for the baseball bats and tennis rackets he kept stored there.

And felt fur moving back and forth against his hand.

He stepped back as the closet door eased fully open, the huge white and yellow-streaked creature coming with him as if its fur were glued to his hand. The cat rubbed the side of its head back and forth against his palm, staring up at him with wide, fixed pupils. With an effort of will, Richard pulled his hand away – the fingers tingled. The cat's zombie stare broke and its mouth suddenly grinned impossibly wide.

Richard ran into the bathroom and washed his hands thoroughly, near delirious with his need to remove the feel of the thing. But the tingling was still there. Another cat appeared outside the bathroom window, its doughy face pressed into the glass until eyes and mouth went loony. Richard opened the back door to the bathroom and made his way down the dimly lit back hall. But from behind each door he passed came a scratching, a sniffing, as if they were tracking him.

A cat passed him from behind, rubbing against the outside of his leg. Richard looked down: the small, multicolored creature trotted ahead, coat changing shade and pattern as the light changed. But the way the cat moved seemed so normal, so innocuous – here and there stopping to snap at a moth, or to lunge clumsily at a moving shadow – Richard tended to think this cat must not yet be part of the others, until the cat glared at him, doubling size with a glance, and Richard recognized this cat as Dragon, Dragon in the eyes and in the teeth, whatever size and shape the cat might take.

Richard stood his ground, or, more accurately, was afraid of what might happen to him if he ran. But Dragon swiveled his head back around and continued to trot down the corridor as if he hadn't noticed Richard at all. Richard turned, indecisive, wanting to return to Serena's front door, but this back hall connected to Serena's bedroom as well. Could Dragon know this? Without a doubt – he'd pretty much had the run of the place since he'd shown up (except for certain corners, certain stretches of floor and carpet, certain thresholds even Dragon knew better than to cross) – and Dragon was headed in her direction. Richard started after the cat, who seemed completely oblivious to him now.

Dragon kept several yards ahead of him, raising his leg and spraying each door before Richard could get there. The odor accumulated, intensified, and it occurred to Richard this was more than one individual cat's marking of territory, but a claim being staked for the whole of the Deadfall, a claim for the kingdom of the cats.

To his relief they passed the innocuous-looking rear door of Serena's quarters. Dragon didn't even bother to mark it (or did the cat already consider it marked?). Richard didn't stop in any case, not wanting to alert the cat to Serena's whereabouts if he didn't already know. They left the hall, and its worn carpets, for a succession of tiled, empty rooms which Jacob always referred to as "the overflow kitchen."

Richard heard the first click-clack, and then a string of them, click-click-clack, an overlapping syncopation of hundreds of clicks and clacks, then around the doorway came dozens of Siamese cats trotting across the floor, their claws extended.

Richard moved into the carpeted back hall. And there was Dragon, suddenly blocking his way, sniffing at his palm, then moving his mouth over Richard's thumb and closing, not too firmly, keeping his teeth back but still holding Richard's thumb well enough that Richard knew Dragon wouldn't easily let his prize go.

Dragon's tongue began caressing the trapped thumb, wrapping around it so tightly he couldn't possibly pull loose. The cat started moving the tongue slowly back and forth, its rough texture grating away his skin. Finally Dragon uncoiled his tongue and walked away slowly with an air of dismissal. Richard examined his thumb: it was bloody. Layers of skin had been scraped away.

"Dragon!" Serena squealed behind him. Richard turned as she rushed past him, skipping across the floor and landing behind the cat, who still would not turn around. "Oh, Daddy, you *found* him!"

"No, Serena!" he shouted, as the cat's eyes became huge and hard, one paw raised, claws gleaming even in the dim light.

"Daddy?" Serena looked back at him, at the same time reaching out a hand to caress her long-lost cat. Richard held his breath. The cat's ears shot up like rigid cones. Richard started running, reached his hands down to scoop up his daughter or grapple with the cat if required. "Daddy! You'll *scare* him again!" Sudden defiance, resentment in her voice.

"Honey, I didn't."

"Yes, you did! You *never* liked Dragon! And he's all I have left!" Serena burst into tears and pulled Dragon to her. Richard tensed, but the cat allowed himself to be held. A low purr filled the room: directionless, and impossibly loud. Even in her upset, Serena must have felt the wrongness of the sound. She held the cat out and away from her, her hands under his front legs. He opened his mouth wide with a loud, snake-like hiss. Serena dropped Dragon, scurried over to her father on her hands and knees, clamped on to his leg. "Daddeeee." She began to cry.

The cat stretched himself out to twice his length, fixed his eyes on Richard and Serena, and then lowered his ears halfway, waiting.

Richard tried to ease himself and Serena toward the back hall, at the same time pulling Serena up along his leg from the floor. She held on so tightly he could barely move. But Dragon hissed yet again, even more loudly, more like his namesake than any garden-variety serpent. They stopped. Serena was rigid against him.

The cat flattened his ears completely and began to circle them. The ears twitched back and forth, followed by two quick flicks of the tongue around the lips. Dragon padded over to Serena's feet and raised his paw. Without thinking, Richard reached down to bat him away.

Dragon's paw pushed against his hand. He could not believe the strength in the gesture. He could feel the claws coming slowly out of their pads. He jerked his hand away and moved his right shoe between Dragon and his daughter.

The cat clamped his mouth over the toe of the shoe. Serena squealed. Richard struggled to pull his foot away, but the cat was like a lead weight, impossible to budge. Richard felt an enormous strain on his lower leg as he yanked. He almost laughed – such a small cat, and yet it was as if a boulder had rolled onto his shoe. He flashed back to a time just after they got Dragon, and the kitten had attacked, and chewed playfully on his big toe, exposed through a hole in the sock. This was insane.

Suddenly Dragon released the shoe, and Richard staggered

back against the wall. Serena was screaming. Richard looked down at the front of his shoe: a couple of inches of leather gone, shreds of blue sock pulled out and dangling, blood trickling from the ragged cavity.

Dragon stretched his mouth into a hideous grin and sniffed loudly.

"Daddy, look," Serena said softly.

Richard lifted his head and looked beyond Dragon, to the doors of a second auxiliary kitchen, and the hall beyond. All of it packed wall to wall with cats. There were breeds he recognized and breeds he did not. Abyssinian, Bobtail, Burmese. An indescribable breed with a yellow-dotted coat and scarlet whiskers. And on the left, pressed against the wall, there was a Cornish Rex (or so he thought – he'd never actually seen one before). An Egyptian Mau, an aged Sphinx. White cats with whiter eyes. Black cats with blacker eyes. A reddish cat with a blue-tipped tail. Two Norwegians. A huge cat, almost hairless, and Richard would have thought it a pig, if not for its teeth and claws. A variety of Orientals. A long narrow cat. A tall crooked cat. A Himalayan, several Persians.

One incredibly large cat with an unlikely amount of muscle was shaking its heavy, bull-like head from side to side, more dog- than cat-like in its movements. Several creatures tumbled out of its ears onto the floor and it lapped them up with a skinny, pale yellow tongue.

But it was the distinctiveness of their eyes that impressed him the most: yellows, hazel-greens, greens, rich oranges, red-tinged whites, the occasional blue. But when Dragon stepped back into the midst of them, creeping in reverse like some grainy silent movie wound back, their eyes all gradually changed, until eventually they took on the silver hues of Dragon's great, brilliant eyes.

Dragon lifted his head toward Richard and Serena, stretched out his throat, and began to purr. The purring quickly fell through the registers into a soft growl, then, as if testing the muscles and sinews involved, Dragon's mouth went through a number of contortions, but with no sound resulting.

Dragon's throat appeared to move differently from a domestic cat's – there was something vaguely panther-like about it, Richard thought. In the next moment, Dragon began to roar like one of the big cats, a large, full-throated sound. But Richard was sure domestic cats did not have the ability to roar, even to to imitate a roar. Dragon cut off the sound with a sudden smacking of his lips. His tongue shot out briefly, and Richard thought it much too large for his mouth. He watched as Dragon stretched on his front paws. For his size, Dragon's muscles seemed massive. He arched his back and twisted around, showing them the grandness of his tail: this new tail was almost four times the width of the one he'd come to them with. The enormous tail bobbed forward over Dragon's head as he pranced in front of his followers. The other cats appeared tense, fixed on him, taking measure of his every gesture. Richard felt as if he and Serena had finally been dismissed, but doubted this was truly the case.

"He's changed, Daddy. Oh, he's changed so much."

"I know, honey. I know. I'm afraid he's not your little pet anymore. Come on, we have to go now. Just hang on to me, whatever happens."

They were able to slip out of the room and halfway down the hall toward Serena's room before seeing Hardy, sprawled dead across the middle of the hall, three tiny black and white kittens tearing away at its insides. Serena started to squeal and Richard clamped a hand across her mouth. Her eyes grew enormous. He moved her into an even narrower connecting hallway, his hand still over her mouth.

They were several yards down this hall (which led, Richard thought, to a door off the front lobby) when he became aware of a tearing sound behind him. He twisted to see a half-dozen cats entering the hall, claws in the wallpaper on each side, tearing their way toward him. He kept Serena ahead of him, moving her along as he picked up the pace.

They pushed through the door at the end of the narrow passage, discovering that it did indeed bring them out into the lobby. Richard locked it; on the other side, the cats began to howl.

"Daddy, what'll we do?"

He held a finger to his lips and Serena clamped her own hand over her mouth. There was a many-layered popping noise, rising in volume. He couldn't imagine what it might be. Where was Jacob? He didn't think much about the fact that he hadn't seen any of the guests the past few hours – they tended to lie low as a matter of course, more so if anything unusual was going on. And was this unusual? Certainly, even for the Deadfall. But he'd expected to see Jacob in a crisis. This *was* a crisis, wasn't it? Under the circumstances, the man's secretiveness seemed intolerable.

The popping noise was growing louder. And there was a bass ripple cascading from above. Then he realized what was happening, turned his head while pulling Serena to him, foolishly clinging to some thin thread of an idea that he might shield her from this.

At the top of the left-hand staircase a wave of electrified cats appeared, followed a beat later by a wave of cats on the right, both floods descending toward the wide landing at the top of the lobby where they would join and overflow the Deadfall's great central stair. Their claws were out as they ran, making the popping noise as they snagged and pulled the carpet threads, sending dust and bits of material flying, a gray cloud of it drifting to the red-tiled lobby floor. Many of them *eeyowed* in pain, or anger, or excitement – Richard imagined claws snagging and snapping, but there was no apparent impairment to their descent.

The registration desk was just a few feet away. "Stay here," he whispered, and the wide-eyed fear that spread through her face almost made him stop, almost made him want to wrap his arms around her and wait for whatever happened.

He tore himself away and hurried behind the desk, slid open a small drawer and retrieved the loaded pistol there. He eased back to Serena's side. The cats had almost reached the bottom of the stairs. Serena stared at the gun, looking even more frightened. "Daddy."

"Just come with me." He grabbed her by the hand and pulled her with him toward the front door. Several cats bounded ahead of the crowd, immediately targeting Serena. Richard pointed the gun in their direction and fired. One of the cats tumbled amid a general shrieking. Richard was surprised at how loud the gun sounded in the high-ceilinged lobby; he'd never shot a gun before.

The great mass of cats still on the staircase sat motionless, heads butting forward, peering. Then, one by one, they stretched themselves – there was a final chorus of popping as they freed their claws, shreds of carpet flying like flowers under a mower. Then one by one they grinned and began to move from the stairs. Richard threw away the gun and ran toward the front door, dragging Serena along by one arm, *eeyowing* her own gritty pain.

They squeezed through the door just ahead of a rainbow-colored tide erasing the lobby. Richard slammed the massive door on a chorus of baby screams, looked down and saw bits of bloody fur and paw sliced off by the smooth steel edge of the door jamb. On the other side of the door was more popping – heavier, softer – as the cats broke their bodies against the carved wood panels.

Serena clung to him and shook uncontrollably. He slipped his finger under her chin and tilted her face up. Only a couple of scratches across her cheeks, nothing serious, but her eyes looked dazed, her forehead white. "Honey, it's okay. They're locked on the other side of the door."

She jerked herself away and shook her head wildly. "It's *never* okay!" she screamed, spit flying off her lips. "Not in this place! It's *made* not to be okay!" Her body twisted – she seemed barely able to stand. She made a staggering turn and started down the front steps. "*Sometimes*, Dad," she threw back over her shoulder, "you're an *idiot!*"

"Serena! Stay with me!" He went after her, stumbling over something on the porch. With a flash of anger, he kicked it, saw soft, bloody flesh flying. He focused on her back, turning gray as she raced ahead of him over the dark lawn. "Serena, we have to stay together!" as he stepped into another lump of flesh. And another. *What the hell?* Blood slimed his shoes. He could barely contain his fury at her. He couldn't believe what she'd just said to him – it wasn't like her – and now she was putting herself into even more danger. She'd been like this since the cat came, more and more unpredictable.

She'd stopped a few yards ahead, was looking around, down at the lawn. Again his shoes went into something soft, with a soft crunching sound. He stopped himself, made himself see more clearly, stared at the hundreds of small lumps littering the Deadfall lawn.

Hundreds of mice, the heads gone, chewed from the bodies. Dozens of birds, opened throat to tail feathers like overripe pods. A dozen or so squirrels, their heads gone as well, bodies stretched and rigid, and flattened like road kill (and when before had he ever seen a dead squirrel that wasn't road kill?). An eviscerated mole. A mound of skunk. A helping of miscellaneous, unidentifiable flesh: well-chewed, and regurgitated. And a couple of small dogs, their dog days past, the attempt to remove their heads not quite successful, so that the flesh of their necks was mostly gone, but the bone remained, and Richard marveled at how snake-like those neck bones appeared, so that in death the dogs had become dragons, transforming into mythical creatures.

He wondered if this mass offering was meant for him – he'd had cats before, and except for the quantity and variety this was not unlike something they might have done – but then he heard the deep-throated purr, and turned to see Dragon perched, gargoyle-like, on the edge of the roof.

Serena looked up at Dragon. She slumped to the ground and began to cry. A smallish white cat crept out of the shadows, walking around her in a circle, spraying the ground, claiming his daughter as its territory.

Richard watched as two huge gray cats – each twice the size of the largest, fattest house cat he had ever seen – approached Serena from opposite sides of the field of carnage. He gasped and started toward her, even more alarmed when he heard Dragon growl menacingly behind him.

Then the two cats appeared to look past Serena, seeing each other as if for the first time. They stared, fixated, fur bristling, bodies in slow expansion, tails fluffing out, until the king came into view – Dragon had moved so quickly Richard wondered if maybe this was a twin cat, but the way he held himself was all too unmistakable. The two huge cats shrank up inside themselves until they seemed practically nothing.

"Daddy, I want to leave. Let's get out of here." It was the soft, broken voice of a little girl inside her bad dream. Dragon trotted over to her, purred, rubbed against her. She didn't move, didn't acknowledge the cat's close proximity. The cat's eyes went from black to steel. Then he turned his back on her and slipped into darkness with a rush as if the film of the world had suddenly speeded up. The two fat cats followed him at a more leisurely pace. And all was silent. Not even a murmur from the hordes of cats locked inside the Deadfall. Richard found himself waiting for the sound of broken glass, for the mass of cats to come crashing in a stream of blood and fur through the Deadfall's many windows, but there was nothing. He and Serena might have been completely alone. He could almost laugh at that. He'd wanted a quiet place to recover, to raise his daughter. Jacob had essentially promised him as much.

Something soft was at his waist, embracing him. The sweet smell of his little girl mixed with something else, a musky odor of cat, the charged scent of madness and terror. "Daddy, where's Jacob? He should be here somewhere, shouldn't he?"

"I'm sure... he's working on this, trying to figure a way to get rid of the cats. He's been doing this a long time – he's been at the Deadfall a lot of years, you know? I know it's scary, sweetheart. But Jacob knows what he's doing." He pulled her closer, feeling like a fraud.

"What will we do? Where will we go?" She turned her face into him.

Richard stroked her hair, felt something wet, sticky. He looked at his hand: there was blood in her hair. He tilted her head: scratches across the forehead, down the cheeks like exaggerated tears. "We're going to get into the car," he said. "And then we're going to drive away from here." She looked relieved, but alarmed as well. "Hush now. Maybe we'll come back later, after the problem's been solved."

They slipped out of the light and into the shadows along the wall. It was ridiculous to feel any safer with that route, of course – cats stayed in the shadows, as did other terrible things. But it still seemed to make them both feel better; at least they weren't tripping over the display of tiny corpses. The garage was recessed into the Deadfall behind a screen of small trees, twenty, twenty-five feet away – you couldn't see it from the drive, you had to know where it was.

Richard eased open one of the great slabs of weathered wood, Serena tucked behind him. The air was stale burlap, and scratchy in the nose. He didn't think anyone had been in here since they moved in. Once at the Deadfall, you didn't think of using an automobile except for leaving.

He drew her a few feet inside, shutting the door but not all the way. He imagined breaking out at high speed, wood splintering everywhere, more easily accomplished if the door wasn't latched. He was reluctant to turn on the dim bulb suspended high overhead; it might draw the cats' attention. Birds fluttered up in the rafters – a good sign, he thought. He pulled Serena to one wall and flipped the switch there decisively.

His station wagon appeared older than he remembered, a snapshot in silver, bathed in low-watt white from overhead. The old look of it made him nervous – he hoped it was still drivable.

The balance of light and shadow changed with each hesitant step into the dim recesses of the garage. Bits of alien equipment hung from pegs on the high walls: fanciful grilles for car makes he had never heard of, hoses kinked into exotic designs, discarded fenders stained garishly, an assortment of pipes, struts, wires and baroque tools. Up in the rafters, the birds shifted in unison, then shifted back again with a synchronous rise and fall of tail feather and wing. The occupied territory of birds.

As he approached his car he began experiencing a strange sort of vertigo. The station wagon seemed already to be moving, rolling slowly through the vague light as if in dreamy anticipation. Shadows boiled out from behind the tires and beneath the chrome bumper. They dropped bits of plug wire, small fragments of black plastic, and shreds of cloth and dingy yellow mats of upholstery pad. No, not shadows at all. Cats, dozens of black cats. Then all the black cats began to hiss, so softly at first it seemed the noise was some distance away, then growing in volume and harshness: tires losing air, steam kettles whistling, calm intention in screeching escape.

A great black mass of muscle and fur leapt from the car's roof and approached the motionless pair. It rose on its hind legs, swelling impossibly, until it seemed it would soon be Serena's size. It opened its mouth to screech when a shaft suddenly entered its throat, pinning it to the side of the car, silencing it.

"Out of here!" a voice rasped behind them. Richard turned to see Jacob standing half hidden by the double door, an ancient crossbow hanging from one hand. "Let's go if you don't want to end up like your car!"

Jacob led them back into the Deadfall through doors and down narrow corridors which seemed vaguely familiar, but which Richard was sure he'd never seen before. Certainly he could have never repeated their steps. But suddenly they were in Serena's bedroom, and there were no signs of cats, except for a few kitty posters on the walls which Serena ripped down immediately and without comment. Then, amazingly, she curled up on the bed and went fast asleep. Richard leaned over to kiss her head, felt himself sliding, and sat down on the floor by the bed instead. He stared up at Jacob, whose face in the darkness appeared elongated and feline. "What now?" he asked.

"Now, we rest," Jacob replied, and busied himself moving Serena's furniture around, pushing it up against her doors.

SOMETIME IN THE middle of the night, Richard heard the voices: low, musical murmurs, a blending of chirruping noises, punctuated by open-throated calls, cries, howls, screeches. Requests, demands, greetings, signals, the most elementary parts of a language. He wasn't sure if he was awake or not, if he heard or had only dreamed he'd heard the cats speak and sing. Abby had been trying to awaken him for hours. The cat needed to be let out, the cat needed to be fed. His turn. He never took responsibility. He never did what he was supposed to. He wanted to clamp his hands over his wife's mouth, shut her up. He was so tired; all he wanted to do was sleep. People murdered when they were denied their sleep – they couldn't help themselves. Waking up a sleeping, dreaming man was a dangerous thing to do. You took your life in your hands. The sleeper was like a cat: basic, elemental, amoral. You couldn't help yourself. Instinct took over. The beast was at home.

He dreamed of hordes of cats being burned alive over great bonfires, and single cats turning black on a spit. An army of peasants at war with the cats, chasing them down and smashing their spines with iron bars. Sackloads of half-dead cats stinking up the courtyards. Mock trials with prosecutors and executioners, the guilty cats strung up on a makeshift gallows.

In the middle of the night the cats howled, and it sounded like human screams, torn from some visceral old world in the back alleys of the brain.

Richard watched as Dragon brought a small fox into the midst of some kittens, and then let it loose. The fox backed away, but there was no place for it to go. One by one the kittens reached out tentatively to swat at the fox. Richard wondered why the fox – so much larger than the kittens – did not attack or fight its way through. But the confused look, the nervous weaving of the head, suggested the fox sensed something different about these kittens.

A few of the kittens began hissing and spitting. Then, with an eruption of noise, they all bolted toward the fox, their forepaws raised. Suddenly the fox disappeared inside an explosion of red mist. Serena's face appeared in its place, eyes wide, cheeks claw-torn and chewed.

He jolted awake, rubbing at the fur collar around his neck, straining against the pressure at his throat, pushing the collar open, gasping for air. He opened his eyes and gazed at the cats piled high around him, sleeping contentedly, except for the one, Dragon, who crouched by his feet, staring at him unmoving.

He knew it was Dragon from the way the cat tilted his head, the way he stared, licked his lips, and looked down at his paws: a kitten with a monster inside. But his physical appearance had changed some. At first, Richard thought the changes were subtle, but as he dared to raise his head for a better angle, more and more of Dragon's transformation jelled from the shadows.

Dragon had become scraggly, with wild long fur in such disarray it appeared randomly glued to his back. Richard followed the improbably long legs and saw that Dragon now had cloven hooves instead of paws. Bumps in the fur above his pink, glowing eyes suggested horns.

"Pssst. Kitty!" Serena's voice. Richard turned his head – too quickly, dizziness made his eyes swim and fill with cats he had to shake and shoo away – and saw Serena inside the doorway of her closet, Jacob's pale old face right behind and above her, surrounded by little-girl party dresses Serena had outgrown but been reluctant to throw away. With a pang, Richard remembered that Abby had bought them all on 'just us girls' shopping trips with their daughter. That it had never occurred to him before why Serena might have kept them made him feel like a creep, not deserving the honor of being her dad.

"Kitty, kitty!" she called out again. Dragon turned his head stiffly toward the closet. Serena held a ball of yarn in her upraised hand.

Oh, come now, Richard thought. The ball of yarn left Serena's hand as if in slow motion, lobbed through the air in a high arc, one end of the yarn freeing itself, trailing a tail. Dragon appeared mesmerized, following the yarn with his head, then suddenly he leapt, caught the ball in midair, tumbling over and over into the middle of the other cats – who scattered as if a burning coal had been cast into their midst – growling softly with the yarn clutched to his belly.

"Daddy, come on!" Serena demanded, and Richard looked at the two of them squeezed into the closet, Jacob's head haloed in little girl lace, and he wanted to laugh. But he surprised himself and climbed to his feet, stepping carefully over sleeping cats, watching as other cats slipped slowly from a hole that had been scratched and torn out of Serena's bedroom wall, saw the cats pause, looking around, hissing irritably, apparently agitated by the rearranged furniture, until – seeing Dragon with the yarn – they bounded over to join in the king's play. Richard chose that moment to leap over the remaining slumbering cats and into Serena's closet like a character in a kid's fantasy novel.

He looked at Jacob with what he imagined to be a sleepy and crazy smile. "So now what? We pass into some other dimension from here?"

Jacob glanced overhead. Richard looked up at an open trapdoor, into the darkness beyond. "I didn't tell you about it because it wouldn't be good for Serena to explore the hotel by herself," Jacob explained. "Closed, it simply blends into the ceiling."

Dragon was still playing with the yarn, looking every bit the kitten, completely harmless. "Time to go now, Daddy." There was pleading in her voice, as if her daddy had gone crazy and had to be brought back to his senses. Richard watched as Dragon's ears moved, following the sound of Serena's voice. He shut the closet door carefully.

Jacob was up inside the trapdoor in seconds. The old man's agility never ceased to amaze. He pulled Serena up and Richard followed, struggling even with their help. Jacob slipped the trapdoor back into place, bringing the darkness down on them completely. Then with a shush a match flame appeared, touched to a candle mounted in a wall sconce beside them. The dusty wall glowed, layered in cobwebs. "I completely forgot about this section while we were cleaning – I must be slipping. Now don't straighten up all the way," Jacob warned him. "The ceiling is quite low until we get to the sitting room."

They followed Jacob through the low, winding corridor, stopping to light more candles along the way. Richard thought these might be the oldest candles he had ever seen: thick as small tree trunks, made of a greasy, yellow wax. The floor sloped downward for a time, which made little sense architecturally, but then what about this ancient hotel pretended to logic? But even as Richard pondered the Escheresque perplexities of the place, the corridor made a sharp left, followed by a sharp right, and then the floor seemed to be on an incline. There were rustlings along the edges of the walls where the candlelight did not reach, but Jacob did not react, and even Serena seemed calm, no doubt taking her cue from him. At one point, Richard noticed faces painted for several yards on the ceiling: women with shapeless, earthworm lips expressing pain or ecstasy or both, and white crosses furiously carved into the wood to scratch out their painted eyes. Then the faces were gone, and there were large sections of black paint, the corridor widened, and Jacob led them into a large room.

This had to be the sitting room. There were an assortment of benches and loungers and Adirondack chairs scattered about the odd, dusty space. A grimy glass with one withered straw perched on a TV tray beside one of the chairs – Richard imagined it filled with lemonade, or some other liquid he wouldn't have cared to drink. In any case, he didn't imagine the place had been utilized in some years, although in the Deadfall, signs of disuse and neglect weren't always what they might seem.

"This spot used to be quite popular," Jacob said as if in answer, "although I won't pretend to know why. You can see the front lawn from some of these peepholes over here."

Richard joined him by a row of white circles, and then realized the circles were painted around actual holes to the outside. He bent slightly and tried them: a number were clogged, and although they appeared to come in pairs, several of the pairs were too widely spaced for the eyes of anyone he had ever met. But finally he found a pair he felt comfortable with: he brought his hands up to the sides of his face and leaned forward. He thought of a peepshow he'd gone to with some friends back in college. You put in your two quarters and were shown things you had never seen before. Some of those things you really didn't *want* to see, but you'd paid your fifty cents so you just had to look.

Dawn was about a half hour past, and there were cats everywhere, their frenzy unabated even after a night's revelries. Cats tearing at the shrubbery, climbing on each other's backs, spitting and howling, fighting over the carcasses of small animals, dragging half-live creatures into the center of the front lawn to become the focal point of a new round of feline play. Richard was amazed that they were still able to discover prey anywhere in the surrounding fifty miles.

A scrawny, ragged cat staggered back and forth near the hotel porch, its skin opened, internal organs on display as if it had crawled off the dissection table of a high school biology class.

Watching the cats spread out over the lawn, foraging, hunting, Richard thought of *meat*, how this was all about *meat*, the hunger for it, the consumption of it, the rapid and efficient excretion of it. Limber cat bodies directly out of the Pliocene, with those prehistoric memories still intact. He watched as they lurked behind the bushes, as they leapt to consummate a kill.

"Why do you think dogs eat cat feces? They can smell the meat inside."

Richard twisted around. "Do you read minds, Jacob? It would be unfair not to tell us if you did."

Jacob smiled grimly. "No more than you, my friend. I simply have a dark turn of mind. It is one of the qualifications for working here. When I'm with other people with similar dark turns of mind, and when we're looking at the same scenes, it's not too difficult to guess what you're thinking."

Back at the peephole, he watched as Dragon trotted out into the center of the Deadfall's front acreage, a line of frisky kittens in tow. The other cats parted before the procession, dragging their victims with them. Within a few minutes they'd made a large, rough circle: Dragon at the hub of a wheel, the rest of the cats arranged around the rim. It was at that moment that Richard realized where this 'sitting room' was, where these peepholes were located.

High above the Deadfall's front entrance was a row of carved heads: a lion, a bear, a dragon, then several abstract-looking faces so fantastic they refused to stick in memory, leaving you only with the nagging question of whether they were based on life, or based on madness, and finally, a head that might have been a beautiful woman, or might have been a young child, depending on your mood and the time of day. The faces had always looked wide-eyed to Richard, intensely observant.

His immediate thought was that whoever watched from here simply wanted to observe new visitors to the hotel. But this was more a lounge, a gathering place. Then he thought of how that front lawn with the activities that took place there was actually the most 'normal' location on the Deadfall grounds. On first arrival, new guests usually did not reveal their peculiarities. They waited until safely tucked inside the Deadfall's plush, complicated interior (although a few came heavily hooded, wrapped in bandages, or masked). Normal deliveries from normal businesses came through the front entrance, as did the mail carrier and the rare salesman. And they had family picnics on this lawn. He'd played with his daughter on this lawn, and she'd played there by herself.

And maybe that was the attraction that might draw a crowd. A beautiful, well-adjusted young girl. A father adoring his daughter. Normal life. For some, it would be the only place they could witness something like that.

He took his eyes away from the cats and scanned the room slowly. Jacob saw what he was doing, but made no comment. Richard noted how thick with dust everything was. Except the chairs, the seats and backs and arms of the chairs. Clean and almost shiny from continued use. He considered this as he pressed his eyes against the peepholes once again.

Involuntarily he cried out. Dragon had come up behind the gathering of kittens, killing each with a bite to the back of the neck. Even at this distance their cries were piercing. Was that possible? Their screams were the agonized screams of young children. The worst sound on earth: babies dying in pain.

The monster cat stood up on his hind legs and grinned with his teeth, his contorted face tilted up toward the Deadfall. "He knows we're up here!" Richard said. "My God, he can find us anywhere!"

"Eventually, yes. We cannot know for sure he knows about this place, but eventually he will, I have no doubt. So far he's worked his way into every other nook and cranny, places I'd not thought possible."

Richard rubbed his face. "So is that where you were while my daughter was in danger? Taking the *tour?*"

"It was important to gauge the extent of their infiltration, to find out if there were places they wouldn't go. Unfortunately I see no area they've avoided, in any deliberate way." If Jacob had taken offense at Richard's tone, he wasn't betraying it. "Besides your station wagon, his cats have rendered the Deadfall's pickup inoperable, as well as my old Ford. They even managed to remove key parts of the riding lawnmower."

"This is unbelievable. I've questioned my decision to bring my daughter here, despite your fanciful reassurances. And now her greatest danger comes from her pet cat?"

"None of us is entirely safe in this world. It's understandable when a father cannot accept that. We do what we can. Our guests here know these things better than anyone. I've also spent a couple of hours this evening checking up on those guests – you may recall that we have a certain responsibility to them, however alien and invulnerable they might appear to our more elementary sensibilities. Many have left, or hidden themselves in ways I cannot detect, but I've found three dead in their rooms, marked and unmarked, with perfectly innocent-looking kittens posted nearby."

Richard tried to keep his voice under control, not wanting Serena to know how wrong everything had become (And how ridiculous was that? How crazy had he become?). "Then tell me what to do, Jacob. Tell me how to protect my daughter."

"Serena," Jacob said softly, his eyes sad, "is the only one capable of protecting anyone here today."

"HOW CAN YOU ask me to put my daughter in that kind of danger?" They'd moved back down the corridor, leaving Serena asleep on a blood-colored corpse of a couch in the sitting room.

"She's already in danger. We're *all* in danger. Deadfall guests we can control, for the most part. I know very little about what to do in this situation, except to keep my eyes and ears open, and pay attention to what my senses tell me. And what they tell me here is that we are simply more toys to this monstrous cat – and what he eats and what he plays with are all pretty much the same to him. He's going to tire of us, and then the play's going to become much more violent, and then he's going to get rid of us. He'd already be tired of us, if it weren't for Serena. Whatever he's become, he remembers what he used to be, and what he used to be has much to do with Serena."

"Does the hotel have anything to do with what's happening here?"

"Not directly, but one of my predecessors had this saying, 'The Deadfall makes you live up to your potential. Good or bad – it's all the same to the Hotel.' I think this little kitty just may have achieved its ultimate potential."

"She's just a little girl. How is she supposed to handle this?"

"She'll handle this by being who she is. She needs to turn that cat into her pet again. Those other cats aren't anything without their king. She's going to have to get him away from the others. That's when the two of us will take over the job."

"And what will the two of us do with him once she delivers him to us?"

"I have no idea."

"Great plan."

"It is the only one we have. I suggest we improvise from there."

Serena's eagerness to pursue the plan appalled him. "We can always find another way," he told her. "You know how clever Jacob is. Remember how he organized things for the cleaning? Pretty amazing, I thought, the way he figured everything out. He'll come up with another way – I should never have even told you about this crazy idea. I'll go ask him right now."

"Daddy." She sounded so much like her mother, struggling to find patience. "It must be the *only* way, or Jacob wouldn't have suggested it. Besides, he *is* my cat."

Richard reached to squeeze her shoulder. "Honey, don't you find it a little... difficult to think of Dragon as a housecat anymore?"

She let go of an embarrassed little smile. "I guess so. But I'm supposed to take some responsibility, I think, whatever he is. You taught me that, Daddy."

Richard tried to think of what stupid little homily he might have let slip that would encourage her to risk her life. "And Dragon still likes me, sorta, I think, and I guess that's all we've got going for us right now. And pretty soon, who knows, maybe he'll change so much he won't care anything about me anymore, maybe he'll even have forgotten how to care."

Her analysis was so close to Jacob's that Richard felt defenseless, foolish for trying to argue against it. She stood up and put an arm part way around his waist. "Let's go talk to Jacob, Daddy. I guess we should do this pretty soon. I'll be too scared if Dragon changes much more."

As they made their way down the staircases they discovered

a few cats no doubt left behind because they were either too tired or too wounded to travel with the rest of the pack. Richard and Jacob and Serena avoided even these non-threatening felines, detouring through abandoned rooms and dusty passageways. Everywhere there were signs of carnage, of cats having attacked other cats: scattered fur patches and rags of scalp, tears and scratches so numerous in the woodwork and walls that Richard feared some sort of collapse. *So much for Spring cleaning.* Light fixtures dangled from the ceiling: here and there chewed electrical wire hung down above electrocuted cat corpses. And everywhere noxious yellow painted over the furniture.

Richard went with Serena out onto the porch. He tried to follow her down the steps but she pushed him back, urging him with her eyes to remember the plan.

Serena stepped out on the front lawn. She wore her hair pulled back into a ponytail, the same way she'd had it the day they brought Dragon to her. She hadn't remembered that, nor had Richard, but Jacob was sure. Richard stayed back on the porch: Serena's idea, and it made sense. She had to establish the contact with Dragon, recall the relationship. No one else could be involved.

He didn't see Dragon at first. There were a number of cats around: slow-moving, fattened, somnolent. They pretty much ignored him: too tired, too preoccupied with the pleasures of digestion. He thought about the possibility that Dragon might be in very much the same state, but surely that was too much to hope for. Then Richard saw the large yellow dog sprawled out to one side, recognized it as the poor old stray that sometimes dropped by the kitchens, waiting until someone – usually Jacob – fed him. The dog appeared to be asleep, but then he saw the cat's paw rising and falling, batting at the lifeless head. Dragon's face suddenly appeared to one side of the dog's, grinning. Richard looked at Serena: she'd spied her old pet as well.

Dragon gazed into the dog's empty eyes. Trembling, Richard could easily imagine the cat looking into Serena's eyes that same way. Serena was crossing the lawn slowly, avoiding piles of sleeping cats. "Kitty, kitty," she called softly. Suddenly the plan seemed ridiculous.

Dragon's purr drifted across the lawn, rising in volume. Mesmerized, Richard didn't want to move.

Serena stopped at the dog's carcass. Dragon gazed up at her, tilting his head quizzically. "Oh." He could hear the shake in her voice. "There you are, kitty." Dragon became very still. "Come with me, kitty. Wanna play?" she asked musically. Dragon tilted his head in the opposite direction. Richard held his breath as his daughter turned, began walking slowly back up the lawn toward the Deadfall entrance. After a few moments, she paused and peered back over her shoulder. Dragon took up the old cue and bounded after her like a kitten.

Serena left the front door open as she entered the Deadfall, Dragon by this point trotting in beside her. Richard followed at a discreet distance, staying just close enough to get a feel for Dragon's attitude, ready to call the whole thing off if the cat became the least bit threatening.

Once inside, Serena headed toward the library. Dragon seemed suddenly excited, started racing up and down the carpet as if chasing an invisible companion, the typical kitten.

When Serena opened the library door, Dragon raced ahead into the dark chamber. She stole a nervous glance back at her father, then reached in by the door to flip the switch that controlled the reading lamps: the green glass-shaded lamp – gorgeous and oversized – that sat in the center of the cherry wood study table, and the brass floor lamp by Serena's favorite Queen Anne chair. These lamps were just the thing for some cozy late night reading, but provided only two pools of illumination, barely enough to see to make it across the room. The rest of the vast library was completely missing, swallowed by the darkness. Yet you could still feel the massive weight of all those books, and the dust that lay upon all those volumes (the weight of a few large men in and of itself), and the centuries of learning, just out of reach, a burden of possibility in the shadows.

Serena followed Dragon into the dim chamber, leaving the library door open slightly, just wide enough for Richard to slide through. The cat would be blocked from seeing him by the bookcase by the door. He brought his head around one edge of it, and saw Serena sitting herself down in the Queen Anne, and Dragon pacing back and forth before a low bookshelf beneath the tall windows. Suddenly the cat pounced at a volume on the bottom shelf, his claws catching it at the top of its spine, his weight tilting the book out of the bookcase and tumbling to the rug below. The book lay opened, the cat rubbing his head into the trough of pages as if reading closely, before circling the book and lunging as if at sleeping prey, clamping his jaws into one corner of the thick leather cover, then dragging the tome across the library toward Serena in her chair.

Richard considered the jaw strength required, and found himself gazing up, at the narrow second floor gallery hugging the walls of books, knowing that Jacob was poised somewhere there in the shadows, ready with one of the ancient fishing nets he'd retrieved from the basement walls. *Don't wait long*, he prayed, and looked back at his child as she leaned forward in her chair to retrieve the book where Dragon had brought it. It was an old, well-used book, the words on the cover in large gold script: CAT LORE. Dragon took his place, erect on his haunches by her feet, as Serena began to read.

"Cats have seven lives. Cats have nine lives. For three they play, for three they stray, and the last three they stay. A cat isn't accepted into Heaven or Hell until he uses up all nine."

She looked up from the book and down at Dragon then, as

if gauging his reaction. The cat swayed and leaned forward, as if needing more.

"On Christmas Eve, the cats get on their knees to pray. On New Year's Day, all the cats in Ohio kneel down to pray."

The repetition and variation seemed a bit strange to Richard, then he realized Serena must be reading from a catalog of cat beliefs, not all of which would be consistent. But all of which, he thought now, the great King Dragon might understand to be true.

Then Serena took a deep breath, and Richard tensed, knowing what was to come. There was a slight shifting in the shadows overhead, the tiniest glimmer (Jacob's buckle?), but before Dragon's attention could be drawn away, Serena's recitation rushed out of her straining lips, "A pink-eyed cat brings bad luck. A three-colored cat is good luck. A five-colored cat is good luck. A white cat is good luck. A white cat is bad luck. A white cat at night is bad luck. A six-toed white cat is good luck." She gasped, as something fluttered in the dark. "See a one-eyed cat, cross and uncross your fingers three times if you don't want bad luck. See a one-eyed cat, spit on your thumb, push into your palm, make a wish that will come true. A sneezing cat is good luck. A black cat is good luck." As the net came down, the weights along its edges clanking against railings and bookcases. "A black cat is bad luck. A black cat seen before breakfast is bad luck. If you see a black cat, oh, *Daddy!*" she cried, leaning away from the net as it covered the floor in front of her. "Spit three times to avoid bad luck!" Which she did, right into the net.

For a few moments Richard remained in the shadows, staring at the tableaux: the net spread across the library floor, dust rising in a haze, the scattered corpses of books ripped from their shelves during the net's descent, his sweet child leaning over the net, her fists balled, screaming. "I was *good* to you! You had no business hurting us! It's not *right!*" He ran and grabbed her, held her close. "Oh, daddy, he's dead, he's dead."

Jacob walked slowly past them and stood by the net. He leaned over to examine the wreckage.

"Stand over by the chair, honey," Richard said, leading her away. He returned and helped Jacob search. They tugged on each link in the net, lifting and peering through the still-flying dust.

"He's not here," Jacob said simply.

"Impossible! He was right under the net! I saw! It swallowed him whole."

"You can see it as well as I, Richard. The cat is not under here."

"Then *where is he?*" Richard pulled on the net – it was so heavy it hurt his fingers. So he kicked at the net, ran into the net and stomped wherever he could. Jacob said nothing. Finally Richard looked up at him, and past him to the chair where he had left Serena. But Serena wasn't there.

"Serena!" Richard ran across the net, stumbled, grabbed the chair for balance, moved it aside, knocked it over, looking. "Serena!" He looked wildly around the library, ran up and down the shadowed areas. "Is there a secret passage, Jacob? Tell me!"

"Hold on, hold on," Jacob raised both hands. "Listen."

Richard tried to silence his breath. He had limited success, but he could hear a faint, descending tapping. Serena's shoes. Jacob jerked his head toward the child-sized door in the darkness behind the chair. "I don't know why they put it here," he said, "but it's another way to the basement."

The miniature door splintered in his hand. He threw away the doorknob. There were tiny stairs going down. He thought about Alice in Wonderland. He required the pill that makes you small. The opening was no more than five feet high, and only slightly wider than his shoulders. Pitch black interior, a cloying mildew smell. He pushed himself inside, feeling like a ragged cork one size too large. He half-fell to the first tiny landing. A change in the air told him that Jacob had squeezed in after him. *Now we're both in the dollhouse*, he thought, and it did not reassure him. *We'll never get back out.* A rapid tapping down the steps below him, an oppressive cat's purr that shook the walls pressing against him, and he plunged forward again without a word.

The passage seemed to shrink even further as they went down. A few feet more and he was crouched so far he had to be careful not to ram his knees into his chin when he moved. He could hear Jacob huffing and puffing behind him, and it worried him thinking that the old man might have a heart attack. *How will I find Serena then?* he thought uncharitably. But he hadn't the time to indulge his guilt – Serena's shoes sounded closer, and the rumbling purr of the cat so loud he felt as if Dragon had swallowed them all, and they were descending the creature's esophagus into its belly. "Serena!" he called, but she didn't answer, and after a few moments more he could no longer hear her shoes, or the cat's purr – just the close thunder of his own panicked breath.

The steps ended before a smallish window. Without stopping, Richard hauled himself up into the frame and pushed his head and torso through. They were in the Deadfall basement. In the dim light, beyond rows of dusty cartons and abandoned furniture, he saw a flash of Serena's dress, and a flash of fur. He forced himself through the window and landed hard on the slightly damp floor. A scurrying in the surrounding gloom, but he had no time to look. He still could not hear Serena's footsteps, but off in the darkness, things were being bumped against, things were being displaced. He moved as fast as he could, dim light from some unknown source illuminating the edges of columns and wreckage, but not much more. He heard Jacob drop to the floor behind him, but did not take the time to turn around.

Things were stacked so high down here that he could not see above them. There appeared to be enough old furniture to equip several homes. Now and then, bits of paper flapped or crackled with his passage. He pressed past shelves full of oddly-shaped glassware, dinnerware of unknown function and origin. They rattled musically when he bumped them, and he feared they might spur some desperate maneuver from the cat, so he quickened the pace. The fact that Jacob was right at his back, sounding equally urgent, did not reassure him. He rushed past an intersection of lanes, not realizing he'd seen Serena at its end. He stopped and stepped back, peered around the edge of a gigantic antique sideboard – *how'd they get this down here?* – and saw Serena standing motionless, staring at something he could not see. Then she began to step backwards, out of his frame of vision, and then Dragon crept into view, advancing, back raised, tail up and whipping side-to-side like an agitated snake. Then Dragon, too, moved out of view.

Richard moved quickly to pursue.

"Careful!" Jacob whispered, grabbing Richard's shoulder. "You don't want to startle the cat!"

So the two of them eased through the narrow space between boxes and furniture, coming around the end to discover Serena facing them, her head outlined by the dark square window behind her. Dragon had his back to them, facing her, his body looking swollen as every muscle expanded and the fur stood away from his flesh. He hissed and appeared to grow some more, rocking back on his haunches, ready to strike.

Richard clutched the floor lamp a foot or so from his right hand, began lifting it from the floor.

"Daddy, no!" she screamed. She looked directly into Dragon's eyes, raised her shoulders and arms, dropped her mouth open and screeched as loud as she could.

"No!" Richard howled with helplessness as the cat leapt into the air, front legs out and reaching for his precious daughter's head.

At the last second, Serena jerked sideways as if shot, the same moment as the cat disappeared through the black window. Serena recovered her balance, and pushed the heavy iron hatch of the ancient Deadfall furnace closed.

Richard stood dumbfounded. The furnace was so huge – six times larger, at least, than any furnace he had ever seen – that he'd always thought of it as essentially filling the basement, with no specific location, no specific door.

Jacob walked up beside her. She'd looked so large a moment ago, making faces at the monster cat. Now she seemed improbably tiny, even beside the shrunken old caretaker.

Jacob put his hand on a large red button mounted on a metal box above the furnace door. He looked down at Serena.

Serena looked over at Richard, an ineffably sad expression on her face. She stared up at Jacob. And nodded.

Jacob pushed the heel of his palm into the button and the furnace exploded into life. It made a terrible, anguished, almost organic sound.

At one time a sign by the front door of the Deadfall stated "NO PETS ALLOWED." It has been missing since before my time here. If I cannot find the original, I will make my own.

I do not believe that any of the three members of the Carter family now residing here will object when I post it.

– from the diary of Jacob Ascher,
proprietor, Deadfall Hotel, 1969-2000

Chapter Four
THE CRAVING

This evening I ate a leisurely meal in the Deadfall's kitchen, without doubt my favorite location in the hotel. My guest for this repast was Ms. Abigail Carter, deceased wife of Richard Carter, the current proprietor. And Serena's mother. I understand that there are those who might perceive some impropriety in such a meeting, and I accept their concerns, declining to use the argument that the bonds of matrimony end with the grave (or, in her case, the scattering of one's ashes).

Ours is not a romantic relationship. Ms. Carter prefers the environs of the kitchen because Enid keeps it spotlessly clean. This is not meant to imply that other areas of the Deadfall are less clean, but they are cluttered, they map the affects of numerous encounters both human and non-human, and so could hardly be called 'antiseptic.' For souls of some sensitivity, such as Ms. Carter, antiseptic matters.

I'm not sure how Ms. Carter would react if she were to step into one of our giant freezers, however, stocked as they are with foodstuffs meeting the rather specific requirements of our many visitors. In the freezers, she would find virtually every meat known to man, including several human cadavers (legally obtained, of course). There are also a variety of insects and parasitic organisms preserved on those frosted shelves, as well as a number of animal and vegetable combinations frozen at specific stages of decomposition. Need I say more? What whets one appetite destroys the appetite of another. It has always been so.

Fortunately Enid is not required to prepare the bulk of these foods. The culinary knowledge required to successfully execute such a range of cuisines would be quite beyond the capabilities of a room full of top chefs, not to mention the, let us say, stubborn tastes of one middle-aged cook. Residents have free access to the kitchen to prepare their own meals if that is what they desire, although schedules must be submitted to avoid unfortunate conflicts. A few years ago I made a serious error, which resulted in a resident entering the kitchen before the previous occupant had completed his dietary needs, whereupon said occupant abandoned the evening's menu for something new and hopefully tastier. This change in courses resulted in dire consequences for all parties involved.

There is a formal dining room at the back of the third of the four sub-kitchens attached to the central food preparation area. But since all staff and residents eat at the chef's table located here, or in their individual rooms, the dining room is used for the storage of supplies and additional furniture (essential, when the furnishings of some rooms are destroyed during, or after, a resident's stay). But the fact that this unused dining room exists at all reminds me that the Deadfall was originally constructed for other, more 'normal' commerce. It was only upon the deaths of the original owner's wife and children, and after the series of stressful transformations following, that the original business plan of the Deadfall Hotel was changed.

Of course, death changes most things, but not everything. It does not change the need for companionship. That is why I take my meals with Ms. Abigail Carter. It assuages a need for companionship I have felt for many years now – she is well-versed in a number of subjects, and as is the case in many marriages, felt able to share only a small portion of that knowledge with her husband. And it provides her with the opportunity to talk: of her fiercely-loved Serena, of the dead infant, of the regrets over a premature death (and although there is, really, no such thing, I do not correct her), of the longing, the terrible longing all the dead feel.

The summer left us some time ago, destroyed by its own heat. Fall is but a whisper, in these environs. With so much death and decay on display year round we hardly notice the autumn, and so it truncates, crawling off sullen and insulted by our lack of attention. Winter normally arrives with a week's snow, oftentimes more, already on the ground. You can feel the frost forming in the blood, but we keep the liquor pantry well-stocked with a large selection of basic and exotic liqueurs.

Christmas at the Deadfall would seem, perhaps, irrelevant, although a few of our residents do observe the holiday in their own manner. In times past, some of the proprietors have even attempted some sort of decoration scheme – and the storage areas contain a variety of peeling and rotting Santas and reindeer, and the occasional moldering angel. Crates full of lights representing a century's changing electrical standards, and all manner of ornamentation from the Victorian through art deco and 'sixties kitsch crowd the corners of out-of-the-way closets. This year Richard Carter chose – wisely, I believe – to keep Christmas confined to the warmth and safety of his family's quarters, where I'm sure he did his best to provide Serena with the traditional holiday niceties.

I did see the occasional, odd, referential gesture toward the holiday in other parts of the hotel this year, however. Outside a door on the third floor, someone had constructed a rather abstract representation of a tree out of yellowing fish bones, which made me wonder, despite myself, if we might still have a stray, too-intelligent cat or two about. And at one point I heard what I could only surmise were Christmas carols sung faintly in unidentifiable tongue in the northeast second floor corridor. There was also a moment out on the snow-packed tennis courts which one might have interpreted as a gift exchange among three hooded figures and a three-legged canine, if one were inclined to whimsical speculations.

Personally, I never celebrate the holiday, but I have chosen to mark its arrival in the same manner every year: sitting quietly in my small room at the back of the hotel, the panes of my one tiny window glowing in opal brilliance from the snow-reflected light, reading the largest, oldest book I can get my hands on. The next day, I know, will be colder, and I have little hope of warmth until spring.

– from the diary of Jacob Ascher,
proprietor, Deadfall Hotel, 1969-2000

IT WAS ONLY a frozen flower, a few curves of red tissue fixed in the white ice spread below the window of his private study. But it bothered Richard to distraction. The flower had lost none of its color.

He didn't know what kind of flower it was; there were a number of them around the grounds of the Deadfall, always singly, never a group of them, a little like a rose, but the color cooler, the edges of the petals ragged, and more open, the insides moist and pale until they darkened into shadow toward the center, where they resembled hungry mouths.

The flower should have been brown, or black. Rotted away, even. The weather had been so wet and cold, the ground frozen solid for over a month now, the snow piling higher each day. But this one flower had retained all its original color, the entirety of its original form. As if the ice had preserved it. Not that it looked life-like at all, not at all. It looked plastic and artificial and nothing you'd like to smell or give to anyone you loved.

Winter had always struck him the same way. There was always something a little artificial about the season, something unreal. Snow had never looked natural: it was too white, too brilliant. Ice was worse, the way it pretended to preserve everything, while preserving very little. The way it cracked if you tried to bend it. Too rigid. Too cold. Winter was someone's dream. Too many of the shadows had gone away. The dream had stripped the trees of their leaves so you could see all too plainly what lay beneath them. The dream made you see your own breath in front of you, made you want to gather it back quickly before too much escaped.

Abby used to fret over the plants outside in the cold. Every year they would have a bush or a young tree that did not make it through. Sometimes you would know even before the snows had melted which ones would make it and which ones would not. There would be a certain way they looked under the ice, a certain way they bent beneath the weight of the snow. They would be dead, and you would know they were dead, and there was nothing you could do. And yet you had to look at them all winter. Every day you had to check on them, even knowing they were dead.

The dream preserved the dead. The dead were always there, frozen in place, and the unnatural ice made their eyes shine with a trapped consciousness.

In places, snow had drifted as much as four feet up the sides of the hotel. Stiff, cold paws had left a tangled scrawl of trails over the otherwise smooth embankments, recording the anxious activity of small animal brains. Sometimes, squirrels or rabbits would climb the embankments to a hotel window and press themselves into the glass, creating brief artificial nights of teeth and quivering fur.

The grove which gave the Deadfall its name was at its starkest, its clearest definition, branches poking in all directions into the clouded fluid of the sky. At the highest, thickest point, the denuded branches were sharpened bundles of sticks. Farther toward the perimeter, certain patterns of limbs became apparent: twisted hands and feet, cartilage strung with filaments of muscle and nerve, narrow-hipped dancers leaping into the sky.

Early in the season, something had disturbed the ever-widening scatter of deadfall, pulling the fallen branches out and dragging them toward the hotel until now they made a huge, deformed backbone half-submerged in the snow. The last scrawny vertebrae wavered in the high winds that came at dusk, claws of wind now and again scratching at Richard's study window. One of the tenants – a bushy-headed man with no cap and split trousers – came each day and took a single piece of the backbone for himself, holding it up to the sky in admiration, exclaiming something unintelligible when some new shape or pattern suddenly revealed itself in the light, then went away with the piece tucked inside his coat, to whatever room he now resided in. Maybe to burn it, or maybe to assemble it with other such found pieces. Maybe to love it, or maybe to worship. Richard should have stopped him a long time ago, but he had never ceased wondering and dreaming about the secret lives of his tenants.

Every day since the snow began, Richard had slipped into fur-lined boots and fur coat – he didn't know who they'd belonged to, but they were hung up at the front of the study closet as if he were expected to use them – and gone out for a half-hour's inspection of the grounds. Jacob said it was important, "just to keep an eye on things," and sometimes joined him.

With the surrounding vegetation dead or diminished, the naked face of the Deadfall had been revealed, its borders unsoftened, its details unblurred. Now he stood examining it, wondering what repairs he might be expected to make, if any. Where the vines along the north corners had receded with the season, great saw-toothed gashes and streaks had been revealed. The stone appeared gnawed, savaged, the broad-leaf vines a bandage. Richard thought he could see large pale ovals in some of the dark cavities, like sucker prints.

"Big Foot did that one," the old man said behind him.

Richard gaped. Jacob was actually attempting a joke.

"He and his friends were unruly. I had to evict the lot."

Richard stared at him. "Thanks a lot. I do appreciate the straight information, Jacob." He thrust his hands into his pockets, suddenly colder.

"It's unlikely to be any warmer for awhile," Jacob said, his voice softer. "From here on out it will be a slow, leisurely slide into a dream of white ice." Then, "You're not sorry you took the job?"

Richard didn't say anything for a while, thinking of Serena, what was or was not good for Serena, thinking of the cats and everything else to be afraid of when you had a child, then he surprised himself by saying, "No. I guess I know this is where I belong."

"For the time being."

"For the time being," Richard agreed.

"Some have said that the Deadfall is a state of mind. You do not have to stay. But you know that already, don't you?"

There was a grace in the slow blink of those pale eyes. "I know. But I feel uncomfortable about dragging Serena into it. She hasn't been outside in a month. All this." He gestured vaguely. "Change. It's scary for her."

"You are her father, so her place is wherever you are. I do not believe she truly wants anything different. And I do not think she really dislikes it here. Children have a way of accepting this place on its own terms. Far more easily than most adults, I would say." Something greenish flew out of the twisted grove and tumbled through the air before slamming into the stone above them. There was no follow-up sound. Jacob paused, quiet with his own thoughts, but appeared unfazed. "The deadness of the winter here," he continued, "it makes everyone nervous at first, even our long-term residents. The sudden... nakedness, I suppose."

Jacob faded back into his own company then, and Richard kept his peace. At the Deadfall, reticence was acceptable, even required.

The air around him bristled. He knew that wasn't just his own anxiety, but so often he felt 'over-sensitive.' Even as a child, he'd been saddened by events others weren't saddened by. The skeletal lines and criss-crossings of the naked trees appeared to expand, extending their fissures into the white sky. There was movement in the dying leaves and trees, but he saw nothing. He tried to focus on Jacob. "You're not going to tell me about what's happened here." He gestured toward the ruined stone wall. "You're not going to tell me what all that deterioration is about."

Finally, when Richard's patience had about run out, Jacob said "No. Deadfall is complex. There are layers of history, layers of experience here. I cannot simply jump around, educating you at random."

"So, why am I even here?"

Jacob's voice was a whisper. "I cannot answer that for you."

Richard could see Serena's face in one of the front windows. She didn't want to be near the trees. Funny how it should come to him that way.

Late that afternoon Jacob requested Richard's assistance

with a new chore: *The Checklist*. "I like to do this every winter. You can do as you like, but I would encourage you to continue this tradition." The Checklist was a booklet of several sheets clipped together, a list of current residents copied out of the hotel register.

"At this stage, all we do is knock on doors," Jacob said. "We don't unlock doors without permission. We certainly don't break in. If more dramatic steps are required, well, we'll make those decisions in the spring."

Richard followed Jacob up and down the corridors with the list, as Jacob knocked on doors, making checkmarks and comments as requested. The vigor Jacob used varied from a gentle tapping with a few fingers to serious fists pounding on wood until Richard wondered if splintering wasn't inevitable. But he had no idea what criteria Jacob was using to justify this difference.

Most of the knocking brought answering murmurs, an occasional *yes*, in several different languages. To each indication of a presence Jacob replied, simply, "Winter survey."

Sometimes a response was more dramatic: an angry shout, a scream, a low, rumbling growl. Once the resident behind the door burst into song.

Periodically, however, there was no response from a room, and Jacob would pause, consider, and instruct Richard to note 'check back later,' 'probably out hunting,' or simply, 'absent.' Sometimes he seemed saddened.

At the end of the day, Richard had made notations by seventeen room designations on the list. Jacob studied them and nodded solemnly. "I'll let you know later in the season if we need to do anything," he said, and walked away.

SOMETHING THUDDED AGAINST the study door. A muffled voice. "Serena?" he asked. The door opened and Jacob pushed his head around the jamb. For a moment, Richard had the uneasy impression that the old man's neck had lengthened during the night.

"I'm sorry to bother you, but are you about ready to tackle that plumbing chore?"

"Sure." Richard stood and walked toward the door, uneasy, wondering what would happen if he suddenly turned around and looked out the window, if the flower would be the same, shining against the backdrop of ice with an unnatural red light, or would it be black and shriveled.

"Are you sure you don't want to get something to eat first?" Jacob asked as they made their way down still another staircase Richard had never seen before. After this long operating the hotel, the experience had by now become as unremarkable as passing from one room to another. "You're looking a little pale, I think."

"I'm eating enough. It seems like I'm eating all the time. I'm just not gaining any weight. Okay by me." Richard smiled tightly.

"Winter's influence on the appetite is unpredictable, and highly variable," Jacob said, leading them down into a still narrower corridor. "And the hotel amplifies the effect."

The air had grown progressively cooler as the corridors brought them below ground level. This coolness seemed to further quiet the virtually silent hotel. A month ago, when the snow had first begun to fall, and Richard had been filled with amazement over the sheer beauty of it – the flakes had been huge – Jacob had come up behind him and whispered, his breath alarmingly warm in these falling temperatures, "Few come in winter."

And that proved true. For as soon as the snow began to fall, tenants began to move out. "Warm weather beasties," Jacob called them. In groups of twos and threes, some Richard had seen around the grounds, some he had never seen, moving out with no, few, or truckloads of belongings, early in the morning or late at night. Once he'd watched from a corner as nondescript moving men in uniform coveralls carried out a seemingly endless string of furniture and boxed and bagged belongings from a room he had always believed tiny, like clowns pouring from a painted Volkswagen at show time. He thought, once, of stopping them to make sure the things they were removing didn't actually belong to the hotel, like any ordinarily cautious hotel manager. But "thievery is not usually among their repertoire of sins," as Jacob had once said.

And every one of these escaping residents had been bundled head to foot in furs and wools, blankets and burlaps, some wrapped so heavily the hired help had to lead them out by the arm. As if the slightest touch of the cold air might erode them.

Many more remained than had left, if any of his estimates of the average hotel population were correct. But fewer and fewer showed up in the kitchen and lobby, and only one or two felt compelled to pace the hotel corridors at night. And only the bearded man made furtive ventures out into the artificial whiteness.

"Winter at the Deadfall," Jacob muttered to himself, for perhaps the hundredth time since the first snowfall.

The permanent residents of the Deadfall settled almost ritualistically into winter. Now and then their soft chants, their too-loud escaped thoughts, drifted along the ceilings of the corridors. Or collected like hairballs in the corners, where they spun into arguments, grew garbled and confused, drifted into dust.

"Winter at the Deadfall," Jacob said once again, as he led Richard down a steep narrow staircase into the underground portion of the hotel. The steel door had stuck, and it required all the strength of the both of them to push it open. It made a sound as if it were ripping the floorboards apart.

The brick around the staircase was warped and the mortar uneven, a combination that made the walls hard to look at for long, the corners difficult to find. The ceiling stretched far overhead into a cold, windy darkness. Richard heard a distant sound like wings splitting the air. The air here was damp, and it appeared that the wood had been coated and recoated with an oil preservative, never quite dry. He held fast to the greasy handrail, his eyes fixed on Jacob's back. They began a slow descent – even the old man seemed to be taking his careful time.

Now and then there would be dark, rectangular openings in the twisted brick. "Whoever built this place, and there were many, mind you, and over no short period of years," Jacob began, "well, none of them, apparently, owned plumb bobs." His chuckle echoed faintly. "They built by instinct, I suppose you'd say."

As the stair dropped lower, Richard became aware of a viscosity between steps and shoes that made walking more difficult, tiresome. The thick carpet of mushy dust sucked the strength from his legs.

"These holes – they're air passages. They permeate the hotel, inside the walls. This isn't simply the cellar stairwell, I would say. It acts like the lungs of the hotel. That's the reason for the cold, and the steel door keeps the lungs sealed, you see." He pointed at one of the passages. "These help the hotel breathe in summer. It would be like an oven, otherwise, and a large number of our charges do not care for windows, so the hotel has relatively few for its size." Jacob looked at him. "You've heard the joke about the would-be suicide who couldn't stand the sight of an open window?" He paused. "No – I guessed as much." He picked up the pace. "In any case, the richest man in the world couldn't afford all the air conditioners it would take, or the electricity to run them." Richard laid his hand on the brick surrounding one of the holes. "Please avoid reaching into any of them," Jacob called back over his shoulder. "They weren't included in this summer's cleaning." Richard tucked his wandering hand into his pocket.

At the moment, Serena was no doubt up in the library, reading whatever looked interesting, even though most of the books were far over her head. But since they had moved here, his daughter had developed a curiosity about all the things she could not possibly understand, all those old books and paintings, all the slightly off-track aspects of the hotel. When he'd asked her about it, she'd pulled herself out of the book she was laboring over, a long, narrow volume with a plush red binding, *A History of Dreams to Come* stamped in faded gold on the cover. "I don't really need to understand," was all she'd said, before burrowing her way back into the text.

Sometimes she wandered the halls for hours at a time, hands feeling the patterns of the flocked wallpaper like someone blind, as if trying to commit them to memory. She'd wandered through vacant, unlocked rooms, until Richard had discovered her and put a stop to that. "Too dangerous," he told her, although admitting to himself he really wasn't so sure. Every now and then, she'd play chess or work puzzles or simply sit with one of the residents – one or both of the dark, elderly twin sisters from the third floor, or the too-pale midget whose hands were always heavily gloved. None of whom he ever heard speak to her.

"They don't really *need* to," she'd tell him, with a tone that betrayed her impatience. But sometimes he would hear her speaking to them, in the monologue voice she'd once used for her dolls. At times like those, he again thought he'd done the wrong thing, bringing her here. It hadn't been for *her*, certainly.

The situations some parents put their children in used to bother him. Unhealthy situations. *Dangerous* situations. They'd move them somewhere way out in the country to get away from the crime and pollution of the cities, and there wouldn't be adequate medical or other emergency help available. Or they'd move their kids in to the city because they liked the lifestyle, and the kids would be walking past pimps and drug dealers to school every day. Or maybe a father's grief had bent him a little too far, and he'd taken the kid to live in the original horror hotel. And the kid is almost eaten by a human wolf.

No one was ever hurt here without a reason. But Richard didn't know if he could believe that.

"If you do not face the wolf sometime, it's likely to circle around behind you."

Richard stared into the darkness, trying to see Jacob. The old man's face floated up out of the black. "She doesn't *have* to be here; I didn't have to bring her," Richard snapped.

Jacob's eyes flashed in the dim light. "You have to look at what scares you, Richard, if you don't want it to control your life."

"My daughter was never scared of werewolves, Jacob. Not until she came here."

"A wolf isn't always just a wolf. A human being isn't always just a human being. And no one really knows what truly frightens another human being, even if it is your own daughter. Shape does not matter. If you stay here long enough, you will understand that. Shapes do not scare you; it is the shadows that move under them. Shapes never scared anyone, this hotel never scared anyone. It is finding your own face inside, being scared nearly half to death by your own face, and still not being too afraid to look into that mirror again. That's what matters. And right now – plumbing. Plumbing is what matters. Serena is not likely to appreciate all your guilt and obsession over how to save her from some place she is feeling at home in if she does not have an appropriate place to go *potty!*"

Jacob's steps dropped him further into gray night. Richard followed, half-smiling, carrying the tools.

The door at the bottom of the stairs was much older: black, oily wood, reinforced with iron. Pieces splintered off the bottom as the door scraped open.

Jacob led him through a maze of rooms crammed with pipes. "Circulation!" he said. "Water, gas, sewer, electrical – it is all here. Blood, piss, and vinegar." At one corner they came across a huge boiler-like device with a multitude of pipes and coils arranged around the top like an elaborate metal hairdo. "One of your predecessors thought he could power the hotel with this device. 'Spirit Trap,' he called it. But I suppose it made too much noise for him."

Jacob would stop now and then to examine the chalk markings on one of the pipes, and then with renewed energy maneuver through a series of sudden bends in the passageways. Once he stopped before a small rusted hatch set flush into the wall, not quite at his head height.

"Here is something I would like to show you." He wedged the end of a wrench under one corner of the hatch and pried it open. He stuck the flashlight in first, then cautiously followed with his head. "Okay. Come here." As Jacob brought his head back out, Richard examined him for spider webs. Jacob handed him the flashlight. "Take a look," he said. "Position your head just inside the door."

"Wait a minute." Richard stared at the hatch. It was pitch black inside.

"It is clean; you saw me check it. Nothing waiting to lay an egg in your head, I assure you."

Richard glared at the caretaker and grabbed the flashlight out of his hand. "Hold the hatch. Just so it doesn't slam back or anything." Jacob nodded, drumming his fingers irritatingly on the egg-shell metal. Richard stuck the flashlight end through first. Bright red brick lined the passage. Warm, circulating air left goosebumps on the back of his arm. Puzzled, he pushed his head through the opening. A breeze of near-hot air lifted his hair. But he could see very little. A vertical column of brilliant red brick, pitch dark on either end. "What is it?" he called back.

"Heating system. That's why the hotel isn't nearly as cold as one might expect."

"Wait. What about that big furnace over in the auxiliary basement? We're nowhere near there." Richard trained the light on the shaft below him. No end in sight. He squinted for a long time, trying to see what might be there, sometimes thinking he saw bits of cloud or dark shapes in the air currents, sometimes thinking he heard a voice sighing, or music, or just the slightest trace of laughter, before Jacob finally answered.

"What you saw was just the incinerator, for burning trash, like unfriendly kitties." He paused, as if expecting Richard to laugh at the weak, grim joke. "We don't use it for heating. There is no furnace here. No furnace anywhere." Richard came out of the hatch and looked at Jacob. Jacob frowned. "I've looked for years. And in the summer that air's ice cold. I've dropped stones into the shaft – they never make a sound. It's the Deadfall Windpipe, or something like that." He chuckled. "I don't know who built it, but he or she was *a genius,* no doubt about that." He took the light back. "We'd best hurry now. Our job's waiting for us just a short distance down this passage, if I've calculated correctly."

They came to a tall room. It was like entering a chimney. A dozen or so pipes, jammed together tight as organ pipes, dropped straight out of the darkness above. At waist-height, they joined other pipes, which entered the crumbling brick and plaster walls at right angles. Each pipe had two valves, one on either side of the angle.

"Here it is," Jacob said. "At first glance, it looks like a random design, I know. I'm always surprised they don't clog more often." Rubbing the dust from the pipes, he tapped a small tube entering the upper valve from the rear. Richard could see now that all the valves had them. "It took me a while to figure it out," Jacob began, "but it appears that these tubes add pressure inside each valve and help push the substance inside the pipe – fluid or gas or solids, whatever it might be – to wherever in the hotel it needs to go." He flashed the light several feet above the valve. An oily, pus-like corrosion caked some of the metal. "These pipes are *old*." A long, segmented bug with near-transparent head waved its greasy feelers at the intruding beam of light.

"Disgusting," Richard murmured. The air suddenly felt too wet, too old in his mouth. He wanted to spit it out. He was a little panicky. He felt like throwing up.

"You'd never make a doctor," Jacob said.

"What's that?"

"I just mean if you were to put your hands inside these bodies of ours you'd find a state of affairs equally disgusting. The hotel has to breathe, heat up and cool down, get rid of its waste. The secret systems of anything, however wonderful, aren't always pretty to look at."

Not for the first time, Richard wished the old man would just shut up. He had a headache, and realized he was hungry again. Starved.

He'd always been easily disgusted by the 'secret systems' of things. His parents had had a great deal of illness between them: rheumatic fever and bad lungs, bad liver, bad kidneys, illnesses that had made them incontinent, ugly, and angry. He'd hated their bodies, and been suspicious of his own.

But his own disgust had given him appetite, made him hungry. From the time he was a child – that was the funny thing, the terrible thing. Even as his parents were throwing up in the other room, their marriage having been reduced to a simple sharing of sickness and anger, Richard had been in the refrigerator, stuffing his face. By the time he entered high school he'd been vastly overweight. And his own disquiet over his physical body had driven him to eat even more.

The only reason he'd lost the weight at the end of college had been a switch in appetites. Sex had disgusted him, in degrees ranging from the vague to the profound: the smell of another body, the look of it, the look in the woman's eyes – desire, apprehension, defiance, an abandonment of self that seemed all too similar to suicide, all of it there together – he wondered if Abby had ever guessed. He didn't think so. If anything, she might have thought him *too* obsessed with her body, too enamored of it. Because his disgust with sex, the repulsion he had felt in the presence of another body, had in turn given him a great appetite for it. Repulsion and excitement, a sourness and a quickening. A hunger for touching, for long nights of bodies alternately defiant and apprehensive.

But maybe she would have guessed if they'd been together longer. He would have hated that. For, with all his confusion, his pitiful aversions, he knew he had loved her, and it would have killed him to hurt her like that. Before Serena, Abby had been all he had.

Jacob's hammer rang on the valve stems as he attempted to loosen them. The sound echoed over their heads, receded rapidly into the darkness above. An enormous white wing that was not a wing seemed to float down toward Richard out of the darkness. A woman's pale gown. Abby's gown. Her face floated just above the gown, lips pulling back, lips pulling back so far they split her beautiful face open and emptied it over his head, the liquid streaming over his face, gathering in his eyes and into the corners of his mouth where he breathed her in, tasted her, gathered her in with his tongue.

Jacob's hammer exploded again. The room smelled of rot and sour decay. A few strands of reddish-blonde hair briefly caressed Richard's face, and then were gone.

"All of us live with the dead," Jacob said. "All of us with memory."

"More than memory." Richard tried to wipe away tears that were not there.

"You see her every day? Some part of her?"

"Pretty much. Sometimes more. And always, in my dreams."

Jacob had been using a huge wrench to loosen one of the valves. Now he pulled down on the bend that attached below it. The metal squealed. The joint held by a thread. He banged on it twice more. "Widowers in British New Guinea," he panted, "*Mekeo*, I believe. They carry a tomahawk to protect themselves from their dead wives."

"She wouldn't hurt me."

"Perhaps not. No, I'm sure not. But memory is a hungry thing, a craving thing. If you don't carry your tomahawk it can eat up your time, consume your life. There we go. Come over here, Richard." Jacob held the flashlight up to the open end of the valve. "Wrong one," he said. "But listen." A thin crying slipped out of the pipe. Richard felt it like a worm on the back of his neck. They tried several more pipes, found water, stale dusty air, laughter and lamentations. Then on the last one, Jacob said, "Got it," his arm and a crowbar pushed halfway up the pipe. "Stuck tight, whatever it is."

Finally the thing came away with a cracking sound, and dark, mushy sewage gushed from the pipe and began pooling on the floor. Richard gasped, covered his mouth with his hand. Jacob struggled to reconnect the joint, his boots sliding a dance through the thick, lace-high goop. "There!" he shouted, tightening the retainer rings so far Richard thought the ancient metal would split. "This is some *old crap*, is the way a professional plumber would put it, I believe." He grinned, slipped on rubber gloves and began fingering through the sludge. The surface of the gloves smoked when he brought them back up into air, the offending object held well away from him. He stroked it gently, like a baby's head, cleaning it off.

It was a small skull. An animal skull. Its lower teeth curved high up over the nasal area, threatening the eye sockets. "I told him not to flush these things down the toilet anymore," Jacob muttered, almost sadly, and dropped the skull into his sack.

They climbed out a way different from the one they'd come – Richard wanted to get to a bath as soon as possible. And after what should have been far too many steps up several staircases, they reached a row of narrow windows practically at ground level, the sills snow-packed to within six inches of their tops. Jacob peered through the glass over the high lip of snow. "I see Serena decided to play outside today after our lessons."

Richard pushed into the window beside Jacob. "It's *too cold* for her out there."

"Please, Richard. Remember that she isn't a toddler."

Serena was out in the snow; he could see her red boots dancing between the stark charcoal trunks of the grove.

The wind was rising. Every now and then a gust would strike the white powder, pick it up like an invisible scoop, scatter it out again in a glistening cloud. Serena ran through it, kicking at the snow as if to force more of it into the air. Richard imagined she was having a wonderful time, but because of the angle and her closeness to the windows, he could not actually see her face.

Her red boots, her blue-jeaned legs, her new white coat disappeared into the brilliant white spray. He waited for her to reappear, and when she did not for several moments, he grew anxious. Then a shadow formed in the middle of the snow cloud. A slight shadow, snatches of red flashing as it whirled inside the cloud. The snow fell and the cloud separated. At first Richard thought the woman who finally emerged was some dream-vision of how Serena would look in twenty years.

The lines of the face were so like hers, the posture, the way she moved her hands.

But then Serena appeared beside her. The woman had one arm across her shoulders, and his daughter suddenly seemed much smaller. He could now see Serena's face; she looked happy. The woman bent over her, hair not quite blonde and not quite red spilling slowly down the side of her face, obscuring her mouth as she leaned forward to whisper something to his daughter, who laughed almost drunkenly, so hard she staggered briefly in the thick snow. The waves of blonde and red hair separated in the rising wind, the wind seeming to build up as the woman whispered, as Serena laughed, until Richard could hear it almost howling through the glass, more snow lifting into the brilliant air to obscure the two figures. He could not stop watching.

He and Abby had always told her not to talk to strangers. If she went off with a stranger, how could he protect her?

The wind died abruptly. The snow dropped into a scattered, ungraspable mist like a juggler's bad dream. The woman's form was revealed, closer to the window, looking down at him. Serena was nowhere to be seen.

Aquiline face and lean nose. Eyebrows a bit too heavy. The woman was ill-clothed for the weather: her dress was a dark blue, near-black, and almost gauzy. Over that, just a darker shawl to protect her. Her arms and lower legs were bare and anemic-looking, a mere shade or so darker than the snow, so that at times she appeared to have no arms or legs – making her just a vision of mutilated torso and head floating above the untroubled snow. Staring at him with dark, still eyes. He thought about the flashes of red he had seen in her shadow, but only her lips were red, too red, as if freshly painted.

Her hair – not quite red and not quite blonde – floated along the edge of her shawl. Somehow it bothered him that her hair had lost none of its color.

"I see Serena has met a new guest," Jacob said, behind him.

"No," Richard said wearily. "She's met Abby. She's met her mother."

BUT HER NAME was Marie Rosenow, and even though her resemblance to his late wife had faded somewhat since she'd checked in, occasionally, in the right light, she looked so like her that Richard could not look at her for long. So he found himself apprehending her with sideways glances, and spying on her reflection, which made the resemblance all the more persistent and disturbing.

"What were you whispering about? Why were you laughing so?" he'd asked Serena, who'd just smiled shyly.

"Woman talk, Daddy," she'd finally said, and laughed. He didn't know what to make of her new giddiness, but he did not like it.

Marie Rosenow had checked in with very little: a couple of bags and a folded leather case more like a tool kit than a purse, which she held tightly under her arm.

And a tall, Nordic-looking man she called John, who stood in the background and carried her bags.

It may have been Richard's simple unease in her presence that made him keep looking at the man: his lean height, bleached hair which appeared to be thinning, pale, downcast eyes. The man held himself like a servant, and no doubt that was his job, but Richard found his subservient manner still unaccountably irritating. Her man – Richard reminded himself to think of him with his name, John – leaned back against the wall, the bags propped awkwardly across his knees. Richard thought of a tired, overgrown child waiting impatiently while his mother dealt with another adult.

When Marie Rosenow smiled at him, her breath smelled, not exactly rank, but rich with food. And Richard thought of

Abby after a late night steak dinner, whispering his name in bed as he explored the secret shadows of her body.

"Let me show you to your room," he said.

The woman's lips stretched, emphasizing the thinness of her face. She was remarkably beautiful. "That really won't be necessary," she said. "John can handle all that. Just give him the room number. I would like to look around a bit first – I always feel better in a new environment if I look around."

"I should at least draw him a map." Richard attempted a professional hotel manager's apologetic smile. "It's a big, complicated hotel."

"I'm sure," she said absently, not a part of the conversation anymore.

The tall, pale man lifted the bags, but hesitated when she tried to hand him the flat leather case. She jabbed it at him insistently and at last he took it in one hand, wedging it under his arm and still holding onto it with that hand, as if he were terrified of dropping it. Embarrassed, Richard gave him the scrawled map.

"Will you please show me around?" Her tone was just slightly imperious.

He looked at her nervously, feeling painfully shy. Finally he moved from behind the front desk. "We can start on this floor," he said.

In the beginning, he felt like a little boy in her company, like a little boy with a mother he had not seen in years.

"There is so much *room* here! I had heard, but had no idea! It's *lovely*. We have never stayed here before, Mister –"

"Richard is fine."

"Very well. We have never stayed here before, Richard, but I am sure we will want to come again. We – John and I – are at our best –"

"John is your...?"

"He's my" – she waved her hand – "my assistant. Of sorts. A male secretary of sorts." Richard was embarrassed that he'd interrupted her. "*I* am at my best," she began again, "in large places, with fewer people."

"Then you'll do fine here. There are few visitors during the winter, I'm told."

"Oh, you are new here, to this job, as well?"

"A short time."

"Then you – enjoy it here."

"Enjoy" was not the word he would have used. "I think I do belong here, I suppose." Saying the words made him feel pretentious, but he knew they were true. As if the Deadfall were his dream, and belonged to him. He wondered if he should warn her.

New or not, she moved through the corridors and rooms as if she, too, belonged there, had always been a part of the Deadfall. They paused in the music room because she wanted a view from the windows. "The sky is very white here," she said. "Do the clouds always lie so low?

"Usually," he said. "In fact, the cover is normally so thick you forget the sky is supposed to be blue. You start thinking of the white sky; the birds, the outlines of the trees – they seem more like shadows against the white."

"Yes, the trees," staring out the window at the Deadfall grove, she raised her fingers to the glass, as if to trace the distant limbs.

"Winter's the only time the grove really fits, I suppose. I mean, the deadfall, the dead limbs." He felt awkward, unsure if he was saying too much, if he was being too personal. "The naked limbs always seem so incongruous in spring."

"But death makes living possible." She looked back at him. "Don't you think? Of course, this is true scientifically: the process of decomposition supplying the elements necessary for future life. But I wonder if it isn't true psychologically as well.

The old die and leave a place for the young, the new ideas. The death of one close – our grief cleanses, allows us to see more clearly, don't you think?"

He stared at her. "That hasn't exactly been my experience."

She looked back out the window. "I see. You find the two worlds to be very different? Incompatible?"

"They just aren't the same. You can't... so many things you can't –"

As she moved into the shadowed areas of the music room, her eyes shifted toward yellow. "The only difference between the living and the dead is the blood they contain. In the dead, the blood is sour or absent. Their envy of the living is for that blood. The memories they inflict upon the grief-stricken are for that blood."

"It seems... unnatural." He wanted to leave the room. And yet he wanted to get to know this woman. He wanted to be with her.

"What could be more natural? Blood nourishes the fetus in its womb. Blood is the true mother of us all."

"I suppose that's true."

"The only true difference between a sleeping man and a dead man is the blood he contains."

He thought what she was saying was ridiculous, but he found it fascinating just the same. Richard gestured toward the door. "Perhaps I should make sure that everything is all right with your room."

Red hair, blonde hair, dropped slowly over one unmoving eye, which had fixed him like a gun sight. "Which one are you, Richard? Sleeping, or dead?"

ALONE IN HIS bed he could not manage to stay warm, even with piles of bedclothes, so every night of this winter had found Richard walking. In the empty rooms and closed corridors of the Deadfall, sudden apparitions of his wife would come to him, like an instant's updraft of smoke, seen out of the corner of his eye. The seeing seemed to depend on the occurrence of just the right angle, the correct tilting of the head.

Other times, her presence was a less palpable thing. She came as a slight mistiness in the eye, fresh air on the lips, a breeze against his chest, abrading his nipples.

At each dawn her transparent form filled with the yellows and pinks of the morning light. The burning outline of her would bleed into the ornate Persian carpet runners, and she would be gone.

Richard's night walks continued after the arrival of Marie Rosenow. More often than not he would find her pacing these dim-lit corridors as well, but she would always be ahead of him, or across a large room with her head averted, so that she did not seem to be aware of him. She looked lovelier in this light – during the day there always seemed something too faded, something disturbingly pale about her. He would follow her as closely as he could, although never for very long, as she was constantly disappearing into the unlit regions of the hotel.

She seemed troubled. There was something vaguely anxious or undecided about her movements. At times, he imagined her as a stray animal trapped inside the hotel, shocked into silence and hesitant to draw attention to itself.

One night, he heard a voice moving through the hallway toward him as he tracked her. But when he arrived where the source of the voice should have been, it was gone. The corridor here was very dark, the air heavy with dust.

"You've followed me." She spoke from within a dark shadow by one of the doorways. Only her ruddy lips and a yellow sliver of face were visible.

"Yes," he said. "I'm sorry. I – well, I have no excuse, really."

She laughed. At his awkwardness, he thought. "Do you make it a habit of following women around your hotel?"

"No. Just you."

Her face rose out of shadow so rapidly he could have sworn the outer edges of her skin began to fray. Her hair was lusterless tendrils, testing his skin before her lips reached him. Again, her breath was rank, and he recognized her desire. Tooth and tongue to neck, to cheekbone, to nape, her mouth danced around him. "You're so *sweet*," she whispered.

As if from a distance, he saw himself flying down the corridor along the ceiling, his arms pressed to his sides with the speed. He saw his mouth fly open as if to scream. He tried to taste the shadows.

And then the appetite was back. He found hair in his mouth, and it tasted of cobweb. He licked his lips. "No, no," he whispered, and pushed her as hard as he could.

She did not stumble, but merely stepped back on her own accord.

"I'm sorry," he said foolishly.

She stared at him a moment, then strode back through shadow, her body now velvet, now dust.

AGAIN, RICHARD COULD not sleep. He began walking the great north-south corridor which, despite its many twists and off-center bends, still managed to run the entire length of the hotel. As he neared the northern end, he discovered that the power was off. According to Jacob, the cobbled-together wiring was plagued with shorts, one system running directly into another, much of the old wiring embedded deep within the complex ganglia of the new.

He drew out the candle and matches from his pocket, kept for such emergencies. After a time the candle flame became transparent, a mere shadow in the shape of a flame. So instead it was his memory lighting the way, as he passed through the night halls of his childhood.

He was in the upstairs hallway of the house he had grown up in, the hallway without a lamp, but he had to use a candle anyway because he didn't want his parents to know he was up. He made his way down the stairs, terrified that he would stumble and fall in the dark, to the coat closet at the bottom where he had found his father's secret treasure of books.

He put his candle down carefully beside the box. The books and magazines were full of pictures of dead women. The women in those pictures were dead. He could not imagine how else someone could have gotten such pictures. They had propped the dead women up in all kinds of strange and distasteful positions. What was worse, they had sewn the eyelids open, so that the dead eyes just stared at you, at whoever was looking at the pictures. It made him feel bad to be looking at the pictures, seeing those dead eyes. Sometimes he could see where the eyes had gone a little cloudy, or an insect had crawled up onto an exposed eyeball. He had seen it all. He could almost smell the stench of the dead flesh on the pages. Dead women had a glossy feel.

But still, he had gotten an erection, and it had frightened him. He went to the bathroom and had fantasies of eating himself, consuming himself one little piece and by-product at a time. He dreamed of nourishing himself with himself, with no more need of other food.

Before Richard returned to his bed after the long walk through the hotel, he went into his private bathroom and stared at himself in the mirror. He looked for places where his skin might betray corruption. He looked for patches of dead skin where he might not have washed thoroughly enough. Perhaps there were pieces of skin he had not seen or washed in years – he didn't know – and now perhaps he was vulnerable there. He looked for signs of cancer.

He thought of Marie Rosenow, and felt the appetite, the beginnings of arousal.

* * *

"I'VE SEEN YOU spending a great deal of time with Ms. Rosenow of late," Jacob said. He'd stayed close all afternoon, so Richard figured he had something to say to him.

"Yes. I guess I have." Richard went back to his newspaper. If the man had something to say, he'd just have to say it.

"I know you've been lonely a long time. But, for heaven's sake, Richard! You know this is no *ordinary* hotel."

Richard put down his paper. "Okay, I admit it. She somewhat resembles Abby – I *know* that. I know maybe that's what the attraction's all about. But I'm not sure there's anything wrong with that."

Jacob scowled. "And I suppose you think that statement expresses a great deal of self-awareness?"

"What's got into you?"

"I understand she resembles Abigail. The dead tend to resemble the dead."

"Oh, *come* now. Maybe you've been in this hotel too long. Not everyone –"

"This is no ordinary hotel, Richard. That is the one essential fact you always have to keep in mind if you're going to function within this environment. *Ordinary* people do not stay here!"

"I'm not ordinary? *Serena's* not ordinary?"

"Don't be obtuse. You *know* what I mean. Think about how you feel with her, the sensations, the things you see. I highly doubt it is an *ordinary* experience." The old man left.

Marie Rosenow's man John was sitting out in the lobby when Richard came out. The sun was high enough that morning to fill the lobby with a brilliant white glare, which so washed out John's color that at first Richard didn't see the man's flesh at all. He thought Serena might have left one of his old suits out after playing with it. Then, when he went over to check it out, he'd seen the outlines of the man's face, the hair so pale it resembled a cap of web spun around his skull.

"Good morning."

The man didn't say anything for a moment, and Richard began to wonder if he might be hard of hearing. Then the faded head slowly began to turn, the edges of the face becoming almost transparent as he edged into the morning light. John's eyes were cotton balls, his mouth a thin wiggle of stitches. "Hello. Morning."

"We've never really been introduced. I'm Richard, and I run this hotel." He offered his hand.

"Yes," John said, pulling at the edge of Richard's hand with a few loose, cold fingers. "I know that."

"I have talked a bit with Ms. Rosenow. Just a bit." John's eyes now looked pink. With nervous, almost palsied fingers, he kept pulling at his shirt and coat sleeves as if they were too short. "Have you served Ms. Rosenow long?"

"She has been... very good to me."

"I'm sure," he said, embarrassed. Perhaps the man had some sort of mental or emotional handicap. Richard wasn't sure he even wanted to know. "Well, I suppose I'd better get back to my work." He offered his hand again.

At first John looked at it as if he'd never seen anything like it before. Then his own hand came up with a little jerk and he grabbed Richard's hand with a convulsive squeeze.

Metal gleamed on John's wrist. Richard leaned closer. A brass affair, looking much like a small mouth organ, appeared to have been stapled to his skin. A small, capped tube protruded. The skin around the device was puckered an angry shade of red.

Richard heard himself make a strained, half-laughing sound, and then he withdrew his hand. "So much to do in a place like this," he said, and left the room.

*   *   *

EVEN WHEN MARIE wasn't in the room, Richard caught himself imagining her presence. He only had to look at any slightly complex pattern – the design of the wallpaper, the nap of the rug, an ornately painted vase – to find her dark, fixed eyes, her ruddy mouth, the fine curve of her pale cheeks. Although he felt slightly foolish, he could not stop himself from making these comparisons. She whispered sweet secrets into his ears with her souring, tantalizing breath.

"What's the matter with John?" he asked. "I saw the metal contraption on his wrist."

She looked at him, her lips pressed tightly together. "He is dying, I am afraid."

"Cancer?" The word fell out without consideration.

She nodded. "He is dying," she said again. "It is *inevitable*, now." He wrapped his arms around her, pressing his cheek to the back of her cold neck.

He spent an hour or so each morning shoveling snow from the front patios. The sky was amazingly white, the light so bright it made the shadows burn. The dark clouds, patterned like human X-rays, twisted slowly past. Eye sockets drifted, seeking eyes. The weathervanes high up along the roofline – crow and cock, cat and snake – turned their dark silhouettes southward.

At night he would lie down but his fevered imagination continued to fire one image after another. Pictures of days past and days to come would scroll across the off-white ceiling, broken now and again by the sudden shadow of a tree limb or separated vine blown across the window. It was like lying in his grave, he thought, conscious through the generations, the world changing rapidly above him, the wind blowing the years ruthlessly past his headstone.

But I'm alive.

Don't leave me, Abby whispered from under the pillow beside him. *You made a promise. After all this time, don't leave me,* then she made a shallow gasping noise as if she were smothering. "I want to love again before I die," he said, but not really to her. "I have a right. I'm still alive."

Marie stayed away from him night after night, running away down the dark corridors, teasing. Irritated at first, now he just wanted to be with her.

One night he saw her coming out of the music room and attempted to follow her shadowed shape as it traveled from room to room, down every short and long corridor in the hotel. He stayed well back so she wouldn't see him. She dragged her gray shadow behind her along the runner and baseboard, a peculiarly pale version of herself.

She turned a sharp corner and left her shadow behind. Richard halted, stared at the shadow as it drifted along the floor independent of its owner. A trick of the light, he thought, and tried to ignore it. It was simply a gray shadow.

But it darkened and fled as he approached. In some distant part of the hotel, a woman's laughter burst and ran up and down the scale. The shadow raced ahead and around the next bend in the corridor, as if returning to her.

Other silhouettes traveled the walls past him, angular and quick. His own shadow grew sluggish, as if sticking to the surface of the wallpaper, dragging one step behind his own movements. One dark shape after another moved across him, threatening his balance.

Finally one latched on to him, pushing him faster and faster down the center of the corridor. He glanced down in panic, and thought it must be her runaway shadow, for it was about her height and bore the curve of her face, the light trace of her hair. He stumbled and fell, but could not feel the carpet beneath him, could not feel the walls, and was suddenly lying on his back, once again as if in his grave, all sensation suddenly ended as he could feel nothing supporting him.

Her face floated above him. "It is time," she said.

The air had grown pale above her, as if she was lying on a pillow, her hair spread out into a nest for her skull, her face a mask of yellowing wax. Then he became confused, and did not know if she was in fact above him, or if she was lying in her own bed and he was above *her*, making ready to kiss her. The ceiling, or the bed, began to dissolve. He could see the pitch-colored sky above them, the clouds drifting over the hotel, the edges of darkness and cloud beginning to fray so that they might float up into it.

Her face fell closer and she nipped at his lips, finally grasping a bit of tender skin expertly between two teeth and pulling. He tried to see what else awaited him in the dark cavern of her mouth, but again could see nothing but the night sky poised above the Deadfall.

She nipped him again, this time taking more flesh from his lower lip. He tasted salt. He thought of Renfield, eating his flies and spiders, laughing that high-pitched, mad, girlish laugh. He tried to push away from her, but gravity wasn't working for him. He only drifted closer into her stinking breath and teeth.

"The kiss begins as a bite," she said softly. "Don't be alarmed. It's not what people say – it can be very pleasurable. Very *ordinary* people do this."

"You're not ordinary," he managed, hearing the fear in his own voice.

"And neither are you, my sweet," she whispered into his ear. "My sugar," she murmured, scraping her teeth across the lobe. He felt an unpleasant sensation along the skin over his spine, as if his flesh were wrinkling, peeling there. As if the snake of his backbone were finally freeing itself of its costume.

His fear aroused him. He felt himself taken by her many mouths. He heard his skin rub.

Her teeth raked lightly at him. "In places where the capillaries are close to the surface," she whispered, "you do not even have to break the skin."

Making love to her, he sensed the beginnings of his own body's decay. He was scared, and he embraced her more tightly because it was the only way he knew to seek comfort. He was terrified of the ecstasy of letting go.

He did not know what might happen to his daughter if he were to let go.

"Why did you choose me?" he asked. "I haven't been *chosen* in a very long time." Her smile descended on him slowly. "But I'm glad, you chose me. That's, the best thing, the important thing."

"Yes," she said, her lips brushing his shoulder, his chest. "I choose *you*, my sweet. From now on *you* will be the one."

Her teeth began to deepen the abrasion she had made on his chest. He could feel her tongue searching for entry beneath a small torn flap of his skin.

His mind floated away rapidly and his body surrounded her. His windows, his doors, the silent passages of his empty corridors, all kept watch, and listened.

THE NEXT MORNING in the lobby, he saw Serena and Marie Rosenow laughing like two madwomen. It reminded him so much of times when Abby had made this crazy laugh, and Serena, still a little girl who worshipped her mother, had tried to ape that laugh, with little success. Marie reached out to his daughter and touched her tentatively on the shoulder. Serena hugged her, still laughing. Richard stared at the pair coldly. In a far-off part of his brain, he noted how happy Serena seemed with this new woman. But he could not help but think of an aged crone of a countess bathing in the blood of countless virgins, her wrinkled skin filling out, her color gradually bleaching to a shade of snow.

After Serena had gone up to her room, Richard pulled Marie aside. "You're *never* to touch her!" he whispered fiercely. "I don't even want you to *talk* to her!" He shook her; he suddenly realized he was ready to strike her.

Marie slipped away from him. *As if she were oiled,* he thought. "I may be a great many things, Richard." She started to leave him. He was already reaching to pull her back, when she stopped and stared at him. "But I am no pedophile." She was gone before he could say more.

Richard believed her. And yet, that afternoon, he still sent Serena away.

"It's not fair!" she screamed, looking like a much younger child, her face red and puffy from an hour-long bout of crying.

"Enid has invited you down to her sister's house in Mad Devon," he said. "And with so few tenants, she probably won't be cooking up here for awhile. It'll be good for you to spend some time with her. And her son – get to know him – he may be a little slow, but he might still make a good friend. I know you've always been fascinated by him. Find out what makes him tick, then you can tell *me*." He laughed and she blushed. "You're growing up. A young woman. Enid can help you more with that than I can."

"You just want to be *alone* with *her!* You're afraid I'll get in the way of your little romance!"

He didn't know what to say. He wanted to be truthful with her, but he didn't know what to say. The taxi had come and gone and he still didn't know what to say. He still didn't *know*.

He did not see Marie Rosenow the rest of that day; he wondered what she did with her afternoons – obviously the light didn't bother her. He spent much of his own day in the lobby, gazing out the tall windows, watching the snow fill the sky in agitated flurries, drifting over the driveway and piling higher against the walls, the Deadfall grove a brooding, distant presence, glistening black through the gauzy whiteness.

"You sent the wrong one away, but I think you already know that," Jacob said behind him.

Richard felt too weary to turn and look, or even to tell Jacob that he couldn't talk about this right now. "I had to protect her – not that I'm positive that she really needs protection – but I don't care to take that kind of chance. Besides, as you've told me so many times before, we don't turn people away."

"That we do not. Perhaps we really should sometimes, but we do not. That is our custom."

"So what are you trying to tell me, Jacob?"

"Simply that there needs to be a marked difference between whom you let into this hotel and whom you let into your heart. Think of this hotel as – forgive the metaphor – a model for your dreams, and it is perfectly acceptable – healthy perhaps, although I'm certainly no expert – to let anything and anyone into your dreams. But that does not mean you sit down and break bread with them. Or share the same bed."

"Hey, now, you're going too far."

Jacob didn't respond.

"I'm sorry, Jacob," Richard finally said.

"No, perhaps you are correct. This is none of my business."

"My business has been your business ever since I got here." Richard sighed. "And I must admit I have needed that. And I don't think all that should change now. Not yet."

"Richard, my grandfather once told me that if you are denied a better love, you will settle for any love. Sometimes in our distress one looks as good as any other."

"Your grandfather was a wise man, Jacob."

"Then you should heed his advice."

"She has an illness," Richard said. "I'm not sure of the details of it, but life isn't a horror movie. I just can't find any evil in her."

"I am not saying you should. Our residents, well, they are *complicated*. But compassion does not have to be a synonym for stupidity."

Richard chuckled. "I'll try to remember that."

"In an earlier, let us say, less sophisticated time, they had ways of keeping the dead from coming back. They might feed them to animals or remove their arms and legs to curtail their travel, or simply tie them up. Gypsies would insert a hatpin through the heart. And some would, truth be told, simply eat them, which seemed to settle the issue."

"You're not seriously suggesting that she's dead, are you?"

"I cannot say that with absolute certainty, no. It is always an error to jump to conclusions with our particular clientele. But as my beloved grandfather would say, 'that is no way to live.'"

"Maybe she has no choice."

Jacob walked over to the front windows and stared out at the rapidly building snowstorm. "There are choices and there are choices. We *all* feed off each other, Richard. That is not always such a terrible thing – perhaps a natural consequence of having a brain that can aspire, and yearn. But like anything else, some creatures take it a bit too far." He stood still for a time as blown flakes began adhering to the panes. "But you should ask *him*," he finally said. "He is the expert."

Richard came to the window and stood beside Jacob. He looked past the violent flurry of white, struggling to find what the old man was looking at. Finally, there at the edge of the grove, staring up at the twisted, convoluted branches as if admiring a work of art. It was Marie Rosenow's companion, John.

The white wind seemed capable of toppling him; his gaunt frame shook. His face and hair above the bright red scarf were the color of the snow.

"He looks thinner, notably weaker, than when he first came. You look at him, Richard. Are you *that* lonely?"

That night, her door was ajar. Peering around, he saw a figure almost the color of the sheets, flesh adhering to the sheets, melting into them like pale butter left too long. Marie bent over the figure like a nun in prayer. Richard glimpsed dark fluid running through a pallid yellow tube. The figure on the bed jerked once, as if in orgasm. Pale fists clenched in pain and a dollop of blood suddenly splattered the inside of the bottle. Marie leaned closer, whispering.

"HE WAS AN addict, when I first met him," Marie Rosenow was pacing. She kept her rooms dark, rugs over the windows, as much to keep out the violent sounds of the storm, she said, as to protect the growing sensitivity of her eyes, redder with each passing day. "I stopped all that. He got clean, through me. But he *likes* the feel of steel in his veins."

"You left your door open," Richard said. "It has never been open before. That was no accident, Marie."

"Sometimes he scratches up his own chest, and rubs his blood on me," she said, in a voice so like a shy young girl's it embarrassed Richard. "Sometimes, during sex, I lap. I lick."

"He's weak."

"Sometimes there is little difference between weakness and passion," she said, coming closer to him. He found himself backing away. "If it wasn't me, it would be someone else, do you understand? He *enjoys* having his blood taken."

"You could take... animal blood."

"I have a need to be loved." She came into his arms. He thought of her body, the paleness of it, the almost inanimate beauty of it. He thought of her body as something separate from her, feeding on all the blood she'd taken in, consuming it, so that she'd become pale again, and needed more. He thought of the monster that was her body. He held her tightly, until his arms grew numb.

A little before dawn the next morning a strange bird was driven out of the skies by the storm. It struggled to within a dozen yards of the hotel's front door before finally collapsing.

"Damn," Jacob muttered, attempting to finish his morning coffee. "You stay here," he said to Richard, then donned his heavy coat and gloves. He had to put his shoulder into the front door to wedge it open against the snow.

Richard watched as Jacob pushed through the icy gales to reach the bird. Now and then a wing would jerk and flutter, but he couldn't tell if that was the bird's weakening struggles or the wind animating the body.

As Jacob knelt into the snow by the bird, Richard thought he saw the bird's head turn and stare at him. Feeling ice inside, a sudden wave of nausea, he went to get his jacket.

Stroking the bird's twitching wings, Jacob peered over his shoulder as Richard came up beside him. Richard stared. The bird's dark wings were painted with its own blood. The head was featherless, a pale flesh color. And deformed, or unformed. There was no beak. It was as if the beak had been torn away, leaving a face much like a baby's. The head lolled, mouth gaping; long red and yellow feathers floated away from the back of its nearly bald pate. It looked as if someone had sewn bloody wings onto the corpse of a huge fetus.

Richard had the strange notion that it resembled him. The two men stood there until dawn made the storm red.

He avoided her as much as possible, but she continued to seek him out. When he said, "I can't do this," she became like a child he could not deny. But he would not let her nip him, or scratch. He would hold her, the storm of her, and let her tell him of things she remembered, long ago parties and boyfriends, the normal things. And the sadnesses, the things she could not have, the absent friendships, the imagined family.

"No one's denied me before," she would say into his chest, in a voice both sad and petulant. "Imagine," she would whisper, her face violet and vermillion in the shadows. At night, he would find animals lying on the sills outside his bedroom windows: dark bodies and too-bright eyes. Eventually he kept his shades drawn all the time.

One afternoon he came across her outside her rooms. She was coughing, choking. When he approached her, she started to walk away. "Marie?"

"He grows weaker," she managed, her back to him. From inside he could hear the shifting of sheets, the slow fall of flesh against bed, the soft groans.

He put his hand on her arm, and she looked at him. Her pupils darkened the whites of her eyes. Dried blood still caked her mouth and part of her chin. She resembled a child not old enough to eat cleanly. He started away.

"Please," she moaned.

He came back to her. She rubbed angrily at her face with the edge of her pale gown. Redness spread into the delicate fibers. It occurred to him how careful she had seemed before, how meticulous. He thought of her cleaning her teeth in the mornings, her sour breath the only indication. "I'm sorry," he said.

"Who do you think you are?" Her face was cat-like. He expected her to spit at him at any moment. "You are dying, just as I. Wouldn't you do almost anything to stay alive?"

"Not anything," he said.

She stared at him, some of her fire gone. "And neither have I," she finally said. "I have never murdered a child. Although I cannot say I could not, someday." Richard chilled. "But to stay alive? To breathe one more day? Your Abby is *dead* – but secretly, deep down, are you not glad it was not you?"

"I wouldn't be human otherwise," he said. "But I'm still not the same as you."

"Oh? What difference is there between the living who is dead and the dead who is living? We come out of our mothers' wombs already looking for our graves."

"I'm not *dead*," he said.

"And neither am *I!*" she shouted. "There is no beauty in death. No noble mouth. The mouth flaps open, Richard. It *gapes*. The cloudy eyeballs grow distorted from the pressure. There is no aging like the aging of death. The skin wrinkles as the body loses water. The skin begins to bruise, the muscles in the eyelids, neck, and jaw go rigid. No beauty there, Richard. Your Abby, do you really think she is the lovely apparition who haunts these halls? Do you think she still reposes so peacefully, even more beautiful, younger than when she was alive? You should have dug her up, Richard. You'd find a greenish tinge over the belly, a stink as the intestines break down, the skin blistering and bloating – I love him, Richard. Just as I'd love *you*. You need not be alone!"

Her voice fell to a whisper, punctuated by hysteria. But Richard had stopped listening. She'd gone too far. He wanted to tell her she knew nothing about him, or his life. He wanted to tell her there was no body – Abby had been cremated. He wanted to tell her she knew nothing, but he held his tongue. He left her ranting in the hallway outside her door.

THE PHONE HAD rung for a very long time before Richard realized what it was. Few people called the Deadfall.

"Daddy?" Serena's voice sounded strange and far away, a memory.

"Hi, honey. How are you?"

"I'm okay. Enid has been taking me places and I've been helping out in her sister's weaving shop."

"That's nice." Her normalcy stirred him. He wondered, again, how he could ever have dragged her into such a setting.

"Daddy, when can I come home?"

"Home?"

"Daddy, I want to come home."

She meant the hotel. She meant him. "Soon, honey. I promise. I just have to take care of a few things first."

"Is that lady still there?"

He gripped the phone. He was acutely aware of the cool bite of the receiver into his ear, the static like a fevered whisper, the faint stench of old, heated wiring. "No," he lied. "She's gone now."

"I'm glad, Daddy. I'm real glad. I'll see you soon. Love you."

"Love you, too, sweetheart."

The hallway still smelled faintly of blood. He wondered if they'd ever get the coppery smell out of the walls, the carpet.

"When it rains," Marie had told him one evening, just before drifting off to sleep, "I imagine that it is raining blood. The full, dark clouds tear, and disintegrate. And no matter what I do, I cannot stop the dripping."

Her door opened, and the cold wind rushed past, leaving a dead quiet. He imagined a panicked flight of souls. *She's left the window open*, he thought. He tasted copper.

She drifted out as if sleepwalking. She went to the window at the end of the corridor and opened that one as well. For a moment, he imagined her drifting out into the storm.

"It's cold," he said.

She said nothing. He looked into her room. John lay on the yellow rug, his eyes open and staring. A drop of brilliant red hung from his chin, then fell as if in slow motion to join the spreading stain beneath his head.

"You've killed him," he said.

She opened her mouth to deny it and John's blood ran out at the corners. "He was so ill." Her voice sounded choked with fluid, as if she had a bad cold.

Richard went into her room and bent over the body. She followed him. The hem of her gown was torn and ragged, the tattered end like long fingers soaked in blood. John's dead hand clutched a torn bit of gown.

"You took too much," Richard said.

"Perhaps. He was so ill. He was dying."

Richard found the metal that had been ripped out of John's arm. He examined the neck where sharp teeth had worried open a rough flap of skin for lapping. He looked up at her. She licked her lips.

"You took too much. But that was no accident."

Her eyes flashed. "I love you, Richard."

"You *need* me. Now. You thought you'd found a substitute for him."

"I *love* you!" She opened her mouth too wide. More blood drooled to the carpet. Her nostrils spread grotesquely. He could hear her smelling the room, smelling him.

"You've mistaken the smell of blood for the smell of love."

"Love?" She laughed. She raised her hands, her gown opening like spreading wings. She was naked underneath. A streak of dried blood soiled the perfect paleness of her belly. Richard was aroused; he stepped back, frightened and disgusted with himself. "This world of yours, it's a world of impersonal loves. You have your media personalities to fall in love with – it's only surfaces you need to know. You do not *know* your lovers, only the lovers you dream of. What better time to return to basic truths? Mine is, at least, an *honest* affection. For my own life, my own passion. My main purpose is to *continue*."

"You haven't escaped death," he said softly. "You've embraced it."

What came from her was something between a sob and a hiss. She stepped toward him, closing in. He got his hands onto her shoulders and pushed her toward the window. "But I *cared* about you," he said. "I thought I could help you. Someday I might have loved you." She fell against the window sill. When she rose, he picked up a ladder-back chair and broke off a leg. He held it in front of him, a screw protruding from its end. "Don't make me, please," he said, on the verge of tears.

She stared at him, then climbed up into the window. She let the storm take her.

Off and on after she left the Deadfall, I followed Marie Rosenow around in the storm. It was almost unbearably cold, even in my heavy parka, fur-lined boots and gloves, so I could do this only in spurts, but it was a duty I felt obligated to perform. Marie Rosenow wore fewer clothes each day, finally reduced to searching the snow drifts for her small animal meals wearing no more than a few silken threads roughly the color of her whitening head and pubic hair. Periodically a tear would open on buttock or belly, but she bled very little.

I watched as she wandered the Deadfall grove, tracing the convoluted limbs with her fingertips. I sought her out on the cliffs behind the hotel, where she moaned her barely articulated laments to the still and unfeeling lake. I stood by silently while she devoured mice, squirrels, and small birds, fewer each day until she stopped eating at all.

Serena came back to the hotel, and I did my best to make sure she never saw Marie, even when Marie watched from beneath a window, or wandered aimlessly the pathways surrounding the hotel. I could have done something sooner, and I wonder now if maybe I should have.

One day I found her body lying face down in the snow beneath one of the twisted trees. It had been difficult to see at first – the skin had gone from white to something almost transparent. Her hair had gone the same straw color as the winter weeds. The body had emptied itself when she had finally given up, the blood seeping down into the snow. The ice underneath her body had melted into a muddy, reddish brown gel.

I won't be telling Richard about this. There are some things he does not need to know.

The body was gone by the end of the next day. The gel liquefied, filtering down through the snow and ice. Perhaps the flowers will be healthier next spring.

– from the diary of Jacob Ascher,
proprietor, Deadfall Hotel, 1969-2000

Chapter Five

IN MEMORY OF HEAVEN

Spring in most parts of the world is considered a time of hope and renewal. The snows have disappeared, the sun comes out, the seemingly dead limbs sprout green buds. Young men's fancies turn to thoughts of love, and all that. Spring at the Deadfall, at least during my time here, has always been late to arrive, a matter of gradual warming trends, subtle shifts in color, a slow struggle out of death and decay.

Tons of vegetation expire here during the winter months. Seemingly healthy trees a hundred or more years old die through to their hearts, and collapse as if felled by invisible axmen. If not for the fact that we have many hundreds of such trees, our woods here would be a thin veil of new growth instead of the dense wall they have become. But even a few trees dying each year in this manner make a dramatic impression. Once one witnesses such a failure, the surprising breadth and depth of the Deadfall grove becomes much more understandable. If anything, one wonders why the elaborate tangle of dead branches has not completely consumed the property.

The thoroughness of this demise extends to all other plant life in the area as well: grass and flowers and all sizes of bush and weed. And when the new, aggressive growth finally does come in, it comes as a kind of scavenging, feeding on the corpse of the old. We labor to haul away as much of the dead as possible, thereby starving the new plants into a reasonable balance.

This year my successor Richard Carter discovered conclusively that my description of this process was without exaggeration as he helped me haul away truckload after truckload of dead plant matter. This was a time-consuming process, not only because of the volume, but because of the care that must be taken in separating the living from the dead. New trunks grow out of the fallen trunks of the old, and if one is to preserve the freshman growth, the senior must be trimmed away without disturbing the new roots. In many areas of the grounds, the dead matter outweighs the new growth by a factor of ten or more, so we shovel and scrape for hours until the fresh, solitary shoots may find their own scope without interference. If we did not take our task seriously, the limbs of the dead would block and strangle these young plants, and we would be left with nothing but a pile of steaming rot by mid-season.

Serena observed our labors for the first week until, bored, she took herself off to invent some new game. Until her departure, I must say I was vaguely discomfited by her attitude. "Get rid of all that ugly old dead stuff," she'd say. "I want to see the new flowers." There's nothing wrong with such a sentiment, of course, but I couldn't help ruminating on just how relatively soon I, and her father, would become "ugly old dead stuff." Am I over-thinking this? Obviously. It seems to be in the nature of adulthood that we venerate the past, grieve its obsolescence, and even live there in the mind far more than could possibly be healthy. Perhaps our sympathy is because we feel life slipping away. The very young, on the other hand, appear to worship every new thing.

There is one spring ritual at the hotel, however, in which Richard is not yet prepared to participate. My predecessor at the Deadfall, Ms. Malachiuk (no first name that I'm aware of), involved me in this particular task only after I had been here for three years. Ms. Malachiuk had been in charge here since the early 'thirties. At the time I arrived, her proprietorship was in its third decade. Her tenure might be considered a quiet one, having experienced few of the dramatic events which spice the hotel's history. This might in part have been due to the times – it would be hard to imagine any resident as monstrous as some of our world leaders during that period, and in fact, many Nazi and Stalin-era uniforms were discovered abandoned in closets during subsequent sweeps of vacated rooms. But I also like to think her very demeanor may have contributed to the placidity of her tenure. A short, quiet woman, she projected more the attitude of a servant than that of management personnel. Clearly she saw herself as in a service role, and behaved accordingly.

She came to my room just before dawn on an early Spring day, her hands folded together, her head slightly bowed in the religious posture I would always associate with her. "Regretfully, I must introduce you today to an unpleasant new task. We commonly refer to it as the annual 'Removal.' You will be responsible for its smooth operation every year at this time. Some years, the Removal lasts only a day or so, but there have been years, I'm afraid, when the task has required several weeks of diligent effort."

With such a formidable introduction, I imagined a task of great danger, and fatalist as I was at the time I readied myself for a potentially life-threatening endeavor. Instead, she instructed me to obtain a shovel, a heavy hammer, crowbar and sacks from the tool shed and join her in front of a room on the second floor. She pulled out a key, unlocked and slowly opened the door.

There was very little smell, but the body lying on the ornate rug had predominantly liquefied, with a more or less solid right hand and incredibly long, multiply-hinged left leg still wrapped in the rotting clothes. The head was an abstraction of not completely unappealing arrangement.

"We have twelve more to deal with this season," she said. "Most years there are far more, each dead in their own way, as befitting their type. We must have had an unusually healthy clientele this year."

In fact, there were thirteen more. I found a small form curled inside a wall sconce at the end of the third floor hall. His tiny tuxedo was streaked with dark brown scorch marks from repeatedly, convulsively embracing the white-hot bulb.

Compared to many who have come here, I must say that Marie Rosenow's demise was a relatively wholesome one.

> – from the diary of Jacob Ascher,
> proprietor, Deadfall Hotel, 1969-2000

SOMETHING WAS LOOSE in the room. Richard was still too groggy to address the issue, still too enthralled with his dream to take action. He'd been up late with Jacob the night before, unsuccessfully trying to trace an electrical problem in the hotel that had been going on for weeks – a random power outage hitting individual rooms or clusters of rooms with no apparent logic or pattern, traveling through the structure like some darkness fairy. He'd been dreaming of this fairy, riding its crisped wings as it soared through the halls, tightly clutching its insect-like shoulders, feeling the arbitrariness of its havoc, worried that it might approach Serena's room and find harm to do there.

There was also something nagging about the dream, some realization he knew he was very close to, but which remained just out of his grasp. It had to do with Abby, he thought, seeing Abby again, their family being together again, and not being confident if she would be happy to be with him again.

Sometimes in dreams the secret way to happiness seems right on the other side of a door you cannot quite get open, falling off the lips of a stranger you cannot quite hear, resting in a dim shadow your eyes cannot quite penetrate. Sometimes you actually do find the way in the dream, but then promptly forget it, finding in its place an all-too-imperfect memory.

Now he was very close to that memory of heaven, this dark sprite taking him right to its threshold, but something was loose in his room, something was flapping, something was shaking him out of his dream.

A bird was loose in the Deadfall. The flapping in his sleep had awakened him, becoming a loud, rhythmic sound that shook him and made him cold, blood throbbing in his ears, so that at first he thought it was the anxious beat of his own pulse that had awakened him, his heart ripping itself apart. That kind of thing had happened to him all the time as a child – sometimes he couldn't fall asleep for hours because of the thundering of his pulse. In adolescence, he'd thought the pulse might be in his arm, so he tried not to sleep on it, and at first that seemed to work, but it eventually came back, now throbbing in his ears. So then he thought his ears must be the culprits, particularly the left one, which was the side he always slept on. So he'd fashioned ear muffs out of heavy socks and the metal reinforcing band from an old winter cap. But then the annoying pulse moved into his head, where it had lived all this time.

As he grew older, the pulsing faded away, and he had no theories as to why. Once it had gone he found he'd missed it, for at least it had been his constant reminder of life, however frightening, late at night when death arrived for so many. His own grandfather had died sometime after midnight, his uncles between the hours of one a.m. and five, and when his father died it had been right after retiring for the night.

Richard pulled away the covers and permitted the night air of the Deadfall into his bed, until the flap, flap, flap of a wing finally reached him. He slipped out of his bed, pulled on his robe and shoes, stepped out into the yellow-lit hall that ran along the back of the manager's quarters.

Bug-shaped baseboard lights placed every few yards illuminated the bottom quarter of the hall. In the distance they flickered as if choking. Sparser ceiling fixtures – shell-shaped, spaced a good twenty feet apart – pulsed. A short, perhaps, no doubt related to the other electrical issues.

Flap, flap, flap.

He stepped more quickly. Soon he was almost running.

Darkness broke and turned away from him. Richard imagined, of course, all manner of apparitions: a rare species of bat, an animated coat, a doll with wings. This was the Deadfall Hotel, after all – the sound wasn't likely to come from a sparrow the cat had chased in.

He couldn't stop himself from grinning then, as terrible as that thought might have been. There were no more cats in the Deadfall and, he suspected, it might be some time before they were allowed back in.

He followed the sound into the darkness ahead of him. The doors to the normally locked music room were open.

Something hit one of the ornate French panels. Inside, the gauze curtains were flying.

Richard moved into the room and stepped to the side, away from the doors, letting his eyes grow accustomed to the moonlight seeping through the large bay window. Something circled him. A lock of hair fluttered across his forehead.

Something white was flapping, flashing its wings, the beat of its wings quickening and its image coming clearer, brighter: white luminescent sides, finely-sculpted wings. The beak gleamed with orange lightning as the small head darted.

Then the bird passed closer to him, and suddenly he was breathing wet air, and smelling the salty thing, the smell all over his face.

"Abby?"

The bird's presence was small, but its effect substantial. Richard could feel it moving the air around in the long-closed room. The bird fell into a glide, improbable as that seemed in such a small space.

Richard reached slowly for one of the curtains. He grabbed it at the middle, began to pull it down. The old gauze panel gave way with a brittle tearing, rotted threads popping, dust raining over his face and arm. With the cloth held carefully in both hands, he crept to the center of the music room, where the beautiful white bird hung suspended and flapping, as if on slow-motion film.

The bird watched as he approached it with the gauze, its wings beating in a multiplied blur. Again, her smell drifted over him, and he felt fear and amazement over the terrible solidity of the bird. He reached out with the curtain in his hands and gathered her in. The bird filled the gauze and made it, too, appallingly solid.

Suddenly the bundle became heavy, too heavy to hold. His arms dropped. The bird opened its wings and the gauze disintegrated into airy swatches and dust.

Abby drifted aimlessly around the music room. She looked more haggard than the last time he had seen her. He couldn't imagine why an apparition should change so. He was careful to use the word 'apparition' in thinking about the manifestation of his late wife. This thing lacked her personality, her attitudes – at best, it was merely a heartless image.

But there was an agitated, nervous quality about her. A pacing, but no foot ever touched floor. Sometimes she turned so quickly pieces of her appeared to break off, float away, and evaporate into the darkness.

"Abby," he said. When she looked at him, her eyes swam with tears.

But this did not move him. He wondered how he could be so heartless with her, apparition or not. When she'd been alive, he would have done anything to keep her, to hold on to her for just a little longer.

She was just a vague presence in the air, a perfume, a lost ray of light. And it still amazed him how much weight a dead thing could have.

Abby turned and turned in the air. He thought about just how far he should have gone to keep her with him. What terrible things he might have been willing to do. And he was thankful that human beings don't get to make such choices. It was just a fantasy to torment ourselves, guilty to be still alive. He wondered where he would be now if Abby had not died. Certainly not managing this hotel.

Richard had come to doubt what it was he mourned. Was he really mourning Abby? He couldn't know what she thought about during those quiet moments to herself. Could anyone make such a claim? A life was a secret thing, even between a husband and wife. Your secret life was completely your own, and because it was unknown, would never be mourned. The secret life of each individual went unhonored through eternity.

She twirled, faster and faster, until she was the white bird revolving in the air. And it was the white bird who passed unharmed through the closed window of the music room, leaving the air behind moist and warm and hard for Richard to breathe.

He walked slowly through the pre-dawn halls to his quarters for a few minutes' snatched sleep. Tomorrow would be another full day of the Deadfall's seemingly endless spring disposal of dead plants. He considered himself lucky that last year's cleanup had been completed before he was hired. Jacob had told him that it had been particularly nasty last year, requiring a month's work and using hired labor for some select, less-exotic tasks. Still, Richard had to wonder how Jacob could have tackled that much by himself. If Richard had faced that chore his first month on the job, he would have been gone, with no regrets.

Although Jacob had carefully explained why all this work was necessary, it still seemed wrong somehow, as if they were so ashamed of the past winter they were doing everything in their power to destroy all its evidence.

THEY WERE DOWN to a few remaining cleanup tasks, the final sweep-up of scattered leaves, bark, trunk fragments, and unidentifiable debris. Close examination of the last was ill-advised, Jacob had cautioned.

"And why is that?" Of course the first thing he did upon hearing that statement was to look at what he was sweeping even more closely.

"With so many fragments, and the way all nature mirrors itself – limbs and root resemble bone, leaf and bark recall skin, and so forth – these final pieces become a kind of Rorschach. And certainly you will find dead animal bits, a variety of decayed forms, without sufficient wholeness to allay your fears."

"In other words, it's best to rein in the imagination when looking at this, umm, compost?"

"Exactly."

"And after it's swept and gathered?"

"We burn it. With caution. In the beginning they were afraid the winds might sweep the fire toward the hotel, so they dumped these piles into one corner of the lake. But over time things began to grow there, and it became a home for various – well, 'vermin' would be a good word. So now we burn this bit. The ashes go into the gardens."

Richard didn't want to insult the man, but he had to believe there was a better, less labor-intensive way. And once *he* was in complete charge, he would find one. But he certainly wasn't saying so now. Instead he said, "I don't think I've ever seen such rapid, out-of-control growth."

"A few times in my life I have worked in jungles. It has a similar feel. You are surrounded by a bounty of lushness, of beauty, and then that beauty dies, and almost overnight you are surrounded by this bounty of death. Which you must deal with somehow, the debris left behind in the wake of paradise. What we are doing here is like cleaning up heaven's garbage, you might say."

Richard found Jacob's way of putting things on the eccentric side sometimes. Sometimes charming, sometimes annoying. But still, there *was* something about spring at the Deadfall that felt very wrong. All that green, new growth seemed like a sheet thrown over an underlying decay, camouflaging it under Mom's best holiday tablecloth. It reminded him of those people who, instead of fixing the dry rot in a house, simply painted it a new color. But he had to admit there was a certain satisfaction in making these tidy piles of debris and then burning the piles, sweeping up the ashes, feeding the gardens. A guilty pleasure, taking solace in burning, after burning had cost him so much in his life. But cleaning up after the dead, making the best of it. He'd become good at that.

The rake Jacob had given him for the job was a big, heavy

thing, certainly the hardiest rake he'd ever seen. Its heavy iron tines proved razor sharp, so sharp Richard had to wonder if Jacob was in the habit of using it against things other than leaves. The rake head was reinforced by ornate struts and the thick handle was beautifully hand-carved. Certainly no everyday gardening tool. But for all that bulk it was amazingly easy to maneuver, shaped to the very contours of his hands. In no time at all, despite the thickness of the plant wreckage, he had constructed a number of tidy piles. Some of the dead vegetation had secreted a salty-smelling substance as it dried, pieces sticking one to the other until a multilayered, foul-looking conglomerate had formed.

Spring had been Abby's favorite season. When the weather was warm and dry enough, they'd had picnics in the backyard, the bright air enriched by the new plants breaking through the soil, releasing an earthy perfume.

But spring had also been known to depress Abby. During these spells of depression, she might pass days without speaking to anyone.

"What's wrong with Mommy?" Serena would ask.

"She's just tired."

"She looks mad all the time." Richard never knew exactly what to say about that, but he hated the stressed look in his daughter's face.

"Oh, no, honey." Richard had picked her up and carried her out of the house. He felt bad for Abby, but annoyed by how her moods were affecting their daughter. Tiptoeing around so as not to disturb her intense silence became old after awhile. Sometimes he couldn't say he knew her anymore.

Even during these depressive silent periods they made love, but she often displayed a bizarrely mechanical affect. "I love you," he said when he climbed into bed, kissing the back of her neck. Abby rolled over and opened her arms. But her face was almost expressionless, her eyes fixed on the ceiling. At those times he knew he should just leave the bed, but he craved the closeness. And so he felt himself fall into this lifeless woman's arms, and made love to the stranger wearing his wife's face.

One of the waste piles exploded into a shower of grit. It got in his hair, all over his face. He coughed, tried to spit the decayed matter out. When his vision cleared he could see something all bone and black skin racing from pile to pile, destroying his work, rocketing up one of the skeletal trees on the edge of the clearing. There it froze, indistinguishable from the tree limbs.

In the destroyed piles were several oddly-shaped skeletons of animals he did not recognize, many of the bones heavily scored, gnawed, or hacked.

"They've been showing up the last ten years or so," Jacob said behind him. "I've never had one slow down enough to see what they really look like. But this seems to be the only time they come around, just for a meal or two. Then they're gone until next year."

Jacob helped him carry the re-raked piles out to the ancient brick incinerator in large wicker baskets. 'Hotel Deadfall' was hand-painted in ornate script on the side of each. They stood and watched as the flames licked up over the chimney, in reds, violets, rich velvety blacks, shards of green. Jacob said they had to wait until the fire was completely out before leaving, for the safety of the hotel and its grounds.

A half-hour into their silent vigil, Jacob said, "By the way, we have a group coming in this week. I apologize – I should have told you earlier."

"A group? Like a convention?" It was hard to imagine – a convention held at the Deadfall. "How many?"

"I believe it was a hundred, two hundred, something like that – I have the rooms checked off in the ledger. No, no conventions here. The Senior Reverend Johnson and his family arrive tomorrow, which includes his father who is also his predecessor, now Senior Reverend Emeritus Johnson."

"Reverend? You mean this is a religious group?"

Jacob looked uncomfortable. "Well. Yes, they come every year at this time, but last year they missed. Some sort of accident, I was told. The day after the Senior Reverend and his family arrive, we will be seeing subordinate reverends, acolytes, members of the council, followers, and the women's union. The vast bulk of the congregation, however, should straggle in on Thursday."

"Acolytes? Followers? They sound, um, *cultish*."

Jacob looked somewhat flustered. "I'm really no expert, but they seem, ostensibly at least, to have a more mainstream religious flavor. So I would answer *no*, but then I have found no understanding, or comfort, in religion for quite some time. They might all be called 'cults,' as far as I'm concerned, at one time or another. It is much like joining a club, I believe. You think that, as part of a collective, you are going to do some good, but then the club wishes you to change the way you wear your hair, or insists that you wear a different tie, and then they shame you when you do not conform, they humiliate you, and some of the members get, how do you say, out of hand, and then you feel that your physical life, or your spiritual life, is in danger. But it is important to be tolerant, don't you think, even when we don't understand? "

"So, explain this to me. Given the nature of the Deadfall's clientele, why would they choose to meet here?"

"Richard, are you thinking in terms of the E-word?"

"Evil? I don't know. We haven't really discussed evil before, have we? Certainly one encounters evil here at the hotel from time to time?"

"My own beliefs are simple, perhaps a bit too uncomplicated. I am sure of very little. I believe that to treat another of our species as if they were not a legitimate human being, that is evil. To take lives with malice, or because of some self-involved need or perversion, is an evil act. Hitler and Stalin were evil men. Jack the Ripper, whoever he might have been, was evil. But the subtleties of modern ethics are beyond me – I feel I understand less and less."

The flames had died down and now a thick, gray smoke slipped smoothly from the chimney. Richard wondered what the EPA might have to say about what they were doing, but suspected their inspections in these parts were rare. He leaned lazily on his rake, feeling vaguely disgusted. "So why here? You didn't answer my question."

"Perhaps they see it as some sort of challenge. Firemen seek fires, do they not? I do not honestly know. They began coming here during my predecessor's time, when Johnson Senior was in charge of their group. There was an arrangement. The Deadfall honors such arrangements. When you are fully in charge, you will find that you, also, will honor such arrangements; you will not be able to help yourself." Richard had an urge to object, but did not. He didn't understand, but he knew Jacob was telling the truth. "I hope this does not cause too much conflict with your own beliefs."

"No. No," Richard said. "It doesn't matter, I suppose. The fact is, I respect people who can believe in something. And I'm not sure how far I'd really trust a person without *any* beliefs. But an entire *group* of people with the *same* belief? Whether it be religious, nationalist, political, whatever. That has always frightened me."

"Then gird yourself, if I may say so. I suspect that, starting tomorrow, we will both be tested."

THE NEXT DAY the Reverend Johnson *et al.* arrived in a huge, vintage black Lincoln Continental Town car. Richard watched from a front window as it slipped quietly through the ornate front gate, filigreed ironwork rearing up on either side of the broad fenders as if reluctant to let the vehicle pass. The

Lincoln drifted serenely up the drive, engine humming as if it had rolled off the assembly line yesterday. It looked so new, in fact, Richard found it a bit startling. No dents, no flaws, no road dust, better than new. *God's car doesn't get dirty,* he thought, then felt a little ashamed of himself.

The windshield and side windows were an opaque, smoky gray, but a small girl – dark-haired, beautiful, perhaps a year or two younger than Serena – had rolled down the rear driver-side window and thrust her head out, gazing solemnly at the passing ground, then the Deadfall grove, which seemed particularly stark today against the new green growth around it. When she looked at the hotel itself, she smiled.

The car stopped in front of the porch. Richard felt compelled to make the extra effort of going out to meet them. Anyway, they might need help with the luggage. Enid's son – whose name, he'd finally discovered, was Frederick – was unavailable, having been ill for over a month. Jacob said it "might be serious."

Richard waved to the little girl, who started to wave back, but then she looked down at the drive, and Richard could see that a small mat of the dead vegetation had somehow landed on the pavement. It was burnt around the edges – he figured the wind had picked it up out of the incinerator and dropped it there. But something moved on it, and the girl ducked her head back inside and rolled up the window. Richard watched as the mat grew legs and walked off into the bushes. He hoped the little girl hadn't seen that.

There were sounds of a commotion from inside the car. The driver's door opened and a man about Richard's age with longish blond hair and movie-star good looks climbed out. Seeing Richard, his face opened into a magazine-ad smile, and he made an economical gesture which might possibly have been a wave. "You're the new manager?" he asked.

"I am."

"I'll just be a moment. It's my little girl, she doesn't want to step out of the car just yet." He mimed exaggerated helplessness with hands and shoulders. "She said she saw something."

"We have," Richard began, not really knowing what he could say, "large... *bugs*... this time of year."

"Of course. It's a time of renewal for so many of the Lord's creatures. It's a new opportunity for *joy*, wouldn't you say?"

"Well, that's certainly a positive way to look at it."

"Gotta stay positive," the reverend said, going around to the rear driver's side door. "We'll be a minute. She's always been... high strung." He opened the door and slid inside. A few minutes later he climbed out again, leading his daughter by the hand, her shoulders slumped, face down. "Everything's fine now." He held out his hand. "The Reverend Tim Johnson. Pleased to meet you."

Richard took the hand. It was large, and very warm, and dry and steady. Richard wondered if that meant the man had steady nerves, or none at all. It was obviously too soon to tell.

"Reverend."

"Call me Tim."

"Tim." *Then why did you introduce yourself as Reverend?* he thought, again embarrassed by his small-mindedness.

"And this is Annabelle. Hold out your hand, Annabelle."

She held up a limp, delicate hand without moving her gaze from the ground. Richard took it carefully with only a few fingers and gave it a soft squeeze. "Pleased to meet you, Annabelle. I have a daughter about your age. Her name is Serena. You'll probably see her while you're here." No response. Richard straightened. "Can I help you with your bags?"

"Very kind of you, but we really prefer handling our own. We just have some overnights. The rest of our luggage is coming with my staff, early tomorrow morning sometime. I always like to come a little early, get the family settled, before all the commotion starts. I get so busy with the congregation; there's never enough time when you're doing the Lord's work! So I prize this family time."

As he spoke, a white-haired gentleman was climbing out of the passenger side front seat. From the resemblance, Richard assumed this must be the Reverend Johnson Senior. The older man nodded in Richard's direction. The muscles surrounding the man's mouth toyed with a smile, then gave up as if out of practice. "Tim," he said hoarsely, "We better get her inside."

Richard assumed he meant the little girl, but the reverend Tim kissed his daughter on the top of her head, then joined his father at the rear passenger side door. With the sun's lower angle, Richard could vaguely distinguish the still outline of a head in the back of the car. The Reverend Johnson's posture withered slightly as he pulled open the door. "Dear?"

A nice man, Richard thought, *but something vaguely irritating about him.*

The two men leaned over, the elder Johnson with an audible grunt. When they straightened, a dark-haired woman in a bright red dress rose between them, like a miraculously blooming flower. Her back was to Richard, her head somewhat wobbly on the pale stalk of neck. There was something about the dress. Richard wasn't sure what, something vaguely anachronistic in the cut of the shoulders, the cuffed sleeves. It didn't quite fit her – it was too tight on the shoulders and upper arms. He wasn't sure what gave him the idea, but he wondered if maybe she hadn't dressed herself.

The Reverend Tim tapped her on the left shoulder, and his father gave her a little push on the right. She leaned quickly toward Richard, and for a moment he thought she was falling, until the head righted itself. She smiled then, but it was reminiscent of the smiles of small babies – having more to do with some physical process, than with sincere feeling.

This was obviously the little girl's mother. She had the same dark, beautiful looks. The Reverend Tim stepped slightly to the side, his hands open and ready by her arm, accompanying his wife as she attempted to proceed to the porch unaided.

She had a pleasant face, and she moved slowly up the steps, as if onto a stage. The Reverend Tim and his father seemed strangely quiet, reverential. The little girl stood perfectly still, away from the steps, watching her mother expressionlessly. Richard saw the window curtain near the door flutter slightly, then Serena's face behind the glass.

There was a slight hesitation in everything the woman did. Even tilting her head, saying "Hello, I'm Mrs. Johnson," had an off-rhythm quality, as if she didn't have quite enough air to move the words. Accepting her hand, Richard detected an unevenness in her grip. Her head swung slowly toward her daughter. "An-na-belle," she said, almost as if surprised. Annabelle said nothing, motionless.

"Go with your mother inside, honey," the Reverend Tim said. "Help your mother."

Annabelle walked over reluctantly and went inside with her mother, ignoring the woman's stiffly offered hand. Watching them leave, Richard was left with a great sense of disorder about the woman. He could see the crooked seams, the way the stockings bagged loosely below her knees, like a slough of skin. But no, not exactly as if she didn't care, but as if she hadn't noticed. He thought about the woman's face, there had been a slight blurriness to it, as if viewing her features through gel – the cheeks looking sanded, a bit too smooth, a layer of pastels painted on, eye shadow and lipstick ever-so-slightly out of their expected borders, as if they'd been applied without benefit of mirror.

"My wife," the Reverend Tim began – Richard was instantly embarrassed; the man had caught him staring – "is not herself."

"I believe there's a doctor, one of the towns," Richard stopped, unsure if Jacob had actually told him this, or if he was just making it up, like filling in the details of a story only half heard.

"No need." Reverend Tim pulled several small bags out of the trunk. His father took them without comment and started, overburdened, toward the steps. Richard moved to help, but the old man shook his head as if embarrassed, hurried on. "She's stable. There was an accident a while back. Her fault, I'm afraid." He looked at Richard and shrugged. "She hasn't been the same."

Then the Reverend Tim slammed the trunk lid with an angry motion – Richard was sure – despite his calm face. The lid popped back up, and he tried repeatedly to close the trunk, slamming it harder each time, but still with that implacable expression. Each time it popped open again. Finally he gave up and leaned back against the rear bumper, staring off toward the grove.

"I'll have Jacob, our caretaker, take a look," Richard said, feeling absurd at this pretense of being somehow in charge. "He's very competent with this sort of thing."

"My wife is very fond of this car," the Reverend Tim replied. Then he stood up, looking renewed. "If you don't mind. I must attend to my family." And suddenly he was energetically striding for the front door of the Deadfall, as if in flight. Richard struggled to keep up.

"WELL, THIS MAY be the problem." Jacob pointed the flashlight into a dark space where several beams criss-crossed.

The supporting architecture down in this level made no sense to Richard. He was used to parallel beams, parallel floor joists, posts supporting the beams and the bearing walls on top of them. Very little here appeared to be parallel, or perpendicular for that matter. Beams and joists were arranged in patterns like Pick-Up Sticks, laid one atop the other at irregular angles.

The flashlight beam wavered, finding its way through the barriers, finally revealing what appeared to be a tattered wig dyed a multitude of colors. Richard allowed his eyes to adjust before making any conclusions. Finally he said, "It's a big tangle of electrical cable. God, don't tell me those are *splices?*" Dizzy, he grabbed a beam, tried to hide just how scared he was.

"I'm afraid so. There may be some sort of metal box at the center of it, just for form's sake, but that may be no more than a tomato soup can with holes punched through it."

"You're kidding."

"There is a peaches can, label still on it, buried in the wall behind a bathroom mirror on the second floor. It's the junction box for the wiring to about twelve rooms."

"So what do we do?"

"We do nothing. Some people find flickering lights romantic. The next time we have a couple of that persuasion in the Deadfall, we'll know what room to put them in."

"How can that be safe?"

"If we tamper with the nerves, then who knows what might happen to the body? Best to leave them alone. We are hardly trained physicians, here. From time to time, I have brought professional electricians in to examine the premises. They shake their heads. They refuse to touch a single wire. A few say nothing – they simply walk out to their trucks and leave."

"So we don't touch, either."

"Not unless there is sparking, exposed copper. That has been my criterion. So far it has been sufficient. Imagine this hotel, its integrity compromised, its senses altered. All due to our meddling. Imagine it as Mrs. Johnson."

"Whoa. Where did that come from?"

"None of my affair, really. I should have kept my peace. I was being indiscreet." Jacob studied the wiring.

"Too late now. What are you seeing?"

"It would be beneath my notice, if not for the little girl. People may do as they like – certainly this hotel is some sort of monument to that sentiment, and I presume this to be a family issue and not indicative of the religion as a whole – but children, well, certainly, you know yourself. Children require care."

"Well, the woman is sick, obviously. But I don't understand. Are you saying she shouldn't be around her own child? Because if you are, that her mother –"

"– is dead, Richard. I am convinced her mother is dead."

"Then who is this woman pretending to be her mother?" He stopped. "Oh."

THE 'GATHERING,' AS they referred to themselves, began arriving early the next morning, about an hour before dawn, and continued to arrive over the next thirty hours or so, Jacob and Richard splitting shifts in order to check them in at all hours of the night. Couples and families, extended groups, lone stragglers, arriving in trucks, cars, buses, bikes and motorbikes, and a single white horse with an ornate red cross painted onto one flank. Richard's worry about the steed was aggravated by the gallon-hatted rider with the badge that said 'Lassoed by God,' which turned out to be his only words. But Jacob said there wasn't any problem, and he led the animal away.

During the final hours of the influx, Richard made it out from behind the registration desk only for occasional bathroom breaks. Now and then, he saw Serena walking around with Annabelle, showing her the sights.

Other than the occasional eccentrics, like the cowboy and an extremely tall, rather homely woman wearing a man's suit much too small for her, the vast majority of the Gathering appeared to be perfectly normal, everyday types. They might have been plucked wholesale from your average mall, or from any neighborhood (pre-Deadfall, of course) Richard had ever lived in. Now and then he'd overhear one call another, "Most Reverend," or "Sister," or once, "Acolyte John," referring to a man who looked no more threatening than a grocery clerk (a perception which, he quickly realized, was perfectly useless, for wasn't a grocery clerk, too, capable of terror?). But they might as well have been Shriners, Elks, or Scouts – fanciful labels applied to ordinary people. He was embarrassed by his prejudice, but there it was: he took comfort in the fact that the aberrations who resided in the Deadfall *looked* the part.

Richard soon discovered the significance of the group's name. Late in the afternoon of that day, just before sunset, all the members of the group went outside, spread across the lawn, sat down among the trees, wandered onto the tennis courts. They looked like any large company picnic, really, loosely organized into parallel tracks of activity, grouped for conversation, for sports, for eating. And yet, viewed from the hotel's front entrance, there appeared to be more cohesiveness than that, as if they were a large organism spreading its limbs, stretching here and contracting there, making itself comfortable. Richard saw Annabelle leading Serena through this group, no doubt reciprocating Serena's tour through the hotel, holding hands the way little girls will, with that talent for making 'best friends forever' at a moment's notice.

He felt he should just let the girls be, tried to make himself feel at ease with it, thinking surely there was nothing wrong with these people, with Serena being out, unchaperoned, among these people, that sometimes you had to let your silly prejudices go for the health of your children. But at root he didn't feel okay with it, and couldn't relax with it. He walked down the lawn and into the congregation, whose members nodded, smiled and waved, sang out greetings or muttered polite hellos, the mix like any other crowd, although perhaps a crowd somewhat friendlier than most.

He chose not to exactly follow the girls, but tried to remain in their vicinity at least, listening to the way the people talked to each other, attempting to interpret what they said, trying to find some salve for his anxieties. The Gathering actually consisted of small bunches of people, conversational groups.

He thought of the couple of cocktail parties he'd been to during his lifetime, and thought them remarkably similar. There wasn't the booze, but there was the air of drunkenness. The subject matter of their conversations, of course, was something different entirely.

"It's about survival, really." This from a bearded man smoking a pipe, a professor type. "No one wants to die."

"There's death of the body, and then there's death of the spirit." A pale woman in a large red hat, looking guarded, and angry.

"Of course. It is the interplay, the balance that is so difficult to achieve."

And a few feet away, a young man of damaged complexion whose tone managed somehow to be both friendly *and* aggressive. "The early Christians, they were guerillas. The real reason Judas betrayed Jesus was because Jesus wasn't being militant enough. But Judas underestimated the Christ. 'Think not that I am come to send peace on earth, I come not to send peace but a sword.' That's from Matthew. 'He that hath no sword, let him sell his garments and buy one.' That's from Luke. He was crucified with other zealots and rebels."

And walking down the hill, pushing between the tight masses, apologizing, but keeping himself moving forward. "Devils and demons, demons and devils. But only one God, mind you."

And down around the tennis courts, separated by the nets. "The need to belong, the need to be loved, becomes the will to power. The faithful give their money, their possessions, but on the other end, they do well financially. I see it happen all the time. Have you read the literature?"

And under the trees, the couples holding hands. "You think about what the group can do for you, and what you owe to the group. What does it mean not to belong? I say it means everything. Who would want to remain in that position?"

And lying on the grass, holding hands, eyes closed, weeping. "One decision and it all becomes clear. The rest will be taken care of for you."

Much of the group was euphoric, some of them bordering on silly. There were small groups participating in 'exercises in laughter,' where they laughed together, at nothing, until one or two had to sit down on the ground for lack of breath. But here and there, Richard picked out some who appeared confused, staring at their surroundings as if they weren't quite sure where they were. They appeared lost, and seriously depressed.

He had made an honest effort not to think much about Mrs. Johnson, but he had been fooling himself, of course – meditations on the implications of what Jacob had concluded about her filled in any unoccupied gaps in his thoughts. Now and then he did see her in the crowd, tottering about, followed around by some earnest-looking young man in a dark suit and narrow tie Richard assumed must have been assigned to her. She appeared lost, stunned, and at times just plain goofy. *Nothing scary here*, he concluded. *Just sad*.

He didn't really know what to think about what had happened to her, not that he had the faintest idea what, in fact, had occurred here, beyond Jacob's vague allusions. But when he thought about his own wife, and the possibility of keeping her on the planet, then it didn't matter what warnings a hundred cheesy movies and a few hundred pulp novels made – he would have done everything humanly, and inhumanly, possible.

At one point there was an announcement for 'Just Desserts,' which was met with laughter and cheering. Young women wearing rainbow-patterned baseball caps came out into the crowd dragging large trash bags full of candies and packaged pastries, which they distributed freely. He saw Serena and Annabelle sitting with a group of children greedily tearing into the packages and devouring the contents, pointing at the sticky messes on each other's faces, giggling uncontrollably. *She's in for a sick night*, he thought. *Headache in the morning.* But he felt no compulsion to stop her. It was good just seeing her acting like any other kid.

He saw Jacob out beyond the edge of the crowd, struggling to put up chairs under the trees among a collection of large antique birdbaths. Not that Richard had ever seen a bird using one of them. Jacob had told him, simply, "Something else likes to use those baths. I've seen it once or twice, from a distance. But no sign of a bird anywhere near them, ever."

Richard walked over, trying not to step on anyone; and when he did, apologizing profusely, the injured party just shook her hand in exaggerated fashion, laughing around her candy bar. A few yards away, he spied Mrs. Johnson sitting on the ground beside her worried-looking keeper: her dress pulled up high on her thighs, her face smeared with thick, mud-like chocolate. She grinned spastically while maneuvering her tongue with impressive skill.

"Can I help with that?" he asked Jacob.

Jacob looked up, smiled, but with a harried edge. "Oh, please. Thank you. Some of the older members sit down at sunset for special prayer, it seems. The Reverend forgot to tell me until a half hour ago."

After a few minutes of quiet labor unloading folding chairs from a cart Jacob had dragged out of one of the storage buildings, trying to find stable spots for them on the uneven ground, Jacob asked, "So what do you think?"

"About?"

"About our new guests? I know you had some reservations, and I believe, some discomfort with religion in general, am I correct?"

"Well, yes. A prejudice of mine, I'm sure, so I'm trying to be more open-minded, which I should be, especially with your – our – role here."

"But?"

Richard gripped the back of a chair and leaned forward, looking at Jacob. "I've just never quite gotten it. Why are religious people always talking about gods and devils? Why can't they stick with the real world? It's hard enough just keeping track of the day-to-day."

Jacob paused in his chore and looked at him. "If it were only that simple. I doubt that I imagine the same God as these people, or the same devils. But I do dream of gods, and veritable armies of devils. The world is full of horror. Our imaginations struggle to keep up. It would be a poor life without imagining. I'm not sure we can have any salvation, in fact, without imagining."

"Imagining didn't stop the Holocaust, Hiroshima, the deaths of hundreds of thousands, or my own wife's death. That's the *real* world, Jacob."

Jacob stared at him long enough to make him uncomfortable. Finally he spoke. "Please do not lecture me on issues of world history, Richard. I have more than a history aficionado's knowledge of the deaths of hundreds of thousands."

"I'm sorry, I didn't mean –"

Jacob waved his hand in agitated dismissal. "No, I apologize. Perhaps I myself am affected by these" – he gestured vaguely toward the crowd – "intense encounters with religion. I *believe*, surely, in the real world. But some factual events achieve status beyond the real. They are as real as the severing of a limb, yet become as mythical, as symbolic, as Saturn devouring his children. And both aspects impact us significantly. Our lives are voyages through darkness. Imagining a divine meaning for it all permits us to love. This duality is essential to our nature. How else do we face non-existence?"

Richard quietly continued putting out chairs. Finally he replied, "I think religion gives me a headache."

Jacob guffawed. "Perhaps it was simply my pomposity."

"No, of course not, I –"

"You were providing me with an honest reaction, which I appreciated. This is a conversation I would like to continue later. For now, could you meet me upstairs in ten minutes? They will be having dinner soon – they have brought their own cooks, of course. There are a few things I would like to get done before they return to their rooms."

"WE WILL NEED to move this furniture somewhere," Jacob said as they rounded the corner. "It might cause a serious problem if someone sets off a, well – sorry – if there were a fire."

"No problem." Richard surveyed the hallway, not quite understanding what he was seeing. Furniture had been dragged out of the rooms and stacked against the walls: ornately-columned four-poster beds with fanciful brocade canopies, the dark silhouettes of high-backed Queen Anne chairs like birds hunkering down for a long rest, assorted Victorian settees and stools appearing too delicate for actual use, a variety of highboys and lowboys with dark, atmospheric stains, arranged with their backs to a constricted meander of exposed Persian carpet which was all that was left to allow passage through the corridor. "Are they cleaning, fumigating?"

"*Exorcising* is perhaps the better word. Although I suspect cleansing and pest destruction are some small part of the process. Their religion is suspicious of other people's possessions. They never purchase items at yard sales, or thrift stores, for example, for fear a devil worshipper might once have owned them."

Richard helped Jacob move a number of pieces into a vacant room. Although he found himself annoyed by the group's general wariness, he thought that, at least in terms of their beliefs, refusing to use the furniture probably made sense. "So what would these people do," he asked, "if they ran into one of our more... different residents?"

"Try to kill it, him or her, I suppose. The same thing you or I might do, perhaps, if we woke up with a snake in the bed. Of course we can't let that happen. Happily, those who come here to stay are usually quite skilled at avoidance."

"Life is a difficult proposition. We have no business making it more difficult for each other. At least, that's what *I* believe."

"Certainly. What other point is there, don't you agree? Most tend to view their time spent here in the hotel as a kind of vacation, a retreat, you might say, from the daily assault of contemporary life. The Deadfall is a *dark* place, of course, one of a hundred or so locations about the globe where darkness, in fact, concentrates, where it is distilled into, say, a few shambling forms. But the darkness here is of an ancient variety, *familiar* somehow, a part of the very blood feeding our tissue. It is the darkness human beings have always faced, and survived. This contemporary variety, so skillfully exploited by the modern media, is no different in kind, certainly, but its implications seem rather more anxiety-producing, I would think. For it would seem that the horrors of the modern world threaten the whole human enterprise. It's a point of commonality for most of us, I like to think."

Many of the pieces were incredibly heavy, and by the time they'd finished moving all the furniture out of the hall, both men were exhausted. They slumped together onto a long Victorian settee, eyes half-closed and sleepy. "So these are probably nice people," Richard offered. "For the most part."

"Certainly. For the most part. But there are always a few –"

"Bad apples. I know. But most of them are just ordinary people, aren't they? Like most of us, they're just looking for something."

"Appealing, isn't it? One decision and all the rest is taken care of for you. You become their possession, but it is a comfortable life. All for the simple price of belief."

"You've never really told me what *you* believe, Jacob. You don't believe much; of what they believe, I mean. Am I correct?"

"Belief is a wonderful thing and a terrible thing. And a frightening thing – because you cannot see into another person's head and know with any assurance what he or she truly believes.

"To be perfectly honest, I have been a crusty old nonbeliever who still had, hypocritically, certainly, some hopes of Heaven. A place of peace and solace, somewhere I might lay my burden down, as the old hymns suggest. But what I have seen among the world's great religions has spoiled that illusion for me. They have convinced me that I will not be seeing any of my favorite people there, but simply more of those" – he gestured – "lifeless, judgmental types. Now I will just have to say, 'No, thank you,' if the invitation ever comes."

"Love the individual. Fear the group," Richard said lazily, raising his fist in a tired, mocking imitation of a defiant gesture.

Jacob chuckled. "Indeed. Fear the group." And raised his own fist to match.

THE FIRST SESSION of the sermons was scheduled for mid-morning of the following day. Richard had had no intentions of attending, but Serena had wanted to go and sit with Annabelle, and he still didn't feel comfortable with her spending large amounts of time with the Gathering where he couldn't see her. Jacob suggested he might want to be available in any case, for 'emergencies.'

The hotel wasn't providing anything for these sermons, except a location, the shore of the Deadfall Lake, in a natural amphitheater down the hill below the cliffs behind the hotel. The Gathering had their own portable sound system they could carry down, powered by two car batteries. Having spent very little time by the lake, Richard was curious about what it would be like to sit there, to take it all in, even though he expected it to be an uncomfortable experience with all the sermonizing.

The morning was unseasonably warm, burning off the typical resident fog in the hour after dawn. Around ten o'clock the entire membership of the Gathering left the hotel and walked around back, beginning a slow descent that wound through low scrub trees and ugly outcroppings of a mottled, white and gray stone. Richard trailed the group, Serena and Annabelle walking a few yards ahead of him, holding hands.

The congregation was focused, murmuring some sort of song, so softly he couldn't make out the words. Their eyes were locked on the trail, the yellowed seam it made in the hillside as it led them down, and on the distant lake below, huge and gray, depthless, looking more like a rainy sky than a body of water, as if the universe had flipped, and they were in ascension.

He was distracted. He kept looking back over his shoulder at the shabby backside of the hotel – the weathered boards, the beaten paint – embarrassed, relieved they didn't appear to notice, and wondering what they would think of the place when they came back up the hill. Once he was comfortably in charge, he would have to make an upgrade a priority.

On either side of the trail, a border of thick brush some six or seven feet high stitched the hill. Now and then, inside or behind it, he heard and caught glimpses of fellow travelers: eyes too large, legs too many, fingers too crooked. Residents, he was sure, curious about the proceedings. He wondered if any of the congregation had noticed, if there would be a panic, if they would hold him personally responsible.

The trail spilled out at the bottom, onto a wide expanse of rocky beach, stones growing in number as they walked toward the amphitheater, where random rock became a deliberate placement of tiers and seats and rows, with a capacity in the hundreds. On the lakeside, a stage of a sort consisting of interlocking slabs rose several feet above the bottom tier. Jacob had told him plays had been mounted here in the old days; Shakespeare mostly, *The Tempest* an apparent favorite.

Richard wondered about the labor involved, and who the actors might have been, who the attentive audience.

The lake stretched behind the stage in all directions, filling the eyes and filling the mind. He found himself looking away, agitated by the sense that the gray water might suddenly rise and consume them.

A group of dark-suited aides had already put up a white canopy over a speaker's stand, with a row of chairs on either side. Mrs. Johnson was led to the front row, seated on the left side with two identically-suited young men. Her handler from the day before wasn't among them. Annabelle led Serena also to the front row, but chose to sit on the far right, away from her mother. The remainder of the Gathering quickly sat themselves, rushing about with deliberation, filling the spaces just so, as if in a drill. Although Richard could discern no real difference in clothing among the group – no sense of 'uniform' – a kind of sorting was taking place, he was sure of it. People somehow resembled the ones they chose to sit next to, whether by philosophy or emotional state or attitude he could not tell.

The program consisted of a series of sermons, each delivered by a different speaker. After a couple of rabble-rousing performances by younger talents that had the crowd on their feet, it settled into a series of boring treatises on fine points of dogma, delivered by elderly academic types. The crowd was quietly attentive, postures frozen, eyes glazed.

When the Reverend Tim Johnson came to the podium, however, everything changed.

"We are the Gathering," he began. The crowd sat up, leaned forward. Here and there, people put their hands up to their faces. Some of them were already weeping. "We are the Gathering, but we are nothing without the Vessel. The Vessel is where we have gathered ourselves, as a drink for the Lord. We will not contaminate that drink with the voices and the ideas from those on the outside. Our vessel is also a ship, which will take us on a marvelous voyage into God's kingdom. Like the pilgrims of old, we simply seek peace and comfort in the embrace of our Lord. Some place away from the plagues of AIDS and venereal disease, the dangerous desires of others, the sexual madness of society."

Scattered "Amens" floated up from the crowd, not like cheers or exclamations, but more languorous, soft and soulful.

The crowd was intent. They sat motionless, locked in place. Richard imagined if he touched one on the shoulder they'd fall over. The notable exception was the small cadre of young men in dark business suits, walking up and down the aisles, smiling, nodding, watching, as the reverend gently laid it all out: the Gathering, the Vessel.

"Our lives are incomplete, disorganized. But now we may pour ourselves into a vessel that will give us form. Then God will take care of us. We will be His angels. And who would not desire such a thing? Who would not care to be an angel?"

And the crowd smiled. And the crowd laughed. But no grins, and no belly laughs. Gentle smiles, soft chuckles, a chorus of good-humored sighs. And the young men in the aisles provided the cues and guided the rest.

"We dedicate ourselves to His service, and in return He gives us the answers we seek. It is our solace for having endured our lives. Not that we should deny the pain and fear of the world. Instead we should take *showers* in our pain, we should *submerge* ourselves in fear, so that fear and that pain becomes a *catalyst* for our transcendence."

Now there were shouts from the crowd which sounded much like anger, but were something different: excitement, perhaps, or a spontaneous expression of the fear the reverend had been talking about.

"When the soul of the Lord animates you, all your worries are taken care of. When the soul of the Lord animates you, all confusion and ambivalence will be resolved."

Scattered through the crowd, many people were weeping. The ones sitting next to them seemed to take no notice, but the young men brought them tissues, brought them pats and whispers.

"Sometimes Heaven is so close, it feels like if you took your hand and rubbed at the air Heaven would appear."

One of the young men raised his hand and said, "Yes!" A cascade of answering *yeses* rose from all parts of the amphitheater.

"This is a world of trouble and hurt. Once you enter the Vessel your trouble is eased, your hurt is salved, but even among the Gathering, trouble and hurt do not disappear, because we are living human beings, and trouble and hurt just go naturally with being human."

"Amen, brother," from another of the cadre of suits. *Amens* rose and fell, punctuated by *brother*, punctuated by *yes*.

"But if you follow the ways of the Gathering, and you allow the Lord to enter you, when you die you become as an angel, and the world of the angels is a finer world than this one, a world transformed and made perfect. You know you belong to that other world, otherwise you would not have been so confused all your life."

And all the time the Reverend Tim spoke, the young men in their crisp dark suits strolled through the crowd, jostling those who had fallen asleep, shaking hands and slapping backs, saying "How are you?" Stroking, patting, massaging the congregation, with smiles spreading broadly across their faces.

"And to follow the ways of the Gathering, I do not mean simply to say the words, but you must *mean* the words. You must commit to the Gathering your undivided attention, all your goods and all your time, and not distract yourself with the words and doings of the unbeliever, whether they be outside the family or inside the family. For those who enter the Vessel are your family now, and all others will damage that family if you are not vigilant, and will spoil your chances to enter into that eternal and perfect kingdom of God."

Isolated in their own section was a handful of people earmarked as 'visitors.' Richard had become aware of them the day before – they'd been brought in, recruited by members of the congregation, treated with the kind of kindness one might show a poor relation, or someone who was seriously ill. Today, these were the ones Richard found most interesting to watch – many of them appeared obviously saddened to be so left out, faces yearning like children with no presents at Christmastime. For much of the sermon, the young men had ignored them, had spared them not even a glance, but now, toward the end of the Reverend's sermon, the cadre had started talking to them. "I am so sorry for you," he heard one young man say, and, "I wish you did not suffer so much."

"Believe me when I say there is a hidden meaning in human history and if we stay in the Vessel together, we will voyage to its interpretation. We will become angels, and fly away out of this world of torment and strife."

At the end of this sermon, the last of the morning, the young men served as ushers, guiding the congregation up the hill. Now the visitors were surrounded by people talking to them, embracing them, holding their hands.

Richard could hear a scurrying in the brush, but he was too busy looking for Serena to worry that one of the Deadfall's residents might inadvertently be seen. Finally he found her, being talked to by one of the young men, Annabelle nowhere in sight. Richard pulled her away, apologetic but deliberate. She did not protest, but clutched his hand.

Near the front of the line, a young woman screamed. People ran to her side. "She saw the Devil!" someone cried. Someone else demanded a search through the brush for demons.

The well-suited young men, with the assistance of some of the speakers from the day's sermons, maneuvered the crowd around with impressive efficiency. The woman who had screamed was comforted, then isolated, taken up the hillside separately.

When they reached the top of the hill, Richard veered off to a back entrance by the kitchens, Serena in tow.

"Mommy, no!"

The commotion came from the vicinity of a small cluster of Mulberry bushes near the back entrance. "Wait here," he cautioned Serena, leaving her by the steps while he trotted into the shaded area.

One of the dark-suited young men lay on the ground. Mrs. Johnson crouched over him, her hands around his throat. Annabelle stood by the wall of the hotel, her face a pale mask.

Richard ran over and put his hands on the woman's shoulders, pulled. She rolled her head back, her eyes unfocused, jaws slack. Her shoulders were like stone. His gaze followed her arms down to the young man's terrified face, where her fingers were sunk deep into his throat. Richard felt panicky – obviously he wasn't going to be able to stop her.

A mass of dark forms rushed around him. Hands pushed him aside. "Sir! Sir, we'll handle this!" The young men swarmed over Mrs. Johnson, slipping a kind of leather harness over her head, wedged her mouth open, tossing something down her throat. Foam dribbled out over her chin. Richard pulled the sobbing Annabelle out of there.

RICHARD FOUND JACOB in the little room behind the registration counter, sitting at an old school desk, paying bills. "I need a better answer about why the Gathering is here."

Jacob looked up, a hint of amusement on his face. "Very well. I do not believe I know anything more than I've already told you, however. What sort of questions do you have?"

"Well, in the first place, how much does the congregation know about our clientele? I assume the Reverend Tim, or his father, know something about what happens here, am I correct? I mean, we certainly don't advertise, and no one stumbles on the hotel accidentally."

"As I believe I said before, the Gathering first started coming here in the early 'sixties, during my predecessor's time. During my tenure, arrangements usually were made through the Reverend Senior Emeritus. What arrangements there were; normally he just called to say when they were coming. One must presume he knew of our particular… mission. There has always been a kind of unspoken understanding among all parties that, at least while their group is here, 'discretion' is the word of the day."

"So the members of the congregation, they probably haven't a clue?"

"We do not provide a 'Guide to Flora and Fauna of the Deadfall,' so I would say no, not at all."

"Then the Reverends Senior or whatever must not mind if their followers become frightened of devils, or whatever?"

"Oh! Yes, I heard about that. It must have been Clarence, don't you think? In 302? I always thought he looked a bit like Satan. And he does get lonely – I imagine he just wanted to be near people.

"But to answer your question – I think it is only logical to conclude that they do not care if their members are frightened. In fact, they must find some advantage in it."

"Advantage?"

"Why else would they be here? If you think about it, they want to impress upon their flock that Evil is real, that the dangers to their spirits are real. The Reverends are holding out this stick with a big carrot at the end of it. It would be difficult to convince your flock to crave salvation, I would think, if they were comfortable in their current existence, if they believed themselves to be safe.

"They depend on a good story to keep their members. You know how powerful a good story can be. You can give your very life over to a good story."

"I think I understand that, but how would they know about this hotel in the first place? What... *qualifies* the Johnsons to even be here?" Jacob started to answer when Richard interrupted. "I know, I know, it was before your time. But are there any records of when they first came, or why?"

"We rarely deal in 'whys,' Richard, but we have ledgers going back to the hotel's beginnings."

Jacob moved the school desk and peeled away the stiff, rotting rug, exposing the lines of a trap door. Pulling up the hatch by its rope handle automatically switched on the lights in the room below. Jacob wordlessly started down the narrow ladder. After some hesitation, Richard followed.

A painting of the White Rabbit from Alice in Wonderland was mounted on the wall behind the ladder. As Richard descended, it filled his view. "Once upon a time someone named this hidden room the Rabbit Hole," Jacob said, in front of him.

Rough wood shelving covering most of the walls held the hotel ledgers as well as reference works on carpentry, landscaping, plumbing and electricity, bound periodicals relating to the hotel industry, bibles, volumes of philosophy. The one wall without shelving was stacked with paintings. Two were exposed: portraits of an incredibly short, squarish woman – Jacob's predecessor, if Richard wasn't mistaken – and of Jacob himself, a much younger version with a silly smile.

"We change the portrait in the hall after the new proprietor is on the job for an appropriate time. There's a blank space out there waiting for yours. I could not wait the usual interval, I am afraid, to get mine down. I swear I have never smiled like that – the painter was drunk, I believe." Jacob went through several volumes before he found it. "July 1, 1961:

Emmett Johnson & Son. Check-out is listed as August 23rd of the same year, so they spent some time with us," he said, rifling through the dusty pages. "She liked to make notes on the guests. A bad habit, I believe. It violates the spirit, if not the letter, of our commitment to our guests for discretion and privacy. The majority of her notes are useless, in any case – she liked to comment on what they ordered from the kitchens, for example, what they wore, the minutiae of habits observed, that sort of thing." He paused. "Interesting."

"What is it?"

"Here she puts 'Father – pedestrian, normal. Son – healer.'"

"I wasn't aware that was part of their religion."

"I do not believe it is."

Later Richard went into the library to find a book on miracle healing. He didn't know if they had such a book, but Jacob had told him he'd be surprised if they didn't.

The door to the Deadfall library was an inconspicuous gray wood panel with a plain brass knob, next to a coat closet off one of the side corridors on the main floor. The walls of the narrow gopher-tunnel of an entrance were lined with pictures – paintings and photographs – of various views of the grounds, particular guests (their faces fuzzy or hidden, shadowed or out of focus), and past managers. Some had engraved name plates fixed to the bottoms of the frames, but most did not.

Jacob was there – a skinny, much younger man caught in the act of doffing the traditional "Deadfall Hotel Recreation Department" baseball cap. Beside him was an oil depicting the vanished Mr. Grant, whose sleepless red eyes and neat beard made him resemble an ailing bird of prey. Then there was a watercolor rendering of a beautiful young woman with a lizard – a live lizard, apparently – perched near the top of her great, pyramid-shaped hat.

There was a dark, murky, black-and-white photograph labeled, simply, 'Mr. Carl.' Richard was at first unable to discern any human figure in the image, but over time realized that the soft smudge near the middle was a man's face, an incredibly long narrow oval of moon-white, hanging in the darkness of the photo's background, his eyes closed.

Except for isolated stretches of progressive or related imagery, the pictures appeared not to be in any particular order. There, among smudged charcoal sketches of obese twins, night photographs of dim gray widows, pictures of uniform background in which virtually no foreground figures could be seen, bright paintings of long-dead men with wide eyes and flushed faces, was a Polaroid snapshot of Richard and Serena entering the hotel for the first time – their slightly blurred faces still clearly apprehensive. The point of view seemed to be that of an upstairs window, but with the plane of ground somehow tilted.

Richard did not like the photograph, did not like the *idea* of it, but knew he would have a hard time explaining to Jacob exactly why he objected.

At last leaving the cramped tunnel, he was invariably awed by the floor-to-ceiling windows that filled the tall wall on the library's far side. At first you might doubt you were in a library at all. Where were the books? But approaching those windows and then turning around, you discovered that the small entrance was like a mouse hole in one corner of a great three-story gallery of finely polished wooden bookcases, the upper levels accessible via wrought metal spiral stairs and ornate catwalks. Several reading chairs had been positioned by smaller bookcases – 'reading islands' Serena liked to call them – on the shiny wooden floor.

Each level had its own separate lighting system, and at night, if you looked up, all you could see was layer after layer of vertically placed volumes leading up into increasingly deeper levels of darkness. During one evening spent in this room, Richard had experienced a terrible, debilitating vertigo, accompanied by the sensation that he himself was warping into the vertical, his body becoming taller and thinner, his head filling with air and floating toward the ceiling like a child's balloon on a jiggling string.

He loved books, and at first had begun each day with an excited visit to the library. But he'd soon discovered that the majority of the volumes here were most eccentric: pseudo-scientific treatises on all manner of strange creatures and belief systems, novels written in bizarre styles, biographies of non-existent people, geographies of non-existent countries. Jacob claimed there was a wealth of useful information here if you knew how to weed out the ridiculous. Obviously, Richard hadn't the expertise.

He found the Reverend Tim Johnson sitting in the Queen Anne, his lap filled by a giant, oil-stained leather volume. "I hope you don't mind." The reverend looked placid, somewhat sleepy. Richard suspected that whether he minded or not was completely irrelevant.

"Of course not. Guests have free access to the library and its holdings."

"Very generous. Very generous." He turned a couple of pages with a delicate wave of his fingers. "You have a wonderful collection of religious writings, by the way. And great old Bibles – the illustrations in this volume are unlike any I've ever seen before. You might think – well, you might even think the artist had encountered angels and devils firsthand."

"Much of great art is divinely inspired, wouldn't you say?"

"Yes; yes, I believe I would. For good or ill. Sometimes the artist allies with the wrong side, I would say. But all these religious tomes, you wouldn't be running some sort of secret seminary here, would you?"

Richard smiled. "I'm relatively new on the job, but I really don't think so. I suppose it's just that spiritual issues have been... an interest, among the proprietors. A wide range of beliefs, cosmologies represented. And many of the guests, well, I believe many of the guests *read*, of course." Richard actually knew very little about such things. He hoped he wouldn't be asked for a recommendation.

The reverend smiled. "Yes, well. Reading opens doors, as they say."

"Serena really enjoys your daughter's company, by the way. I think she may have found a friend."

The smile diminished slightly in the face of this revelation, but still held. "Your daughter appears to be... very well behaved. Annabelle sometimes can be a trial. 'Pre-teen,' I believe they call it. But your daughter is a good influence, I think. I compliment you."

"Oh well, I'm not sure it's my doing. She was born with that temperament, I think."

"Oh, please don't minimize your influence. Fathers so often set the tone, I think. Not that mothers are unimportant."

"Of course."

"I'd like to apologize," he said.

"Oh." Richard felt instantly uncomfortable.

"My wife's behavior. Sometimes it's a problem, and that influences Annabelle. She becomes upset."

"That's quite all right."

"Ever since the accident. We had that serious accident with the car and, well, we all knew any one of us could have died. An experience like that can have a serious effect on a child. A very serious effect."

"You were in the Lincoln? It appears to be in great shape now."

"I took it to some very good people. They knew exactly what to do. You'd hardly know there had been damage."

"Hardly. No one was injured?"

"Scrapes and bruises, and then my wife's injuries, which were more severe." He waved as if to dismiss the question, but his hands were ill-controlled and exaggerated the gesture. "My wife's recovery required some time. And during that time, of course, Annabelle was without a mother. It made for a very delicate situation, interrupting that bond between a mother and child, especially a daughter. I have prayed over this many times – we came so close to losing her."

"Your daughter?"

"No, no, my wife. She might have died. Luckily I knew what to do in the situation."

"You knew first aid."

"Well, yes. I had some knowledge, which I applied. Knowledge flows from the Lord. He showed me what to do, and I followed."

Slightly embarrassed, Richard nodded.

"But she's just fine now, my wife. A little shaken up, certainly. Her behavior has been... a result of the stress. Post-traumatic stress. A *terrible* accident. And of course that can encourage fantasies in a child, especially in a sensitive child."

"I see." He decided to leave it there.

"I saw you at the sermons. Did you find them edifying?"

Richard felt vertiginous with the sudden change of subject. "It was... interesting. I'm not a terribly religious person."

"None of us are, until we hear the right things. That is why this work is so important. We must share our witness. People must hear our words."

"They appeared to be listening."

"And why shouldn't they? I have given them something they can feel a part of. How many people feel like they *belong*? The members of the Gathering suffer as all people suffer, but the Gathering provides a solace for being human, the solace of finally having the answer, of being *right* for once, and the hope that there will be something good at the end of all this suffering. How could I deny them that? How could I deny them their escape from death?"

*   *   *

EACH MORNING, THERE was another round of sermons, followed by studies and discussions late into the afternoon. Dinners were generally held outside, and the Gathering retired relatively early, which allowed, Richard supposed, other residents to walk about, but as far as he could tell very few ever took the opportunity. He did run into Mrs. Johnson now and then, always accompanied by two or more assigned guards, as she wandered the halls silently, her eyes in constant movement, reacting to stimuli. He'd noticed red marks around her wrists, her lower arms, her neck, and he imagined that periodically they must strap her to her bed in order for her keepers to get some rest.

The Reverend Senior Emeritus was out and about a great deal, talking to members, laughing, leading small, spontaneous prayer groups. Richard rarely saw his son, who, he was told, was "in prayer." The few times Richard did see him, it was in hallway encounters with his daughter, who was usually tearful, the Reverend Tim breathless and irritated from having to chase her down. This evolved into a tableau Richard had seen many times, but had somehow avoided, personally, for the most part: father lecturing somewhat sullen daughter.

"Anna, you need to be with your mother now. At least try talking to her."

"It makes no *difference*, Daddy!" the child wailed.

Later he actually saw the three of them together, sitting in the old wooden lawn chairs under one of the great maples. Annabelle sat back with her arms folded, in contrast to Reverend Tim Johnson's eager, forward-leaning posture. Mrs. Johnson sat stiffly in the next chair, head tilted as if listening to the ground. Two of the young guardians stood on either side of her. The reverend appeared to be waving his hands about in false heartiness, patting Mrs. Johnson on the shoulder at intervals, gesturing to Annabelle as if to invite her into the conversation.

Serena continued to spend most of her time with Annabelle. It was only when Annabelle's mother was around, or when her father came to take her back to her mother (he appeared to have no other reason for seeking her out), that Annabelle returned to the pale, large-eyed child who had first arrived at the Deadfall.

Richard was a little less nervous about Serena's time with the Gathering, but he'd been relieved when Enid came to him and said, "I'm not cooking much these days. I'll sit with your girl, wherever she goes."

"But your son? I wouldn't want –"

"He is in good hands – my sister is watching him. There is little good I can do for him, and to see him like this – I should have time away from him now. I must steel myself for both our sakes. I will watch your sweet girl. I would like nothing better right now."

He wasn't sure this was necessary, but it was still reassuring. Whenever he saw the two little girls now, Enid was with them. Sometimes when he passed them in the hall, the two girls holding hands, walking quick as lizards, Enid huffing as she attempted to keep up, Serena would glance at him and roll her eyes. But he didn't think she actually minded that much – most of the time he saw the three of them they were sitting companionably, sharing a sandwich or a game, softly conversing. The officious young men the Gathering had employed for watching, for goading, for herding, tended for some reason to avoid Enid (although he couldn't imagine why), and therefore the girls.

Jacob wandered by the front desk in the middle of that afternoon. "Things appear to be *handled*, I assume? At least as much as possible? There is a sense of *equilibrium* in our little hotel?"

Richard wasn't positive, but he thought he smelled just a hint of wine on Jacob's breath. Of course that didn't really mean anything – he'd probably just had it with lunch – but Richard was surprised just the same. "I believe so. They're not the rowdiest bunch, for their numbers."

"Indeed. Well, then, I have a chore it is time you learned. Our private cemetery – it must be weeded and cleaned once a year. It will only require two or three hours, so I was thinking I would suggest now? If you are available?"

"Oh. Well, of course." Richard had never really thought of that plot just beyond the tennis courts as something of importance, requiring maintenance.

Entrance to the private cemetery was obtained via an ornate, bronze-colored gate. The cemetery was laid out on a surprisingly sharp slope ("for drainage purposes," Jacob explained), which skewed the gate and warped the bordering fence, so that the gate never entirely closed, and whole sections of the fence were broken or down altogether. Great trees grew in the gaps, the cemetery situated around and inside one of the older groves of trees on the property. The graves in the central, cleared area were arranged in a series of concentric circles with occasional spokes, a more-or-less uniform spider web.

As they approached the central web, passing through a tight wall of trees, Jacob stopped him, gestured toward a row of tall oaks on a serpentine mound which ran near the downslope edge of the cemetery. There Richard recognized a few of the long-term tenants proceeding single-file along the mound: the two old sisters in their dark choir robes, the incredibly emaciated man who wore a different hat every time Richard saw him, a gray-robed figure who never spoke, whose face had never been seen. A final figure trailed the line, its face wrapped in rags, carrying a grass sack across its back whose sides bulged. Jacob walked down for a better view, and after a brief hesitation Richard joined him.

The grass sack was gently laid beside a pre-dug hole. The old sisters opened the sack, and several hands went in to ease the body out.

The body was all bone and black oily skin, reminiscent of the thing that had disturbed the leaf piles earlier. Richard looked away despite his burning curiosity, feeling much too much the intruder. He proceeded back up the slope and to the central clearing, began the work of clearing vegetation from around the graves. After a few minutes, Jacob joined him, silently bent to his labors.

There were dozens of graves, the vegetation thick and stubborn around each one. After a while, Richard asked, "Who's buried here?"

"A few members of the founding family, managers and other staff, the occasional resident, if request was made, the even rarer wayward traveler who never made it, technically, to check-in."

Most of the names on the stones were virtually unreadable, others lettered in some foreign tongue. Some were simple piles of stones, others complicated and intricate constructions suggestive of abstract sculpture.

Richard carried an ordinary rake, with some clippers tied to his belt. His job was weeding around the markers, which produced considerable anxiety, especially around some of the more delicate sculptures. And he had no sense of what was considered appropriate etiquette for the task, where he was supposed to stand, what was or was not proper to touch.

Carrying a giant old-fashioned scythe, Jacob had his sleeves rolled up and wore bright red suspenders and tie, coal-black pants. He had the physically harder but more desirable job: mowing down the tall weeds that filled the open spaces between graves. He was enthusiastic, even aggressive.

Richard winced every time the rake clinked against a headstone. Perhaps it was this anxiety which made him discount the flashes of color, the rapid movements, between the trees in the upslope part of the cemetery, until Jacob put a hand on his shoulder and pointed at the dark coppice in the far corner, and a small girl's form passing under the low-hanging boughs.

"Was that Annabelle?" Richard asked.

Jacob put a finger to his lips and motioned him to follow. They put down their tools and made their way slowly between the graves and onto a diagonal path. At the tight grove of trees they had to turn sideways in order to squeeze past the trunks in the outer layer. At the center was a grassy area where they found Serena and Annabelle sitting beside a small cluster of graves. The girls sang softly to themselves and to each other. Enid sat in a folding chair a few feet away, working at a canvas bag full of knitting. She glanced up and nodded before returning to her work.

Richard and Jacob were practically over the girls before they noticed their presence. Richard could read the marker nearest Serena, a wooden plank jammed into the ground, inscribed with black marker:

Abigail, Loving Wife and Mother

The crude image of a flying bird had been drawn beneath the words. The grave was awash in fresh flowers.

Serena looked embarrassed, but said nothing. She probably thought she was in trouble. Richard didn't want her thinking that, but he was at a loss for words. He looked at Jacob, who apparently had no help to offer. Finally, as tears began tracing their way down Serena's cheeks, he said, "Honey. Your mom – she died back in the city. I don't think – your mom won't be *there*, in the ground. It's very nice, but that piece of wood just has her name on it. That's not her grave."

"She's here. I know. You know it, too, Daddy." Serena set her mouth.

The board on a similar small grave in front of the Johnson

girl read 'Here Lies Helen Johnson,' and below that, 'I love you,' signed 'Annabelle,' as if it were a letter.

"But your mother," Richard began, then stopped, feeling he had no right to speak to this.

There was a drawing on Mrs. Johnson's marker as well. The draftsmanship was crude, but it appeared to be the image of a vicious, snapping dog.

"I once knew a woman in the old country," Jacob said. "A friend of the family, a short time before* –" He paused. "When I still *had* a family. I was just a child. Once she told me that upon the death of some unlucky people, the soul goes into the body of a vicious dog. There it is free to attack the living, wreaking havoc among the mourners. I remember I was terrified. I cried for days. It was one of the last times I ever cried, I believe."

Everyone was quiet walking back to the hotel. Serena and her father led the way; Enid trailed behind to accompany Annabelle, who was lost in thought.

Richard grasped his daughter's hand and said, "You could have told me you needed the grave. I would have helped you make it."

She shrugged. "I know, Daddy. But it was for me, and it was for Annabelle. We talk and we bring flowers to their graves and we tell stories we make up. It makes us feel better – I don't know why."

"What kind of stories?"

"Annabelle has a story about how her mother transformed into a bad, mad dog and then tried to eat her."

"And you?"

She looked up. "I tell Annabelle a story about how sometimes dead people sleep in the trees, until they become angels. I tell her we need to make sure our mommies climb up into the trees. If they're not in a tree when God comes, then they don't get to be angels."

Once they were back at the hotel, Jacob and Enid took the girls inside for dinner, while Richard carried the weeding tools around to the side. An angled bulkhead door set into the foundation covered the steps leading down into the part of the basement they used for tool storage. But one of the reverend's private guardians was sitting on the door, arms folded. "Sir, I'm sorry, but I'm afraid I can't permit you access right now," he said, not looking or sounding sorry at all.

"Get away from that hatch." Richard tried to sound as cold and menacing as possible. He was feeling anything but cold, however – he was furious. "You're a guest here. You don't *own* the place. Doesn't your reverend teach you anything about courtesy? Or are you folks so special you think you can do anything you want?"

"Mr. Carter, I'm sorry, could I please have a word?"

Richard looked around. The elder Reverend Johnson was sitting on a nearby bench squeezed into a sliver of shade, looking as if he'd collapsed there – his hair disheveled, his shirt unbuttoned to expose a sweat-stained T-shirt, his suit coat abandoned on the ground.

Richard threw the tools down. "What's *wrong* with you people? There are other people in this world, you know, other people with other beliefs."

"Please don't blame the boy," Johnson said. "I ordered him to stay there and not let anyone in. My daughter-in-law is feeling ill, and I didn't want –"

"I know all about your daughter-in-law," Richard slid onto the bench, noticing with some surprise that he was actually shaking his finger at the old man. "I would say she is a bit more than ill."

"Well, I'm not sure what you're trying to say."

"You brought your son here when he was a boy – maybe you thought one of the residents could teach him how to better use his talent, or maybe you thought he was a monster and so he belonged here, I don't know. Is that what you're promising these people – that if they get sick, he'll heal them? That maybe they'll live forever if they just follow *your way?* 'Your faith has made you well.' Luke 17:19. Isn't that the verse? Are you promising these people Heaven?"

"Bringing him here, a child, was no doubt a mistake. One of many I have made with my son." He looked down at his hands, which trembled noticeably until he grasped one with the other. "We all have hopes of Heaven, I think. Even you, Mr. Carter. I certainly try to help people get there, but I make no promises. How can I? The world is a mystery – you know that better than most."

"And the healing?"

"They come to us in search of healing, that is certainly true. They come to us in pain, requiring our understanding and acceptance. But what we offer is a *spiritual* healing, Mr. Carter. Some profess to heal in other ways, to mend limbs, to cure ailments of the stomach, liver, bladder, to rid the body of cancer, yes, yes, but I do not traffic in such promises. That sort of healing is not something I ever mention in my sermons. Nor does my son. It gives people the wrong idea. All those charlatans in tent shows and on TV."

"But you brought him here that time because he could heal, right? Isn't that what he at least *tried* to do with his wife? So what is it, for the select few?"

"I swear it is nothing like that!" The old man rose, then sat down hard. Richard felt guilty, if not unjustified. But what if he gave the man a heart attack?

"I'll get you some water. I'm sorry," he said softly.

"No, no. Let me just say my piece." He took a tearing breath, then stared at Richard with sorrowful eyes. "He never had control of it. I recognized early on that people felt better around him, and that it was more than just his pleasing personality, but it wasn't because of anything he actually did.

It just happened. *I* was the one who encouraged him to learn how to use it with purpose, and I pushed him, even when I saw that it was frustrating him, and making it even harder for him to control. We had a handyman at the church who fell off the roof, broke his leg. But instead of calling an ambulance, I had my son work on him. My son was terrified, he kept looking up over his shoulder at me again and again as he repeatedly laid his hands on the man with no result. But I kept urging him on. I caused that poor man unnecessary pain, and my son a terrible humiliation."

"But still, you didn't give up."

"Oh, but I did. After that I apologized, I told him not to try it anymore."

"But he didn't listen."

"He didn't listen. Why *should* he listen to me, after what I put him through? I don't think he tried it all the time, but every now and then I'd see him out in the yard, crouched by a dead bird, or a squirrel, crying, putting his hands all over that dead thing, and praying, begging for its deliverance, his deliverance. And then one afternoon his beloved red setter, Sean, he called him – his only friend, really, he was such an isolated, inward boy – Sean was run over by a truck right in front of our house."

"And it worked," Richard interrupted, "This time the healing worked."

The old man stared at some spot on Richard's face, as if seeing something terribly wrong in his skin, some foretelling blemish, some imperfection presaging a future trauma. "Well," he finally spoke, voice cracking, "that would depend on your definition of 'worked.' By the time I got there Tim had Sean in his arms, staggering under the dog's weight as he carried him out of the street and around to our back yard. I don't think he wanted any of the neighbors to see what he was going to do.

"The dog was clearly dead, of course. When the truck hit him he'd been carried up into the wheel well. His neck was broken, his back, and most of the other bones as well, I think. Massive internal injuries. Blood everywhere. It looked like my son was carrying an arm full of soiled rags.

"But in the back yard –" Reverend Johnson stopped, looked around. "Tim was hysterical, screaming. He lay down right on top of the dog, pulling every bit of that broken animal up into an embrace. I tried to break his grip, but he was much too strong. And after a minute, maybe less, parts of it, and there was enough damage I really wasn't sure which parts, began to twitch. Another minute more, and there was this sound, a whine, but not like an injured animal; like the belt on a machine, or a worn-out bearing, giving way."

The reverend moved his hands to his knees, began rubbing as if having discovered some new pain. He stared at the basement bulkhead, the young man still planted there, looking bored. "Tim kept that animal out on a blanket in the garage. I wouldn't let it in the house. It was the first time I think I was glad his mother wasn't alive.

"Eventually the dog could move off the blanket. It didn't walk exactly. It was hinged, in places where there had been no joints before. And where there had been joints, many of those had reversed themselves, or had acquired a greater range of motion than was natural to them, so it wasn't walking exactly – I don't know what it was doing, but a kind of locomotion did occur."

"You should have killed it."

"Oh yes, I should have done a lot of things. After a month of this, even Tim wanted the creature dead. But Tim couldn't make himself, and I couldn't make myself go near it. That's when we got the call from the manager here."

"Ms. Malachiuk."

"That's right. Jacob's predecessor. She said there had been a referral. She seemed to know all about our situation. Of course, under normal circumstances, I would have hung up the phone, but I was desperate. So Tim loaded the dog into the trunk and we drove here."

"You brought the dog?"

"Oh, yes. She said the dog could stay here; 'needs to stay here,' I believe were the words she used."

"Did someone treat the dog, or help you learn to deal with it?"

The reverend didn't say anything for a time, just stared at the basement door. "You know it's a funny thing," he finally began. "After the first couple of nights here, I never thought much about Tim's dog. And I don't believe either one of us ever saw Sean again, unless Tim did, and didn't tell me."

"How did Tim spend his time here?"

"I can't say that I know. I was terrified – I remember sleeping a lot, staying in the room, drinking a great deal. The Deadfall had a wonderful wine selection in those days."

"Still does."

"Oh, I'm sure. But I mustn't partake." He smiled wanly. "I've discovered I have a bit of a problem with the *vino*.

"But I didn't see Tim much. Yet another way in which I've failed him, I'm sure. But it was like walking into a funhouse, only you never leave. Living a dream, not exactly a nightmare, but a very disturbing, disorienting dream, not unlike being on a bad, paranoid drunk, I would say."

"Was it that way for Tim as well?"

"I certainly can't say for sure, but I don't think so. Once I asked him, 'Aren't you scared, Tim?' And he said, 'Yes, but that's what I want, Dad; that's what I need right now.' And he'd be out all night, sitting outside, walking around in this dark hotel. 'I'll tell you when it's time for us to leave,' he said. Can you imagine?"

"I believe I can. Living inside the fear."

"Yes, yes – those were approximately his words as well. Later, of course, that became an important part of his ministry. 'You can't leave your fears behind,' he'd say, 'until first you live inside them. You have to live inside your house of fear.'"

"Your daughter-in-law –"

"Tim was driving the car. Annabelle was knocked unconscious, so apparently was unaware of most the accident, thank the Lord. One of the assistants drove Annabelle to our private physician – we've been seeing him for years – who examined her. *Perfectly* fine, a blessing. I don't believe she even saw the damage to the car, and her mother didn't even have to make a trip to the hospital."

"Of course not. And that was –"

"Nine months ago."

"And now you're back at the Deadfall once again."

"Yes, yes, that does seem to be the case." He looked suddenly stricken. "You know, they were very much in love. He used to say he was in paradise. He just wanted to have that time back."

"So what's your plan?"

"Actually, since you're the manager here now, I was hoping you would know."

RICHARD WALKED SLOWLY down the steps into the basement, the reverend following closely behind. They held their rakes tightly, tipped forward and ready, although he hoped they wouldn't need them. The reverend had sent the officious young guard away, and at the moment Richard regretted that decision.

A few bare bulbs lit the interior. The wood-beamed ceiling and clay-caked rock walls gave everything a reddish tinge.

Some of the floor was paved in concrete, some of it paved in stone, and some of it in bare dirt.

A figure rested on the dirt: rags for clothing, mannequin-like. The mannequin's hand moved, crawling up the rough wall like a pale mouse.

She wore a flimsy red dress. Richard didn't imagine she had worn it much, as a preacher's wife. What was it his own father used to say? *Every preacher's wife needs a red dress.* Maybe the dress reminded her of better times.

She moved her right cheek against the dirt, the movements growing steadily larger until she was rubbing her entire head into the dirt in a slow rhythm. As they watched, Mrs. Johnson opened and shut her mouth again and again. No sounds came out. He noticed that one shoe was missing, the other wedged onto the wrong foot. She opened her mouth again and again.

She rotated her head toward the light from the doorway, her jaws working in slow-motion. She began eating the dirt.

"Shouldn't we do something?"

"What can we do? She has left the world behind. In her own way, she has done what the Gathering dreams of doing."

"You make it sound like Heaven."

The reverend shrugged. "What is Heaven? Each man or woman finds his or her own."

"That doesn't sound like a preacher."

He made a sad smile. "I am retired. Let my son do the preaching."

"I don't think Heaven is like that, if there is one. I don't think it means retiring from the world in fear."

The reverend gazed at him doubtfully. "You and your daughter, you have an isolated life here. When was the last time you listened to the news, watched television, opened a newspaper? Why have you chosen such a life?"

"I'm not one of your flock, Reverend. Don't think that you understand me."

"Of course. I apologize."

Mrs. Johnson made soft, infant-like choking sounds. Richard looked away. "What does your son do about her at night? Does he lock her up in one of the rooms? Or down here?"

The reverend gazed down at his feet. "Whatever she has become, they are still a married couple. There is a sacred bond," he trailed off.

"I loved my own wife," Richard said. "I still love her, but I no longer feel married."

"Some people believe" – the reverend paused, scratched at his cheek – "that you can bring the dead back to life by making love to them."

"I don't understand what you mean. What are you trying to say?"

The reverend looked embarrassed. "They still share a bed. I don't actually know any more than that."

IT WAS THE final day of the Gathering, the final sermon, and although the Reverend Tim was supposed to deliver this address – his crowning moment, according to his father – he was nowhere to be seen. Richard and Jacob stood at the back of the crowd. Serena and Annabelle, still chaperoned by Enid, knitting bag in hand, sat somewhere near the middle. Mrs. Johnson was in the front row, surrounded by a phalanx of the young, pimply-faced men in their black suits and ties.

"I feel like we should do something for Annabelle," Richard said. "I can't stand that we're just watching this happen. But then I haven't exactly been heroic, have I? All I really want to do is get on with my life, and forget that the fire ever happened."

Jacob sighed. "We do not need any heroes working here. They tend to keep their fear at a distance. I'd rather see them shake hands with it, whisper to it, become – what is the word

– 'buddies?' The Reverends... the things they say are not entirely without merit. Perhaps that makes them more of a danger, I do not know."

"I just can't seem to get through it," Richard said. "How long is it going to take?"

"People are always wanting to get through things, to get over things."

A murmur rose from the crowd. A large number of women in white aprons were passing through the aisles, handing out morsels of food. "Take, eat," the women said. The crowd looked like one great, milling hive.

Johnson Senior gingerly climbed the rocks to the platform and faced the crowd, his suit so dark it looked like a hole burned through the background of water and sky.

"I haven't done this in a while. I hope I still have the knack." This was greeted with scattered laughter. "This'll be from Mark six, verses thirty through forty-six. Also John six, one through fifteen. You all know this one, it being about Jesus and those blessed loaves, and those equally blessed fishes.

"And Jesus said, 'Let us go to a quiet place and rest awhile.' And isn't *this* the quietest place you've ever been?"

The crowd murmured their agreement.

"And the people saw Jesus leaving. They saw where he was going, and so they took a shorter way to the quiet place. Because even back in those days, people did love a short cut."

Someone shouted, "Amen!" There was scattered applause.

"Because, you see, these people were like lost sheep, and Jesus knew they needed him to be their shepherd. He comforted them, and he healed the ones that were sick.

"And Jesus said, 'Give them something to eat!'

"But the disciples, they said there wasn't *enough* food to feed all those folk! And back in those days, don't you know they weren't blessed with the Big McDonald's, the Kentucky Frieds, or even the all-you-can-eat cafeteria buffets!"

Some of the crowd laughed heartily, but others looked serious as death.

"And Jesus told his disciples to seat the people, like it was some kind of big sit-down dinner, with five thousand men, and many women and children. Can you imagine that many people dropping by your house for dinner? Now what would the wife say to that?

"And Jesus took the five loaves and the two fishes, and he looked up to heaven and blessed those loaves and blessed those fishes, and then he broke them, and then he broke them again, and he gave all those pieces to his disciples to give to the people.

"And don't you know that little bit of food was passed, and passed around, and it reached every last one of those guests. *And* they had to use twelve great big baskets to hold all the bread and the fish that was left over!

"And don't you know I bet that was the best meal they ever had!"

And with that the crowd burst into cheers and applause. And the preacher's wife, leaping up from the front of the crowd, dove past the desperate hands of her guardians and bit into a child's arm.

A LARGE GROUP of the young men had been deployed to guard the basement bulkhead door. Richard really had no objection this time, but it still angered him. He occupied himself with keeping the little girls away from the basement. He was going to have to talk to the Reverend Tim soon, if at all possible. The Senior Reverend had sent some men out to find his son. Richard wasn't privy to the details of whatever commitment the Deadfall had made to these people, but he couldn't let this go on. Jacob might not approve, but there were children involved.

"Daddy, Annabelle and I made a wreath. Could you give it to her mom?"

He was holding it before he figured out how to reply. It was rough and uncomfortable in his hands, made out of dried branches, leaves, and other matter fallen out of the trees, made out of dead things.

He didn't like to think about his daughter and her friend making such a thing. They stared at him from a few feet away, not saying anything. Still, it was a beautiful wreath. They'd made it with what they had. That was the whole meaning of it.

Richard saw Jacob motioning to him from the corner of the hotel. He walked over. Jacob looked at the wreath in his hand. "We'd best get down there," Jacob said.

"Into the tool storage? You know, I don't think those young men are going to let us this time."

"There's another way," Jacob headed toward the front steps.

Of course there is – what was I thinking? Richard hurried to keep up with him.

He followed Jacob into a coat closet near the front door, through a narrow side panel, then down a rickety metal spiral staircase that swayed alarmingly with every step. They came out into the basement from behind a curtain of hoses and long-handled garden implements.

Reverend Tim and Mrs. Johnson lay entwined by one wall, their flesh gouged and torn, Mrs. Johnson's right hand rammed far enough down her husband's throat to dislocate his neck, as if to snatch out all his solicitous words, his desperate entreaties. A knife handle sagged from her left ear canal. She smiled the smile of the dead, muscles relaxed by the absence of pain. In the orange light of the grime-painted bulb, a line of wet earth glistened from one corner of her mouth down to just beneath her pale chin.

Richard and Jacob climbed out of the basement through the bulkhead door, surprising the young men gathered there. Annabelle ran forward, saw that he no longer had the wreath. She ran to Richard, wrapped her arms around his leg, and cried.

There were some in the crowd who wept, and some who prayed. Someone laughed inappropriately. Words were thrown, blessings were shared. But no one spoke of Heaven.

I do not know what kind of guardian Annabelle's grandfather will be: the loving grandfather he appears to be, or a distant caretaker more than content to give up the raising of his young charge to boarding schools.

It is apparent that much damage can be done to children in a relatively short time. Children's ability to survive, and thrive, is nothing short of miraculous. I do not know what kind of young woman Annabelle will be, but I can hope. Some flowers grow best in the worst soil.

I have read that there is a survival mechanism at work in the fact that the young of each species are 'cute,' according to the standards of the species. There is an arrogant, human-centric air to this theory – for how can a human being postulate a concept of 'cuteness' as it applies to another species? Some people, I am told, will not eat anything with a 'face.' What I believe this actually means is that they will not eat anything that reminds them of 'people.'

But for the moment, let us assume this is a valid theory. We cherish and protect our 'cute' children. But as these children grow older they lose their cuteness, gradually forfeiting our special protection, until the 'ugly' adult loses our special consideration completely.

I find this quite disturbing. And it troubles me that this, simply a part of the ongoing flow of life, is what Annabelle and our Serena have to look forward to.

– from the diary of Jacob Ascher,
proprietor, Deadfall Hotel, 1969-2000

Chapter Six

PHANTASMAGORIA

Some residents, or relatives on their behalf, have elected to be interred in our little cemetery in the event of their demise. It is their right; it is one of the benefits of a forty-eight hour minimum residency at the Deadfall. The Senior Reverend Johnson did not choose this benefit for his son and daughter-in-law, although they most surely would have been welcomed. Instead, he took them with him when he and his granddaughter left the premises with the rest of the Gathering. I do not believe this group will be back next year. I cannot say I am sorry, although I found the granddaughter to be quite charming, and good company for our Serena.

Our cleanup of the cemetery was not quite complete, but we may finish the job at a later time. Richard did not notice the small stone on the outer perimeter of the Grand Circle, the one inscribed simply 'Sean,' with the crude drawing of a dog beneath. And I chose not to point it out to him. The dog stayed with us for many years – he was already well-ensconced by the time I arrived. He was one of Ms. Malachiuk's favorite pets, and often lay beside her as she sat in her rocking chair reading and writing, late into the night (In her spare time she was an aspiring, and unpublished, author of children's books – unpublished for obvious reasons, I would say). He died – if that word has any meaning at all in this circumstance – only hours after his mistress's death. In her honor, I buried him on the Grand Circle with other beloved guests, just as I buried copies of her unpublished manuscripts in the Deadfall library.

Personally, I never cared for the animal. I hated watching him move across the Deadfall lawn, like an ambulatory pile of hide and sticks. Even more, I hated watching him eat.

Another summer approaches. I trust we will not have a repeat of last year's unfortunate incidents, and so accordingly I have shooed all cats, dogs, and other similar strays off the property. If Serena wants a pet this summer, she will have to settle for a goldfish, or perhaps a stone with eyes and a mouth painted on, which I think can look quite lovely when sitting upon a shelf.

Richard has worked out well here, although I have my doubts as to whether his tenure will be a lengthy one. Perhaps he is too sane for a life in the Funhouse. Certainly his devotion to his daughter suggests that, eventually, a position somewhere else might be more appropriate for them.

I have had to break it off with the former Mrs. Abigail Carter, or rather the ghost thereof (but again, I assure you, our relationship has been strictly platonic). My recent encounters with these men who have lost their loved ones is no doubt a small factor, a sad coming to terms with the fact that my own feelings, as crippled as they are, simply do not measure up, but Mrs. Carter's increasing anger has been in fact the primary wedge in our relationship. I wanted a nice person I could talk to *about important matters. It has become increasingly apparent, however, that the former Mrs. Carter's main purpose in un-life, in afterlife, is to rage. Like many of the dead, she has reached that stage beyond acceptance, that stage of true hatred and resentment concerning the living and all that they have that she does not.*

I have recently seen evidence of a deterioration in the Deadfall's infrastructure unlike the usual wear and tear one might expect, if expectation is even a relevant concept in relation to this hotel. In any case, large sections of the paint we applied last summer have begun to peel like a seriously aggravated skin condition, pipes have swollen, doors and windows have shrunk to a degree beyond that explainable by seasonal climatic change. The deadfall grove is, well, unchanged. The situation warrants my close, unbiased observation.

– from the diary of Jacob Ascher,
proprietor, Deadfall Hotel, 1969-2000

RICHARD SHUDDERED AWAKE, the dream falling away like rotten gauze. He'd been in the morgue, making the identification. But the face revealed as the sheet pulled away wasn't Abby's, but Serena's, lips chapped and blue, face pale as a fish's belly.

I want her to go to Heaven, Richard. He remembered the way Abby had said that, looking at him as if he were denying their baby medical care. *She has to be baptized.*

Their disagreement had made him so angry – he wasn't sure why. But Serena had only been in this world six months and here Abby was talking about her possible death. And Abby seemed to have no conception as to why that might upset him. *We start to die the minute we're born.* Another jewel.

Apparently Abby's religion made her feel better about the grim possibilities. But that wasn't for him.

He wasn't proud of himself for it, but now he couldn't see any benefits Abby had gotten out of her religion. She was *here*, wasn't she? And the Deadfall was hardly Heaven.

Sometimes he wondered if Abby hadn't believed in Heaven, she might have been able to hold on, in the end. If she believed that was all there was, and she was about to lose it. But she left both of them. Here she was but a breath, half a dream away, in the next room, just up that staircase. But for him to go to her now would simply mean pain and sorrow for all of them.

But Richard had let Abby take their baby down to the local church. Let her be baptized, as long as Richard didn't have to witness it. Anything to make Abby feel better. Perhaps that showed a lack of principle on his part, he didn't know. But why would he care, really? Most of what people did to assuage the simple pain of being human was just a bit of hocus pocus, wasn't it? Psychology, religion, nationalism, a belief in 'ghoulies and ghosties and long-leggedy beasties, and things that go bump in the night' – it was all pretty much the same.

Back then, bottom line, he believed Abby was the better parent, so he almost always went with whatever she wanted, eventually. He didn't really know what to do with a baby. What would a baptism mean to a baby anyway? He didn't understand how infants thought – he wasn't even sure they *did* think, at least not in the way he understood thinking. Kids felt like pets, really, until a certain age, until they started showing their own personalities and desires, and understood what they wanted out of the world, out of their fathers, out of their mothers.

But whatever it was Serena wanted out of her mother, he couldn't, shouldn't make it happen.

Richard's fondest memory of his own mother, the grandmother Serena never knew, was when she'd come in to say goodnight, and he'd been reading in bed as he did every night, and she'd leaned over, kissed him, whispering, "Books are safer than dreams." Later he'd wondered if she'd actually meant "nightmares," but that wasn't what she'd said. So maybe even a good dream was a risky thing. You could always close a book, but dreams had their own engine – they could keep you asleep even as you struggled to awaken.

Once, when she was eight, Richard had found Serena in bed reading, and he'd been so touched, it seemed in so many ways she was becoming just like him, and he'd said that same thing. He'd leaned over and kissed her, said, "Books are safer than dreams."

She'd stared at him solemnly before replying, "Oh, but Daddy, they shouldn't be."

The Deadfall was like a dream you lived in, a hotel for castoffs, wayward thoughts and desires. What you saw in the mirrors that lined its hallways was both utterly strange and exactly as you expected. It made sense only now and then, but this was your house, so you made the best of it. After all, your head made sense only now and then, but you were pretty much stuck there, as well, weren't you? It was by far your most precise address.

"Daddy, I can't sleep. Could you *please* find that picture of the sheep? *Soon?*"

Richard moved his head on the pillow. He hadn't heard her come in, but there she stood in her pajamas, looking not much different from when she was eight, except she didn't carry Teddy anymore.

"Can't sleep?" She shook her head. He got out of bed and took her hand, guided her back to her room. "I'll look tomorrow. I promise."

More and more like him every day, and now an insomniac. He didn't know if he should apologize, or blame it on the hotel. Their first couple of weeks here, neither one of them had gotten much sleep, but that was hardly surprising, being in a strange place, the strangest of places.

Abby, too, was up, not requiring sleep. He caught just a glimpse of her in the hall as he led Serena through the bedroom door: a floating bit of that rotten gauze, the flesh of dream, shedding gray filmy pieces of itself as it swept above the ornate carpet, always moving, looking for whatever it was the dead always seemed to be looking for. Restless in anger. She did not speak it, but he heard it just the same. Now and then, he'd seen her pause in front of one of the mirrors, and he always wondered what she expected to see, but from the flickering expression playing over her transparent features it was clear, whatever it was, that it terrified her.

He touched the edges of his daughter's hair, leaned closer to smell it. Sometimes he couldn't remember the simplest things about Abby: how her hair felt, how it smelled, a particular expression, a specific gesture. This floating phantasm might have her face, might have something reminiscent of her personality, but more often than not it was just a bad photograph. If something happened to Serena, would he remember precisely what she looked like? Would he be able to conjure up her smell? Could he have collaged it together from smelling her books and toys and clothing, mixing her memory with his tears?

But Richard wasn't haunted by Abby, however resentful she might be. He was haunted by impermanence.

In the halls beyond, lights flickered, glowing yellow, then brown. They highlighted the deterioration of the walls and ceiling, a rash-like spread of brown and gray spots, a steady decline into shabbiness. He'd seen the phenomenon of these shorts and surges before – as if the Deadfall's poor wiring were in sympathy with Abby's deadened mood. Or maybe she did it just to aggravate him. He was supposed to be in charge now – couldn't he at least make the lights burn steadily?

He tried to make some gentle, romantic interpretation of Abby's presence near Serena's door: she was watching out for her daughter, she was craving some sort of contact. But he had learned better. The dead were full of their own concerns and destinations, and although she had come here when they moved, it was no doubt only because she had no other place to go. And because of him. Because she wasn't done with him. She hadn't yet forgiven him his mistakes. How he had fantasized about other women, how he had let her slip from his thoughts until their marriage had become drained and bloodless.

For his part, she might as well leave. Memories, eventually, become just another part of the household goods.

WHEN THEY'D FIRST moved into the Deadfall, Richard hadn't wanted to store their things in the cellar, despite the fact they couldn't fit all their possessions into the manager's family quarters. The cellar was a vast, underground place, walls both earth and stone, and he hadn't wanted to bury what he had left in that enormous grave. He and Abby had acquired those things together, and until their remodeling was done they'd stored them in the garage. Now the house they'd worked on all their married life was ash and cinder, and these remainders had made this trip into a new life: the antique china cabinet, the depression glass, chairs and tables and eccentric-looking paintings. He and Serena could have used the money more, but Richard just couldn't bear to sell them.

Finally, Jacob had convinced him of the environmental security of the Deadfall's cellar. "It has become traditional, in fact, for incoming managers to store pieces of their old lives in this place. The things from my own former life are stored here as well. And as you can see, the managers never seem to retrieve all of their possessions upon their departures, which makes this cellar, I suppose, a kind of museum of the Deadfall's managerial staff."

The three of them had spent half a day emptying the trailer and carrying everything through an outside entrance into those dark, subterranean chambers.

Now he needed to retrieve a piece of that hoard: a rather primitive painting of fat grazing sheep, with purple mountains in the background. It had been Serena's favorite picture as a small child – gazing at it had always helped put her to sleep – and now she wanted it to hang on her bedroom wall, hoping it would have the same effect.

The problem was that Richard hadn't paid much attention to the way they had arranged things in the cellar. It was a crowded, chaotic place, and finding one small painting in all that had become an onerous task.

The cellar confirmed Richard's impression that none of the Deadfall's long succession of managers had bothered to throw anything away. But relative to the Deadfall's history, yours was only a temporary responsibility. Every manager had left a mark, and none had known everything there was to know about this hotel. Throwing away what another manager had put into place would have seemed arrogant, perhaps even dangerous.

Rickety stacks of boxes and crates made floor-to-ceiling columns throughout the vast room. The containers at the bottom were likely to be more ornate, with elaborate hinge and lock devices, and apparently dated back to the time of the original building. Personal possessions from all eras hung from walls and hand-hewn beams. Richard could see a number of antique bicycles, household appliances, dress forms and bundled curtains, lamps and end tables, dress coats and uniforms, toys and canoes and skis and ancient school books, television cabinets with the tubes removed, hoop skirts alongside jumper cables alongside rolls of barbed wire and an entire stuffed menagerie – from beavers to yak heads.

Many of the items were indecipherable. There was a long metal rod with spikes radiating out like spokes from its entire length. A metal bar which might have been a handle was attached to one end. Richard assumed it was some kind of weapon, but he couldn't imagine the sort of creature it was meant to control.

There were several squat glass containers filled with foam, miniature ladders protruding from their tops like novelty straws. In one corner stood a dead potted palm with dials and knobs on the surface of the clay pot. Hanging from much of the ceiling was a huge, continuous fishnet. Jittering shadows danced on the other side of its thick strands.

Their furniture appeared undamaged, although the dampness in the air caused concern. Parts of the wall had disintegrated, exposing the dirt it. There was, in fact, a general sense of sponginess here, of bits missing, of hidden gaps. Richard looked into an antique, green-stained mirror, saw bits of his face falling away.

He stumbled back with a tight, childish cry, arms flailing into stacks of dusty boxes. The towering stacks wobbled, held, but a fall of thick, ashy dust covered his face. He bolted upright, choking and sneezing uncontrollably. Dizziness made him drop to one knee. The room wobbled left and right. He reached up and held his burning nose, blew hard, frantic to clear his nasal passages.

He stifled another cry – Jacob had come down to help look, then been distracted by one item or another. Richard could hear him rummaging through the items at the other end of the basement, muttering to himself. Of course, Jacob was likely to understand these nervous outbursts, but it embarrassed Richard that he still had such moments. Finally he found the little painting inside a collapsing cardboard box tucked under some old bookcases.

"Richard! I have something I think you'd like to see!"

Metal and wood squeaked and rattled as something rolled across the floor. He came out from under the collapsing bookcases, made his way around two red mahogany wardrobes, and found Jacob standing in the middle of a cleared aisle beside a complicated box-like device mounted on a four-legged wooden stand with large wooden wheels attached at the bottom of each leg. A chain belt ran from the left front wheel to a cog under the cabinet, which turned a flywheel and a rod contraption attached to the telescopic lens on the front of the cabinet. The cabinet itself was decorated with scroll work and inlaid veneers, and a small door in the side bore the carved face of a devil in the center. A three-inch stove pipe with a conical lid rose out of a hole in the top of the cabinet.

"Very impressive," Richard said. "Or, 'neat,' as Serena might say. But what is it?"

"They called them *fantascopes*. They were used before the invention of film to project images onto a screen. They were used in the production of phantasmagoria; 'horror shows,' you might say. The operator would project a series of spooky images onto the back of a screen. Since the screen was between the operator and the audience, the people watching did not see the source of the images. The story goes that a Frenchman showed up with it one day at the Deadfall, a year or so after the hotel opened. He offered to entertain the guests for a small fee."

"A horror show?"

"A phantasmagoria, yes."

"That would have been quite interesting, given our clientele."

"Actually, it was rather successful here. So much so that the manager at the time – I think it must have been during Clarence Peabody's tenure – paid the man a large sum of money for it, so that he could put on a phantasmagoria for the guests whenever he felt like it." Jacob patted the cabinet affectionately and opened the small door to reveal some sort of lantern and a metal framework. "It is really quite clever.

There's an oil lantern inside, and a series of hand-painted slides or mechanicals create the images. The belt attached to the wheel controls the distance between the movable front lens and the fixed condenser, so that the proper focus is maintained when you move the fantascope forward or back. But it wasn't a perfect focus, of course, which only added to the effect."

"People found this clever?"

"Oh, people were terrified."

"Really?"

"Indeed. They screamed, fainted, some ran out of the room. This entertainment, you see, was *intended* to generate fear and panic. More than a few deaths were attributed to it, due to weak hearts."

"It seems so primitive. Surely they didn't react that way here?"

Jacob laughed. "Oh, you'd be surprised. It would have thrilled our guests, I imagine, simply because they didn't understand it. But they would have believed the images, in any case, and now and then a particular image would resonate with a guest, I imagine, and prove too much to bear. And for the normal audience member, well, they *believed* in ghosts and demons and monsters, so imagine them seeing one, with no other explanation for its manifestation other than it must be *real*."

"And today, when you go to a horror movie, you don't really believe what you're seeing, but it's entertaining anyway. At least for some people."

"Because it's safe. It reminds you of what really frightens you, but you don't believe in it; you understand *it's only a movie*."

"But the people experiencing the phantasmagoria, they had no such understanding," Richard said, nodding. "They must have been completely overwhelmed."

"They believed," Jacob said, "that Hell had come up to claim them."

* * * *

Richard didn't really want to sit through this, but Jacob had seemed so eager and insistent, and Jacob had insisted on very little since they'd moved in. Richard sat in a rickety wooden folding chair, his feet planted firmly so as to minimize the wobble. Approximately twelve feet away from him, Jacob had stretched a gauzy curtain. Richard would have helped, but he'd been so repelled by the look and feel of the cloth – it reminded him of the dreams he'd been having, of Abby, and death, and transitioning flesh – he had avoided Jacob's preparations. That end of the basement was pitch black. Jacob had left a low-wattage bulb on at Richard's end. In some ways the dim light was worse than none – around him, the shadows transformed in sympathy with his unease. He kept Serena's painting on his lap, gripping it tightly, reluctant to lay it down on the floor.

The soft sound of tinny bells floated through the darkness. Richard supposed it was meant to signal that the show was about to begin. The light dimmed a little more. He fixed his attention forward, but he really couldn't see the curtain anymore.

A ghostly image of Napoleon Bonaparte suddenly floated in the air in front of him.

"Napoleon Bonaparte!" Jacob intoned in a false, deep voice from the end of the basement.

Napoleon dissolved, replaced by the classical image of a naked man collapsing in a woman's arms. "The Education of Achilles," Jacob announced, still in that low voice.

The show proceeded through a number of slides – 'The Winged Devil,' 'Skeleton with Scythe,' 'Medusa' – each announced solemnly and over-dramatically in Jacob's false voice. Despite the fact that they were nicely painted, and of just the right degree of blurriness to be eerily convincing, Richard was beginning to wonder how many slides Jacob had back there.

A robed woman carrying a bloody dagger loomed ahead, so close she appeared to be actually in front of the screen, unless the screen had been moved in the darkness. She looked as if she was right on him – it was disorienting. *"La Nonne Sanglante!"* Jacob announced. "The Bleeding Nun!" And then, in his own, somewhat excited voice, Jacob said, "Interesting. Inspired by Matthew Lewis' *The Monk,* I believe. We have a copy in the library. Have you read it?"

"Um, Jacob, perhaps it would be better if you didn't speak."

There was a long pause as The Bleeding Nun stayed up far longer than the other images. Then, Jacob's voice, "Oh. Of course. You are absolutely right."

The Bleeding Nun went to black. Another long pause made Richard worry he'd dampened Jacob's enthusiasm for the performance. But then there was a sound as of clanking chains, beginning as if at some distance and rapidly increasing in volume. A shimmering pale figure came out of a corner of the dark basement, glowing red as it approached, finally manifesting as a demon in chains, quivering in rage, yet speechless, fading in and out until it disappeared entirely.

Richard knew, of course, that this was simply a painted slide, and he'd even heard the whistle and creak as Jacob wheeled the fantascope around to achieve the zooming effect. But it thrilled him just the same, and made him realize just how devastating this display would be for someone who actually believed in such things.

Another long pause, a soft whispering, and a glowing, half-transparent figure moved swiftly through the air, garment and remnants of flesh trailing in eerie slow-motion. Her head tilted, eyes rolled back. More terrified than terrifying, she gazed at Richard, screaming as fire raced across the darkness in pursuit. Her face was an emotional puzzle, reminiscent of Serena, his mother, every beautiful thing he'd known in women. Richard was brought to tears, convinced this was Abby, even though he could see that it was obviously a painted image. Fading in and out, his memory of her, as insubstantial as reflected smoke.

*   *   *

RICHARD STRUGGLED AWAKE with a powerful shudder, his heart and lungs tearing themselves from the nightmare's grip. He held onto the bed with both hands, shaking his head as if to dislodge the images that had settled there. Jacob *had* introduced him to the phantasmagoria, that had been no dream, but no doubt his natural anxieties had magnified its effects.

For the first few seconds of wakefulness, he thought he was still in the cellars, having fallen asleep on the floor, but the cellar clutter slowly dissolved, the clutter of his own bedroom replacing it. He looked at the clock: 3:00 AM. He was reluctant to try sleep again just yet, not desiring to revisit either the cellar or the morgue. So he did as had become his habit on sleep-interrupted nights; he pulled on robe and slippers for a trip to the library, where he would read until sleep became appealing once more.

With his first few steps out his bedroom door, Richard realized he wasn't entirely awake. Scattered brain cells, apparently, were still sleeping, and he found himself moving with a kind of pleasant drowsiness. This alerted him that he probably should take his perceptions with a grain of salt. He was sure that was unhealthy in some way, but necessary if you wanted to maintain your equilibrium within the Deadfall environs.

Almost immediately he was impressed by the air of decay in the corridor. Oftentimes, during the day, the walls and furnishings of the hotel appeared worn, well-used, but nothing so bad as this. Tonight, he could not help but notice the fraying edges of the carpet, the places where designs had faded, become obscured by some wear or stain, how the wallpaper had begun to peel at the seams, to separate from the borders near the ceiling, to bubble in places where the windows had allowed decades of sunlight in. The vast patchwork hotel appeared to be separating into its composite pieces, its additions and planned additions, its rooms of dream and its fevered spaces.

The few pieces of upholstered furniture in the hall, and the delicately-turned occasional tables, also appeared less impressive than he remembered: fabric worn thin at the corners, threads snagged near the floor as if by feline mischief, veneers flaking away from some sudden atmospheric change.

Peering up at the ceiling was almost alarming: bulbs were blown or missing from fixtures (was Jacob actually shirking his duties?), plaster had begun to threateningly bow.

And beyond the deterioration, Richard felt a certain uncleanliness walking here. He could sense it adhering to his slippers, slipping through the air into his lungs. He felt an urge to spit it out. He was careful with his hands, not wanting to touch anything.

A drifting beside him. A breath, a frown. He turned his head slowly, caught Abby's eye. He found himself breathing in, searching for her smell, some indication beyond the visual that this was indeed her. She looked at him, and yet she didn't look at him. Something about her transparent eyes suggested she *was* seeing him, but there was much more to it than that. She might be his memory of her, but he also suspected that he was somehow her memory of him.

In many ways, this had been the strangest part of the Deadfall experience. Abby had no business being here, and yet here she was, looking both like and unlike herself, both as if she'd never died and as if she'd never lived and had simply been his hallucination. He wanted to touch and hold her and say how terribly, terribly sorry he felt, but at the same time he wanted never to see her again. He couldn't *grieve* her, really, as long as she was still present. His wife had become a ghost, and yet his relationship with her was still quite real.

A soft sigh and a rush of air, vertiginous apprehension. At first he thought Abby had transported herself and was now approaching him from the other end of the hall. Then that there were two, three Abbys, coming at him in a line, their ghostly hair and limbs and clothing fluttering, as if blown by a spectral wind. But the posture of the figures distinguished them: slumped, depressed, bony shoulders, and their ghostly substance of a different, bluer shade.

One of the figures glided past him, the smoky blue orb of her right eye rotating in his direction as she apparently noticed him, then her mouth unfolded, blue glass tongue tasting the air in surprise, although he had no idea how he might have come to that conclusion. But just as quickly she went away, ignoring him, and he watched her as she glided up to one of the walls, with its associated chair, framed pictures, antique lighting sconce, and raised her dress slightly with both almost-invisible hands, whereupon dozens of gray, millipede-like things, a couple of feet long, at least six inches across, glided out from under her phantom petticoats and swarmed over the chair, over the wall, thousands of thin legs churning, and everything they passed over became a lighter shade, cleaned and renewed.

The fabled housekeepers! so excited to have finally witnessed them in the act, he looked to Abby to tell her who they were and discovered that Abby was no longer there. *Of course.* He felt foolish and sad.

Then he was aware of a soft weeping. The spectral housekeeper had been joined by the other two, and all three now stared at the recently cleaned wall, which appeared to be rapidly filling in with dirt, handprints, deterioration. The millipedal cleaners swarmed the wall several more times, and each time the dirt and wear came back more quickly than the time before, and the housekeepers sighed, and the housekeepers wept, and eventually they floated away with heads bowed.

Obviously the system had broken down. Richard's alarm was padded by drowsiness and a buzzing incoherence. He needed to inform Jacob about all this, but knew that, at least at that moment, he would be unable to frame the right sentences. Maybe after he'd read a little, gotten a bit more sleep. He continued on to the library.

At first glance, there was never anything particularly outré or strange about the Deadfall library, other than the fact that it was an unusually fine and impressive example of bibliotheca to be found in a hotel. The room itself, unlike most of the spaces in the Deadfall, had never given Richard an uneasy moment, and he'd always found that a relaxing read was easily achieved. The books housed here, of course, were unusual in and of themselves. There were a few standards of American and European literature, limited and first editions for the most part, and a nice selection of fairy tales, folklore, geography, philosophy, religion, and home repair. But the bulk of the volumes in the library were items Richard – who considered himself well-read – had never heard of before. Shelf after shelf of 'scientific' treatises examining, literally, everything from ants to zebras. Memoirs by people he'd never heard of, many of them having little labels on their spines inscribed 'ex-resident,' including a small volume full of nonsense syllables titled *Memories of a Frog*. A dozen or so histories of the Deadfall, most of them completely bogus, according to Jacob, who said the hotel's "true" history "has yet to be recorded." Shelved in this section was a slim volume entitled *The Autobiography of Clarence Peabody*, which Richard quickly skimmed, seeking some mention of the fantoscope. There was none – beyond a few basic statistics, the pamphlet focused almost entirely on missed opportunities and complaints about the few opportunities actually obtained.

A large collection of cookbooks exploring cuisines Richard had no interest at all in sampling filled an entire bookcase. Partially completed novels which for some reason had been bound and distributed anyway. A book of transparent pages. Several large volumes of photographs of feet. First aid manuals for 'Species of Dubious Existence.' And a one-hundred-and-twenty-three-volume set of *The Recorded Dreams of Ruth M. Gammetier.*

When they'd first arrived, Serena had been convinced the Deadfall library must hold every book ever written, but quickly found that it did not include any fiction written in the last fifty years or so, and certainly none of the young adult series she'd come to love. It did, however, provide tantalizing glimpses into the unknown and the unimaginable, to the extent that Richard insisted that she show him any book that interested her before delving into it too deeply. That was no doubt an unenforceable restriction, but he at least wanted to alert her to possible dangers that might be found in these pages. Happily, she'd been content so far to restrict her reading to the numerous volumes of fairytale and folklore.

It had become Richard's habit to peruse the shelves, focusing primarily on the more out of the way cases, selecting books to read at random or by hunch, sit, and read. Sometimes he was pleasantly surprised, as with *The Monkey's Final Haircut*, by Wilma G. Crawford, which he concluded was the best novel he'd ever read. Other times he wasted hours on indecipherable prose which he honestly suspected might have shortened his life.

Tonight he climbed the staircases to the third level, walked nonchalantly in front of the shelves, intent on pulling a book out with unstudied impulse. But his eye was drawn by a thin sheaf of papers bound under a clip, pulled half-way out from between two huge medical texts: *Maladies of the Invisible,* Vols. 1 and 2. It must have been recently disturbed – he would have noticed it before, otherwise. He spread the volumes apart with both hands and slipped the papers out.

The Crooked House, A Story for Children, by M.M. Malachiuk. A crude cartoon of a house with enormous red eyes had been hand-drawn under the title. He thumbed through it:

more crude drawings, a minimal use of words. Some sort of handmade picture book. He took it down to the ground floor and began to read.

ELAINE COULDN'T BELIEVE a thing the squirrel was saying. She'd always heard that squirrels were notorious liars.

"Your house has eaten all my food!" the squirrel declared in a high-pitched, whiny voice. "It popped its top and a great tongue came out of the attic, and licked my food right out of the hole in the oak tree! Now what will I do this winter?"

"Oh, bosh and bother," Elaine replied, pulled out a butcher knife and cut off the squirrel's full, glorious tail. The squirrel jumped up and down, furious with Elaine because of the insult and furious with himself because he'd let his guard down. The squirrel tried to bite Elaine on her knees, but a swift kick put him in his place, across the road and into a ditch half-filled with raw sewage. The squirrel crawled out of the foul ditch and lay gasping on the edge of the pavement, shaking with the vibrations but blind to the traffic's merciless approach.

In the meantime, Elaine skipped onto the porch and nailed the severed tail to the door. After an appropriate period of admiration, she went inside for cookies and cream.

That night, while Elaine slept, the squirrel stood up on the first stone of the long walkway that wound its way through the huge yard and up to the front porch. The shades in the two large front windows were about half-closed, the left one noticeably lower than the right, giving the house a drowsy, drunken look. The roof that hid the house's evil, greedy tongue lay relaxed and sunken, conveying a deformed, feeble air to the house's posture, and the way the porch sagged, lopsided and collapsing at its most extreme before the front door, reminded the squirrel of the ugly, drooling lips most human beings possessed.

The squirrel made a tight, tiny fist and raised it into the air.

From her bed, Elaine gazed out the window (which had a flaw in the glass, just like her astigmatic eye) at the recalcitrant squirrel. She knew her house looked drowsy, comatose, but that was simply a ruse. It was every bit as awake and prepared as she was.

She had her butcher knife beneath her pillow, along with cudgel and cat's claw. Her house was ready with splinters and nails and dry-rotted planks. Squirrels, never having lived in houses, did not understand them.

Elaine had not only lived in this house since she was born, but the house, once basic and small, had grown with her, had grown up around her, so that now they resembled one another, they were sister and sister. The house had her eyes in its windows. The house opened its front door and her mouth yawned in its place. The house's furnace was her heart, and it was her blood that ran through its plumbing. Squirrels have no chance when house and sister work as one.

RICHARD READ TO the end of the book, through much murder and mayhem and clouds of extracted fur, then skipped back to previous passages, seeking some semblance of understanding. The book, finally, was a hymn to the mean-spirited, illustrated in the scrawl of a psychotic child. He supposed it had served some cathartic purpose for its author, but he could not imagine permitting any child of his to read such a disturbed screed. He was fascinated, however, by the way the house had come to resemble the child who lived inside it, and toward the end, how the old woman who had been the child slowly deteriorated in the manner of an ill-maintained home.

The reading did little to encourage sleep, and despite the heavy exhaustion in most of his body, his head was aflutter with anxiety. As he shuffled back to his quarters, his eyes wide, attention scattered, he made note of new peels in the wallpaper, heavier layers – he was sure – of dust on lamps and upholstered backs.

He made a couple of wrong turns – nothing new for him, particularly at this time of night. What was new was the dead end. He couldn't even be sure what floor he was on, but he knew he'd never seen this before: a dead-end hall with a tall door. The top half of the door was green glass, and beaded with moisture. Painted on the wall above the door in deteriorated lettering: POOL.

The pool room appeared to have been designed to suggest an underwater cavern. The walls were rough and warped, here and there, by fake stalactite and stalagmite columns. The lighting was dim and greenish, recessed near the tops of these columns and behind outcroppings along the ceiling's edge. The illumination had that reflected pool look, although he hadn't yet seen the pool. He did hear the dripping. His footsteps echoed, but not as loudly as he would have thought. He wondered if there was something spongy about the walls that absorbed sound. Scattered about the floor were slimy gray and black bars of soap, shampoo bottle empties, stiff, moldy towels, several torn pairs of men's swimming trunks.

Somewhere beyond the entry, Richard heard a splash. He walked carefully, watching his feet, listening for more. The pool's edge began abruptly, a three-inch border of white stone, followed by a foot-high drop into the inkiest water he'd ever seen.

His eyes adjusted to the brighter illumination here, its source an ovoid of blue in the ceiling to match the size of the pool itself. Tides moved through the black water, revealing ridges of black silt. The pool was thick with pollution, and things moved slowly through it, feeding. Now and then an eye expanded open, oil dripping across the whites and milky iris, then closed.

"I'm afraid we... have no... lifeguard today. Frankly... I... think he's... been eaten."

The man was thin and naked except for his tiny black swim trunks, the sides of which appeared to be strings merely painted onto his bony thighs. He lounged on the edge of a deck chair, its webbing frayed and drooping. His huge hands almost covered his knees. He was bald. His throat had been cut, but apparently some time ago, as no blood issued. The wound appeared slightly infected, the edges puffed up like lips. He was somewhat difficult to understand, as everything he said with his mouth was preceded by a split second with the same words from his flapping wound.

"I'm sorry," Richard said. "I didn't mean to intrude."

"No... intrusion. It is... your job... or not? You're... the new... one, I believe."

"Yes. But I've been here several months. I'm sorry. I didn't know we had a swimming pool."

The skinny man laughed. It was confusing to hear, terrible to see. "Not much... for swimming... these days. As you can... see... hasn't been... cleaned... in years."

Something pushed its way through the dark sludge just beneath the surface. He thought it might be a hand.

He looked up. The skinny man with the cut throat was gone.

RICHARD WAS UP early the next day. In fact, he hadn't even tried to get back to sleep. He hoped, at least, exhaustion would take care of the problem that evening. He found the right staircase with the narrow door tucked underneath. No number, but he knew it to be Jacob's quarters. He'd never bothered him here before, although he hadn't been cautioned not to. He knocked lightly and a weary voice told him to come in.

It was a single room, not very grand, but interesting, unpredictable. It appeared to have been carved out of an empty cavity in the structure: behind and underneath a stairway, in the seam where two sections of the hotel met, around passages for pipes and wiring. It consisted of a number of crannies and loft-spaces, accessible via ladders from platforms above the smallish floor. Paintings hung everywhere, as did oddly-shaped bookcases, masks, unidentifiable pieces of taxidermy, photo collages, signs, and an assortment of orphaned architectural elements – papal, Celtic, and Maltese crosses, linen fold and tracing details, Spanish and ionic capitals, beak-head and cat's-head molding, nailed or screwed or cemented to the walls. A couple of tall, narrow windows near the ceiling let the light in, augmented by lamps everywhere. This surprised him – was it possible Jacob was scared of the dark?

Jacob sat at a battered Mission-style desk, alongside a narrow cot. As Richard came closer he could see that Jacob was mounting stamps in a book. "You're a stamp collector," he said.

"You sound surprised. I imagine you expected to see me pinning butterflies to a board – living ones, preferably."

"Well, no."

Jacob looked up. "Sorry. That was supposed to be a joke. I keep forgetting that my sense of humor is... questionable." He paused, closed the book. "So you're up early – is there a problem?"

"Jacob, do we have a pool?"

He stopped what he was doing. He appeared to be searching his mind for something. Could this be such a difficult question? "Well, occasionally."

Richard sighed. "What does that mean?"

"It's only there, *occasionally*, when we need it to be. It's a time share, you might call it. The rest of the time it's at some other, similar hotel. Haiti, perhaps, or the Black Forest."

"Okay, assuming that makes sense, what determines its location?"

"I don't know, actually. Need, I suppose. I take it you have stumbled upon it?"

"Last night. I couldn't sleep again."

"I am sorry to hear that. Were any of our residents using the pool?"

"There was one fellow in trunks, his throat was slit. He wasn't swimming – I don't know if he could, the pool was full of black, oily sludge. But there was a hand – someone might have been in the pool."

"I'm searching my memory, but I don't think I know him," Jacob said. "He may have been from one of the other hotels. Not a very secure system, is it?"

Richard shrugged. "I don't know what to say."

"Yes. Well, I'll make some calls. By the way, I'm glad you dropped by. I have to travel for a few days, talk to our contributors."

Richard hadn't felt stupid here in the hotel in some time, but today the feeling was back. "I don't know what you mean."

"Oh? Sorry. The financial base of our operation relies on some key donations. Every year I must visit those donors and, well, express our appreciation."

"I see."

"You'll be making this trip next year."

"I will? Oh."

"Is something wrong?"

"Have you noticed the deterioration in the hotel lately?"

"Oh, yes. I'm studying the problem."

"So nothing to worry about?"

"I won't know that until I have completed the study."

"But it's okay for you to leave?"

"A building is much like a living thing. It grows ill. Sometimes it dies, but usually there is something you can do before that happens. The Deadfall has been ill before, but still, it survives."

*   *   *

RICHARD SHUDDERED AWAKE, his chest wet and cold. He could not move his head. He blinked his eyes to clear the fog, and saw Abby stretched out on the metal table with him, her eyes open and empty. Overhead, the dingy bulb flickered and buzzed. He sensed the figure moving around him, glimpsed the shadow of its arm, held his breath as the cold spray rinsed him, rinsed Abby. In the blur beyond, he sensed the other table, and although he could not see, knew that his little girl was on it, and if he hadn't already been dead that knowledge would have killed him.

Richard shuddered awake, gazing at the destruction of the ornate green and gold wallpaper: a pastoral scene, sheep wrapped in clouds, the woman in the ball gown with her long slender neck, the man bowed, caressing her hand, kissing it, and Richard was pretty sure the man was weeping, his heart was breaking, and this scene, repeated hundreds of times in this Deadfall hall, this oh-so public display, was a humiliation beyond bearing.

How had he gotten himself out into the hall? Had he fallen asleep here, unable to make it into his bedroom?

He tilted his head back, stared into the brilliant ceiling lights, bright suns in the cerulean ceiling. He could feel the floral carpeting beneath him, drying up and dying. And everywhere on the walls, this idyllic scene of courting lovers, complete with sheep and pastel pastures, was decaying, dissolving into the horsehair plaster, into the rotting lathe beneath the surface, stating oh-so-frankly that love was a lie and could not survive.

He examined his hands and forearms, fully expecting to see this same decay, this inescapable plague of nonexistence, but although his flesh was pale, and his hands trembled, he appeared to be whole. He willed himself to get on hands and knees and crawl into the bedroom. If Serena found him like this, whatever would she think? If he died, what would happen to her? But he could not move. He was weak and a coward, and he could not make himself move.

A clarity rose like fever from his extremities, into his belly and spreading into his chest, irritating the skin of his shoulders and neck before rushing to fill his head. He considered the possibility – no, he was *sure* of the reality – that this was just some ordinary hotel. Rundown, sparsely populated, poorly managed, but ordinary. These guests were ordinary people, with jobs to go to, and families and relations at home. A furious man, a desperate widow, an abandoned pet, a damaged soul, a troubled heart. Figments. Simply because these creatures were lost and unattractive, as most people were lost and unattractive, as he, himself, was lost and unattractive, had led him to imagine them monsters. Most ordinary people, certainly, were monsters. Their skin was scarred, their recesses stank, they hid their motivations behind tired, pain-stained eyes. When they looked at themselves in mirrors what they saw was strange and unpredictable, and yet nothing unfamiliar at all.

They dreamed all their lives, and in almost every instance they settled for something less than what they dreamed. They took the job they could get, they married the person who would have them, they did the things they knew they could do without pain or humiliation. They lived haunted by the ends to come. They did not recognize their own lives, which seemed pale and without passion. They could not hear what their children were saying. They were in terrible trouble, and ordinary, banal trouble. They could not imagine how, they could not imagine when. They settled. Most of them could not even achieve a fanciful, horrible death.

He sobbed. He was sure that when he opened his eyes Serena would be sixteen, seventeen, unable or unwilling to put up with his madness anymore. She'd leave him lying in bed, the television groaning on in excited complaint, and as terrible as he found its sound, it would still comfort him.

"Mr. Carter, Mr. Carter, you okay? Mr. Carter, stop crying. Are you hurt? Mr. Carter, open your eyes."

He did, and saw the monster rushing out of the darkness to float above him, looming over him, sadness gripping the monster's eyes. Not Enid, although he looked like Enid. Enid's son. Richard shuddered, and closed his eyes again, and shuddered himself asleep.

THE TELEVISION WAS on, and for a brief happy moment Richard thought he was home again, home being somewhere in the past, with Abby in the kitchen and some mindless show embarrassing itself in the living room. And embarrassing him, because he really wanted to watch it. He knew Serena would already be there, sitting on a pillow a few feet away, snacking on something. Abby wouldn't be pleased about it, but also wouldn't want to make it a big issue.

But happiness quickly passed as he realized this couldn't be. He rose from the cot where they had placed him, supporting himself with a sore arm. Enid was at the small stove, cooking something. He still felt a little disoriented, because he could still hear the television set, and as far as he knew there were no televisions at the Deadfall – certainly he hadn't seen one before now.

Then he heard Serena's laugh coming from another room. He looked through a nearby doorway, saw Enid's son standing there, looking the other way, and heard Serena's laugh again, over the television, coming from that same room.

"You may sit up, I think. And in another five minutes, but no less, you may come over to this table and eat some food."

He pulled himself up, struggled to his feet.

"Frederick!"

Enid's son came rushing in, put his massive hands on Richard's shoulders, and pushed him back onto the cot before he pitched forward onto the floor which, he realized, he was about to do.

"Mr. Carter, while you're in my place, you'll need to do what I say," Enid called from the stove.

"Thanks. Of course," Richard said. "And thank *you*, Frederick. I'm still pretty weak." He forced a smile.

Half an hour later, Richard sat at the table eating stew and biscuits, while Enid worked on her knitting. Uncomfortable with her silence, he said, staring at his bowl, "I must have caught some kind of bug."

"I suppose you could call it that. A bug. Some kind of bug that's going around."

"You sound skeptical."

"My Frederick almost died last month. I have a right to be skeptical. I just know that buildings get sick, just like people get sick. You don't usually hear about people catching house diseases – dry rot, paint peel, loose foundation, flickering lights, brown out, short circuit, whatever – but we don't live in Usual, USA, now do we?"

"Jacob is looking into it."

"Hmpf," was her reply.

Her knitting might be the same garment she'd been working on for months. He heard Serena's laughter from the other room, punctuated by a hoarse boom which he assumed must be Frederick's own merriment.

"She hasn't watched TV since we've been here," Richard said. "I know she's missed it."

"I told her to stay in the other room," Enid said. "I told her you needed to rest. She'd much rather be sitting here with you, I assure you." She flashed the needles rapidly. "But it's good for her to laugh. Jacob doesn't appreciate that enough."

"I don't expect you've told *him* that."

"I certainly have." She waved a needle in his direction. "He tries. But he doesn't know everything. Not even about this hotel. The Deadfall may be a grand, unusual place, but just like any other big hotel, the staff knows things management doesn't know; this cook has *seen* things that old maintenance man wouldn't believe."

"And the housekeepers?"

She frowned. "Oh, I imagine they know plenty, most of it things the rest of us don't want to know."

"Well, obviously *I* have a great deal to learn. For example, right now, where are we? Is this Mad Devon?"

She laughed. "Heavens, no. Mad Devon is okay, you know my sister lives there. But we're still in the hotel. Didn't Jacob tell you Frederick and I live in the hotel?"

"He may have – I wouldn't swear. He tells me a lot of things."

She chuckled. "Where, exactly, we live in this big old hotel has always been my secret to share. Not all the managers, or staff, have been people I'd care to have in my home. After today, you'll know how to get here. You and Serena are welcome at any time, and of course now you know I have the only television."

He laughed. "Maybe someday I'll have secrets to share, or not share."

Enid looked at him coolly. "No secrets? That is hard to believe, Richard."

He dropped his eyes, unable to meet her gaze. "When I'm in the hotel longer, maybe I'll see some things you haven't seen."

"Oh, but you have. Jacob asked me to check in on you while he was gone, Frederick and I. We were alerted – that's why we found you."

Richard grinned, feeling a little ridiculous. "He thought I needed babysitting?"

"You met The Pool Man."

"Jacob said he was unfamiliar with the fellow."

She put down her knitting. "I doubt that, although anything's possible, I suppose. Or maybe he just didn't want to make you anxious. Too much anxiety in this place always works against you. The Pool Man, and that awful cesspool of his, has appeared from time to time, over decades I believe. I've heard his pool reaches deep. Let us say, much deeper than these rocky foundations. I'm thankful never to have encountered him."

When Richard walked into the other room, Serena yelled "Daddy!" and ran into his arms. She hugged him so hard it somewhat frightened him, and he found himself stroking and patting her hair the way he had when she'd been a small child.

The teen comedy she and Frederick had been watching ended, then the news came on. They hadn't heard any news since they'd moved. Richard had an immediate impulse to reach over and switch off the TV, but why? He didn't want her to hear about those awful things – which made no sense to him, given the situation he had decided to bring her into.

There had been terrible floods in Germany; hundreds of people had been killed. A mass grave had been uncovered in the Middle East. In Colorado, a man was accused of dragging his girlfriend behind his car and then dismembering the body. In Florida, a press conference ended with an on-air suicide. Horrors of the times, Richard thought, horrors of the moment.

And then he thought of the dark and depthless Deadfall pool, and the Pool Man with his doubly misleading smile, and the faceless things that swam there.

He had brought his daughter to live in the Funhouse, but hadn't they always lived here? Serena loved scary movies, just like her mother – he'd hated those movies – they seemed to have nothing to do with him. As a child he'd fantasized disastrous things happening to him and his family: murderers breaking down the door, wolves dragging them out of their beds, lava flows sweeping the house away. But none of those things ever happened.

In the Funhouse you work up terror for things that have nothing to do with you. You feel safe enough that none of this is going to touch you – it's going to be a respite from your daily anxieties – it's going to be fun. But instead you find it is a return to terror, to the fears that are always with us, whatever happens in the *real* world.

Serena went to bed early, exhausted. He had done that – she had been worried about him. She asked him to stay with her until she fell asleep, which he did, and long after, holding her hand, whispering stories to her that she'd enjoyed when she was little, mixed in with adventures she'd had with Mom and Dad, remarkable things seen, mysteries wondered about, comical disasters. Finally, when she was grumbling in her sleep over his incessant noise, he let go of her hand and left the room.

Exhausted himself, he could not sleep, could not bring himself to lie down and shut out the light. Dreams had too much to tell him, and he was tired of listening. He just wanted to move along with his life, to care for his daughter and raise her in peace, safe and away – for a time – from the horrors of the world. Illness and endings would descend upon her soon enough, couldn't she just have this brief time away?

The walls and rugs, ceilings and furnishings of the hotel did not appear so shabby to him right now. Not of brochure quality, certainly, but what is? All things wear. What is needed shows its age. The wear patterns in the wood grain – on the chair arms, on the upper edges of tables, along the carved details of leg ends, in the flat stretches of base board and wall panel and window and door frame – had the beauty of use, of encounters with living things. The gentle separations of wallpaper were memorials to the passage of cold and heat and seasonal revolution. Fighting time was futile and a waste.

Residents he had not seen in months drifted down the hall, signaling greeting with a wave or raised eye. Some he had never interacted with even had words to share, and although he didn't always understand, the effort pleased him.

Two figures in tuxedos, their faces wrapped in coarse gray hair, played chess at a small table near the front windows. Ill-matched couples (she with the elongated torso and strange turns of hip, he with slanted face and never-ending fingers; she with the large eyes, he with no ears) strolled up and down the grand staircase. An elderly gentleman stood by the front desk, leaning low to the counter, laughing with multiple lips. Moving in and out of the crowd, a young man in a gray, homemade uniform practiced amateur pest control. Two women of remarkably short stature and incomplete hair lay curled in a corner in a complicated embrace.

Off to the side could be heard scattered shouts and cries, as someone operated the fantascope for a small seated group. Phantasmagoric imagery spilled into the surrounding crowd, climbing the steps, dropping off the vaulted ceiling of the great lobby.

Richard suspected the hotel had recorded it all, had played it back hundreds of times over its lifetime. It didn't much matter to these folk, now or then, so why should it matter to him?

Someone had left a window open. A cold breeze moved slowly across the floor, wrapping around furniture, wrapping around legs, wrapping around *his* legs. He began to shiver.

He recognized some of the furniture. Someone, Jacob perhaps, had moved his old furniture up from the cellars. He was pleased, such a pleasant surprise, everything he and Abby had worked for, everything remembered become real.

Now if someone could just close off that draft, everything would be perfect. He began to shake.

Jacob had once told him they used to offer room service. Then they had to stop because they kept losing staff.

"Someone *please* shut that door!"

But it was too late. He began to shudder.

THAT NIGHT, RICHARD shuddered, and shuddered, and woke up in the pool. His arms and shoulders were covered with such weight he thought his bones would snap. Overhead, looming in a double grin, was the Pool Man.

"How? How did I *get* here?" Richard shouted, struggling.

The Pool Man bent his neck incorrectly, and impossibly swiveled his upper torso around for a better view, close enough to sniff Richard's face. One of his mouths was rank, the other smelled sweet. Richard wasn't sure which was which.

"Sleep... walk, would be... my theory," the Pool Man said. "Once... folks see... the pool... they can't wait... to come back."

"No!" Richard wiggled his feet, kicking up. But it made him sink deeper. He gasped as sediment, fiber, blood lapped his lower lip.

The Pool Man wagged his finger, *No, No, No.* "Think... quick... sand," he double whispered.

Richard closed his eyes, but could not contain his panic so easily. It burned the inside of his eyelids, its black claws scraped against his brain, it forced his eyes open, and he was gone.

HE HAD WAITED a hundred years on this hillside, patience his only option, then a few years more, the people running in and out of his mouth, gazing out his eyes, rearranging everything inside him, all in their desperate, pitiful need to make a meaning of what happened to them, as if weather and rock and ground had a story and a plan. They wore him out from the inside, then they fled into the night, never to return. It happened this way, again and again.

What is this? They hide in his rooms and they weep and he is sick to death of their crying. There is nothing he can do for them, so why do they stay? He has lasted two of their lifetimes, and with luck he will last many more. They cannot last. They cannot last. It is sad perhaps, but there is nothing to be done.

But inside, there is a pain he cannot ignore. Inside, a human has latched to a wall, has opened its mouth and gullet and all, has howled out air older than its days, older than these walls or anything growing on this hill, such emptiness and loneliness that even walls must take notice.

And he is there, looking at the thing, with eyes that cannot see beyond its own poor life, then back out again, into insects flying in the room, in spiders gathered in aimless make, in all creatures hungry and scurrying through this room, not knowing if this poor thing is predator or prey.

And then to parts unknown, flying through his own veins, the air ripe from a hundred years' humans' breathing, furnished with things accumulated, paid and bled for: things to sit in, things to lie on, things to put things on, things to hold and look into and hope for a better return and a meaning that will not come, no matter how much they hold and look into and sit on and lie on and moan. Nothing comes, nothing comes, except the resignation of the barren.

And he is gliding over the floor of his world, over the foundations, over the bottom line, over the feet. And there is nothing he can't see, or feel, or hear. And it is not enough. He races away. He takes the broader view: these walls, this hill, this sky, this ground. These bones, this muscle, this flesh, these eyes peering out of an over-occupied skull.

Inside the Deadfall grove, the dead things accumulate. Limb and torso, the natural cast-offs of the world. Seeing becomes a complicated process of ignorance and simplification. The limbs mesh one into the other – you trace their paths round and round. Before you know, you are buried in it. Before you know, you are covered in dead things, and no ax in sight.

The limbs grab him and lift him out. His name is called as if from a great height.

RICHARD RAISED HIS head off the floor with a great, heaving gasp, choking on the invisible. He sat up dizzily, leaned on wobbly arms. He was back in his bedroom. Brilliant light made the window look on fire. He saw the drop glide across his hand and disappear into the phantasmagoric pattern of the rug, and realized he was crying. He leaned his head back and stared at the water-stained ceiling, the frayed wiring twisting into the tarnished brass neck of the ornately-winged light fixture, and took a deep, shuddering breath, as if he'd been holding it far too long.

His vision blurred, and he was suddenly anxious about what might be creeping toward him out of the corners of the room. But then his eyes cleared, and there was nothing, and he loved the way the light filling the window spilled to make everything in this space glow.

He wondered if Serena was in her room. They had a lot to pack, but there were certainly belongings they might leave behind. Now, and over the next few years, there would be much he would have to say to her. Once back in the real world, they would have to live with what had happened, and what might happen, as family.

"SO, HOW DID it go with our investors?" Richard sipped at the tea in an antique, expensive-looking cup. He'd never been much of a tea drinker, but he hadn't wanted to offend Jacob, especially after all he had done. Actually, he was surprised to find it quite tasty. He might have to take it up.

"*Patrons* would be the more accurate term. They made the usual cautions about expenses, deteriorating standards and the like, just to make it sound as if they knew what they were doing, and that they might some day choose to withhold their funds, which they will never do, I can assure you. It would be like Catholics refusing to fund the Vatican. They made the one arbitrary demand. Every year there is always one arbitrary demand."

"What was this year's?"

"I have to put a bench outside against the wall by the front entrance. Never mind that there's little shade there, that it's going to be too hot to sit on about four months out of the year, and none of our residents would want to display themselves so openly in any case. But I will do as they instruct."

Richard nodded, putting the cup down on the small lacquer tray. Jacob's quarters were really quite pleasant – he liked the way the light fell out of the upper windows and yellowed the shadows below. He wished he had been able to spend more time with Jacob like this. "It was kind of Enid to help Serena pack," he said.

"We're all going to miss her, and you as well."

Richard nodded. "She cried when I told her."

"I'm sure she did, but didn't you also detect, if I may say so, some glimmer of *relief* in her face?"

"Yes. Yes, I certainly did."

"A difficult decision, but the correct one, I think."

Richard didn't say anything for a time, and it wasn't Jacob's way to push him. Finally Richard did speak, the words coming surprisingly easily. "We were childhood sweethearts, Abby and I. For the longest time, I couldn't even imagine myself with another girl. I imagined she felt exactly the same way; it was a key part of our story together. And maybe she did – I certainly have no reason to think she didn't. Except for the fact that I came to understand people know much less about each other than they think they do.

"We first started thinking about that house when we were in high school. We'd draw pictures of how we thought it would be. She made a lot of collages, from magazines and cloth samples, that sort of thing, to represent how each of the rooms would be. She added rooms and took away rooms, she rearranged the elements until sometimes our dream house became a real mystery to me – I barely recognized it from one version to the next. There would be rooms whose functions were completely impenetrable to me, and the very next day they would be gone from the plan, and replaced by other, equally mysterious spaces. I think maybe she could have been a designer, if she'd only imagined herself that way.

"I looked at all the home owner's magazines I could find, *House and What-Not*. Of course I didn't let on to any of my friends. I took a few vocational classes at school, carpentry and plumbing. The electrical class was always full. I could have taken a summer course, but we both loved the beach. Summer was our time.

"We got married right out of high school and we started putting away money. We knew it would take awhile, a house like what we wanted. A house like that doesn't come cheap. After a few years, Serena was born, and that was okay, that was what we wanted, but obviously our dream house would have to wait awhile.

"But we couldn't wait, not really. The idea of that house had *ripened*, you see. Our desire for that dream had peaked. If we waited any longer it would be *over*-ripe, if you know what I mean. It would never have been so good again. Abby had a little inheritance, and there was that money we saved, so we looked and looked and found a house of the right size, the right form, the right impression, but it was all torn up inside. A lot of damage. A lot of potential."

"A 'fixer-upper,'" Jacob said.

"What?"

"Sorry. I believe they call them 'fixer-uppers.'"

"Exactly. That's exactly what they call them. We didn't have much money left after the purchase, hardly anything really. But we had all these books on construction and home repair, all those magazines and drawings and plans, and collages, all those dreams on paper. And I was a pretty good carpenter. And Abby, Abby was just *inspired*, you know?"

Jacob nodded. "Inspired."

"So we went for it, got materials on the cheap, worked nights and weekends on it, just using our labor, our efforts, instead of money, just to see how far we'd get. And we got pretty far.

"But do you know how much electricians cost?"

"Quite a sum. I've hired a few, or *tried* to hire a few, I should say."

"There's no way we could afford that, unless we saved for years more, but we couldn't save anything because we were having to rent a place at the same time. But I had all these books, my own little library. And I checked out a bunch more from the library. I read everything I could – I thought I knew exactly what I was doing, how to make it safe. Electricity, it's such a *wild* thing, you know?"

"And no inspectors were involved, I imagine."

"No, it was all undercover, behind the walls. We couldn't get the city involved, because we couldn't hire licensed people, and besides, we were afraid they wouldn't let us do what we wanted, that it might violate their codes.

"Abby was nervous about the electrical, but I told her it would be fine. I told her I could do it. And I believed I could do it.

"By that point, our nerves were worn pretty thin. We were tired of being poor, and we were arguing all the time. Serena started having trouble in school, and we blamed each other. Abby said I was too busy, I didn't spend enough time on it.

"Which was true. But I just wanted to get things done, get us moved in. I knew what was safe and what wasn't safe. Those codes, they're always stricter than they need to be, or so I said. It made me mad that she would question me like that. I knew what I was doing – I'd read all those books, and we really couldn't *afford* to hire anyone. I wanted to spend that money on other things. I kept telling her it would be okay."

"But it wasn't."

"For about two years, it was fine. I was *so* pleased with myself. I figured I could do anything. Then we started getting shorts, brown-outs. And I didn't want to call anyone in, because I didn't want them to see what I'd done."

"And there it is."

"And there it is. Nothing dramatic. Not the kind of thing you write books about, or turn into movies. No big thing. But then it's everything." Richard stared at his hands. "And there's the other thing."

"The other thing?"

"Childhood sweethearts. We'd known each other all our lives. But you love someone all your life, you start forgetting exactly why it is you loved them. You love them because you love them. It gets to be like breathing. Abby was pretty angry with me that last year, and for the first time I started wondering. I started imagining, and during those long nights working on the house, that imagining became my escape. I started imagining myself with other women, in other lives. I almost started *hoping* for some other life. Because everything I imagined, you see, had a lot more color, a lot more blood, than the life I actually had."

"And did you act on that?"

"Never. Maybe if I'd had an opportunity, but it never happened."

"You know, you're not unusual in this."

"Oh, I know. But when I think about the fire – it started by the bedrooms. There wasn't that much time. I got Serena out first."

"Parents put their children first. It's why the species survives."

"I *know!* I don't know if I would have done it differently, but when I think about it, you *know* you love your children – it's there in your *body*, you can just about *touch* it. You *love* them. But a husband, a wife, you don't always *know*. You don't always understand. Especially when you've dreamed of this other life, wondering how it would be.

"And maybe that slows you down. You grab your child. But beyond that, you don't know. You've imagined so many other things. And now you've run out of time."

"And now it's time to leave?"

Richard didn't think he meant it as a question.

"And now it's time to leave, to leave all these beasties and ghoulies behind. To come out of hiding. For myself, and for Serena."

"You do what you can do," Jacob said.

"That's right. You do what you can do. I really appreciate the opportunity, but now I can do something else. I went into the Funhouse to see what I could see, and believe me I saw plenty. I didn't think I'd find my way out because of all the mirrors.

"Then I figured it out. Sometimes in the funhouse, a mirror is just another door."

EPILOGUE

Some are not meant to live in the Funhouse, nor are they suited for the rarified entertainment that is the Phantasmagoria. That is perfectly understandable. We do not always know who may live and thrive here and who may not, and what effect they will have on us. We must use caution, for we may come to resemble them, and they us.

Earlier this week, I bade a sad farewell to Richard and Serena Carter. I trust their time here has been useful for them – I know it has been for me. I will miss Serena – she reminds me what a joy children can be, what a comfort as one grows old and faces what must be faced. It has been a bittersweet time with her, as it recalls old losses, old wounds.

Of course I will miss Richard as well. Some day, I think, we would have been friends. I have not had a friend in many years.

Ms. Abigail Carter has made the decision to remain here with us. I have not attempted to influence her decision, but I find that I am pleased. Her struggle with her husband and daughter has ended – she is ready to move on. I believe *this is best for everyone concerned. I look forward to future conversation with her.*

The small changes – an alteration in the light, the quality of the air, the movement of shadow, the pressure on the eye, a dangerous shift in mood – occur so rapidly they disorient, and make us doubt our ability to cope. The larger changes – like the pattern of dark limbs filling and refilling the Deadfall Grove, pushing it further toward the Hotel, and closer to cliff and lake – take a lifetime to complete. Someday we will lose this structure entirely to that greedy reach of dead limb, but not yet. Not yet.

We carry our fear with us, from forgotten pasts into unimaginable futures. It is not so much a burden or hindrance, but who we are. No one wants to be incidental; we struggle against irrelevance. But our days are short; for most of us, there is not enough time for more than a too-hasty stroke of the brush.

It is not that most of us are unable to accept such a fate. Most of us cannot even imagine its possibility.

The horror is in the not knowing, and in the knowing all too well. The horror is in the breathless and the breath, the loss of a future in order to be a shadowy figure in someone's past. We become the furniture in the picture on the great grandchild's wall.

We look at our world through holocaust eyes as Hiroshima flowers in our brainstem. Our Jack-the-Ripper hearts dissect every emotional pledge, as if counting on deception. We cannot see all that is at stake, because all is at stake.

We shudder when day becomes night and night becomes day. We shudder when our eyes close and we cannot tell if it is death or dream arriving. We shudder when lovers drift away and what we see in the mirror has no resemblance to our understanding. We shudder down all our days and nights, in hope of the one embrace that will take all this cold away.

– from the diary of Jacob Ascher,
proprietor, Deadfall Hotel, 1969-2000